The Popish Midwife

The Popish Midwife
Fourth Edition published by Dustie Books in the United Kingdom 2017
First, Second and Third Editions published by The Conrad Press in the United Kingdom 2016

E-book ISBN 978-1-9998173-0-5
Paperback ISBN 978-1-9998173-1-2

Book jacket design by Carmen Christensen

Formatting for paperback and Kindle by Timothy Savage
twitter.com/timsavage66

Reach author Annelisa Christensen online:
twitter.com/Alpha_Annelisa
www.scriptalchemy.com/
www.facebook.com/scriptalchemy
www.annelisachristensen.com

The Popish Midwife

A tale of high treason, prejudice and betrayal

ANNELISA CHRISTENSEN

Table of Contents

To my parents, David and Signe Green,
who taught me to be true to myself

'I hope the God of Truth and Justice will protect me,
and bring me through them all,
and pluck off the vails,
and discover both Truth and Frauds barefaced.'
-Elizabeth Cellier (1680)

'If I did say so I lyed'
-Elizabeth Cellier (1681)

Preface

London, England

'Hurrah! Hurrah! The King is taking his throne!'
On the 29th day of May, 1660, eleven years of Oliver Cromwell's strict puritan rule that had begun with the execution of the first King Charles in 1649, ends with the restoration to the throne of the second King Charles, his son. A weight is lifted from London's people. For the first time in eleven years, groups meet openly in taverns and coffee houses without being arrested; lords and ladies dare to wear colour again without fear of a turn in the stocks; and the assembly of people at fairs and celebrations is actively encouraged after years of bans.

Even Cromwell's men tired of the strict soberness and austerity of the period, the Interregnum, following the end of the Civil War.
Suppression had been the only way for Cromwell to prevent reprisals from the Cavaliers, Royalist supporters, but now Cromwell is dead. His own parliament would rather the rightful King Charles II were fetched from exile in France and returned to the throne than have the country run by Cromwell's weak son, or any longer bear the chaos reigning since their leader's death.
It is time for England's people to heal.
Though there is rejoicing for the return of the King, there is a darker side to London: there is no sanitation. All human garbage and waste is thrown to rot in the streets, attracting large numbers of rats. And with the rats comes the Black Death, an epidemic of the bubonic plague, killing thousands every day. Fathers, sons, mothers, daughters leave their dead in the street for the death carts to collect and dispose of.

1

From Sunday, the second day of September to Wednesday, the fifth day of September in the year of 1666, the plague is ended by a baker's accident. A small fire begins in his oven and, fanned by strong wind, soon spreads through the wooden city, burning most everything in its path.

The plague had wiped out over seventy thousand of London's people. The fire erases more than thirteen thousand homes.

People have already been through so much, yet there is more to come. With regular news of the ongoing war with Holland and, further, the torture of Protestants in Mediterranean countries and on the continent in the continuing Spanish Inquisition, people fear for the safety of their religion and their way of life. Strangers and foreigners are potential threats. Catholics are seen as worse than any other, for surely their ceremonies of eating the Lord's body and blood are sacrilegious, their use of trinkets and idols violate the law of the Church of England, and their devotion to the Pope is traitorous to the King and his religion?

As the decade proceeds, anti-Catholic hysteria heightens: Catholics are banned from any government or civil post and even from the city itself. Catholics not yet gaoled are often beaten in the street. Priests are hanged; drawn and quartered for treason, for it is clear they cannot be loyal to both the King and the Pope. Loyalty must be to one or another.

Titus Oates is embittered by his expulsion from the Jesuit training college in St Omer for Sodomy. He quickly plans his revenge on Father Thomas Whitbread, and gathers to his side all those against the succession to the throne of the Duke of York, James, brother of King Charles and self-professed Catholic. Oates 'discovers' a Popish[1] plot, allegedly devised by the Catholic Duke of York to murder the King, his brother, and place himself on the throne. He produces papers he'd apparently found, naming and incriminating many priests, with Father Whitbread on top of the list.

Charles himself is reluctant to believe a man who cannot keep straight even simple stories, or descriptions of royalty and gentlemen he claims to know on the continent, whom the King knows well. However, the Government presses King Charles to allow full investigation, and he has Oates swear an affidavit to the magistrate, Sir Edmundbury Godfrey.

Sir Godfrey mysteriously disappears and is later found murdered. Oates is quick to point out how his death gives credence for the Popish Plot against the King. Soon, Oates and his men set out to accuse every priest and Catholic that ever crossed his path, until the gaols are overcrowded with the unjustly accused.

Into these gaols, a few charitable gentlewomen bring alms to prisoners, along with news and information from the coffee houses and courts. In exchange, they leave with vital accounts of the prisoners to share with families and other interested parties.

One of these women is Elizabeth Cellier, once midwife to the first Duchess of York, Anne Hyde, may her soul rest in peace.

1

26th day of March, 1678

Halfway home, the putrid smell of the cages in the Enchanted Castle of Newgate still stifled my nose. Though the street odours were vile, their comparable sweetness cleared the gagging substance that stuck to my airways.

His Majesty's gaol overflowed with those falsely accused of plotting against the King. How those poor wretches lived on such solid foulness day after day I could not tell, but could only surmise the body, being a wondrous thing, must alter itself to survive when the spirit gives it strength to do so. At the least, being free to leave, I was not forced to test this idea for myself.

Unlike in the countryside, where the winter season tests a person most fully, I pondered whether the worst season in the city is the summer, when a lavender soaked hand-kerchief is small protection against swarms of flies circling unavoidable shoe-deep waste. Unavoidable only if you are not well enough placed to use a coach or hackney carriage. Moreover, the best season in London is the frozen winter, when ice locks tight all noxious odours beneath the feet, and casts the Thames in such ice that it becomes the place of the Winter Fayre.

That time was past, and now regular rain had washed much dirt into the river. Despite the vernal purging, there still remained a single stream of sucking mud in the middle channel of the street that, in my distraction, I stepped deep into. The putrid dregs of city life drenched my shoe and spilled over the top of it. The awful day might have ended there, with my thinking that the day had shown me its worst had it not been for the sky squeezing out a sudden shower, but I would yet be downtrodden by Dame Nature, for the rain was a blessing to me. I raised my face and thanked God for the cool, clear water that washed over me and cleansed me, lifted my skirts out of the gutter to lessen the spattering and splashing of the muck and continued walking, trying to wash my filthy foot as much as I could in any fresh puddle before I reached home.

Even as it purged the stench from my nostrils and clothes, the rain could not reach inside and expel every persistent sordid memory of the day from my mind. I blinked equally persistent raindrops from my lashes as I remembered the morning's events.

'Madame Cellier! Madame Cellier, aidez-moi s'il vous plaît!' Marie Desermeau, the young Huguenot midwife that lived near by me, pleaded as we left Newgate.

Though my French was much improved, she spoke fast in her mother tongue, and I did not comprehend all she then said.

'Parlez lentement, Marie. Je ne peux pas vous comprendre,' I said. Speak slowly, Marie, I cannot understand you. The French my husband had taught me was little enough to comprehend his people.

Using a combination of gestures and the occasional English word, she asked that I call on the wife of a local carpenter, Mrs Potter whom, she feared, did not receive proper care as she should. I did not question that the woman was Catholic, else I would not ever be asked to visit with her.

Nor would a Protestant midwife do the task of a Catholic sister. Each tended her own. That strict law caused the death of many a poor mother and infant, but was, nevertheless, the law we abided by. Religion had no bearing on success in the art and, indeed, some of our kind on both sides had no training at all and dealt us badly.

Marie communicated her fear that the one tending the carpenter's wife was such a one. She gestured until I understood that this was a wicked, wicked woman and I should not tarry, so I did not.

My arrival at the house was greeted by screams that rent the air, with so much urgency that I deemed the woman already in delivery and the baby wrongly placed. The cries and howls were such that my heart stopped, for no person hearing that unparalleled noise expelled from living flesh could believe life would remain long in a body! My knock was unanswered and, fearing the woman to be birthing alone and in danger, I went in.

Manners and civilities be damned, I hurried through the house, following my ears to the source, though at times the noise perplexed me by seeming to come from all directions. I barely noticed the man kneeling beside the fireplace, praying. He stoked the customary fire to keep evil spirits from taking the innocent newborn soul. Kneeling beside him, a boy of six or seven covered his ears with his hands and cried.

No child should hear such agonies in his mother!

I did not waste time asking if I might enter; the woman's cries were invitation enough. Neither stood to stop me as I continued to the back chamber. I expected to find the woman with gossips – kinswomen or neighbours – but found a lone midwife, performing heinous rituals banned from the craft for a matter of centuries, if ever they were acceptable.

Her red cloak lay over a nearby chair, but she may as well have worn it for all the red that covered her. Every part of her was stained with the blood of the woman, or maybe the unborn child's; it could have been either. In her hand she wielded as a sword an instrument, the likes I did never wish to see in the hands of such a one, or any other. She poked the long stick, unsmoothed by any carpenter, curved at the end like a shepherd hook in and out of the woman's womb to hook out the baby, missed and tried again, oblivious to the pain she caused the mother. The pool of blood laid testimony to how ineffectual her method. She murdered the woman with ignorance.

'Desist, woman! What hellish deed is this you do!' I shouted, surprising her into stopping her abhorrent act. 'Unhand that devil's stick!'

'Stay out of my business, Mrs Cellier, this is my task!'

Her meaning was clear. She would take payment for it, not

me, with nary a thought for mother nor unborn child. How she knew my name I did not give a thought to.

'I cannot allow it. You murder the woman and her child!' I grabbed the stick as she made to start again. She slapped me with her bloodied hand, but I held fast and pulled. Then I slapped her back. She put her hand to her cheek and bloodied it. She let go of the stick.

'Do not dare teach me my job, French leech! Some of us must eke a living from the poor, and some of us must take any job, even a doomed job as this. Go away and drink from the gold cup you keep in the palace!'

'Remember your oath, woman. Rich and poor alike! And if this woman is doomed, 'tis all your doing!' I spat on the floor.

'Oath be damned!' She spat toward me rather than the floor. 'I took none. When they denied us licence, they took our living. This stubborn baby must come forth now. I have another laying in today.'

'Then let me have this one,' I said. 'You cannot be in two places at one time.'

'No, this one is mine. 'Tis I that tended her these last months.'

'You deserve no payment for your foul work here. Leave now, or shall I call a magistrate and have you indicted for assault.' I tried to snatch the stick from her hand, but she held fast, and pulled back.

'What! But you cannot be serious. I have done the most work on this!'

'Still your busy hand, woman! Your work here is that of the Devil, and you cannot take pride in it. If that woman loses more blood she will surely die.' If I could not save this one's life, I might at the least prevent further torture.

'Her baby refuses to come forth, and is stuck fast as Excalibur in the stone!' The woman stopped her jabbing, freed the bloody stick from my hand and pointed it at me. I grabbed it again.

'Stuck? Has the baby released its waters then? It was my understanding she was to lay in another month.'

"Tis her time, I tell you.' She tried to raise the foul hook once more, but I held tight.

'Well, if it is her time then leave me to tend her, for you are not fit to be at her side!'

Something in my voice must have warned her of my intention. She looked at me warily. 'I will not leave until I have taken payment.'

Without a thought, I opened my purse and gave her some coins.

'Take these and begone.' I meant no reward for this devil, but wished her leave so I might attend the poor tortured creature atop the bed.

The moment she had silver in her bloodied palm, the evil incarnate dropped the coins in her pocket, threw down the stick and wiped her hands on her filthy apron.

'You may clean your hands with my grease,' I said, thinking of the next woman she would attend.

She paid me no mind, but took her red cloak from the chair, donned it, then left saying no more. I intended to relate the story of this woman to all that would listen, that none other would give her custom. Her future prey would be only the innocent and ignorant my word did not reach.

Looking to the bed, I felt shame to wear the same red cloth. Mrs Potter had stopped screaming and lay bleeding and still. Her silence was ominous. I doubted if there was any single thing I could do for her or the baby.

I took the pot of goose fat from my bag and cleaned my hands, while shouting to the husband to boil some water as a matter of urgency. Soon thereafter, Mr Potter came in wary as a man found guilty of treason awaiting sentence, and looked to the bed.

'Does my wife live? Never have I heard such noise in childbirth!'

I thought of the boy covering his ears, rocking back and forth with wet cheeks. He might be motherless tonight, and the man a widower.

'She is direly wounded.'

'Has that creature murdered her?' he asked, gesturing towards the door.

Betraying my kind, I nodded, but comforting words hid from me.

'Will the baby…is it…?' He did not have to finish. I shrugged. There was no way of knowing what damage that monster did until I examined the poor woman.

'Bring the water as soon as it is ready,' I said, as I returned to the bedside.

I did not wish the man to see what I was to do to his poor wife.

It did not take long to confirm Mrs Potter's heart no longer beat, and her breath did not wet the looking glass. I should look to the unborn child.

With no reason now to think of the mother, still bleeding over the bed, I reached my hand deep inside and felt the baby's soft warmth… and a movement so small I might have missed it had I not stayed steady. I could not feel the head – it was breech, perhaps that saved it. If it would survive the inflictions of that stick it must be taken from the body now. When a woman had no life left in her, the child would not choose to come out the customary way. I must cut her open and take it out.

I considered my tools in the open bag. Amid small glass lotion bottles and articles for a poultice were a knife, forceps, a needle and cloths, as well as some alcohol. I took the knife, honed sharp for such times as this. Had the woman been alive, I would have set it in the fire to cleanse, but such a time-consuming task was needless now. I opened the poor woman's mouth, so that the child might receive breath, rolled her onto her left side and cut smart and neat into her belly.

I withdrew the infant. It no longer moved. Was it too late?

I wiped the remains of the sac from the face, stuck my finger into the tiny black mouth to check for blockage, and then took the tender little ankles in one hand and hung the small body upside down and slapped it hard to clear its lungs. I did not know if it was still warm from its mother or from its own self. There was damage to its legs from that woman's stick but it seemed otherwise whole.

Still it did not move.

Had that devil given Mrs Potter a potion that reached into the baby and stopped it breathing? She knew less than cared what she did, so it was possible.

The door opened, but I was too busy with the baby to throw a sheet over the sliced belly and save the husband's eyes. He had the boiled water, but quickly saw his time was wasted. Times like this were too frequent and disgraced me.

'I grieve for you, Mr Potter, for no woman should ever bear such treatment and no man should ever suffer his wife do so!' I said. My voice did not sound as if it came from myself.

Holding the pail of steaming water, he looked at the open staring eyes of his wife on the bed, and the still form of the baby hanging from my hand. It was as if his very soul was taken from him. He cried then. He cried like an animal in pain.

'Why, Lord? Why do you take my wife and child without me?' Wide eyed, he fixed on the discarded mortal remains of the woman so recently his life companion. 'Has the dark of night come to claim my day? Wake me from this, my worst nightmare, or take me, Lord! Take me to her!' In horror, I watched as the man dropped to his knees, spilling scalding water on him, then plunge his hand into the water and scream, 'Are bad dreams come to life? Take my pain that I know I dream!'

I fast placed the dead baby on the bed beside its mother and rushed to aid the living. When I kicked over the pail, some spilled onto my leg. As if the action brought reality to the man, he collapsed over, his knees bent double, his head to the floor, and howled.

The man's grief was too great and could not be stayed by me, so I returned to the still form of the baby. If I did not try one more time, that woman would have the lives of two, and that I would not allow! The man had lost his wife and the boy his mother. I would not see them lose the baby without every effort to save it.

The infant had turned black. I once saw a midwife bring a

child back to life by the slapping of it from the bottom of the spine to the top, so I held firm its greasy feet and slapped it hard in the way I had seen, gripping hard to stop the slippery skin sliding through my fingers. There was no movement from the baby, but the man looked up, his jaw open, a frown upon his brow, the question froze ere it was full-formed. 'Wha-?'

'I must try, see?' I told him, not wanting to waste breath talking.

He shook his head and winced each time I hopelessly slapped its tiny back again, and again. Nothing. Letting go of hope, the man returned his head to the floor and continued weeping.

I should have stopped, but a deep part of me had to purge the shame of what that midwife had done, and another part of me imagined the midwife there before me, so I was possessed by an urge to hit her until she could hurt no other. But she was gone, and my actions had no benefit. Neither did my anger abate. I slapped the baby hard on the back one last time. Perhaps it was the strength of the strike that forced the small ball of black liquid from its mouth, but no other thing happened, so I carried the body toward the bed to lay it down, knowing I had now done every Earthly thing I knew of.

As I placed the body down, I near dropped it in surprise when it whistled like wind in the trees. But the man's crying made me uncertain of what I heard.

'Hush,' I said to the man, more severely than I meant. 'Hush!'

When he realised my urgency, thick silence filled the room, pushed back the walls and the windows, so all I could hear were echoes of the woman's screams. I let out my breath. False hope. Even the bodies of newborns sometimes passed through the final throes, and gurgled and rattled when Death came for them.

As the life had gone from the infant, so it went from me. My shoulders slumped. I lay the little body next to his mother, made the sign of the cross, and murmured the Pater Noster so that the Lord would receive these innocents into his Kingdom. When the husband saw I prayed, he bowed his own head, but then resumed his wailing the moment I finished.

11

What more could I do but clean the room? The Almighty God knew Mr Potter was unable. Perhaps He was the only one to know why this little one was taken before it had lived any time, but the Devil it was that used such an evil woman as the instrument of its death.

This woman called into question my life's work and pride – all I had ever done or wanted to do. In this moment, the craft my mother had passed onto me, as I had passed it onto my eldest daughter, burned me with guilt and the wish to divest myself of any tie to it. Wearing the red cloak once more could only lay my own claim to that she-devil's actions. I looked at my cloak, lying where I did not remember dropping it, and imagined throwing it, along with my prized bag of lotions, medicines and ointments, into the deep Thames River when I left there.

Perhaps I stood there a long time, perhaps no time at all.

The man cried still but, perhaps sensing my stillness, looked up, his face wet and so red that he might have plunged it in the boiling water as he had his hand.

Suddenly, the bed made a squealing, hissing sound like a fresh cut log thrown in the fire. In the silence that followed, I searched for the cause of that noise. Then, when I thought I had imagined it, a yell tore through the air, so loud it caused me to start. The baby. A miracle had brought the baby back! My prayer was answered. He was alive, his little soul returned to us. For a moment I could do nothing but take in the sight of the baby, unable to credit it. The man, equally incredulous, came to his feet and moved to the other side of the bed and, for a while, we both simply stared down at the infant.

The baby moved and waved his hands weakly in the air.

I shook my head and forced myself into action.

With the Oath I had taken before it was forbidden came permission for a midwife to baptise where necessary. This baby lived and cried, but if only our Father knew why he was taken before, then only He knew if He might take him from us once more.

Without further ado, I cleaned every orifice and swaddled the baby, then asked the man for the gown he should be baptised in, likely the one either the father or mother had been baptised in too. He found it and brought it to me. I fast made a cross over the water in a bowl and thanked God for the blessing of this child's return. Then I dipped my fingers in the still water, spoke the necessary words and administered the sacrament.

That done, I took the baby up, and once more swaddled him, and offered him to the father.

The man no longer bawled but took a step back from the infant, as if it had the Devil in it. I had seen it before. Some fathers might not take to a child when their wife had lost her life for it.

I ignored Mr Potter's red hand, which I would deal with shortly, and pressed the infant into his arms, shoving at the man's chest when he did not at first take him. The balance tipped from reluctance to acceptance and he folded his arms around the bundle with surprising tenderness, new tears falling gently, quietly, on the baby's tiny face.

Later, once I had tended the man's burnt hands with an ointment of plantain, comfrey and thyme, and dressed them with bandages, I took time to sew the woman's belly that he would no longer have to see the insides, then cleaned up the day's mess as best I could, scrubbing blood from the floor and wall and placed fresh sheets beneath Mrs Potter.

Wouldst that I had another pair of hands to help me.

Finally, I laid out the corpse and cleaned her from head to toe, and dressed her in fresh clothes the best I could without help, ready for her family and friends to pay their last respects. It would normally be the job of the womenfolk of the family. I finished and wiped a stray hair from my eyes with the back of my forearm.

Before leaving, I collected my paraphernalia together, and gave Mr Potter a bottle of burn lotion and instructed him in the use of it. He still held the baby, and the boy child by the fireplace peeked out from behind him.

'I am indebted to you for my child's life, Mrs... I beg your pardon, madam. I failed to ask your name?' For the first time since I came there, I looked fully at the man. I could not recall such a plain face. There was nothing remarkable about it at all. His nose was small and straight, his mouth not too large nor too small, his eyes were a good distance apart and of common colour. He did not wear a periwig, for he was not in society, though it was likely he frequently wore one, for his brown hair was shorn tight to his head. Despite having no mark of distinction, his face was of a good man, and I warmed to him.

'The name is Mrs Cellier, Mr Potter. Elizabeth Cellier.'

'My gratitude will always be at your side, Mrs Cellier,' he said.

My heart heavy and body worn, I would have done more, but no words of comfort for his wife came to mind, so I merely nodded. It was usual, at this point, to ask for payment, but I did not have that sort of uncaring heart.

I still intended to find a neighbour to stay with him and, of course, a wet-nurse for the infant. Mr Potter informed me that the unusual lack of gossips at Mrs Potter's bedside was because the so-called midwife had sent them away; a most peculiar thing to do. If I had to scour the whole of the city, I would find that woman and hold her accountable!

'Thank you, Mrs Cellier,' said Mr Potter. 'That woman has taken my wife, but you have given me back my son.'

'Only God can give life back, Mr Potter,' I said. 'He must have use here on Earth for this child.'

That was ere noon and now, coming from Newgate the second time this day, I turned right from Old Bailey Lane into Ludgate Hill towards home and wished the rain might purge the image of that devil's minion in the red cloak and the dreadful carnage she left behind. Women of that nature should not dare to call themselves midwives, but murderers.

Dwelling deep on such horror, at first I did not hear the footsteps follow in mine, but as I became aware of them I naturally quickened. I had safely walked the streets at all times of day and night for so many years, my midwife cloak protecting me, I had become accustomed to doing so unchallenged, as well I maintained a respect for the characters that travelled them.

Foolishly, I did not even yet imagine the footsteps had any relevance for myself until suddenly my cloak was grabbed so that I near lost my balance and fell.

'You! Whore of the Frenchman! Plague of the city! What say you on the plot against the King? Talk witch! What know you?'

I spun full round at the growl to find a hostile woman holding my cloak. Beyond her stood an equally unfriendly man and three children, any mask of civility removed, so that even the faces of the children held the raw purpose of a pack of hunters cornering their prey.

'Tell me why I should know the answer to your question?' I asked boldly, pulling myself upright, and grabbing back my cloak.

'Do you deny you befriend Papist plotters?'

'I do no such thing. I know of no plotters.' Drops of rain dripped from the hem of my hood as I raised my head and tried to walk past.

'But I know you! You are thick as thieves with Papist priests and traitors to the King. I doubt not how you hide wicked Popish charms, amulets and idols in your basket under the sham of alms and carry treasonous notes between the villains of Newgate and their plotting accomplices in the city.' As the scowling woman said this, she stepped forward, as did others of her family. The woman grabbed my wrist.

'Unhand me,' I said, putting all the authority I had ever learned into my voice and pulled free from her hard grip, an action made possible only by the greasing of the rain.

The woman barely reacted. She stayed too close to me and again growled in my face like a dog. Such hatred and suspicion was common in every Protestant that feared a Catholic should sit on the throne and bring the abominations of southern countries to our own three Kingdoms. As of late, any not of this country or of the Presbyterian faith were condemned on the street without trial, and many an innocent man and woman was beaten for their religion or origin. Being both Catholic and married to a foreigner, I was doubly condemned. This one seemed to know me, but I did not remember her. I doubted reasonable voice would sway her but nevertheless I spoke out.

'I have wronged no man and intend none to any.'

She ignored my protest, so convinced was she that I was guilty of foul play. Without further warning, the woman struck me with some hard thing she had in her hand I had not seen. My head spun and bile filled my mouth. The woman did not strike once, but followed it by another and another before I had the chance to recover. I shielded my face from her brutal fists, but when her husband and children joined her, hitting and kicking me anywhere they could, I had no defence.

'You bloody Popish toad – take your vile venomous husband back to the putrid bog you came from!' I heard the man say, muffled by my arms wrapped around my ears to shield my head.

'I am of this Kingdom!' I shouted without hope my words would find a mark. 'This is my land…' My words were cut off by the next hit.

'Take that for the King, you foreign whore!' The smack was smaller, but the young'un's voice mimicked his parents' words.

They did not stop even when I fell into the grimy water. My chest made a breaking sound as the woman's boot kicked it hard as any man's. There was little strength or will in me to fight back and I let them have me. I could do no other.

Then there was a shout, the sound of scuffling feet, followed by stillness. I was left to die in this place. I lay unmoving in the cold water soaking into my clothes and shivered violently.

'Are you harmed? Can you stand?'

Was I harmed?

Of course I was harmed.

The man, a rotund man of the law, grabbed my arm and laboured to lift me to my feet with less strength than a spider. I yelped loudly and he released me, then I screamed when I hit the ground. Whatever was broken in my chest pierced my innards in a

16

cage of pain, so that only some of what happened around me after this slipped through the bars.

The man of the law seemed not to know what to do. He left me lying in the blood-filled puddle while he took the names of the attackers who, it seemed, had the impertinence to still be nearby, and the name of witnesses that, I noted well, not only did not prevent my beating but now came forward to vouch for the attackers. The officer of the peace swore my attackers, a family by the name of Atterbury, to abide by the law. Once one witness had vouched Mrs Atterbury would appear in court the following day, they were free to leave.

Free to leave!

Theirs was the freedom to assault some hapless passer by until damaged beyond fixing.

I could neither walk nor stand. It occurred to me I might die this night, my injuries being internal. Those bigots may have punched my insides into gruel and I might die before I could see my dear Pierre once more. Years of midwifery had taught me, it was not the wounds on the outside that killed a man, but those on the inside.

Through a closing haze, before I blacked out, I heard the man of the law direct someone fetch a cart. My heavy eyes closed until strong arms lifted me from the ground and placed me in the aforesaid cart. The agony of being moved was nothing to that by each torturous bump the wheels encountered along the road. My chest yowled in protest, but all that came from me was an occasional groan.

At some time the pain stopped. The next I knew, strong arms lifted me oh so gently from the cart and into the warm, familiar smell of my home. I knew they were Pierre's arms. Only he could provide such comfort through the pain that filled me then. And I knew it was home. Only home has such superior effect of closing around one like a womb; it swaddled me as a newborn infant.

My childhood showed that protection might be as superficial as external injuries, and that a marauder might, like internal bleeding, as easily enter your home to pillage and attack a family as if there were no walls or doors. A house was but false security, yet, though my family was regularly attacked by Puritans during the reign of the present King's father, home remained safer within than without.

Perhaps it was the comforting crackle of the fire in the grate, or being cosseted by the love of my family, that gave me leave to relax the moment I was brought through the door. My husband fussed, as I knew he would, and directed the men to carry me to our bedchamber, where I was laid down.

'My clothes,' I might have said if I could speak, 'they will drench the sheets'.

'A surgeon has been sent for,' came a gruff voice I did not know. I wanted to curl away from it, but could not move. The pain was only still when I was. Each part of me became solid as the winter Thames, as if blood refused to flow through it. I tried to tell Pierre what had happened, but my mouth, though uninjured, would not form even a mere whisper.

'Is she dead?' Pierre asked over and over.

'She has heartbeat and breath,' said the deep gruff voice, 'but we lost her when we carried her into the cart and she did not return.'

'When is the surgeon to come?' The warmth of a blanket covered me, but I could not thank Pierre for his kindness. My limbs were so cold.

'A man was sent to fetch him but a half hour ago by the man of law that found her. The people who did this knew her name, so he will know where to come. He will come soon enough.'

'I offer you thanks, monsieur.' I heard coins jangle, no doubt into the men's open palms. Then the voices faded as Pierre saw them to the door. 'If you see the surgeon, tell him to make haste,' he urged them as they left. If they answered I did not hear them. The door latch clunked into place and Pierre's footsteps returned to the bedside. A hand pushed the web of tangled hair from my face and stroked my cheek. Something warm moved over my cheek as light as a feather and I knew it was a tear tickling a trail to my ear. Did he cry because I was dead? I must surely be alive if my skin felt that exquisite touch.

Then it was day. Familiar sunlight painted window squares on the wall telling me it must be late morning. Cold night still touched my face and turned my breath into clouds. Pierre did not lie beside me but slept upright in a chair next to the bed.

Every laugh and frown line of Pierre's sleeping face was more familiar to me than my own. I cherished the curl of his surprising dark lashes, the deep-set greying hairline, the slant of his crumpled narrow lips, and how his ageing skin hung loosely from his cheekbones onto his hand. This man had saved me over and over, and for him I would surely give my life, as I knew he would for me.

That Pierre had watched over me was all the more endearing. I watched his stillness for some time, and the warmth that travelled through me had me try to reach out my hand to touch his face. But I could not move my arm, and I could not touch my husband's dear face. I tried to speak. I still could not. Nothing came but a croak.

Though barely audible, the noise was enough to wake Pierre. His eyes came upon me the moment he opened them as though he had never slept. When he saw I was awake, he sprung to his feet, took my hand in his, knelt by the bed and thanked God for my deliverance.

'Lizzie. Lizzie, *ma chérie*. You are returned to me!'

Not waiting for any reply from me, he told me I was lost for two nights and a day, and he had feared for my life more than he had ever feared for anything. The doctor had come and bandaged my chest tight, and all he could do was pray, he said, and pray he had. All he could do was hope, and hope held his hand as he had held mine. Memories of our every time together had given him strength to pray such times would continue.

On the eighth Instant[2] of April, almost fourteen nights after I nearly died, I insisted on being carried in the coach to the Sessions of Peace to see Susanna and John Atterbury found guilty of their violence against me, only to be insulted by the paltry sum of twenty shillings they were fined for my grave injury and for my husband despairing for my life. Their children – John, Sara and Elizabeth

– though they had intended me harm and attacked me, were out of britches but not considered old enough to be charged, so they were merely cautioned. I made sure to give them the evil eye throughout the hearing though I had no doubt from their gestures and expressions they had no remorse for what they had done.

As far it concerned the judges, the Atterburys' attack on me was merely another chapter in the growing book of such assaults.

That I took a foreign husband made it worse to some than being foreign myself. Foreigners were first to be hoisted and beaten, along with Catholics, for the cause of any calamity, whether plague or fire or other. Again, I say, I was doubly condemned, and the judges spared no sympathy.

With the advance of the Catholic faith across the continent into Holland, many feared its poison would soon infect our Kingdom through the war with the Dutch. The judges told me I could have suffered the fate of other unfortunate Catholics all over the city. I should be grateful, they said, I had not finished my life dangling from the nearest sign, or at the end of a dark alley with a knife in my back.

'Tis thirteen years since the plague,' I said when I was allowed to speak, 'yet those of my religion are unforgiven for so many carried away in dead carts and thrown into common graves of every parish. Tis a dozen years since the Great Fire, yet we are still blamed for a lazy baker's folly. One nature's disease, the other an accident. I ask every one of you, when will truth be unveiled? When will blame for Spain's death, torture and inquisition fall where it belongs, in Spain?'

My speech only served to act as bellows on embers.

But now I knew the fear of persecution.

Such persecutions, of the Protestant minority by Catholics in Spain and other places, were repeated here by Protestants against the Catholic minority. 'Twas the very same oppression and torment with roles merely reversed. What difference the matter of sides but the place the sides are taken?

2

9th day of January, 1679

I made it my habit, on occasion, to break bread with prisoners of the debtors' prison so that I might appreciate something of what they must endure. The sparse meal was all they would have, but barely filled a space in their stomachs nor kept them warm. I would not eat more than each of them was given, as I sat with them awhile and heard the latest prison news.

On this bitter, bitter day in January that I would tell about, I left the room they called The Castle, and tightened my cloak against the cold, and outside met Marie Desermeau and Mrs Mary Ayrey, who came hither from other directions. Although we were glad enough of the company and greeted one another cordially, recent memory of the conditions inside removed any reason to smile. This group of good women I had established a year ago had the common aim of alleviating the suffering of prisoners in whatever way we could.

'What is the debtors' lot? Fare they well?' asked Mrs Ayrey.

'Well enough, considering they are starved, frozen and filthy,' I said. 'They will die of cold before they die of dysentery, though their souls may die from lack of light ere that happens. How fared those you saw?'

'Dire, Mother Cellier. As with the debtors, they are so cold, the rags they wear barely cover half their skin, and the other half is damp and exposed to icy stone that saps any warmth they might glean from meagre rations.'

'We must find more blankets for them.'

'I know a stable where some sit on the side unused.' This came from a youngster with Mrs Ayrey, who I knew to be barely out of the schoolroom. Her father had died in prison, and she now tried to improve the lot of others that were equally undeserving of their fate. 'I could take maybe one or two, if they are still there tonight?'

'An excellent idea, Miss.' I took out my purse and gave her a couple of coins to cover the cost of the blankets. 'But we will not become thieves, no better than some inside these wall. Please offer this recompense to the owner.' She wore no gloves, and her hands fumbled to clasp the coins as she put them into her drawstring purse. 'Is there any other urgency?' I asked the women, noting their ruddy cheeks and noses.

Prison work was hard on the stomach and hard on fair skin, but we never forgot we could leave that place at the end of the day, and we would warm our hands by a burning fire and eat hot broth before we slept. Those left lying on the cold stone floor, their own water soaking into the tattered remnants of their clothes, had less chance to see the morning each and every night they remained there, especially during the winter. Summer brought its own problems of stench and disease, but they were not the problems of now. The cold and lack of food were immediate and demanded our attention.

'We will find whatever we can to cover them up and keep them warm. Will the Turn-key let us give them?' Mrs Ayrey rightly considered.

'I know not the answer to that. They have been stricter lately. But we must try,' I said. As the eldest, they often deferred to me as if I had every answer, and I allowed them to do so since, more times than not, it allowed me my own way.

The winter sun already sunk behind the buildings as we talked, and so we walked towards the Gate-Lodge.

'Might I ask if you are full recovered, Mother Cellier? Our concern for you has been diligent.'

'I am most grateful for your concern. I am much recovered.' I considered the pains I still suffered in my joints, particularly when the cold wind bit through the layers. My convalescence after the beating had been long and arduous, and even nine months after the episode, my chest continued to complain when I exerted myself too much, but worse was how jumpy I had become when I saw any huddle of persons in the street that looked as if it might have a purpose other than good.

'*Écoutez. Qu'est-ce que?*' said Maria, stopping suddenly. She moved her head as if to locate an elusive sound and frowned.

'What is it?' asked Mrs Ayrey.

'Perhaps 'tis a dog.' The young woman with Mrs Ayrey held up her finger, signing for quiet.

We listened to the silence so intently, when the sound came it caused every one of us to jump with fright.

'Hark! What noise is that? Can it be an unnatural animal of the night?'

We listened some more. Our ears were assailed by sporadic sounds: horrible groaning interspersed with a terrible squealing and screeching that sent shivers through my scalp, skin and into the base of my stomach, making me want to expel what little I recently ate.

That was no animal, of that I was certain. It was a sound I would never forget. It was a sound that echoed a woman tortured nine months since. Poor Mrs Potter. It was sound caused only by the agony of body and searing of spirit that one man could inflict on another man or animal, the sound of a broken, or breaking, man.

'It comes from in there.' The young girl pointed towards the Condemned Hole, or simply The Hole as it was called, the dungeon where unspeakable acts took place, so they said.

The sound came once more, and again brought to mind the midwife I had yet to find in this city, that should be charged for murder if I did. Harris, the rough and toothless turnkey, stood near the entrance, looking the other way, his occasional flinch and the tightness of his features clearly demonstrating his failure to ignore the sound.

'Harris,' I asked. 'What goes on in there?' Harris had worked there a long time, so I was surprised to see any thing disconcert him. He could not hide his guilt as he informed us, "Tis old Mrs Turner having a long labour.'

23

'If that is a woman on her birthing bed then I am old Mother Hubbard! Are you ashamed to tell us the truth, Harris?' He knew I knew he lied. I looked at him closely until he looked away.

'Tis a woman in labour, I tell you.'

'In that case,' I said, calling his bluff, 'I am a midwife and I will aid her with these good friends of mine.' I started towards the source of the noise.

'You cannot go in there.' Harris had the decency to look to his feet as he spoke.

'Harris, if there is a woman needing my skills you had better let me past.'

Perhaps he foresaw himself as the next poor soul in the The Hole, and on the wrong side of unspeakable acts, for he straightened and became sharp and scathing in his response.

'What! What can you do, woman? You cannot do anything for that one! Go! Go back to your servant filled homes and stop your pretence with the lives of villains!'

I did not waiver.

'If it is a man in there, Harris,' I persisted, 'what is he called?'

There came a scream, like a hundred wolves at night, redoubled by the inside of that cavernous entrance.

Each of us stood silent and listened. I could barely breathe. That cry was of a man in more pain than any woman giving birth to a sideways child, worse than a man with his leg crushed beneath the iron wheel of a cart. The sound would stretch winter nights in the coming weeks longer than they should ever have been, a gentle torture in comparison, but one that would replay over and over into every silence.

I took hold of the cross around my neck and gripped it tightly, praying for the fellow's soul, and for the strength to save him. My fellow alms givers also assumed a stance of resolve. Heads bent, we prayed together for his deliverance from pain. When we had done, we confronted the turnkey once more.

'Let us down there, Harris,' I said, confronting him face on. 'We must stop this now.'

Harris had passed the moment by when he might be

sympathetic to us, and came down on the other side. 'Return to your own business, Papist whores. You are not welcome here. Begone with you!'

'Some of us be Catholic, but some are not,' I said. 'If we are or are not makes no difference to our charity, nor does it alter our resolve. Where is your compassion that you can stand by here and do nothing? That man is worse than dying!'

'Papists or Papist-lover, the one is as bad as the other! Begone from here!' Then with a more urgent gesture, 'Begone, I tell you!'

I sensed his imperative nature was not that his job required him to be sharp, but that the screams, enough to make any man weep, made him jittery. Indeed, the women standing before him, tougher than many, cowered at each harrowing howl. The screams mingled with the screeches of some metal thing grating against metal, or perhaps stone, was enough to make us all wish to run.

I rarely took notice of Harris – a useless scab that spent half his time looking into an empty ale mug, and the other half engaged in achieving that view – sparing only obligatory pleasantries to keep in with him. He was far from sweet-talking now.

We were no longer mere gadflies biting his back, a nuisance to be swiped away, but witnesses to some heinous act, outlawed and renounced in this country for more than one hundred years. If he were discovered marking time with us he might lose more than his job. His own and his family's lives might depend on his ridding us from this gate. Later, when I thought of it, I knew how fear played the larger part in his next actions. I did not condone what he did, but I understood it.

'Get thee gone from here, Mrs Cellier! Take your women and go!' With which he took up the broadsword he had left lying in the shelter, an unnatural weapon for him despite his occupation, and swung the heavy iron round him like a madman. Then he raised it above his head and ran at us, screaming in a way we could not ignore. In horror, we also screamed and fled towards the gate, with him flailing the blade back and forth in the air behind us, more dangerous for his lack of authority over it.

I do not know when he stopped chasing us, but we did not

stop running until we had left the Lodge behind us, and escaped through the main entrance.

There, the four of us stood outside the gate with our backs against the rough stone wall of Turner's Shop. Heaving with exertion, the cold banished from our bodies by the effort, the bellowed air from our mouths hung suspended in a vapour cloak before us.

Even as I caught my breath, another scream chased after us. Other passers-by stopped to hear what sound that was, asking each other if they knew. Obviously puzzled, they waited a while to identify it when it came again but, being quieter here, most walked away shaking their heads unsatisfied, the mystery unsolved. It was not a sound anyone expected to hear, nor recognise, since it so often stayed behind closed doors.

Or in isolated houses in the countryside, as I remembered from my own childhood.

More than Mrs Potter's dying screams, it conjured up every worst nightmare in me from my younger years: the large, wooden entry door bursting open to admit Cromwell's men; their taking whatever they wanted in the way of possessions or the body, violently and without permission. I saw my mother held down by those men. Then there were cries and screams as well.

Those attackers were the very ones to cause me to question both my own religion and the other. I could not deny, I did not wish to be in league with such cruel devil-beasts and, upon my soul, their very actions against those of their own kind turned me to the religion they reviled, and put me into a religion that gave meaning to my life I would otherwise never have known.

But, terrible as were those far distant memories, I could not recollect any night that I could match what noise came hence from the dark entrance of The Hole. Not one of the horrors I imagined the poor wretch suffering could match the severity of these screams. Perhaps unimaginable horrors were always worse than imagined ones. Whatever that man experienced was the worst Hell and had no right to be found on this Earth.

Without warning, footsteps came fast towards us from the

gate. Marie heard them too, because we both stood out from the wall together and stepped in the way of the runner. He was dressed in the garb of an officer of the prison, a ring of keys jangled rust against his fitted coat, mud clung to tight breeches and his cheap periwig was sent askew by such a fast pace that he would not have slowed down if the two of us had not stood in his way. Even then he tried to pass through us, as though we were insignificant in his need to escape.

Mrs Ayrey caught hold of his arm and said, 'For crying out loud! What hounds chase you so fleet-footed from the prison?'

Big eyed, the officer looked at the hand on his arm, momentarily taken aback that he was stopped, as if he had not seen us there. 'What?'

'I asked you, what are they doing in there?' Mrs Ayrey said emboldened.

The officer looked back towards Harris guarding the door, shook his head and pulled his arm from Mrs Ayrey's grasp. 'I dare not tell you.'

I interjected, ''Tis a man upon the rack. I'll lay my life on it!'

Again the officer shook his head. 'I know not, but I do know that if I stop here those demons will surely come for me.'

'Who is it? Is it the silversmith? Is it Prance?' I asked.

I heard there were some none too happy with the goldsmith of Covent Garden. A short time since, he took the part with Titus Oates as a witness to the murder of the anti-Catholic knight, Sir Edmundbury Godfrey that London was in such a buzz about. They said the murder was under instruction of some Catholic priests.

Having first denied any involvement, Prance then turned about to confess his part of the murder, only to recant it all once again before the King, proclaiming the innocence of himself and those he had named. It was to be supposed, it was one thing to lie before the council, and another to perjure yourself before His Majesty. They said the King promised him a pardon to allay his fears, for what was to become of him if he spoke the truth?

Word in the prison was that the lives of the three men– Mr Hill, Mr Green and Mr Berry – rested upon his not spinning another time, for he had claimed to hold guard for them, and two others, whilst they strangled the knight and ran him through with his own sword. When Prance denied his part the second time, he was returned to Newgate, whether for the first lies or the next, and kept in the insufferable coffin-cell they called the Little Ease, so that he may decide against his foolishness and speak another time for Oates.

'Please, Madam, do not ask me, for I dare not tell you. Everything I know is that I cannot more listen to this noise. Release me.' He had already released himself from Mrs Ayrey's grasp, so his request was to release him from our company. With clenched lips, my neck stiff with strain, I could barely nod, but with this, and another scream from yonder, he took his leave, running in the direction of Holborn faster than before, as if the Devil himself were after his soul.

Was there no let up for the poor tortured man? If we had authority or courage, we would have stormed that cold dark place and put an immediate end to his suffering, but none dared do it. A few women were no match to the strength of men.

But neither could we leave. Even though the groans and screams and cries were unbearable. Somehow, by hearing those screams, we suffered with him. None of us considered leaving him to cry into the night alone. We could not turn our back on him, much as it would allay our own discomfort, for we were women of charity. We had taken it upon ourselves to alleviate pain and hardships of those wrongly imprisoned and must stay dedicated to our cause. If we could not prevent pain, we must suffer with those that had it.

Though he had perjured himself, Prance was one of those unfortunates.

So we listened, trapped in that place by conscience until nearly seven in the evening. The screams became more sinister once the dark night came upon us; like a wounded or hungry animal they were perpetual and soul destroying. Paralysed by impotence and despair, those of us that dared uncover our ears could not help but cry for the man. Several times I had thought the groaning stopped and removed my hands, only to hear the fullness of the next tortured howl. My last meagre meal forced itself upwards and I turned to the wall for support as I wretched.

Then, at seven by the church bell, voices alerted us to men approaching along the street. Three men walked past us, without manners enough to either nod or raise a hat to the ladies that stood shivering by the wall, and turned into the Lodge. By his dress, the shorter, more portly one was a Minister. In the flickering orange light of his torch, his grey hair flashed orange, and the shadows of his face altered what might be the semblance of man in daytime to unnatural sinner by night.

Some of us peered through the gate and watched as they entered the Hole.

Shortly after, the noise stopped, and I could only thank God for the silence! I hoped the end came because he was no longer tortured and not because he had died, but I could not suppress the thought that if he had died, that would be a final end to his suffering, that they could do no more to hurt him.

My teeth chattered noisily in the sudden quiet, my bones ached as only old bones know how to, and I became aware that my old injuries were nagging me and that I could not tarry much longer in the cold.

Metal clashed against metal as the doors in the distance were locked and bolted for the night, the prisoners closed in. Occasionally, a muffled shout or laugh or cry came from within, but mostly we were left to stand in stillness. Then Harris pulled shut the big metal door into the Lodge with a loud clang making our cold bones clench in fright, and we could watch no more. A key turned in the nearby lock and Harris's footsteps quietened as he walked away on the other side.

'There is nought more to be done here this night,' said Mary

'I would gladly sit before a well-stoked fire now,' said Mrs Ayrey, through clacking teeth, 'perhaps with a dish of broth to warm my hands and insides.'

'I, too, am ready to leave,' I said, 'but I am loathe to leave without knowledge of what has occurred this day. Is there any willing to stay longer to discover something more?'

Mrs Ayrey wrapped her arms around her and said, 'There is not use to it. We should take to our homes now'.

'It is unlikely this night will reveal more, Mother Cellier,' said the youngster. 'I will come back first thing in the morning and see if I can discover more then.'

As their elder, they again looked to me for guidance, and I suggested we take turns to watch the place when we could.

The silence was eerie after the screams. It was as if they had torn open the air, filled it with violence and filled my whole body with such torment it reverberated deep inside me. The likes of that noise I never wished to hear again. But in that I held false hope, for it followed me home through the streets and, whenever I became complacent against it, woke me in the night many years ever afterwards.

Did Prance die? Or did he merely have respite from a fate worse than death? For the answer, I would have to wait, for there was no answer here tonight.

3

11th day of January, 1679

For the next two days, my hands were kept busy with visiting women ripe with child, or trying to conceive, or with a newborn infant. Whilst delivering these women, my mind could do nothing but stay on my task, but whensoever my hands became idle, my thoughts lingered on what we saw and heard at Newgate. The echoes found me wherever I found myself.

On Friday, I did not hear a thing from the prison, and I was too busy to discover any thing for myself, but on Saturday night, relief came knocking in the form of Mrs Ayrey. The cold, wet dark whisked round her and tried to enter the room with her. As soon as I saw who it was, I took her arm and quickly pulled her in. I closed the door on the night behind her, and bid her tell me the news.

'Tell me, Mrs Ayrey, what did you learn?'

As she spoke, she shook the dripping water from her cap, and accepted the cloth I gave her to dry her face and hands. 'You were right, Mother Cellier. It was Miles Prance. He suffered monstrously.'

'Does he live still? '

'Yes, ma'am. They've tortured the soul out of the poor man, but his body survives.'

'So, what has happened since we were together at Newgate last?'

Mrs Ayrey wiped wet tendrils of hair from her eyes and smoothed them back to the edges of her sharp but kind face, missing a drop hanging off the edge of her nose. Without interrupting her as she spoke, I beckoned her closer to the warmth of the fire to dry herself.

'I spoke to divers prisoners last evening and this morning, ma'am. They were full to bursting about it all, and informed me that the gaolers took him, heavy with irons on his wrists and ankles, to the Lodge. It is common knowledge they examined him for many hours and tried to turn him to confess falsely once more, but he would have none of it. One prisoner told me the interrogators said he had only to give in to them and he would not worry any more about a living; but if he did not, he would not worry more at all!'

I frowned, 'His cry is testament to his ill treatment, may God protect him and give blessing on his soul, but if they have a confession from him and he should perjure himself once more, he would name another to be condemned, and they in turn another. Too many are falsely condemned this way.'

"Tis as maybe, Madam Cellier, but I wish the malice on him might draw to a quick end. I have slept none of these past nights for the noise of Friday searing through my skull.'

Remembering, my lips thinned and I nodded agreement. 'We must pray they end this madness!'

'Well, the poor man was examined on Friday morning from hours before the cock crowed to past noon. The ears of the prisoners burned with his loud protestations.'

'Did they hear any of what was said when he was in The Lodge?' Was it a vain hope that he did not implicate any other? Enough had already suffered in this whole bloody mess.

'They did, ma'am. They said he shouted such things as that he did not know any of the matter, that he was innocent and would not perjure himself for them. He said, and I tell you as I was told, "What will you have me say? Will you murder me because I will not belie myself and others?" They crouched low so they could hear through the floor, and what they heard was that he was in great agony. Hard men said they had never heard the like!'

'And has it ended now? Have they finished with him?' I could hardly keep the tears from my voice.

'No ma'am.' My young friend also failed to prevent tears. I took her hands and she also held mine tight. 'Before dawn this morning they started again, and again the prisoners who lay on a spot above the Hole heard him cry out. I myself saw the Turnkeys carry a bed into the Hole. Even knowing the answer, I went up to them and asked for whom it was for. They told me it was for Prance, and…' She gulped hard and tears clung to her lashes. '…and… they said he had gone mad, ma'am, and tore his bed to pieces!'

'Oh, how the poor man suffers!' I could not help but exclaim. 'And is that an end to it finally?'

'Nearly, but not nearly enough. Tonight Prance was taken to be examined again for an hour of the clock. At the end of that hour they carried him towards the Press-Yard, and that is all I know.'

'I hope that brings the curtain down on this matter. This is nothing but a common witch-hunt, with confessions and accusations sought from tortured men in the stead of women. What difference is there! No man deserves this treatment. We must see if we are able to help him, and how we might alleviate his pains!'

My vehement exclamation woke baby Maggie in the crib and she whimpered.

'I tried before, ma'am, but they refused me. They said he did not want visitors.' She paused for a moment before adding, 'The keeper had fresh blood on his shirt.'

Knowing the manner with which they had misused the poor man, the idea of blood on the keeper's clothes sickened me – me, a trained midwife. It turned my stomach and brought bile to my mouth.

'You have done well, Mrs Ayrey. Won't you treat with me awhile? The pot is hot. Sit and have some tea and tell me more. Does anyone keep watch now?' Not allowing her to deny my curiosity satisfied, I poured us each a cup.

'Yes, I did not leave before Marie arrived, and thought you would wish for news as soon as I could reach you.'

Maggie became restless and her whimper turned into a low cry. I walked over to the crib, saw she was sleep-crying, and leaned over to rub the little one's back until she quietened. 'I give you thanks,' I said, hiding my wet eyes by looking at the baby. 'I have hungered for news. I will not rest easier for knowing, but at least I have the truth now. We must continue our efforts to reach him.

What of Francis Corral, the coachman accused of carrying Sir Godfrey's body?'

Mrs Ayrey sat in Pierre's chair before the fire and clasped the cup in both hands, a puddle forming around her boots.

'They say he also wishes for no visitors, not even his wife.'

I thought on this. 'And is he likewise treated?' Leaving Maggie, I took the chair facing the woman I examined as relentlessly as any judge quizzing a witness.

'He is condemned as one would expect an abetter of murder to be treated.' It was apparent by her dismissal, she also condemned him, though he be not judged.

'He is not even to trial!' I scolded. 'The evidence against him is not yet examined. He may yet be proved innocent of the charge.' I rested my teacup on the arm of the chair to steady it against my angry shakes. 'It might be that Corral is as guilty or as innocent as any other of carrying the body, as they say he is, but it is not for us to decide, Mrs Ayrey. It is for none but the judge and jury to discover what happened that night, and that they have not yet done!' Even sitting, I stamped my foot, and managed to spill my tea.

'Mother Cellier, calm yourself!' She held up her hand to stop my tirade. 'Let the men do their job and find the guilty ones, and we shall do ours, and that is to administer to the poor prisoners. It is not our place to prove or think one way or the other!'

'Mrs Ayrey, you cannot think that we know nothing of it. That is most incredible. You have seen what I have seen, and heard what I have heard. Surely we are not to disregard everything that comes to us for the want of being the wrong sex!'

'Whatever we think is neither here not there. It is not our place…'

Mrs Ayrey trailed off and sat rocking forward and backward in the chair.

'I will not credit you with that statement, ma'am,' I said decisively. And I did not. For she knew as well as I of the false witnesses with pockets heavy with coins to belie the innocent.

'That as may be, Lizzie, but we know not that Corral did not carry the body.'

I sipped of my cup and the tea was a tonic to me.

'If that is the case, I shall discover the truth of it,' I said, already planning how this might be done.

4

28th day of January, 1679

I jumped back when an icicle shattered into several pieces on the ground in front of me. Did someone try to murder me? Hands shaking, heart pounding, I looked up and saw many other such icicles hanging from the edge of a snow bulge, suspended from the eaves of this newly finished building, and the space where one had cracked off. It might have near killed me, but it was only Dame Nature having fun with me!

I did not wish to deviate from my path – I could think only of reaching my destination – but moved further into the road to be sure no other ice-daggers would fall on me. It was not a sign, of that I was certain, merely the weather.

The cold permeated my cloak, through the many layers of clothes I had donned that morning, and into my ageing bones.

I barely noticed the flat, blackened areas between the new houses and taverns, built since the terrible fire of sixty-six, untouched reminders of that awful week. Shells of once thriving houses, shops and inns, still mere charred remains, were now playing grounds for street children. New buildings would stand there some day, but too few carpenters and brick-layers had the largest city to restore. It was a matter of note that, where they had built, the fire was a lesson well learnt and new houses were of brick and stone.

Sometimes, catching a glimpse of blackened wood, I could still smell the smoke pouring from whole lengths of streets. And when I looked into a crackling fire, in my mind's eye I could see the sparks fly from roof to roof, spreading faster than could be doused, and then I relived the night we fled to safety along with friends and neighbours.

My good friends helped me keep my then five children together; the streets were so packed with panic and fear they were continually dragged from my side. If times were ever hard, those were the hardest. It was before I had met Pierre, so I had only myself to rely on. Happily the Lord provided me with the means to earn a living and my midwifery saved us all. Now they were grown and married, except for Isabelle, who lived with us still.

I reached the house I was told belonged to the man called Francis Corral.

I prayed Corral would inform me of the abuse he had suffered in Newgate to write it in my book of evidence. From talk at the prison I heard he was released, finally, after more than three months of suffering: six long weeks in the condemned Hole, with none allowed to see or aid him, and left to starve to death; then seven further weeks in a common prison cell, but still denied visitors.

And he an innocent man, so said those in the prison that knew all what there was to know. They also said the man, that witnessed a coachman carry away the murdered body of the magistrate, Sir Edmundbury Godfrey, falsely accused Corral only for that he happened to be a convenient hackney-coachman at the time, a haphazard scape-goat.

My knock echoed back to me, as it should not have done if the house was occupied.

I banged the door a second time. The house stayed clammed shut. All was quiet and still inside.

I thought about what Corral was accused of. I had prayed for Sir Godfrey's murderer to be discovered and captured as much as any other.

Since the judge's body was found, fear was palpable on the streets, in the coffee houses and in the homes of persons both rich and poor, but to accuse a man for convenience was a terrible crime in itself, worse, perhaps, than the original crime, for every innocent that was implicated.

Even having a witness swear to your whereabouts was no guarantee to prove innocence these days. I heard some had more than a single witness, yet still their proofs were discarded. The false accusers were determined to rid the country of Catholics with whatsoever means they had to hand, even if they used criminals, and criminal ways, to do so.

I knocked hard on the door a third time. If there was anyone at home, they did not answer. My journey was wasted.

Then I spotted the slightest movement in the corner of the upper window, nearly out of sight. There was someone at home. No doubt they feared I was come to return him to prison. There were no sounds of children. Children rarely stayed so quiet unless they feared for their lives or those of their parents, if there were children there.

How might I let them know I meant no harm? I had no token to prove myself safe. I had nothing.

Nothing but my midwife cloak.

Perhaps if I could show it at the window, that might be enough to give confidence in me... I needed a pole, or something tall, but such perfect things as a jouster's lance or a flagpole were not readily come by in the streets of London! However, in my mind was something I had seen in the debris of a burnt house I had passed a small while ago.

I walked back to where lay some lengths of beams, blackened and mostly burnt through. I did not need one to be strong, only long, so I picked up a length I could lift. I could not help but screw up my face at what it would do to my beloved garment but, if I wished to follow through on my plan, do it I must.

Was it enough of a symbol of life that they would believe it did not bring them death? I had to try. I took off my well-worn, cloak, more than mere symbol to me, more than the mark of my trade.

Other than my children and my husband, the cloak was the thing I cared for most. Maybe other midwives did not care for theirs as much as I, and there were some that had sullied it with crimes of indifference, but from the first, when I put it on, it marked more than a career and a means of supporting my family after my first husband deserted us. It was my pride and self respect, and my life.

Now I hoped they would take it as a mark of trust inside this house.

Hooking the shoulders of the cloak over one end, I winced at the charcoal blemish made where it hung against charred wood, and where it rubbed along the beam's length. It was for the good of my cause.

With my lips pressed together and resting the pole on the floor, I knocked one last time at the door. Then I held up the pole and waved my red cloak as a peace flag so they might see it. There were not many folk on the street, or I would have feared that I drew attention to myself. I should not risk being caught with one so late released from the plot.

My arm ached trying to balance the pole, so I rested it on the ground. It was bitter cold and I had begun to shiver. I should put on my cloak again. My efforts were fruitless and of no use. The signal had not worked and no one had come to the door. They were likely in too much fear to come out of hiding. At the very least, I had tried. What more could I do!

I leaned the pole against the wall, and put the outer garment back on, immediately warm and of my own character once more. I should go home and see if any had called on me. One last look at the window confirmed the stillness inside, no hint that they had seen me. I took the pole from where it leaned against the wall, turned and retraced my steps along the road from whence I came.

I had gone not more than ten paces when I heard a call.

'Midwife! Midwife! I beg you come back!'

I turned to see a woman stood on the threshold of the house that had looked deserted shortly before. She held a youngster close in her arms, pressed to her chest to keep him quiet. Without a word, I turned and walked back to the house and introduced myself to her.

'I am Mrs Cellier, an honest midwife. I come to see your husband and offer my assistance to him, and to let him know there are some of us that would dearly see him proven innocent, as we know him to be.

'Can you dress wounds?' she said, shaking and jittery. I have need of a doctor, but dare not call one.'

'I am able. Is it your husband?'

She merely nodded. The tightness in her face told me she held back a great deal of feeling and was in need of some calm conversation.

'I visit the prison and there heard talk of your husband and the wrongs that have been done him. They said he was released today, and I came to offer him and his family assistance.'

'You are the one they call The Popish Midwife.'

It was a statement rather than a question. Mrs Corral did not react to my nod, but to stand back from the entrance and let me pass. She did not hold my name against me. Once in, she passed by me and led me to the living room at the back of the house.

I was accustomed to the differing smells of homes, but here I was made to work hard not to retch at the smell of fetid meat. Curled under some bedding on the floor was a skeleton bare covered with living flesh and labouring to breathe. This man was closer to death than life. Though I did not need to ask, in my shock I asked anyway.

'Mr Corral?'

Again, a nod from the wife sufficed.

Two more children, girls of about eight and five years of age, appeared from wherever they were hiding. They held their mother's skirt and warily regarded the blanket as if the man bent like a hairpin was not their father, but a sleeping monster that might wake and devour them at any time. He was covered with a wool blanket, so I could not see any injury and did not want to disturb him any more than necessary.

'Where does he need dressing?' I said.

'"Tis his legs.' She bent down and shook the skinny shoulder. 'Francis. Francis. Here is someone come to dress your wounds. I will let her see.'

Francis stirred, and murmured, 'What use is it. I am already dead.' His voice crackled scarcely above a whisper.

'Do not talk that way, Francis! You are far from dead. Now you are come from that place you will recover. You must. Our need of you is beyond what you imagine! I will take care of you and you will be up and driving your horses in no time.'

Mrs Corral moved the blanket back and I gasped. The rotting flesh of his legs hung away in places, and stank the more for not having a cover of any sort. I clenched my teeth as, with his wife's help, we slowly moved him onto the side of his back. We could not move him entirely on his back, because his body was set in the way he had formerly lain, his legs at an awkward angle. If he had turned fully over, I surmised, his legs would point into the air over his body.

'What dreadful thing has caused this?' I cried. I had only ever seen such a cruel thing in old and bed-ridden people. It was a terrible disfigurement in a young, strong man.

'They did this to him! They chained him that way so long he cannot stand,' Mrs Corral did not attempt to conceal her anger. 'Thirteen weeks! Thirteen weeks he was cooped up in that foul, foul place, and he an innocent man! How do they dare do such atrocious thing to any man, let alone an innocent one? How, I ask you!'

She knelt next to her husband and tried to hold him, but could not, for he lay in that awkward position. Instead, with her apron strings high in the air, she lay her cheek against his and wet his face with her tears. From there, she looked up at me and begged me bandage his legs and aid him as well as I could.

Not every family could spare a fire in every room, nor even had more than one room. The door to the wooden box bed on the other side was open, and the bedding moved here on the floor to be close to the warmth of possibly the only fire in the house. I was thankful he was not inside the bed, for the bad air around him would surely have killed him in such closed space.

I had to get down on my knees to be close enough to examine his legs, as if he had not been 'examined' enough, so I hitched my skirts and lowered myself carefully down next to him. The stench this close turned my stomach so I wanted to retch more than ever, I that was used to the prison.

I could barely look, but forced myself to look anyway. I was glad for the grey of the day. I could already see more than I wished to see. Where hard shackles had gripped the legs, beneath

41

a thin layer of ragged bleeding flesh, I saw white bone. The flaps of skin hanging from the wound were already decayed and that, I surmised, was what smelled so putrid.

'Call a surgeon,' I said. 'This is no job for a midwife.'

'No! I will not have any man in the house,' she cried. 'How could I trust a man? Just see what they did to my husband!'

I understood her. Who might a person trust? When the finger pointed any which way, at both guilty and innocent, without reason, distrust became widespread. And who was I to tell her to place her trust in one that might as easily turn a person in for a few coins, when I myself had come to distrust all but a few! This family had suffered too much already.

'The wound must be cleaned or he will lose his legs. Bring me some boiling water, a knife, a candle and some garment or sheet I can tear for bandages.' I could lose my midwife licence for doing this, but what else in God's name could I do?

Gladly, I watched the woman get off her knees, move to the fireplace and hang the kettle on a hook; it was best she was kept useful. Then she bustled over to the linen cupboard and took a sheet from a meagre pile of bed wear. When she handed it to me, I knew it was her best. There were few worn patches and the edges were not frayed like the one her husband lay on and they had probably shared at night.

It took a while for the kettle to boil. In that time, we tore the sheet into strips – she did not flinch the slightest at destroying her good sheet – and talked quietly.

'I took him bread and milk. He would not let me give it to him.'

'Who would not?'

'The wicked one at the door. He threw the milk on the floor right in front of my poor Francis. Right in front of him, when he was dying for want of a drink! I tell you, the soul of that one is already in the hands of Satan!'

'What was his countenance, that I might know him?'

'Ugly as the Devil's own. I cannot say how he looked, only how ungodly and wicked he was!' Mrs Corral tore a strip of cotton with the roughness of one avenging herself on the man in her thoughts. Thrice she ripped the sheet from end to end and dust filled the air. 'But I will say that I never wish to see him again.'

'Was he distinguished by any mark?'

'He had a hard hand,' she said, touching her own hand to her cheek.

'He hit you?'

'Divers times. Once for my audacity in giving my husband bread…'

'Oh wicked! So wicked! What kind of man was he, that he would not allow simple fare as that to a starving man!' I could not help but exclaim, though I knew it to be commonplace.

'That was not the end of it,' she said. 'He most cruelly denied me to see my husband when I came to the door of the cell. He made me look to the floor and told me that if I looked upon my husband he would make sure Francis would not see his children for a long time.' We both knew what he meant by that. 'That was when he threw the milk in there. He would not let me enter the door. My poor man was in a sorry state even then! Though I was denied sight of him, I heard him groan and cry in pain.'

If the poor woman was outraged at the horror of this, I was just as so. It was inhuman!

'Then he sent me away without my ever setting eyes on my poor husband. Could a man be so cruel?' She echoed my own thoughts.

'If you did not see your husband, are you certain it was he?'

'As certain as he now lies here before us. It was his voice. And here is proof of their work. What will become of us now?'

'Believe me, I will discover who did this to Mr Corral. They must not be allowed such barbaric freedom!' It was as if the man that lay before me was the source of those screams, three weeks earlier, that dreadful noise that still lived in my head. It was beyond belief such brutal things continued even in this enlightened time, and they happened with the blessing of those who had the power to stop them.

'We must give all attention to these wounds now, but I will

find out what I can, and I will return to check on your husband tomorrow,' I said.

Before I left, I took out my purse and gave Mrs Corral coins enough to buy food, for the children looked as if they would otherwise take after their father and waste to the bone. Sense and hunger had long outweighed pride in her and she took it gratefully, curtseying as if I were a lady of high society.

'Be sure to eat something of it,' I added. If I did not say so, it was likely she would not. A mother would oft feed her children and have none for herself.

5

3rd day of March, 1679

Over the next days and weeks, I became known at Corral's household and was often greeted on arrival by the children, whose faces showed less fear of losing their father as Father Time ushered Death out the door. Sometimes I brought them sweet cake, and they would run to sit by their father to eat it whilst their mother and I dressed his wounds.

Two days after my first visit, I noted Corral had little more colour in his cheeks and was set to die. The holes in his legs did not heal, and so I insisted Mrs Corral call on a surgeon to clean them properly. I could do no more than put salve on it and bandage it, and the rot was spreading.

At first, the good woman argued against me, but soon conceded she would lose her husband if something more were not done and so agreed to send for someone. She would not have a surgeon, she said. A surgeon might tell the authorities, who might believe her husband was delivered home already dead, and they might not be happy to find he still lived.

Finally, she allowed that perhaps the apothecary husband of my daughter, Rachel, by the name of Henry Blasedale, might have more skill than I in medicine and would be acceptable. This decided, we sat and drunk ale together.

As fortune would have it, Henry was able to discover that the only way to properly clean a wound such as this was to wrap it with worms. This he did, while explaining they would eat only the rotting flesh and leave the living. It was an effective treatment that I would never have thought of.

Thinking of those three men – Green, Berry and Hill – tried for the murder of the magistrate, Sir Edmundbury Godfrey, I thought how it was surely a shame there were no such creatures that could do the same for London and rid the city of rot, leaving only the good. There was not a wit of proof against those men that stood the test of court, yet still they were hanged.

Three weeks later, Francis felt well enough to talk a little. I did not expect him to say much about his ordeals in that dark and icy cell. He started by saying he was indebted to me for saving him and for my loyalty. Later, when he recovered more, he told me the things I wanted to know. I asked about the holes in his legs and he described heavy irons called shears that were so far apart they made it impossible to walk.

'I could scarce move but a few inches, and that took all my strength,' he whispered a little louder than the first day he spoke. 'My legs were shackled by irons weighing forty full pounds or more, though the limit of the law is half that!'

They tried to have him confess to carrying the body of Sir Godfrey away after his murder, and the more he denied all knowledge of it, the more they beat him and pulled his hair. They threatened to run him through with a sword, then put him in a thing like an animal trough, where he was cruelly bolted in and squeezed until he fainted. Not only did the gaolers overlook his torment, but a minister added to it.

'Then, when they could not make me own what I did not do, they offered me a large sum of gold – five hundred pounds, they told me – to name the one who employed me to move the poor man's body. I would not do it. I would not belie another for my own gain! Nay, I must live with myself or die.' I nodded my agreement. I had a growing respect for this man.

'When they discovered I was no dog to be trained to do tricks, they chained me in the cell like a wild beast, so I could not move more than a yard in any direction. I was left to die without food or drink.'

'How did you survive so long?' I could not fathom the horror of it all. Perhaps every day I met the men that did this, that did not have a soul, but I did not know what such a man looked like.

Corral looked away to the children, and blinked a few times, before turning his head back and saying in a low voice I could barely hear, 'I was forced to sip my own water to wet my mouth for want of any other drink. The only time I saw victuals were when my brave wife dared bring some – the milk cast on the floor soured out of reach, and the keeper made me watch him eat my bread.'

'Wicked! Wicked, wicked, wicked! How is it that one in the Devil's service lives on this Earth and not where flames sear his beard?'

'It is not only those in prison that are bad. There are some in high places and some in low, I cannot tell who they are, that would point a finger at any they would have taken down.'

'Tortured until you confess, then tortured more to accuse others so they also confess. 'I say, 'tis a witch-hunt!' I said.

'Aye, that's exactly what it is,' agreed Corral. Only this time there is no line drawn between men and women; all are equal marks for gaol.'

As I sat there, I was overcome by the size of this. It was bigger than him, bigger than me, and bigger than each and any part of the whole could do a thing about. There was little for a person to do but keep his head low and watch it play out; but so many innocents would die before it did, as so many had already done.

But why should I only discover the truth of it! I put it to Mr and Mrs Corral, 'What if I should petition the King and ask him to look to his gaols? What if I should tell those that can stop it? They could demand proof, and I would give it to them.'

Warmth grew in me as I told Corral and his wife my idea of why I desired to collect all the details of his awful time. I became excited by the difference I might make.

'And what if every man and woman on the streets, and in all coffee houses, were told what happened in those places…could not that make a difference?' To discover it, they had only to go to the gaols and see for themselves, or attend the courts and hear for themselves.

Sitting next to this man, broken by the law of the land that should protect him, gave me strength to stand up for the truth.

'Will you let me tell your story, of what happened to you in the cells? What they did to you?'

'What do you mean?' he said warily.

'I must tell the truth to all people. If they know, I am certain they will stop it!'

'And maybe they would use it against you, and you will find your self in my stead.'

I raised my head, and said, 'I am a respected citizen. They will not harm me.'

'They would throw into gaol any that stand in their way. Do not believe they would not have you as well as any man, because they would.'

'It maybe so,' I thought about it, 'but I must try.'

'And I must protest! You have done so much for me, I would not see you put your very life in danger like this!'

Despite his words, I saw hope in his eyes. He wanted people to know what happened to him. If his story was not told, he would merely be another silent, tortured soul amongst many; and his story would be of interest to the rest of London. They would not care unless they understood it was innocent folk such as themselves that were in gaol and hanged for acts they did not commit. Only then might this atrocity be stopped.

'I will do it. People must know.'

His wife piped in, 'I have been in the city, Mrs Cellier. I know what they say about the one called The Popish Midwife. If you do this, it would be all the reason they would need or want to hang you from the rafters, or rip you limb from limb if they had half a chance. You must not give them that chance…stay low and live quietly, is what I say.'

'I have lived my life persecuted for my beliefs, Mrs Corral, for my parents being Protestant royalist when I was a child, and for being Catholic now. There need be no more reason than my living to find cause against me, but living should not be reason to hide my beliefs, or the truth. If I do not stand up and speak out, they will only find another reason to persecute me. I may as well stand.'

'I did not know you were a turncoat. How did you come to the Roman Catholic faith?'

'Tis a story too long to tell at this time. I have a woman heavy with twins I must visit,' I said as I stood, not wanting to think of my young days. 'I told her I would call before dark.'

I thanked the Corrals for their hospitality and bade them goodbye. Before I closed the door on the way out, I turned back to Mr Corral and asked him if he would write an account of his ordeal. He told me he did not know how to write, so I said I would come and be his scribe, if that was satisfactory to him. At his agreement, I nodded my approval and left.

Walking home, I pondered on the rightness of doing a thing so provoking. Our Almighty Father had brought me in the way of this cause, and it was not my place to question my place in it, only to divine what I should do about it. It was right that a person knowing something wrong should speak out, but I had children, and a husband I might put at risk by doing so.

The ones that had the reins of this had shown over and over they did not care about such things. They deprived prisoners of seeing their spouse or parent or child without compunction. It was true my family had need of me, but was their need more than those poor wretches in gaol, separated from their own families, and tortured in body and mind until they could stand this life no longer?

My knowledge of this atrocity made it my duty to make something of it.

I had an urge to see Pierre. I fondly pictured his face yesterday after we had bid good night to the boys from St Omers, the witnesses brought over for the trials at the Duchess of York's bidding and staying with us. I could not deny the pleasure as he spoke of his home country.

Still wanting me to return to France with him, he told me stories of his childhood, and of how he came to be such a fine merchant. At times such as these he reminded me he was not always the old man he had now become – he was once a strong man with a thriving business – and I loved to listen to his joyful tales of a youth so different from my own. As he spoke, the flickering light of the fire could not match the warmth memories that lit his face, and I happily borrowed them and made them part of mine.

I would take counsel with Pierre when I came home. He was a wise man and would know whether it was right or not I should do as I intended.

6

28th Day of March, 1679

'Will I ever carry again?' asked Lady Cholmley, trying to see what I did.

I held firm my thoughts and gently swabbed her female secrets with the oil of early summer Garden Tansy, then wiped down my hands with some rags I had in my bag for that purpose. The likes of this work brought to mind that done on poor Mrs Potter a year ago. The gentry were no more safe from inept practice than the poor.

'The Lord does not take me into his counsel, My Lady. If ever I discover the answer, you will surely know of it but, until then, we can but pray.'

'I see. I did imagine it was that bad,' she said. I knew her understanding was full.

Changing the subject, I said, 'How does your wet-nurse seem to you? Is she suitable?'

Having nursed all my own infants, I normally disapproved of the common practice in the higher classes taking a wetnurse without reason, but sometimes necessity demanded it. This mother was still too weak to feed her own, having suffered greatly during the birthing.

'I believe she does a fine job, but I fear the infant is ailing.'

'Oh?' I asked. 'In what way?'

'Maryanne says she has digestive trouble.'

'Does the infant yet eat meat?' I asked. Perhaps the nurse had not followed my instructions on what victuals the infant ought to have.

I thought of the meal that was being prepared for my family and our guests at home and a groan echoed throughout my empty belly. I did not break the night's fast when I woke, being fearful for Father Lewis on trial this day for his life. Word was that some malicious persons in Newgate spoke out against him, and if it were to be proved he practised as a priest he would surely be hanged for treason, as was the law.

'She does. I watched her prepare wheatgrass bread, soaked overnight, and boiled in a little milk as you instructed.'

'Has she eaten any other thing?' I asked.

'I believe the nurse follows your instructions implicitly,' she said with little enthusiasm.

'I will talk to her on the way out. Perhaps it is herself she does not care for.'

Payment for service was left in the usual place for me to collect as I left, so I wished Lady Cholmley well and went looking for Maryanne. I found her on her own in the nursery, holding a sleeping babe. I had mind to be quick here so I could return home and have news from Master Townley, who this morning had plans to attend the trial at The King's Bench.

'Good morning, Maryanne. How fare you today? I understand the infant child is ailing?'

'It is not much, Mrs Cellier, but a little looseness.'

'I see. Have you any soiled clothing I may see?'

Maryanne looked around the room, then pointed to a few items at the cot-side that had not yet been washed. I went over and picked them up.

'The colour is wrong. Are you unhappy?'

'No ma'am, I am not.'

'Have you eaten any such thing I instructed you not to?

'No, I have done as you said.'

What about your husband, have you laid with him lately?'

'You mean, in the intimate way?'

'I do.'

'No ma'am. You told me I must not, and so I have not. I would not do a thing to forfeit this job you found for me. Nor would I ever do any thing that would harm the infant.'

'I must inspect you.' Another time, any woman of breeding might have been shy to show herself, but Maryanne had been opening and closing her upper garments for over a year, suckling first her own infant, and now Lady Cholmley's, and was used to me checking all worked as it should.

She faced me with her top open, and I saw she was full and well-shaped. I walked over and took one protruding nipple between forefinger and thumb, and squeezed until a few drops of milk trickled out and caught them on my nail.

'You whey is too thin. I believe there is rhubarb in the garden. Eat some cooked for breakfast for three days and you will find the little one happier.' I looked at the young woman. A wet-nurse was at her best after the second child. This one was on her third, but she was healthy and robust, and I knew her brats well. She tended them lovingly as a gardener cared for his flowerbeds, and they grew strong.

'I give you thanks, Mrs Cellier. I will do that,' she said with respect.

I took my leave of her then, and walked home fast.

Momentarily, shining silver veins flashed beneath dark clouds and then there was a long low rumble. A storm approached.

By the time I reached home I was drenched. I handed our housekeeper, Susan, my dripping cloak to hang in the closet to dry and, in the absence of Anne, my maid, instructed her to join me in the bed chamber to help me dress for dinner. Before she left, I asked her if Peter was already laid to sleep.

'Yes madam,' she bobbed. 'The babe crawled himself to sleep.' With that she was gone and I went to my room.

My clinking bag of medicines and ointments seemed heavier than usual today. I dropped it on the bed and opened the large, carved oak wardrobe doors.

A loud crackle of thunder came fast on the heels of blue light that filled my room and called to attention the ravages of my full fifty years in the looking glass over the fireplace. It passed as quickly as it came, though the impression in my mind did not, even when I tried to shake it away.

I chose an evening dress suitable for company and struggled free from the wet fabric that clung fast to my cold skin. As I turned to drop my wet clothes onto the bed I fair jumped in fright. I did not see my youngest daughter enter. She stood by my bag, fiddling with the leather handles.

'Hello Maggie. What have you done today?'

'Only playing. What is this?' Having undone the catch of the bag, my child of four years proceeded to pick out items one at the time, and inspect them.

I could not wait longer for Susan. Struggling to squeeze my arms into the tight sleeves of the spring blue evening dress I had chosen, my eyes finally emerged from the lace rim neck to see Maggie holding in one hand the bulging purse of soft brown kid leather I always carried with me. She opened the string tying the top and from it took a plain white, egg-shaped stone and held it in the air between finger and thumb to inspect it.

'That is called an eagle stone, dearest, from Africa, fetched out from beneath a nesting eagle.' I came and leaned over her to look at the stone she held in her hand. 'It is special. There are others in there from different places. Shake it.' She shook it, and was surprised to hear the rattle. 'It carries an infant in its belly,' I told her as she puzzled over it, 'a small stone within the larger stone.'

'Will you birth it?'

'No, but hung round the neck of a woman with child, it will protect her from miscarrying and keep her safe.'

'What is in this one?' She took another leather purse, bound with threads, from my bag and opened it.

'Lodestones. They have power the unborn child cannot resist. Sometimes an infant is too comfortable and does not want to leave the mother's womb, so I show it the stone to change its mind. It is drawn to it, see?'

From the bag, Maggie then took one of the grey, noduled stones, speckled with red iron and placed it onto her upturned curved palm, studied it, then held it to her cheek. I did not expect what next she said, 'I would not leave your belly for this. So ugly.' I held out my hand for the stone and also studied it, though I had seen it, or one the like of it, since the day I followed my mother from house to house, dreaming I would one day follow in her footsteps. Seeing it through my daughter's eyes, it did indeed look plain.

'Do you wish to see some power of the stone?' Maggie nodded, staring at it as though it would grow wings and fly like a bird.

I went to my bedside and opened my wicker sewing box lined with red silk, and drew forth the fine needle I had last night used to fix an indignant button Pierre's new-grown girth caused to jump from a shirt that was happier in his younger days.

'Give it to me,' I said holding out my hand. Maggie placed the innocuous looking stone on my flat palm. Here,' I indicated to her to follow. I cleared a space on the dressing table and put the stone on its surface. Then I placed the needle nearby. Nothing happened. I rolled it gently closer; not much, only enough. Suddenly the tip took on a life of its own and spun round to touch the stone. Maggie's mouth hung open, her eyes wide, then she exclaimed, 'Such magic!'

'Nay, Maggie. A midwife does not cast spells. We need no magic to care for mother and child, but nature's own garden: herbs and spices for ointment, medicine and poultice, and stones such as these to assist us in our task, or ward off bad happenings. The Lord's garden holds all we need for our work, we do not borrow the Devil's hand.'

'But... but... this is magic! Are you a witch?'

'This is nature, child, a midwife's instrument. I am not a witch, and I'll thank you never to say such thing again! Those of our craft are often tasked to expose witches and give evidence at the town counsel of our findings.'

'Do you use this low stone to discover them?'

'Lode-stone,' I corrected.' No, our privilege to visit a woman's bedchamber gives us this position.' Susan came in then, and I asked her to fasten my dress, turning my back so she might do so. 'And also the trust and respect a good midwife gains for herself,' I added to Maggie, speaking over my shoulder. 'And, between us in this room, I am not certain any woman has that kind of power. Only the Lord.'

'Do the men from Flanders come to find a witch?'

'Though I might oft call it a witch hunt, for it is surely that in deed, nay, these young men come overseas to save the lives of their friends.'

'Are they witches, the ones they come to save?' Impressed as she was by the stone, she could not seem to let go the idea of magic.

'They are some of our faith, and for that they are condemned to gaol. Their only crime was to befriend a snake, to take him in and care for him, and for that they are accused by him of ungodly things, even knowing them to be untrue.'

'What did the snake say? Was it the snake in the Bible, the one that spoke to Eve?'

'You should ready yourself for supper.' This was not for a young child's ears.

'But Mam, was it? Was it the same snake?'

'A different snake, the same fork tongue. He accused them of trying to kill the King, though his proof is imaginary.' I spoke my thoughts out loud but, as usual, I spoke too openly. 'Enough now. Go ready yourself for supper, Maggie.'

'Yes Mam.' Maggie looked at the lodestone again. She raised her finger and went to touch the needle but, some distance from it, withdrew her finger as if it were burnt.

'It will not hurt you, Maggie. It holds only good spirits.'

'But Mam, why did Master Palmer cry? Did his friends die?' The question took me aback; I had thought she would ask further about the stone.

'Did he cry?' I asked Susan. At her nod, I pursed my lips. That did not bode well for news of Father Lewis.

I must raise the spirits of these young men. If they stood in court with heavy heart, it was sure to be read as guilt, or desperation to save their friends. Their testimony would be thrown out. It was how the mind of the accusers worked. The boys must be confident in their Testaments, not fearful of failure, though failure was the most common outcome these days.

'I will talk to him,' I said more to myself than any other. 'Go now Maggie, or you will have no supper!' Maggie skipped out fast at that.

'Why did master Palmer cry, Susan?'

'I know not, Madam Cellier, I did not ask him.'

'Perhaps we shall find out soon enough.'

Susan nodded. ''Tis dangerous to talk of Mr Oates so openly. You should be more careful.' Then, suddenly remembering, said, 'There is a message from My Lady, The Duchess of York, Madam.'

'What? Where is it?'

I should admonish Susan for her impertinence in chiding me, but she was right. She fetched the letter from beside my bag on the bed, where she must have laid it down when she fastened my dress.

'Here it is, Madam Cellier. A messenger delivered it this afternoon.'

I took the letter eagerly. Any message from the Royal Court was cause for excitement, but to be singled out by the King's sister in law was a great distinction.

'Thank you, Susan. That will be all.' She did not hide her disappointment as she left.

I took a thick, blue woollen shawl that matched my dress from the top drawer of the curved fronted walnut chest and drew it close round my shoulders. But it was not the chill evening air that caused me to shiver.

My mind had returned to Father Lewis and all those cooped up in gaol for no other reason but the lies of that evil man, Mr Oates, and his cronies. How many more were to suffer for that dark man's work I could not know, but plenty with his beliefs would readily point their finger at any priest that dared to take communion. The Welsh priest was on trial for no more than being saviour to the poor and holding mass for his congregation.

Squinting my eyes so that I might better see the words in the firelight, I read the instruction to come to St James's Palace in the morning. Perhaps the Duchess had discovered I tended her husband's first wife, and would ask me to tend her also, for Fortune did not smile on her child bearing. I held the letter to my chest with momentary pleasure that I might have been singled out for such honour. I would have Margaret lay out a dress for the occasion.

A short while later, I had to hold my news close as we sat at the table to eat. I wished to tell my husband of it first.

Before we could begin, the bell to the outside door rang. My family were used to the harsh sound, but the young masters from St Omers that did not live there winced. I made note to have the blacksmith fix that broken bell casing. He had twice promised to do so, and twice he had failed to do so. If it weren't for that the man was in need of work to support his large family, we would take our business elsewhere.

We waited to see who had come before we said grace. We did not have long to wait. Very soon the door to the dining room was opened by one of the boys from St Omer, with Susan following close behind.

'Come, Master Townley. Come forth and dry yourself. Tell us the news while we eat,' said Pierre to the dripping youth silhouetted in the doorway. A gust of damp air reached the table from the hall, accentuating the cool spring rain splashing against the window.

'My news may remove your appetite.'

'Then we will eat first, talk after. We have had little enough appetite today as it is,' I said, needing food in my belly.

'What, are our manners hiding along with our good humour? Susan, be so good as to take our young friend's cloak,' said Pierre.

Patiently, we waited while Susan took the wet cloak from Townley's shoulders, deftly folding it in three to cross the hall and hang it in the closet without, I suspected, a single drop wetting the floor. Townley trod heavily on the stone floor to the empty place laid for him and leaned on the back of the chair for support, catching neither the eyes of the other young French visitors, nor mine, nor Pierre's.

'A wet evening, my friend,' stated my husband unnecessarily.

Townley paused before sighing. 'The weather is rougher out there than you dare imagine.'

His tone said he talked of other than the weather. He blinked twice then wiped the drops from his lashes.

'Where is the storm centred?' I said.

He looked to me then, and answered.

'The King's Bench has its eye.'

'Seat yourself and eat, friend. Let us all eat.' The young Jesuit needed no further invitation to sit, and when he sat, he sat heavily.

'Your dish, Master Palmer?' I took the offered bowl from the young man, filled it, and returned it to his outstretched hands, noticing his eyes did indeed show the marks of earlier tears. Had he heard Master Townley's news already? I did the same for Master Cox and Master Fall. One by one I filled each dish around the large table. Margaret, who had cooked tonight, had allowed plenty to go around. My husband nodded as I gave him back his bowl, and Isabelle, my unwed daughter from my first husband, questioned me with her large eyes. I shook my head. It was not yet time to hear the news.

'Maggie, perhaps you will say grace this evening?' I hoped the naiveté of young Maggie's innocent prayer might lighten the mood but a little. Besides, I suspected that none other felt much like talking. As I thought she might, Maggie threw herself into the task with enthusiasm.

'We thank you God for the blessing of this food we eat. We thank you God, for giving us plenty to share with our friends from over the sea that are not friends of witches nor snakes! Please God, may it taste as it smells!' she declared.

When the prayer was said, nobody ate. There were no sounds of the picking up of cutlery, or metal on plates, or of chewing. Nothing. I opened my eyes and saw every person, without exception, looked at young Townley with expectation. His eyes stayed closed and he leaned his head on his tightly clasped hands. None was prepared to take a mouthful while he moved his lips in noiseless prayer. There was no doubt his heart was heavy. I dared not ask him to reveal the cause of such weight, for I knew the reason must indeed be as we feared that morning, as we feared each and every time a Catholic was taken to trial.

The proof was weak against the good and kind Father Lewes, the Welsh Jesuit also known as Father of the Poor to members of his parish, but whose real name was Father Baker. How had he been imprisoned this last four months with no evidence against him except the word of a couple of common villains? Truth must win over lies! The purity of witnesses speaking before God, sworn on his word, must surely defeat the word of a viper hissing sham tales in the court garden.

When, at last, the youngster opened his eyes, his lashes were wet with tears that did not fall, by which time we were all similarly afflicted. His eyes stared unseeing towards the jug of ale. Instinctively, I took the handle to pour some for our guests. Broken from his morose reverie, he shook his head and looked around the table and, seeing where he was, came back from that dark place.

'Come, gentlemen,' I tried. 'Let us eat this food, provided by the generous Lord Castlemaine. We will bear the news better with our bellies full. 'Tis no reflection on the hardships we bear that we eat to keep us strong.'

We soaked morsels of bread in gravy to wet parched throats, but thoughts of the day's deeds still yet made them hard to swallow. Not a word was spoken.

'Did your day's work go well, Lizzie?' Pierre was uncomfortable with the silence. This was not the way we were wont to pass supper, even on the worst of days. Outside our home, there were many ways of beating us down, but here we had each other and in that way stayed strong. I found this dolour no less hard than my husband did.

'A day as any other,' I answered, keeping my eyes on his face and ignoring the down-turned ones around the table. If any words could silence us again, it was those words. A day as any other could only mean more sore news.

'Now tell us, Master Townley, for our stomachs are full but cannot take this waiting longer. What news from the priest's trial?' My husband broke the ban on the topic once we had eaten.

'He has been brought to Newgate for examination by Oates and his kindred tormentors,' said Townley.

'Is he free now? Have they finished with him?'

Pierre knew the answer before asking. We all did – it was the reason the mood was so low – but we all needed a dam of hope to shore up the river of relentless persecutions; even one Catholic to be believed and released would give us new strength. But the wicked current was always stronger, and the dam was close to collapsing.

The case of Father Lewis was strong in his favour. He had good witnesses to prove his character and the truth of his innocence and, if any person might be set free, it would be him. His trial had become symbolic of our cause. What happened to him might be the fate of any one of us.

'His freedom now lies in release from mortal bounds,' said Townley, resting his forehead on the balls of his fists, elbows on table. Talking down at the table, his fingers grasped the roots of his hair.

'He was found guilty of being a priest, and so of treason. He will be executed as a traitor.' He was equally angry and perplexed, and more than a little bitter. 'And we all know the death of such a monstrous betrayer! He will hang until nearly dead,' Townley said strangely flat, 'but not quite. Zounds no! He will be snatched at the last moment from peace, sliced open and his entrails will be cut from his belly and burned before him, oh, to be sure he realises the wrong he has done. And he will die knowing his body is to be cut into four by the hangman and his quarters shown in the four corners of the town.'

This was the required death for treason, so he told us nothing new, but the bitterness in his voice contradicted the demeanour of hopelessness. His anger was something I had not heard before in one so young. 'All this trouble for one harmless Good Samaritan.' Townley stopped speaking and looked up to stare somewhere at the far side of the room and beyond, then finished, 'God only knows what they would do to a real traitor!'

'What is this place, that it counts a priest as a traitor for merely being one?' said Palmer, with utter disgust for the way of things. 'What madness has taken this country!'

The boys from St Omer had often talked of how uncomfortable they were in England, where they were unaccepted and unacceptable. In Flanders, as Roman Catholics, they were accustomed to thinking of themselves as of numbering amongst the most fortunate of people, feeling safe walking through the street, being respected and envied their calling to God.

'Will it be here in the city?' I asked, sickened such a devout holy man as he could die in this way. It was hard to understand how God could allow such terrible dealings to his best followers. Yet, he let his own son die in innocence, and his son's death reminded every Christian of his own morals. But Jesus returned to life. Those falsely hanged for treason would not.

'No, he is to be taken back to his home town in Wales. His only reason for being here is so that those lying ghouls might force him to name others.'

'Has he done so?' This was Master Cox, one who oft stayed silent, and who had been so until now.

'Word in the court was that they have tried many ways to coerce him to fabricate lies and corroborate the ones they tell, but he has stayed true. His conscience is clear. No deaths will ensue from his mouth.'

More than one of us released a sigh, relieved his death would not be the cause of others, as was often the way with the weak, unscrupulous or those that lost their way.

But those who broke could not be wholly blamed, when the instruments used against them were as wicked as any in Spain or in the rest of Europe. None that lived in the prisons believed any proclamation by the King or government that our three Kingdoms were free of such atrocities. It was common knowledge there that daily torment and afflictions were used to coerce good Catholic men and women to name their enemies, friends and neighbours, no matter how often denied.

Indeed, whensoever I was apt to blame Prance for his earlier outrageous lies against his fellow man, my thoughts were strangled by memories of his screams. How could I judge such a one when I had not been tested myself! But still I did. I could not, would not, believe I would take the lives of others to save my own, nor, if I knew I was to die, could I take others to the death with me. I prayed I would never be tested.

Two months ago, after I came from Mr Corral's house and revealed my scheme to Pierre, he forbade me to discover and reveal the wickedness and sin that occurred in the prisons to the King, and warned me against meddling in such things that were nought to do with me. He was fast in his opinion and would not be swayed by my deep feelings on it. And so I did not tell him of the enquiries I made, nor of the records I kept. Though I abhorred to keep any secret from Pierre, the task had been set in my way by the Lord and I should not fall short on it.

Master Palmer then gulped, and wept openly. 'I talked...I talked to him. He is the best of men, too good for this... this travesty! His trial and his false conviction cannot be overturned, but the truth should be known by every man in this city! He did nothing – nothing, I say! – to harm a single person, but has only done honest deeds to save those who needed help. They say he...he never turned a body away that wanted for food or a bed to sleep on, and he travelled by night to give alms to the poor. I must tell the truth of this. I did tell him he must write the truth to prick at the conscience of the wicked, but he said the wicked are the ones who would not read that truth, nor would they recognise it if they did.'

None spoke whilst young Palmer talked, but questions clawed for answers.

'No doubt, he is right,' said Master Cox. 'Who are the deceitful witnesses that brought him to trial? I have a desire to look them in the eye as they watch him die and, if they are unrepentant, I would gladly do unto them what is so casually done to such an innocent man walking abroad, and beat sense into them!'

'Master Cox!' said Pierre, 'I understand your wish, for I have had it also. Madam Cellier was beaten near to death a year or so since, and, in a madness that followed her treatment, I could so easily let myself take the lives of the whole family –the man, the woman and their children – if Lizzie herself had not reminded me we are all God's children, and they knew not what they did, any more than those who crucified Jesus. They only follow the ways taught to them by their society.'

As Pierre spoke, I regretted my forgiveness of a year ago. I had thought myself a good woman then, but the continuing deaths might have been stopped if some brave soul had stood against these men and told the truth ere now.

Nobody spoke, so Pierre continued.

'We must not blame the ignorant for their ignorance. They know not how wrong they are any more than those that carry out terrible deeds in the name of our church in Spain. This cannot excuse deliberate falsehoods, only can it provide the scenery in which they concoct their deceits. It matters not whether a person is born here or there, fear runs as deep throughout all countries, but there it be in Protestants when here it be in Catholics.' Pierre paused in thought. 'We are all victims of our birth and where we are born.'

Cox still bunched his fists, and I expected him to bring them down hard on the table. Perhaps it was only that such action would violate the protected space formed by master Townley's elbows on the table, and Townley's face looked deep into it, that stopped him.

'Those false witnesses had a grudge against him!' Townley burst out. 'They even admitted the man had sworn to make Father Lewis repent; his wife had sworn to wash her hands in his heart's blood, and make a pottage of his head,' he mimicked her voice with derision, 'all because they could not extract money from him! What sort of malicious monsters are these that they would take his life for a few pennies!'

'Do they have a name, these monsters?' asked Pierre.

'James. They were William and Dorothy James.' Townley's face, like that of Cox, was red, and within the sadness strong anger was barely kept in check. 'As has happened more than once, every witness for the priest was spirited away before they could testify. 'Tis reprehensible!'

'Were there none then to support him?' The idea of no person to stand by him was appalling.

'The trial was designed to see Father Lewis fail.' Townley spat the answer. He still supported his heavy head, with fingers curling and uncurling in his hair. 'Yes, the ones who revealed the grudge of the James pair stood up, but when one who had previously spoken against him was called upon to speak for him, he had already 'disappeared' before he was called.' The youth took his hands from his hair and laid his palms on the table, his eyes now shining and staring at something we could not see. 'In his favour were two witnesses that bravely unmasked the prosecution witness, a man called Price. They swore he had declared not to recognise the Father when he left the cell where Lewis was kept, yet in the court identified him as a priest and spoke out against him. Their testimony did no good for him, for the jury did not care for it.'

The rest of our questions stayed quiet. Townley looked round the table at each of us; his eyes wide, his face wet and hardened. 'And the worst of it all? If there were no doubts his trial was fair from what I have said here, this one fact reveals its travesty: The man, Arnold, that was his chief prosecutor, chose the jury himself! What think you of that!'

'Is this true?' Having stayed silent, as in shock, Palmer ejaculated as though he could hold it in no longer. 'What mockery is this!'

''Tis as true as I sit here at this table!' said Townley.

'Then he has not had a jury of his peers, and that cannot be!' Cox scraped back his chairs and stood. 'We cannot let this be! We must stop his execution and demand a fair trial!'

The boys added to each other's outrage and became more and more vengeful. I had to admit, I too wanted to see this wrong righted, I too wanted vengeance, but when they started towards the door, I had to join Pierre and protest they should wait til the morrow. They should plan how they wished to achieve their end before finishing the day in the same noose.

It galled them, I could see that. It galled me also, and no doubt Pierre, but we would likely be thrown in the prison right along with Father Lewis, were we to arrive there in anger and protest wildly at his immoral trial and prosecution. We must plan our protest.

'Brothers, heed me! Do not go now. You will not make your mark. Father Lewis will still be in prison, and you will lie there with him!' I said. 'We must design a better way to stop these lies and this persecution. Too many rot in gaol for another's false tale, whether by willing or not, and more will follow. Cannot we change the course of this atrocity our selves? Cannot we find a way to turn the tables?'

I had not known what I would say before it hung in the air, but once said, the truth and rightness of my idea gave me a peace I had not known before in this. What I sought was a reversal of the tide, or was it vengeance? I could not tell, but I knew I could not stand by one more day without doing any little thing. I could see from their faces the others agreed. When they returned to the table, we talked through the night until some time before the cock crowed, long after Pierre had found his pillow. He slept heavy, worn from protesting against our lack of wisdom, though his protest be half-hearted. He was with us on this, even if he did not desire it.

As well as finding proof of the bad things that happened in gaol, we would find proof that the Catholic plot against the King was a sham, and that men had died and more men suffered for the lies of false witnesses. We would find that proof and empty the gaols of innocent men, if it meant placing ourselves at risk.

That night, we agreed that we would take advantage of connections I made through my profession, as well as my capability of visiting Newgate, to further our cause.

I was stirred by a tingling sensation at the thought that I was to be entrusted with such vital tasks and I trembled that I might do something more valuable than merely feeding poor prisoners. Perhaps I might free them! Perhaps I might save their lives.

In the dawn light, I found my place next to Pierre, but I could not close my eyes. Even though they were open, I did not see the ceiling, but so many designs and plans we had made this night. Despite all that went on before them, as my eyes closed I remembered that I was invited to St James Palace this very morning! I would not have long to sleep, but my profession gave me many waking nights and I was used to taking my sleep where I could find it. Margaret would wake me in good time to ready myself for my meeting with the Duchess.

7

12th day of April, 1679

I hitched up my dress and petticoat, retrieved the note from my drawers, and handed it to Lady Powys. Far from being shocked by this uncouth display, she held out her hand solemnly.

'You say this is a petition from the prison? How came you by it?' she asked warily, rather than curiously. Her suspicion was warranted. Gentlewomen, such as myself, did not normally frequent such places. Indeed, the place would have remained foreign to me had I not had reason to attend a women I delivered there a year or more previously. Now I was the most regular visitor to His Majesty's compulsory dwelling, discovering and recording all the wrongs I could of the place.

'I had it from a man called Willoughby in the debtors' prison. He had heard of you through a priest that is in Newgate, that you and our mutual friend, your cousin Roger Palmer, the Earl of Castlemaine, are of generous character, and he bid me give you this, though it put me in danger to do so.'

'You say his name is Willoughby?'

'Thomas Willoughby, Your Ladyship.'

'Is he of Percival Willoughby's blood?'

'The physician? I know of him and his newfangled ideas he foists on midwives. I have great respect for him. But the writer of this letter is not of that family, ma'am. I asked him.'

'What is his purpose in writing?'

'I think you will find the purpose inside.' A witless question. She had the letter in her hand, and could so quickly find his purpose, but she continued to look to me for an answer, and since I knew one, I told it to her. 'I believe he asks for your pity, your mercy and some relief from his position. I believe he tells you he is wrongly accused.'

'Is he an honest man? '

'I believe so, Your Ladyship.' That seemed to satisfy her. She nodded.

'Then I will read it.' Lady Powys took the letter to her desk by the window and sat at the seat with her back to me.

I looked around the reception room. It was far bigger than my own, and the trimmings were more luxurious, many more gilded threads in the tapestry cushions and curtains, and gold leaf highlighting the plasterwork relief. The chandeliers were clean with no spider webs of dust, and the knick-knacks on the mantle shone with care. That she had many servants was obvious. No single person could keep the place in such good care. Our own four servants, whilst considered a respectable number by most, presented as paltry in comparison to that of the Powys household.

From her seat, having finished reading, she asked, 'Can I trust you?'

'If I were to declare myself honourable,' I replied, 'you will be none the wiser, ma'am.'

She looked surprised by my intelligent answer.

'You are right. It was a nonsense question. She looked out the window while saying this, her eyes distant but, on finishing, turned back to me. Her eyes searched my very soul for the answer to her question. She seemed to like what they saw and smiled.

'You will do. You say you are a midwife. Will you take a reply? '

I ignored the first question – it seemed it was rhetorical – and answered the second. 'If you wish me to.'

'This must go to the man, Thomas Willoughby, and none other, you understand?'

By that, I knew she meant 'not the keepers' and understood why a short while later, when she added a few coins to her note and sealed it. She added, 'Since Willoughby trusts you, then I find no reason not to. A man's trust, these days, is hard to earn, so you must have given him reason. Take this to him. Keep it under your skirt.'

Her meaning was clear, both physically and metaphorically.

'Yes, Your Ladyship.'

'And here's something for your trouble.' She put a coin in my hand with the letter, but I refused it.

'I have money enough, Your Ladyship. I have no need of yours.'

'Well, then, give it to some deserving soul in the prison. It is my understanding charges are dear in there, for even removing irons for the relief of the ankles and wrists?'

'Even for putting the irons on, My Lady.'

'How preposterous! Why would a person pay to have irons put on?'

'It is a simple choice – pay a fee to wear the irons offered, or wear some that are so great they weigh down the feet until a man cannot walk. The keepers can charge all they wish for doing as they want, whether it is to the prisoner's advantage or against it. They take money for victuals and drink, and for a pot to sit on, and for emptying it. If a man has no coin for a bed they will take it away. You can get the driest, warmest cell if you have coins enough. The rich may pay to bend treatment in their favour but, for that, their veins of inheritances are bled dry. The poor are simply punished for having no means to line the pocket of the gaoler.'

Once in the flow of this, I could not stop myself from expounding on the appalling conditions in the prison, and how prisoners were charged for every smallest right a person should have naturally, and how that rubbed biting salt into their wound of unfair imprisonment without any healing.

Lady Powys walked back to the seat by the desk at the window and sat stiff and upright, staring sightlessly at the spring downpour. If she had a conscience, she would take a moment to digest this information, for we all liked to believe such things remained in lands far away and had long been eliminated from our own country. Most of the gentle classes had no reason to visit the prison, and if they did, they were shown nice cells, where their well-to-do kith or kin could afford to be. Rarely did they see where the most of the condemned were holed. They would not bear it for the overwhelming stench. And, smelling that stench, they would likely think some animal is kept there, as I did before I went inside.

The first time I had entered the prison, I was called to attend a woman, Mrs Whitley, who, with the insistent hunger of carrying a child, had been caught stealing a single apple from a cart loaded with ripe fruit. And for that, she was thrown in a cell until a judge would see her, but not knowing his whereabouts, the infant did not wait until he might present himself in more appropriate surroundings.

I heard Mrs Whitley's labour cries long before I reached her, but they were combined with groans and moans and yells and sobbing from other cells along the way. The stink affected me greatly – I retched though I covered my nose and mouth with a hand-kerchief – but the noise of neglect was loud and turned my stomach. A dirty, ill-fed man supporting himself by the iron bars, held out his hand for money, or for food. When I went for my purse the guard ushered me on past him with the warning, 'Do not, Madam. You will not reach your target'.

I was conscious of my good clothes, and expected such niceties to rile the prisoners, because I had what they did not, but their needs were so great they only wanted food and basic care and had no care for me. Many lay down in their own filth on the floor, no longer having the instinct to move out of it. That was likely the cause of death of more men and women in there than from starvation.

As we walked, I asked the keeper why these men were in such conditions.

'They have no money,' he said.

'Surely bread and water are a right?' I asked. 'They cannot get these for themselves.'

'If they cannot pay, we ain't got bread to feed 'em. They 'ave to pay for stuff 'emselves. We ain't a charity, m'lady. They did sommat wrong, that is why they're 'ere. They shounta done nuffin' wrong if they cannot pay!'

In fact, their greatest malefaction was their birth into poverty. No matter what their crime, the affliction of these poor men affected me so greatly that I was compelled to return the following day with loaves and money. As I entered the gate, the keeper checked my basket for weapons or notes and, finding none, waved me through with indifference.

If he was surprised by my visit, he did not show it. He truly did not care if they did not eat, neither did he care if they did. He simply did not care about their well being at all, his only task to keep them there. Any other satisfaction he had was to torment them and see them suffer.

That first time, I broke pieces from the loaves and fed them to as many as I could. They were so grateful, I nearly cried when they scrabbled for the crumbs like animals. I had too little for all of them, so I returned later with more. The ones who ate before begged off me as earnestly as those who had none, so it was difficult to tell which ones to give to.

There were some that had given up hope of victuals and lay on the floor waiting to die, who did not try to take any bread from me. I could not reach them for the bars, so I found a gaoler seated in the sunshine on an upturned ale keg, and asked him if I might be let inside the cells. I could not persuade him to take leave of the sunshine and enter the dingy den of the inmates with words and pleas.

'For tuppence I'll let you look. For a groat I'll let y'in,' he said. This was a common scheme, I fast found, for turnkeys to make more than the King paid them. I gave him silver enough to enter the cells and he tested it with his teeth, jangled the keys importantly and then let me enter. That was the last time I paid for entry. After that time I obtained official papers to give relief to the prisoners whensoever I desired it.

The prisoners on the floor would not take victuals at first, not because they refused, but they appeared to have forgotten how. Once I put a small pea-sized piece of bread in their mouths, the reflex to chew slowly returned. I had also bought with me a flagon of water and spooned some over their tongues to wash it down.

There was one that was beyond help that did not chew, even with a morsel of bread placed in his mouth. He did not swallow water either. Though he had no illness that other prisoners could catch, they stayed at the far side of the cell away from him.

To them he was death; he was what they would become if they did not eat and drink. He was as a ghost in their eyes, if they looked at him at all. His presence was a painful reminder that they had nothing to feed themselves, and that they could not afford this fellow inmate pity nor kindness. Whether he had family, and what he was in the life outside, nobody knew or cared. He was simply a dead man.

After that day, I returned regularly to Newgate, bringing food, water and, occasionally, money to buy a better outlook for a person. The dead man, the ghost, I paid to be moved to a better cell with a bed and then visited him daily. It was so little, but if he must die in that hole, he should die with some respect, not as an animal.

My money was little used; it was but a short time before his body was carried away on a cart to God only knew where they took him, I did not ask; and I never knew his name though I did ask. That man's soul now belonged to God, or the other one, depending on what the man had done. It was better that I did something for the living.

The prisoners and the keeper became used to my visits, and soon I was greeted by name.

'Good morning, Mother Cellier. Sun's been shinin' hard today. We will let them in the Yard later, let them have some air,' said the turnkey, already fumbling the hook of keys from his belt and finding the one to let me in.

It was joy to me he should say so, so I commented as I walked through to the dark, damp air inside, 'That would be a fine thing to do, Mr Harris.' I was not in the habit of talking to the man that I now knew went by the name of Harris. He was thoughtless and uncharitable when I first visited, and I believed he was still. So I pondered on this as I walked along the passage to the cells. But perhaps I had influence over this coarse man as well as the prisoners.

'Mrs Cellier, I beg your assistance. Johnny has passed out. Have you some water?' This from a man who had been more concerned for his own health than any other when I first came by here, confirming the idea my visits had swayed hearts as well as bellies. The thought that I had brought a little humanity to the prison, where I had previously seen none, pleased me. I had found a use for myself. My charity might not change the way of it all, but it might alter the lives of some few men and women in my life, and that must satisfy me.

Lady Powys had not seen what I had seen. I did not know if I should say more but, contrary to my usual demeanour, I decided against it. I took the woman's silence to hitch up my skirt once more, and hid the fairly heavy note in the specially made pocket in my knickers. It should be safe there. Few would disturb the modesty of a gentle woman. The lady stood and went over to an ornately carved, wooden box on the mantel. From it, she took several silver coins, and laid them in my palm. 'Give these to some people who need it.' I looked in my hand and saw two half crowns and and three sixpence pieces, and thought of the bread that might give the good persons inside. It was an unexpected kindness.

'Thank you, Your Ladyship, I will do it in your name.'

With that, I was shown to the door.

'Will you come back and tell me what difference it makes?' she asked suddenly.

I nodded and smiled. I had not expected the goodness of this woman. 'Yes, I will do that.'

As I walked down the road, with a mission in my knickers, I pulled up the hood of my cloak to keep the cloudburst of rainfall from my head. This was an interesting day. Apart from the intrigue of carrying notes between the prison and this Lady, I had the feeling that this woman and I might become known to each other, and that could not but be a happy circumstance.

8

13th day of April, 1679

I contrived to see Willoughby the very next day.

It was not Harris at the gate on arrival. It was a young man barely out of schoolroom breeches, though I had doubts he ever had any schooling. He had the hard-eyed, soulless face that took most many more years to ripen…and a nose that was so bulbous it brought to mind an onion. He was a sassy brat, not much older than my middle children, but he was the brat holding the key to the lives of all the men and women inside.

'You leave that bread 'ere, Missus, and I'll be sure they geddit later, if yer know what I mean.'

'Pray, do tell your meaning,' I said conversationally, sure his intention was to have the bread and pass on some divers joy as the irons, a drubbing or other torment.

The boy had the 'beat 'em or be beaten' appearance of the poor, whose family had so little that the parents would often be without so that their children might have some supper; and then brother might fight brother over that mouthful and the strongest or cleverest would grow stronger. Mostly, those pickings were made into broth to feed both parents and children, but the nourishment was thinned so much it made little difference to the ache in the bellies of any. The boy was a survivor. He had come this far by beating the fight out of his siblings and winning that last piece of bread or cabbage stalk, or whatever was brought home that day.

'What I mean is what I say. I'll take that basket o' bread to the pris'ners. You go on 'ome, and I'll make sure they geddit.'

'In the year I have come here I have met most keepers. You are new here, boy. I am sure you are keen to keep your job? Just you

74

let me pass without any lip and I will tell Richardson your service to me was favourable. Don't and, well, just you see what he will do if you do not!'

There was not one man in that infested place that did not fear the ire of Newgate's keeper, a giant, sadistic man, more likely to break bread with the Devil than with men. It was not only the prisoners that feared him, but the guards as well. Whispers of his dark deeds were not hard to hear. They filled every corner of the place. Most prisoners would tattle for a morsel; fresh water would have the whole story. Every man knew him for a cutthroat scoundrel that ran a bed of thieves. Not one that I ever spoke to had seen him smile, not even with satisfaction.

'Have t'see your papers.'

I showed them.

His puny body told me it was rather his head than his muscle that aided his survival, so he was as fast as I suspected he would be to realise the sheriff held the purse to his job and he quickly moved to open the door with the familiar jangle of keys. I also completely expected his face-saving words as I passed through the door.

'Ain't ya got a piece of meat fer me, Missus?'

'You know, boy,' I said, looking skywards while I remembered, 'I do believe I remember birthing you. You are one of the Bowden boys from Cheapside, are you not?'

I knew I had found my mark when his eyes widened with surprise. He had the distinctive Bowden nose and big ears, both on a scrawny little face. He stared at me open-mouthed, as if I had used super-natural powers and, with that satisfaction, I continued walking. There was nothing like a little 'midwife magic' to smooth the passage to many a place most ordinary folk could not venture.

'Do carry my kind regards to your good mother,' I said, without looking back. I would be sure to keep a small bite of bread for the lad for on the way out. If I gave it going in, he would think it payment and ask it every time. This way, it would be a gift I could choose to give, or not, depending on how much benefit he was to me.

I once walked through the corridors with a handkerchief soaked in lavender oil over my nose, else the contents of my stomach would have been expelled. I soon found this distinguished me as an outsider more so than my clean clothes, and compelled myself to breathe the air unfettered. The stink of gangrene of unhealed limbs was dire, and sometimes bodies of the executed were kept in a cell, then left there so long the stench of them rotting was more than a prisoner living there could bear.

I remembered how, when I first went to that place, one man had to share a cell with a quartered body writhing in maggots and so putrid he held a latrine bowl to his nose as relief from the smell.

I had a lot to say to Richardson about that! He did not listen at first but, when I did not stop, he found it more comfortable to his ears to move the carcass. They moved the body parts to the yard near the strong room and have kept all bodies there since. It disgusted me to see lives of the poor finish on such a heap, yet it was better that they no longer kept company with the inmates.

But it was hunger that was of continual importance. I could never provide enough for the prisoners; they were always starving, no matter how much I brought with me. Even with all the coins I could spare, it was never enough. I did what I could, finding other good souls to help me, but still it was not enough. So many mouths made quick work of as many baskets of bread we could bring in a day.

I distributed loaves to prisoners, giving each a larger chunk than normal. With the money from Lady Powys burning a hole in my pocket, I intended buying more that very afternoon. It was but a meagre portion, but two scraps of bread in a single day was a feast to these folk, a kindness that should have been theirs by right.

I gave them nearly everything I had, allowing, as was my wont, enough for the poor families of those who dwelled here that were not provided for. The prisoners had themselves asked me to do this. Not long after my first visit, prisoners started begging me to look after their wives, husbands and children as well, many of whom were only better off for not being locked behind bars, their hunger nearly as great as for those in the cells. Their numbers were so many, too many, I could do but little. I did what I could.

Perhaps Lord Castlemaine might give me more alms for them. He was a generous man and had given often. Or perhaps I could find other persons with money enough to spare for these unfortunates. Lady Powys had given willingly when she had heard of their plight. I would ask her. I would ask her tomorrow.

Captain Willoughby was not in the crowded debtors' cell where I met him last. A man with no front teeth and eyes so sunken they disappeared into his skull told me Willoughby had spoken out of turn to a keeper. If there was one thing I had fast learned, a person inside here should not talk back to a turnkey. Punishment was often swift. The keys hanging from their belts gave them licence to retaliate with far worse punishment than the perceived crime, and most would as readily strike a man with an iron or nine-tails as deprive him of the sun or food, or fasten them to the wall or roof with chains.

I retraced my steps to the gate and the Bowden boy. I asked him where the captain had been taken.

'Give us a bit o' that loaf, and I'll tell ya.'

'Tell me and you will have some,' I said, easily recovering power over him. I had the measure of him. He paused but a moment before answering.

'They put 'im in the Strong Room on 'is own, for a bit of quiet, outta the goodness of their 'earts,' he said.

Gaolers never did anything for prisoners' benefit, only for their own, but I did not argue with the boy and give him reason to deny me.

That Willoughby was now in a cell away from the crowded debtors' cell might at first seem like a good thing, but it was not. My stomach lurched as I remembered two months back finding a man alone in a the strong room with his face eaten by rats. Prisoners told me he was only lately gone from the commoner's cell, and must have died mere hours before. The Strong Room was a foul place to put a man on his own and one of the worst punishments.

'Show me,' I said, with all the authority I could muster. My fifty years easily overwhelmed his fifteen, and mere tone of voice had him lead me to where Willoughby crouched in a dark room with his arms wrapped around his raised knees and his forehead leaning on the top of them. His back was pressed to the wall, a wise position I knew afforded him one less direction to protect himself from the rats.

If the stench of the commoners' cell made me retch, here was the worst smell I could ever imagine, and would never have wish to imagine. The Strong Room lay close to the pile of rotting bodies, in sight of the door, awaiting burial. I averted my watering eyes from those persons that once filled the gaol, but were now tiresome waste to be disposed of before disease and maggots found their way inside from the yard.

How a person might bear being that close to death and disease without losing their mind I did not know, but I saw the man before me could easily fall into that despair, if he had not already done so.

His demeanour was much darkened since last I saw him. At that time, his jaunty, 'Release me, madam, and you will gain yourself a servant of superior quality for a year, and an ardent admirer for all eternity!' implied that, though his body was caged, his spirit was free, but now his hunched back and dropped head was more than a physical position; it was a statement of his place in this prison and in life. It was most unpleasant to see any man so consumed by despair and so lacking in vitality.

He raised his head as our footsteps approached, and greeted me, 'You came back. I knew you would.' His voice told me he had known no such thing, nor had he even believed it. He searched my face to see if I had brought news from his hoped-for benefactor. I could not pass Willoughby the message from Lady Powys with the young turnkey standing beside me so, searching in my basket, I found some victuals to send him away with.

'Here, young Bowden, I have some bread for you and a carrot from my garden. Maybe you would prefer to eat them away from here?' I looked pointedly at the young gaoler – it was a stroke of luck recognising him – and at the rotting cadavers.

He took the food and the hint and nodded then left us. I did not think I could have eaten so close to such fetor, but a person could become used to it with time and hunger, and Bowden proved this by eating some of the loaf as he left us. The way he hunched over it confirmed my earlier image of him fighting for his food, and probably keeping his back to others so they could not snatch it.

Though he was only a young'un, he had the power to make life very difficult for those inside, and could also make things difficult for me. But, with care and time, he might as easily be taught the simple necessity of treating a person with dignity to the satisfaction of us all.

'Quick, does she send me a message?' Willoughby's eyes were crazed with a mixture of hope and despair. He begged my answer before I was ready to give it. He pushed himself to standing and wobbled to the bars that stood between us, kicking a dead rat into the corner. I saw two live ones scurry to where he had been sitting and search the area with their noses. The fire had burned most from the City, but numbers had increased again since then. These odious vermin had no shame, showing themselves whilst we stood right there! However, I did not cringe; I was used to seeing the creatures in the cells.

'Eat first,' I said, fearing Bowden might still be close by. Neither did I wish for him to see where I hid the letter.

Trying not to retch at the smears of filth on the hand that took it, I gave him a chunk of bread, which he ate voraciously. Under the dirt on his hand, I saw what looked like the letters 'N' and 'G' that I did not have time to wonder at. 'Turn your back,' I said. His puzzled look gave way to understanding; he remembered I had asked him to turn his back when I hid his note to Lady Powys.

Willoughby took the opportunity to stuff the remaining bread in his mouth more in the manner of a beast than refined rearing would dignify.

I quickly retrieved the heavy, coin filled note and said, 'This is for you,' then watched as an eager Willoughby took it, felt the weight of it, then opened it as if it might contain a summons to the court, without knowing whether it would be as a paid witness or the condemned.

He looked up with such hope that would make a cloud smile. Tears pooled in the bottom of his shapely eyes and, when he blinked, stuck to his eyelashes and made them pretty like a woman's, strangely more masculine on a man; and despite loving Pierre with all my being, an unexpected rush of adult affection shot through me and brought me closer to the young, handsome fellow.

'Thank you, madam, thank you! You are kindness itself!'

'Am I kind that I am merely the bearer of good news?' My smile was a match for his.

'Aye, you are indeed!' he said. 'The good Lady Powys has given me enough to get out of this damnable place and to a better hole at the King's Bench. She has also declared herself to have sympathy for me.'

'That is indeed good news. Shall I call the turnkey back? '

'He has no authority. He can do nothing. A man will return at sundown and I will charge him to release me from here then.' Willoughby paused only a heartbeat then said, 'I owe you a great debt, madam; a debt I shall repay you before the end of my days, as surely as I stand here now.'

'That you can leave this dreadful place will be thanks enough,' I told him. 'You also do me a good turn when you collect stories of bad treatment here. How goes that?'

Clasping the read letter in one hand, and coins in the other, he still managed to hold the iron bars and press his face into the gap. Checking the door, he lowered his voice. 'I have started the article, as you asked.'

Satisfied, I privately extended gratitude for the written evidence to my friend, Mrs White, that had told me of her good fortune in acquainting herself with Willoughby whilst in prison. She had told me that he had sworn vengeance on Captain Richardson for his excessive severity, and she had been right.

'I will put the accounts of torture and ill use in this prison before the government and the King so they can know the Devil does not choose instruments of his work from only men far away, but also from amongst our own.' I paused to reflect on how God and the Devil were equal in not favouring countries, nor even favouring religions, only the instruments they would use each to their own end.

'Perhaps I can repay your kindness sooner. Are you able to keep a secret? '

'It might depend on what importance it has.' I will not promise to conceal something if I do not know the content of it.

''Tis of the greatest importance, and to do with the King.' My ears pricked up like a dog's on the scent of such mystery. 'What do you know of the King, is he in danger?'

''Tis a plot, Madam, of the direst sort.'

'Have you proof of it?' I asked. Many bragged they had information since the King had declared he would pay for it, and if all versions were true, as many plots prevailed as there were persons in the country!

'Aye, I have. There's a man I know at the King's Bench that has evidence,' he said.

'And do you know who is involved against the King?'

'I do, Madam. Do you swear to hold my secret close?'

'My lips will not release it unless it is to save the King,'

'These words I tell you hold great weight,' he reiterated so quiet that I needed to hold my head closer to the bars and take down my hood, that its rustle against my hair did not prevent my hearing his whisper. 'If the words found their way into ears of plotters, they may act prematurely and none would be able to stop them.'

''Tis understood,' I nodded.

'Good. You are the one they call The Popish Midwife, whom they speak well of in here, which satisfies me you will keep good your oath, for this plot is made by some who have positions close to the King, and who are trusted by him.

'Tell me who they are!' I could stand it no longer. If the King was in danger I must discover all I could and prevent it.

'Patience, Madam. I must tell you, when I give you these names, you must not run to the King or his men with this story. There is no proof but what I overheard in the prison there, and that from a man named Strode, who is now too clammed up to let loose such information again. He only revealed what he had when he was woozy with liquor.'

'He spoke in his cups? Perhaps his word cannot be trusted.'

'Aye. But true or not I must reveal to you what I know. The men I tell you of huddled together to hatch a most horrendous plot. Their plan was to kill the King by several means, but to make it appear to come from the Romish[3] side, the Catholic side. The Popish Plot is nothing but hatched from their imaginations. 'Tis the Presbyterians who should rightly own it! I am further told, Sir Godfrey's death has been turned on the priests and My Lord Bellasis, that is in the Tower, by Oates, for the magistrate knew Oates lied in the affidavit he made to him of the plot.'

'What? Treachery! And it was their plan to lay it on us? With what method did they plan to carry out this dastardly act?'

'Poison, perhaps, or maybe the sword. The man did not say.'

'But you are certain it was not a creation born of too much ale?'

'The details are not certain. The plan is too early, I think, for details to be known. All I am sure of is they use the accusations of that false man, Oates, to direct the finger of the law at the Catholics and away from them.

'So, you know no details of the carrying out of the plot?'

Was I disappointed? But, yes, I would as lief be the discoverer of it, and to bear this news to King Charles and his brother, James, the Duke of York. I would have proof that I, as a Catholic, not only would not kill the King, as many would believe, but would defend him with my life and save him if I could. Furthermore, I yearned to be accepted back into the Royal Court.

When last I was summoned to the court a fourteen-night ago by the Duchess of York, it was merely to satisfy which of two recipes she should best use to strengthen the womb against the unbearable burden of miscarriage: a potion of cinnamon, nutmeg, sugar and eggs as she had heard from her mother, or a powder of dragon's blood[4], red coral, amber grease[5] and bezoar[6] in burnt claret wine, a recipe told to her by Mrs Wilks, her midwife.

Wishing no disagreement with either woman, I told her both were perfectly acceptable, and that, if it so pleased her, she could occasionally lay on her naval a bread poultice of Camomile flowers,

Mastick[7] and Cloves, bruised and mingled well with some Maligo Wine and rose Vinegar. My own recipe and advice was received with gratitude, but as yet no further invitations were issued from the palace.

Willoughby's information would place me in a position of goodwill and trust, and I might be welcomed as once I was, when I had waited on the first Duchess of York. To be so vindicated would be the greatest boon.

'Not the details, but the men involved for certain.'

'You had better be sure of your facts.'

'I am as sure as I stand here, I tell you.'

'Well, then tell me.'

'One, you will be surprised to hear. That is Lord Shaftsbury.'

'Shaftsbury? No, this I will not hear – he is tight with the King!' His face fell, for he thought I did not believe him. I did not doubt him, the man, only the truth of what he said.

'He is the head of them. He is the one that gathered them together.'

'If you say so then, but he is a knight. It is hard to think of a more honest or decent profession.'

'Does that not make it of more concern, not less?'

I thought about this, and realised he was right. One that appeared honest might be given more power than one not trusted; allowed into a position where he could hurt a person, because they did not believe he would. Shaftsbury was such a man. His closeness to the King disguised the harm he wished him. A coldness ran through me.

'Have you other names?'

'He mumbled a few,' said Willoughby, 'but I did not know them. If I ask him now, he would suspect me of angling for them.'

'Can you insinuate yourself into closer acquaintance with him and discover the truth of the matter, Captain?'

Willoughby thought for a while, then said, 'Drink loosed his tongue once, so it might do so again. When I go to the Bench, will you find me a bottle of something strong that I might tempt him and unfasten his tongue?'

'We must do all we can to discover this plot and expose it. I will bring what I can, perhaps my son in law can make me something. He is an apothecary by trade. Will you become familiar to this man and be his companion? He might be willing to talk without inducement.'

'I have tried that. His lips were locked tight as a Girdle of Venus without a key.'

I laughed at his crude wit, surprised I could find humour in this terrible place. Willoughby's eyes creased at the corners, and for a moment I saw a glimpse of his teeth – yellowing, but even and whole, though needing a good clean. What came forth was more of a cough than a laugh. This man was an open speaker and did not hide behind the pretended morals of the gentry even coming from the same. I liked one who spoke freely of the world as they saw it and with good humour.

Another rat ran close to Willoughby's feet and the stench of death reminded me where I was, so I stopped laughing.

Willoughby also stopped and his face became desperate once more. These surroundings could not but weigh heavily on him. After all, he was a debtor not a criminal, and even one that deserved greater punishment did not deserve such foulness.

The Strong Room was designed to keep a man solitary. Though I had come here ere now, I was not certain I would be let back. I was only allowed this visit because the Bowden boy was a greenhorn and knew no better. Veteran gaolers might not let me come.

'Willoughby. It is of vital importance we discover this plot as fast as we can. We must let the King know of it. I will talk to the turnkeys, and see what we might do to get you moved from here. You have payment enough, but it will take time to move you to the King's Bench, if they will let you go.'

'You are too good, Madam. Your kindness is a tonic to restore me.' Then, before I could step back out of reach, the rascal took hold of my hand in his mucky fingers and raised it to his lips. Repulsed by the touch of one so dirty I nearly snatched it back, yet a bolder part of me, the one that fluttered with adult affection when he shed a tear before, would have liked him to hold the cherished hand longer.

The jaundiced whites of his eyes, bright against his dirty skin, could not diminish the sapphires that peered directly at me through long lashes as he raised his lips from my hand. Even then I did not withdraw my hand, but waited for him to give it.

'I am ever your servant, Madam. If ever it is in my power to be of assistance to you for all you have done for me then I will use it.'

'Thank you, Willoughby. In my turn, I will do all I can for you.'

'Your kindness will not be forgotten, Madam.' For a moment before I remembered myself, I was beguiled into thinking myself a lady romanced in court, but it lasted only a moment. The Bowden boy came and told me I had to go. I became a common almoner in a stinking prison once more.

The Bowden boy said Richardson, the head gaoler, was on his way, and I must not still be in the Strong Room when he got there. The lad did not wish to heap trouble on his shoulders if I was found here, it being forbidden for me to have such a run of the place. I surmised that, if he was found to do wrong, he would likely receive some of the same treatment as the prisoners. Any not as rough and cocky as the other turnkeys was fair game to be slashed by their spurs. He might as well be beaten as lose his job.

I did not wish the boy harm for his sympathy to my cause, so I bid Willoughby farewell and promised to find him again soon. I left him with another chunk of bread, which he ate ravenously as if he had none before. I had not thought to bring ale to wash it down, but would bring some next time.

I gave one last piece to the Bowden boy going out the gate. It was gratefully received. I had much work to do.

9

26th day of April, 1679
(late morning)

'Heed me well, *ma chérie*. Take good care.' Pierre took my hands and held them to his lips, then continued to hold them, reminding me of another time they were held in that way, not so long ago, in a different place. We sat at the unlit fireside talking. Moments before, I had told him of my plans to release Willoughby this day with the assistance of Lady Powys.

'Lady Powys is of good blood,' he said, 'but 'tis dangerous to stand in her company. There are spies everywhere. And though we know it be false, her husband is held to account for the plot against our King.'

'I am acquainted with all this, Pierre,' I said, 'but she is a good woman. It is with her aid I have helped more innocents in gaol than I could have alone. She is generosity incarnate. If you saw how grateful are those in need for her charity you would not doubt her.' I turned my hand to hold his hand as he held mine. Pierre was so patient with me, and my quest to better the lot of prisoners where I could, but he feared too deeply for my safety.

'I do not doubt her, only her company, Lizzie. Any associated with the good Lady will be tarred by the same brush as her, for she is painted with that of a conspirator along with her husband. It is said, the true reason she was not herself taken is not because she is believed innocent, but only that proof could not be found against her. They will continue to search for any proof, even false proof.' Pierre paused, then asked, 'She is very interested in this Willoughby. Why is that?'

I did not know how much to tell Pierre, not because I did not trust him, but because I did not wish to gather his disapproval.

He would not like my meddling in politics. 'The man has laid bare himself to be employed by Lady Powys, and she has seen fit to set him a task.'

'What sort of task?' His suspicious attitude was warranted. I stayed quiet for a moment whilst I tried to order my thoughts. I did not want to keep secrets from Pierre. Not telling him before was an omission not a falsehood, but now he asked outright, I must reveal what we, or rather I, had done.

'Willoughby is compiling an article.'

'What article is this you speak of?'

'He gathers evidence of the ill treatment of Catholic prisoners, with the names of witnesses.'

'What will he do with it, once compiled?'

'My dear, I have to break my mind, and admit it is I who will do something with it.' I could not prevent grimacing as a puzzled frown crumpled his forehead along well-worn lines, shadows made deeper by the flickering firelight.

'You? What is this article to you?' When I did not answer, he said with strong voice, 'Again, I ask you, for what purpose will you have this article?'

I was obliged to tell him all.

'I will send it to Parliament, Pierre. What do you think of that!' I raised my chin in defiance of the anger I knew would come.

'I think you are mad.' The look in his eye told me he spoke truly. 'Our religion is the most reviled since that snake, Oates, hissed out his lying accusations. He has much to answer for, and he will answer in the eyes of God, but we must answer to the King and his government, and if we give them reason, they will be glad to offer us extended stay in the very prison you visit and decry!'

He was right, but I was compelled to defend my actions.

'In faith! Yes, I am mad, if being mad means being driven to distraction that they close their eyes and look away. They say we are better than other countries and do not condone instruments of pain and extortion, yet they will not stop the use of them. Worse! Evidence is that our government employs the keepers to use this foul practice to extract false confessions and accusations against others to their own end. Oates has only given them reason to use these methods, but they enjoy their task too much and absolve their actions by saying it is in defence of the King.'

''Tis not for you to reveal this abuse. You are not in a position to do so. You are a Catholic, a midwife and a woman combined.' Pierre softly pleaded. 'To me you are perfection, but the eyes of others are marred by prejudice against you. They will find reason to turn this onto you.'

'Do you think I should leave those innocents in prison to suffer, when I can help them?'

'I think you should pass your article to one who is not so disadvantaged.'

'If you think so, tell me who should do it! Gadbury? He talks loud, but does not have backbone. Who then? Lord Castlemaine? Lord Peterborough? They are even now at risk for their acquaintance with those in the Tower!' Though I knew he would not like the idea, I was disappointed in his dissuasion. Some secret part of me had hoped he would approve and applaud my desire to help.

'What of your Lady Powys – does she wish to present the article?'

'And how, pray, is that different from my doing it! Is she not in a worse position? As you have said, her husband is even now held as a plotter. Less provocation than I can give will turn others onto her. Surely she is more of a target than myself!'

'Perhaps you are right,' Pierre said quietly, a little defeated.

'You must know I support your charitable ways, *ma chérie*, but I cannot support you in this. You will bring danger to us all: to you, to the children, to me, and to any that know us. Remember how badly you were injured before, and they had no reason against you then. Think what they might do if they have.'

I well remembered the Atterbury family and how they had called me 'The Popish Midwife' with such venom as they maliciously pummelled me to the ground for no other reason than my faith, and that was before Titus Oates shook up the hornets' nest and brought such stronger revilement against us. Though they were found guilty of assault, it did not detract from how I had nearly died. Without Pierre, I would have. He had given me the will to live.

'Will you not then support me in this, Pierre?' I said. 'I will do it with or without your support, but I would rather have your blessing.'

I had gone too far along this path to turn back now, so close to my destination. I had proofs and witnesses, and must do something with them. Pierre did not dismiss my plea out of hand, but thought deeply on it. He looked down at my hand held in his. I expected more discouragement.

''Tis wrong what they do. If a man, or woman,' he smiled at me in a way that wrinkles appeared all over his face, 'does not stand tall for his fellows, if he or she does not defend the rights of those more vulnerable than they, then they cannot be seen as honourable nor worthy. Action might be the only thing that separates one with decent heart from one that stands by and allows foul play. If a person does not do what he can to prevent wrong against others, who then will defend that person when the same wrong is done to him?' Again he examined his thoughts in quiet, then suddenly declared, 'I will not prevent you from your path but declare I will be your strength in this venture.'

'Thank you, oh thank you, my turtle!' I kissed him strong on the lips. 'Your wisdom is most honourable!'

'You inspire me, *ma chérie*. But I must ask a thing of you. You must take care of those you would conspire with and against. The latter are not weak, nor are they slow to act. If you rile them, they will as lief have your life as invite you to dine.'

'There now!' I said. 'I near forgot! Lady Powys extends an invitation to myself and Willoughby to dine at Powys House tonight. It would give me the greatest of pleasures if you would accompany me?'

'By the bones of St. Becket! Did you not comprehend my warning? 'Tis not safe! You would place your life in danger for the sake of civil niceties?'

'It was but a moment since you said you would stand by me and be my strength,' I said reproachfully.

'But to be cosy with Lady Powys, *ma chérie*! Do you not think that goes too far?'

'I am to introduce Willoughby to Lady Powys and it would benefit the task if your presence was felt; you are a wise and calm influence. Perhaps you could also offer Willoughby a contract, or some employment to occupy him, to keep him from returning to the debtors' prison?'

Pierre paused before he said, 'I am a man of honour, Lizzie, and I will do it for you, for you are my wife and a good woman, but I would not be a good husband if I did not warn you of the perilous path you take.'

'I know, my dear, but if I do not take it I will not find my destination. Those poor folk in that Palace of Horrors have none other to speak for them. The prisoners cannot speak for themselves for fear of retaliation on themselves or their families; and their families cannot speak for fear of punishment on the prisoners. I am not of them, and I can exploit this position. I have knowledge of many genteel women that I can ask to use their influence in my quest.'

'Again I say take care, Lizzie. Position is not a guarantee of safety. In fact, some might use this as the very excuse they need to trap those in such positions when they could get them no other way.'

He was right, of course. His wisdom was a thing that made him dear to me. I must be careful.

'I have more to unburden on you, Pierre,' I added, knowing I must reveal everything if Pierre was to be involved. 'The man, Willoughby, has discovered a plot.'

'What? Another plot? Are there not, even now, more plots than there are Kings?' Pierre laughed, until he realised I did not. 'You are serious. What is this plot?' I told him how Lord Shaftsbury planned to kill the King and blame the plot on the Catholics.

'I trust you have inspected the facts. 'Who are those involved?' he asked, worry and tiredness etched deep in his wrinkled face.

'We know a few, and are discovering more. This task we have given Willoughby, by reason that he has a talent in this direction.'

'This man has too many such talents,' Pierre commented gruffly.

'Perhaps. But we must be glad for this blessing. He has of late set himself to discover more of the plot at the King's Bench. Although,' I mulled aloud, 'he is now returned to Newgate; another of his talents, I am told, being to escape most every prison he was ever held in.'

'I shall come to dinner to meet this man, and the good Lady Powys, if only to ensure your safety. I intend, also, to discover this man's agenda, and what he will gain from this. I fear someone must also take care you do not extend your actions beyond what is safe!'

'Merci, dear flittermouse[8]. My adoration for you is founded on firm ground. Together we will build a good case.'

Pierre lifted my hands to his lips once more and kissed them.

'Believe this deep in your heart, Lizzie, I would die for you, if need be, though I'd lief as not.'

I prayed I would never test my husband's declaration.

10

26th day of April, 1679 (afternoon)

'Captain Willoughby! I have it, Willoughby. I have it!' I said, barely keeping from shouting and already drawing attention to myself from other persons nearby. 'Willoughby, Come hither, and look what I have done for you!'

The first time I saw him, Captain Thomas Willoughby informed me he was disowned by Baron Willoughby of Willoughby in Essex, for disgracing him with bad debt. I did not know of this family, but my thoughts were not charitable toward any relative who would throw off one for simple debt that was not of that person's making.

None is given life without resistance, for that is what makes us strong, yet some have it more tolerable than others. It appeared the Captain was tested early in childhood, and that my mothering disposition responded to his call for aid.

Now, however, Willoughby did not respond to my call. He did not move at all. He merely sat on the floor with his arms wrapped around his knees, and his head resting on them, as he was before, except this time his stillness gave cause for my words to carry both urgency and authority.

'Thomas Willoughby, take your rump off that stinking floor and get over here!' I said sternly as a mother talking to a child that did not get up on a cold morning to do their chores. After much calling and chivvying he looked up. Straight away I saw streaks of clean skin from beneath his eyes and running over his cheekbones. I feared that, though he was no stranger to the wrong side of iron bars, the monstrous place had reached its barbaric claws inside of him, in the way it reached into most every inmate in time, and was ripping the soul out of him.

I had expectation that my good news would return some of his spirits to him. I would have him wipe those streaks from his face and bring him back to his natural humour.

'Madam Cellier,' he said with a weak tremor, but also with a faint hint of hope.

'I have news that will cheer you Willoughby. Come, do not be shy of it!'

He did not stand, but continued to sit unmoving. It seemed Willoughby's life force had left him and gone elsewhere for it was not in him. When everything a man had to live for was another day of wallowing in his own filth, he would not be the first person nor the last that this place would destroy the will of. Even his appetite had faded by the day. Some prisoners went down faster than others, but this one needed to be the wit and charm of society, any society, to prosper. He would not survive a long duration in this place. I had heard a prison had never held him so long, such was his dislike of being held and his wont to escape.

His dejection took his charms from him…how could a woman be anything but maternal towards a young man with his backbone removed. Instinct would bid me hold him in my arms until the shaking stopped and I could wipe his face clean. Any flutter that might have surprised me in earlier meetings had been long bedded down beneath a blanket of compassion.

'I have bread for you, Willoughby,' I said. Having found the smell in that place too much of late, I had revived using a lavender-scented handkerchief in order to breath freely, but now removed it from my face so he might see my smile. 'I have something that will satisfy you a whole lot more. Come closer that I might give it to you.'

I deliberately slipped a little sauciness into my tone for the benefit of Harris, who was standing out of sight, behind the corner. He would hear us, but would not see our actions, unless his suspicion brought him forth. Did he not have wits enough to observe how the rushlight[2] behind him cast his dancing shadow into the corridor?

None doubted Harris doubled as a spy for the Government, to discover any plot or any indiscretion that could be held against a man already doomed for his religion. I did not wish him to think Willoughby and I had but a charitable or flirtatiousness acquaintance. Nor did I wish him to pursue his examination of that morning of why we stayed 'yoked together as two cart horses'. It was easier to have him suspect the only use I had for Willoughby was as a sinful woman of the street, and play to the common belief that all midwives were whores, but it was not a part I enjoyed playing, especially since it did not help to dispel that false belief.

Again I gestured for Willoughby to come over, but still his puzzled frown showed his confusion, and still he did not move. He was too far from the bars or I would have reached out and grabbed him from his slump.

At last: some comprehension in his countenance. He put one hand against the wall and used it to balance and support him as he pushed with the other on the floor and rolled first to his knees, then up onto unsteady feet. Once-healthy, smooth skin had paled and sunk to the bones of his face and hands. He now resembled every other prisoner here, to whom the meagre bread I and my friends brought was little but a way of forestalling death.

'Aye, my dear, come on over here where I can see you. You are a skinny one, ducks,' I said, falling into local slang. 'Come on, don't be shy.'

With my hand, I continued to gesture madly for him to hurry. I did not want the busy-body Harris coming round the corner and seeing what I would give him; he would take and examine it. Willoughby almost fell against the bars, and took hold of them to balance himself. His weakness was no weakness of character, but of body.

Lowering my voice to a whisper, I said, 'Give me your hand.' When he proffered it, I placed some coins into his palm and, because he simply looked at them, closed his fingers round them and pushed his hand down by his side.

Perhaps that we were too silent and his curiosity was piqued, Harris came round the corner at that point, his nose for gossip right perky, for he immediately sized us up and saw me holding Willoughby's hand. I did not dare let on I had given the captain money; there were no witnesses if he took it away. Not only might he take what was Willoughby's, but he might also take what was mine too, a thing that had happened before.

The turnkeys had no more compunction about blackmailing a visitor out of what they had than taking it from a prisoner. They saw a prisoner's family and friends as responsible for the charges they extorted as the prisoner himself.

Stories were rife and detailed about the divers ways the keepers thought to extract many pecuniary benefits for themselves. As I had told Lady Powys, they would take everything owned by a prisoner's family. At the right price, every human thing could be brought, from the luxury of a less crowded cell, where one might lie down, or even a private cell, to having straw or a blanket to lie on at night.

I had not told Lady Powys how those heavy irons they made a prisoner pay to put on not only prevented movement, but ripped the flesh to the bone. And when they took payment to have them unlocked again, like a knife the irons would take the flesh with them. I could not help but remember the white of the bone of Prance's leg and the ragged, putrid edges of flesh surrounding it.

Another thing I had not told Her Ladyship, for it was not a thing for her gentlewoman's ears, was of such luxuries as the bucket. For a fee a prisoner might have the privilege of a bucket for his waste, without which he must lie in it. Of course, when it was full, he must pay for it to be taken too.

Families of inmates often watched their loved ones thrown into debtors' prison for want of money to pay bad debts, only to be further forced to watch them die inside for want of a crust of bread, and no monies to pay for necessities.

It was not unusual for scarce-found payments meant for food to jingle in the gaoler's pocket against his keys, with no bread given. 'Twas the same for water. No water without money, and sometimes none with it either. And since it was the breadearners who most often found themselves locked up, so it was their fate, in turn, to see their families suffer and starve only to join them inside, leaving their brats to survive on the streets.

I saw these things with my own eyes. It was no less ill to see the lot of debtors, whose only crime was poverty, than to see that of Catholics, whose only crime was their faith. All were equally punished and bled dry for the privilege of being so trapped.

My daily visits alleviated their lot so little, at times I wished I had tears left to cry. When a man lay down determined to die, that he might end his and his family's servitude to the prison leeches, he would refuse my alms and no argument could change his mind. I wished to alleviate his pain, but I understood his desire to die quickly rather than make his loved ones suffer longer. The plight of most would not change for want of time. Those would never have more funds, and what might come to them was best used to feed the children.

A prisoner could only pray his fortune might be changed by an unexpected sum of money coming to him, or by a wealthy gentleman paying his debts and taking him as a servant until the debt was repaid.

Since Willoughby's prosperous family had cut him off from his inheritance, he was in no better position than a pauper that had spent his entire life surviving the street. Nay, perhaps worse, for he did never learn the street ways to cheat death that poverty taught, nor what character he should play in fate as it was dealt.

In a family of as good fortune as his own, Willoughby would have had expectations for a fair deal, and would never have needed to watch for the crooked croupier of life hiding the good cards by shuffling them up his sleeve. The scales against him to play straight would weigh heavier on this man than on one who knew a fixed game was inevitable and had no expectations honesty.

Willoughby clasped the coins as I straightened the front of his jacket, trying not to cringe as I touched something wet on the lapel, making certain to look as if we were caught in intimacy.

'He might have been a passable catch when he came in, Mrs Cellier, but you would not want him now, if you know what I mean. Look to his hair, Missus, see if you can find better company in what crawls there!'

Unwillingly, I looked at Willoughby's hair and indeed saw it move. My instinct was to recoil, but I made myself place a hand to his forehead and wipe a lock from his face.

'There is a fair bit of game in this one yet, Harris.' I laughed in a bawdy fashion. If they expected lewd behaviour from me then I would play that game, as if my only interest in this man was to bed him. At this time, there was naught further from the truth. Apart from his stink and mucky skin and lice crawling in matted hair, I had my Pierre at home to satisfy me. But as long as lewd thoughts filled the gatekeepers' heads they would not suspect my true intentions.

'Well, don't mess the goods about, unless yer willing to pay, of course,' he laughed with a baseness that put us on the same low level. 'Give 'im bread if you want,' he added generously, 'and be gone.'

With that, Harris walked back around the corner and away to make some other person's life a misery. Finally, we were alone.

'Captain Willoughby. Thomas,' I tried, as the man's eyes had glazed and he stared lifeless ahead, even standing as one of the living. 'I am having you out of here.'

At this, there was a tiny flicker of something that might have been recognition, or might only have been him blinking at the piece of dirt caught on his long lashes.

'You must find yourself, Thomas. I will pay your debt for you today, and you will be released as soon as I have that done.' His dark brown eyes came to focus on my face, not yet in hope, for the news had not reached his heart, but the words were in his ears now, trying to reach his mind.

'And I have my maid, Margaret, fetching some fresh clothes for you to wear.' Only now realising his state, Willoughby slowly looked down at the filthy rags he had worn since pawning his own good clothes.

'You have done this for me, Madam? Why would you do so?'

'You have honoured your deal with me to collect important information. I believe you might be of further assistance to my husband and myself.'

'As I once said to you, I will do anything to repay your kindness, my fair lady.'

It is no small wonder how, when hope reaches the heart, it gives life back to the body. Already a spark had returned to Willoughby's eyes and flame to his cheeks. I silently thanked God's hand for reaching inside him and relighting the fire; remembering that I was his instrument for doing so filled me with happiness.

I told Willoughby of my scheme, that he must pretend to be my plaything if I should show interest, so that they would not charge me twice over, or even thrice over, his worth to release him. I had other uses for my money than to add to a gaoler's over-spilling coffer!

I looked at the state of him. Lady Powys would see him today, but not before he had the prison washed off him, and not before the creatures eating off his skin and scalp were scrubbed away. If we must shave his head to rid the infestation, then a periwig would have to be found. He could not stand before the Lady like that!

'I will come back for you shortly, when Margaret gets here, and you will come with me, clean yourself and put on your clothes. Then I will take you to Lady Powys, who wishes to see you.'

'Indeed, I am forever indebted to you, madam.'

'As I have told you, your payment for this kindness was given in advance, and will perhaps save many from worse treatment. It is I who owes you for your labour on the article, and also for your aid in exposing the design to fix the plot against the King onto our faith!'

'I am glad to have been of assistance in those matters. May all men of all faiths one day walk free!'

'Aye, and may we be a small part of the history of it!' It was indeed an uplifting idea, that what we did today might shape the future, even if only in some small way. 'Now, I have bread to feed to some that need it. I will be back to see you soon.' I gave him a chunk, and left him staring sightlessly down at his open palms, bread sitting on one and coins on the other.

11

26th day of April, 1679 (evening)

What a sight we were that evening: I, a midwife, stood with my husband, a merchant, and Willoughby, an ex-convict, outside the grand Powys House at the northwest corner of Lincoln's Inn Fields and Great Queen Street. The magnificent mansion was prominent in London's largest square, only rivalled by Lord Lindsey's splendid home further around the common. Never having visited the residence before, Pierre was suitably impressed and Willoughby was so affected by the size of it that he took time to count the windows.

'Twenty six including the two on street level,' he said, rubbing his hands together. 'One, two, three, four, five floors! Odd's fish, in truth this is a palace!'

Noting his improved demeanour, and ignoring his expletive, one that I had heard the King himself use, I turned to look at the building, a thing I had not done since first I visited it. The imposing front did indeed seem fit for royalty rather than an Earl, but I was witness that, besides their seat in Wales, Lord and Lady Powys had possessed this town house for seven years and were quite comfortable here.

To both the left and to the right of the ornate iron gate and railings was set an arched entrance into a stone passage, each leading to an inside side door for trade callers and servants. We stood outside the closed gates considering if we should use the dignified front door at the top of the broad stone steps normally reserved for callers of their own class, or whether, as I was wont to do when I came on matters of philanthropy, we used one of the two arched passageways.

'We should call at the front entrance as is fitting for dinner guests,' I decided.

The three of us approached the immense fine-carved door that five persons might walk through side by side without touching shoulders, and Pierre took the wooden hand pull and tugged hard until it came from the wall. Three times he pulled and three times the bell beyond the door rang. Seeing Willoughby waiting tall and clean and handsome beside us on the steps brought forth images of that afternoon tumbling one after the other through my head.

Bargaining for Willoughby's release surprised me as being the most effortless part of the day. The lewd comments of the turnkeys gave credence to how well I acted the part of a doxy, made easy by how little was already commonly thought of a midwife and her life. So long as they received a slice of the fees that went to the King they cared little for any other thing! As I expected, thinking I wanted the man as a plaything, they demanded over the payment of his debt but, as I hoped, did not consider him important enough to charge double, or even triple.

Once we reached the street and both breathed deeply of the spring air that smelled sweet after the cells, I found even I could not bear the smell he carried with him. I determined that, if I was somewhat used to the stench inside of the prison, out here it was too overbearing. The delicate nose of Lady Powys would be affronted by such abhorrence. It was fortunate that I had earlier begged of Pierre his permission to take Willoughby home and clean him thoroughly before this night!

It was further fortunate I had the good sense to dismiss the household staff that afternoon to prevent the wagging tongues of the tattle-tales[10] and twattlers[11] amongst them. They might talk too free of this man's presence here and ask questions too complicated to answer simply. With luck, none of the boys from St Omer would be returned home and we might make free with the house.

Soon my arms ached from carrying pots of boiling water enough to fill two bathtubs, then from emptying the water away again. The first full tub, and a good deal of soap, took the most dirt from Willoughby and his under clothing. I could not help but be satisfied by the many crawling creatures swimming in the greasy scum on top of the foul water I tipped into the gutter. At the least there would be less lice to comb out after. Into the second tub I splashed some of my expensive oil of lavender from Paris to cloak the stubborn prison smell.

I thought of the captain undressing.

Without shame, and with his back to me, the captain had unbuttoned a still grey shirt and removed it so that he stood in the tub wearing only baggy breeches tied at his skinny middle and that clung to every scraggy part of him. As he dropped the soggy shirt to the floor, I gasped at his back covered from neck to waist with ribbon scars that could only be made by the bite of lashes. Some wounds were yet unhealed.

Turning his head at my noise and seeing how I looked at him, he turned his full body so I could not see more and said, 'You are shocked, madam. Does your husband not take penance from his flesh? I have found it the singular most satisfying means of atoning for my sins.'

I shook my head. I had seen skin stripped from flesh by the tails before, but this man's back was more discoloured skin than that of sun-browned youth. I swallowed hard and tried to regain a more dispassionate disposition.

'Does not confession to a priest absolve your sin?' I said.

'The extent of my wrongs cannot be undone by confession alone.'

Once the bath was empty and Willoughby had on fresh, dry underclothes and Pierre's nightgown, I had him sit whilst I worked on his hair. Some goose grease aided me in untangling some of the matted knots but, even after much heavy combing, his hair still moved in a way it should not, so I resolved it must be short in order to use my fine-toothed comb and remove what insects held fast. Finally, what was left of his hair no longer had life of its own and some more lavender oil removed any last smell of confinement.

To distract us while we worked on his ablutions, Willoughby told me how he came to have torn ears, having had nails hammered

101

through them into the pillory for counterfeiting. I resolved the periwig he should have must hide such shame.

I then told Willoughby of my meeting with Percival Willoughby, a man-midwife of Derbyshire. Despite interfering a little much in the business of a trade meant for women, he struck me as having more wisdom than I normally gave a man credit for. He would be about eighty now, and probably long in the ground, but I had met this worthy man when he practiced in London in the late fifties.

We had both been called to deliver a lady of standing, my mind cloaks the identity of her. I had been impressed by his uncommon sense in waiting 'til the baby was ready to come, unlike some midwives, who would as soon wrench it from the womb, rip open a mother's body than wait for Dame Nature. He did not hold with many traditional midwife customs that I was taught by my mother, but the reasons he gave were sensible, and his influence on me had since saved, I believe, many babies and their mothers.

The man still held my greatest respect and I would have been honoured to know Willoughby as a relative of him, but the answer was still 'no'. He did not know any such a man, though he may be distant by blood, he imagined.

A knock on the door admitted Margaret; back from completing a task for me.

'Do you have them? '

Instead of answering, Margaret took in the half-dressed, hairless young man behind me, and nodded curtly. It was unlike her to be silent. Like Susan, he usually had much to say on any matter, whether desired or not. I held out my hand for the clothes she held in hers.

Finally she answered, 'Yes madam, but they are overmuch large.' This, I presumed, was after a fast assessment of how little flesh was left on Willoughby's bones.

'They will have to do. A few good meals is what he needs.'

'My coat! Where did you find it!'

'In the pawn shop, where you left it.' I answered him. I showed him our bedchamber, and then Margaret and I left him to dress.

A short while after, a young gentleman emerged from my room. Margaret and I stopped to appraise him. His clothes were obviously fitted in better days when his body had some flesh; there was no single place he now filled them as they should be filled and they hung on him as if he was a stick. But still, the difference from when he arrived two hours since was as a tree in spring is to a tree in winter. In his finery, he was a gentleman once more.

'Close your mouth, Margaret,' I told my maid the moment I remembered to close my own. 'You will do, Captain. Are you hungry?' We were to meet Pierre at Lady Powys's house in half an hour, and we appeared to be ready.

'I most certainly am, My Lady. It is a delight to be my own self once more!' he said, eying his reflection in the looking glass above the fireplace.

'Mrs Cellier,' I answered absently, watching as he turned first one way then the other, pleased with what he saw. Indeed, his graceful movement was a delight on the eyes.

By happy chance, the arrival of our coach at Powys House had coincided with Pierre's and, after introducing Pierre and Willoughby, we proceeded to the door where we now waited. I had allowed Margaret the rest of the day for her own entertainment, once she had taken care of one last message to Lord Castlemaine, asking him if we might meet to discuss the best way to place my petition about the prisons in front of the Government.

Eventually an old, bowed man, who I owned must regularly walk beside the reaper, opened the door and showed us the parlour, where the Countess of Powys stood to greet us.

'Mrs Cellier! It gives me rare pleasure to reacquaint myself with you.'

'The pleasure is wholly mine, Lady Powys. If it so please you, may I introduce Monsieur Pierre Cellier, my husband?' Pierre took Lady Powys's proffered hand and bowed charmingly over it.

'*Bon soir*, My Lady,' he said. 'I could not be more delighted to make the acquaintance of both beauty and Samaritan in one fell swoop.'

'And this must be our friend from Newgate.' Lady Powys was too impatient for me to introduce him properly.

'Indeed, My Lady. This is Captain Thomas Willoughby. Captain Willoughby, Lady Powys.'

'Enchanted, to be sure,' said Willoughby, echoing how Pierre took Lady Powys's hand and leaned over it; but he bowed so low and with such an embellished flourish of his hands even I, who had seen him there, could not imagine that this afternoon he had graced Newgate with his presence and was in such a sorry state. His shakiness did nothing to reduce his charm. Then he raised her small white-gloved fingers back to his full standing height and kissed them elaborately. Lady Powys should have grabbed her hand back at his audaciousness, but it was obvious his flamboyancy and charm, as it did me, captured her straight away. 'It will be my eternal happiness to repay the kindnesses you have shown me,' he said, echoing the words he had told me over and again.

After the requisite pleasantries, Lady Powys said. 'Shall we adjourn to the dining room? Dinner is, I believe, ready to be served,' and proffered her arm for Willoughby to take in his. Pierre, in turn, took my arm and we followed a few steps behind our hostess.

We ate a sumptuous meal of soup served with bread rolls, followed by divers meats, such as pheasant, pork and lamb from the countryside, and the season's first asparagus served in verjuice[12] dressing, made from the last season's crab-apples, as well as some pickled vegetables and sauces. Each course was served in the finest ornate silver dishes, the likes of which we were not so advantaged to have in our own home. The closing course was a jam rolled sponge covered with sweet fruit sauce bottled last autumn.

Between courses, Lady Powys was so good as to show off her two pretty servant girls, dark as any I saw in Newgate, and as colourfully dressed in their finery as any I had seen in the palace. The father of this exotic pair, she informed us, came to England on a merchant ship from Guinea, and now worked as the Powys' head groom. When we had finished admiring them, they left to fetch the next dishes.

Though I warned him against it, I expected Willoughby to

betray his previous dwelling by engorging himself in the manner of an animal, as he had so ravaged the bread I had brought to the prison, but he conducted himself with the civility of a gentleman. In fact, he ate delicately and surprised me by declaring himself full long before the rest of us. My husband, seeing how perplexed I was, and with more knowledge of such things than I, spoke.

'It is commonly said that a man's stomach will shrink when he does not partake of victuals for a long while.' His harsh tone surprised me, considering where poor Willoughby was recently held, and his look toward Willoughby was equal in severity. The topic of prisons had not been opened, but now it was no longer to be avoided.

On being asked, I told a little about some prisoners in Newgate, amongst them that most delightful man, Charles Baker, that was accused of being a priest in Wales, I had met on several occasions in the time he had lived there.

'They call him by his birth name, David Lewis, and the turnkeys tell me he is to be further examined with regards to the Popish Plot,' I said. 'What right they have to condemn an old man like him for his goodness I do not know for, even in a gaol, he already has a reputation of being the kindest man. With my own eyes, I have seen him give another his last bite of bread, and also give his only blanket to a sick man that could not stand or sit!' Familiar anger when I thought of his treatment took my appetite.

For a while we quietly discussed this deed, then Lady Powys delicately probed Captain Willoughby, 'What terrible sights must a man see in that place?'

'Indeed, My Lady,' he gave nothing of them away. 'And it is my honour to be in the company of the good Samaritans who rescued me from such sights, and to whom I offer a most fervent hope of repaying their goodness.' The sincerity in his eyes warmed every person at the table, but how oft he repeated the words begun to be tiresome, though I was pleased he determined to do so.

'Tell us about this Strode character you have acquainted yourself with. Did he speak to you more of a plot?' Pierre and I looked at each other at this indiscretion; she had not even checked if any servant was nearby. Mere mention of a plot by her might give authorities cause to charge her with conspiracy, and worse, her loose talk could put us all at risk. Any servant might be pleased to turn her in for a few coins.

'He did not, My Lady, though it was not for want of trying. Neither spirits nor ale nor opium released his clam-mouth hinges.' For a moment Willoughby leaned both elbows on the table as if weariness might better him. It was apparent he would sleep long and deep once he was allowed the luxury of a warm, clean bed. 'But, for the price of freedom, he has vowed to come around and to no longer perjure himself. He has also vowed to give up to us proof of the perjury by Oate's man, Bedlow, a letter to him from Bedlow that he keeps at his house.'

'And this letter will prove the Catholic plot false?' asked Lady Powys, her eyebrows raised.

Willoughby leaned further across the table, his face momentarily lit by inner zeal. 'The proof within it is that Bedlow was paid by Oates to speak false and will disarm him'.

'That is for the exoneration of all who are wrongly accused,' said Lady Powys. She would, of course, be thinking of her husband and the other four lords, who every person knew had been in the Tower many months in fear of their lives.

'Indeed, My Lady, it would be advantageous to have such proofs of the double-plot, but we will have none unless we have that letter. In it, Bedlow admits to knowing nothing of the plot but what Oates told him, and shows he is therefore a false witness. All that he has said in court – to cause the death of Coleman and Ireland and the ones erroneously hanged for murdering Sir Edmundbury Godfrey, and others since – all of this was fabricated by Oates.'

'We must give aid to him then,' she said. 'Such proof may save the lives of so many others!'

My husband interjected here, 'Nay, My Lady. You must not say what I believe you say!'

'The King has proclaimed that any who discover the Catholic plot against him should be rewarded. I merely propose, any who can provide proof that such is a dastardly plot against the Catholics should be rewarded handsomely. Is that not fair?' Her jaw firmed as she clenched her teeth stubbornly together. I had underestimated the Lady's inner strength.

Pierre studied Lady Powys for some while, also knowing the truth of her words. She would pay well for such proof, but I suspected she would not care where that proof came from, or even if it were honest, so long as it would release her husband. Pierre saw this too, but did not follow with further questions or reproofs. Perhaps he also realised Lady Powys's desperation.

'Just as long as it comes from a good source, My Lady,' he said, settling on a reminder to play close to truth.

'I am sure Captain Willoughby would mark his sources well. Is that not so, Captain?'

Willoughby had followed the conversation closely, and knew well what Lady Powys asked. He did not hesitate even a moment to answer. 'My Lady, for you I will find witnesses against the sham-plot, though I have to search every corner of the land!'

'Start at the house of Shaftsbury!' I said, once I had finished my gulp of wine. 'If he is the ringleader as you say, he will be a fruitful source, of that I am certain.'

'Indeed, Madam.' As Willoughby turned his whole attention to me, my heart pounded in my chest; and though I was long past the first flush of youth, heat flamed my face just as if I were not. I hoped it would be put down to that I was passing into the other side of child-bearing years, or the wine and warmth. He continued, 'I will begin there, and then examine the business of every one of his cronies until I discover all of their wicked plans. Mark me, I am a man of my word.'

He was so ardent I believed he would too.

A bell rang twice somewhere in the large house. As if by consent, we fell to silence and listened to hear who called at this time. Not much was revealed by the sounds through the door but, shortly after, Margaret, still wearing her cloak, was admitted to the dining room.

She brought with her a draught from the cool evening

outside and also a written reply from Lord Castlemaine. As ever, she revealed little but calm. If ever she knew the content of the notes she carried she kept them close to herself and acted as if she did not.

Without a word, she simply handed the paper to me with a bob, and kept her eyes lowered, as she should in polite company. It was not sealed, merely folded, and I begged pardon while I read the brief message to say he would meet with me on the morrow before noon, and that I need not reply but arrive at his house at a time that suited me, for he would be at home the whole day.

'I thank you, Margaret. You may take your leave now,' I dismissed my maid and she left.

'Another message, before I go ma'am.' Margaret leant her face close to my ear. I barely heard her words. 'The coachman, Prance, has sent you a gift of a weanling colt for your trouble. He calls it Thor, and it awaits you in the stable at Arundel house.' Then she was gone. As the door closed on Margaret, I folded the note and unobtrusively tucked it into my dress pocket for safekeeping. How kind of Prance to thank me for my services to himself and his wife with a young horse. But, perhaps I should not accept such gratitude, for it could bond us together in a way that might have tongues wagging, for any person might recognise it as one from his stable.

'That was my cousin's writing, I will warrant,' said Lady Powys.

'Lord Castlemaine,' I nodded agreement. I told her I would meet him the following day, and she asked me to convey her regards to him.

This settled, Lady Powys asked after several of the Catholic gentry with child she had interest in and that I had recently visited. When we finished the meal, we adjourned to the drawing room for coffee, a drink more popularly to be found in coffee houses these days, and not often drunk past afternoon, lest one must keep company with the stars. We passed the time pleasantly, and no more was said on plots or sham plots.

As we were taking our leave, Willoughby revealed he had

no place to sleep. Demonstrating she was not herself unmoved by the handsome young man in our midst, and perhaps it was the association of Willoughby and bed, a somewhat discomposed Lady Powys proclaimed, 'Caution demands that you cannot stay here else you would be most welcome; but conscience will not allow your release from one hell only to be set in the middle of another! We must secure a room for your stay!'

What could only be considered a mischievous gleam came into Willoughby's eyes, a gleam that revealed he not only had knowledge of his potency but also of his ability to influence circumstance in his favour. Indeed, I near expected Lady Powys to insist beyond good breeding that he should stay with her, since it was obvious she had more than rooms enough for the purpose, but Pierre's intervention prevented her from committing an indiscretion she would later regret.

'There is an inn under the sign of the Goat in Drury Lane that might have a room. I will make enquiries if they have a bed for the night.'

By good chance, they did, and after giving Willoughby ten shillings Lady Powys had generously bestowed upon him as a weekly allowance, Pierre and I continued by coach towards home. And as we went we talked.

'You must be careful, my love. Lady Powys is a desperate woman, and she would have Willoughby wrong truth for her own ends.'

'The truth is,' I said, 'we Catholics are falsely blamed for deeds we have not committed, plots we have not hatched. Is it so wrong to seek the truth of it all?'

'Nay, *chérie*. Not if it is truth that is sought and found. But I do not trust Willoughby to find only the truth,' he said, echoing my earlier thoughts. 'You must discover if he is trustworthy.'

'Pray, how should I do that?'

'Find how the stars were aligned when he was born,' Pierre crooked his arm around my shoulders and drew me towards him as the coach swayed to the sound of turning wheels.

'You mean Gadbury?'

'Perhaps our astrologer can tell you which way his personality lies.'

'Do you think it necessary; can you not learn to trust him from past actions?'

'There is something too charming, too fluid, about the man. He seems to flow into this role from another all too easily. I wonder if he would not fill any mould as long as it were lucrative enough.'

I felt myself bristle and defend him, 'I do not see what gives you cause to say so, but I vouched for him when I paid his debts.'

'You are perhaps too trusting, Lizzie, but you must yourself know how spies are everywhere; especially where poverty daily holds hostages for ransom. Are you certain you should vouch for him when you know nothing of him?'

'I will ask Gadbury. Distinction in his art gives me hope he can advise me wisely.'

'And when you do, please remember me to him, Lizzie dearest.'

He had known Gadbury for more years than we had been married; indeed he had introduced me to the astrologer, but Pierre's confidence in the man's skills remained uncertain.

'I will tell him it is for one who you might employ to collect debts,' I said, not wholly hearing Pierre. 'Have you another message for him?'

He laughed and said, 'Not that he will not already have foreseen in the stars.' And on that lighter note, I placed my head on his shoulder and enjoyed the remaining journey home in the security of his embrace.

12

13th day of June, 1679

'I wonder to whom that rather dashing footman belongs?'

The courtroom was crowded with people squashed together as in a compress, come to see the Jesuits on trial for their lives. They were accused on two accounts of treason – for being priests and also for conspiring against the King – and for either crime their hopes for acquittal were small. The lives of many had already been taken for much less, and Chief Justice Scroggs was sitting today, and he was not known for either fairness or leniency. The crowd would have their blood no less.

Such large assemblies of people, sensibly prohibited with threat of severe punished in the year of the plague, had become commonplace once more. Though thirteen years had come and gone, they did not remove the unease of being tight with so many. Like visiting the gaols, I must every time decide if the good of being there outweighed the danger I placed myself in. This day knowledge of how the Jesuits faired in court tipped the scales against the risk.

I turned to see to whom the man referred and was caught off my balance by how close the gentleman stood to my skirt. I could not step away; there was not any spare ground to move into, it being full of quality shoes treading on bare toes of some likely not long out of the debtors' prison, or soon to be in it.

Even for June, it was a hot, thirsty day, and what little air there was had been gasped deeply and without satisfaction into dozens of lungs before, and lay like a heavy cloak suffocating the courtroom. The sweat of so many tightly packed, riled-up onlookers glistened on faces like rain, and made dark patches under the arms of men, women, gentlemen and ladies alike.

The room quivered with the activity of men and women cooling their flaming faces with anything to hand, whether pamphlet or book or fan imported from southern climes. Seeing the heat on others, I wiped the sweat from my own brow and unfolded the sticks of the very latest of fine paper fans, depicting a coach travelling through a rural scene, that Pierre had recently imported for me from France, and fanned my own burning face. I was never more thankful for a thing that I had so recently thought a luxury but I now considered a boon.

Still wondering to whom 'the dashing footman' belonged, I followed the direction of the gentleman's eyes towards the spectators and witnesses yet to be called, which included a large group of young men, our guests from St Omer, and saw that Captain Willoughby did indeed cut a dash as he leaned over to serve some gratefully received beer.

A fair periwig altered his appearance dramatically from the dirt smeared, dark-haired, bony wastrel staring out through the iron bars at me with pleading eyes. Though he had not yet gained much under his skin, and his bones still dominated his skeletal appearance, he had regained an air of finery no gaol could eliminate from his blood. The pearl on his ear caught my eye, and I wondered that he should use his money on such frippery, though I could not deny he was looking rather dapper.

The captain was here, however, in more than the capacity to serve the fledgling Jesuit scholars, which I had asked him to do. Our Lady Powys was good enough to talk with her husband and the other lords in The Tower, and when they found how nicely Willoughby was able to take dictation, they elected to make good use of him, and now employed him, for a good wage of three pounds a week, to write a fair account of this and other trials, and to carry messages for them.

Now he took the empty beer glass from master Townley and, as he stood, looked in my direction, saw me watching him and winked. The refinery he had regained came with an element of cockiness. Rather than respond, I turned my attention back to the gentleman that had noticed him and said, 'Indeed, he cuts a fine figure, does he not? That footman is my husband's man, but has kindly offered to serve our guests from Flanders in court today.' I hoped my flush was not visible amongst so many flushed faces.

'You are acquainted with the Jesuits?' he asked.

I was hard-pressed to fathom whether the increased interest in his voice was for good or bad. It would be a fine day when suspicion of spies did not colour every conversation.

'I am acquainted with the Duchess of York, and she appealed to me to take in the boy witnesses as a favour to her.'

'So your loyalty is not with the Jesuits. They are guilty, I own?'

'Am I a judge of that?' I said, drawing on inner composure since in this heat I had none to support me outside. 'How do you suppose I might decide their guilt before the trial has begun and if the jury is not yet to make a decision? I am sure, as any fair-minded person, I would hear their testimony and that of their witnesses before making any judgement, for we are not so knowledgeable of more than the indictment at this time. Is this not so?'

I hoped I cloaked the scold enough to avoid reproach. I imagined myself in the scold's bridle, an iron muzzle that sat round the head with a spike in the mouth that prevented the wearer move their tongue. It was a cruel device that was brought down from Scotland, designed to punish those that spoke out of turn, or those that were thought to. Good fortune had the man distracted as the judges and spectators returned to the business of the court by Judge North banging his gavel on the table.

I held little conviction this gentleman was more than a spectator of other people's lives, and was certain he would not have a thing to add to any. I excused myself politely, hardly noticed by my brief conversational partner. I would lief have been with the St Omer's boys, but the crowd would not allow my reaching them, so I shuffled to a position I could better see. I was close enough to the door so that, if a breeze happened by, it might make my acquaintance.

A dozen judges and court officials sitting at the Bench,

all wearing long, grey periwigs except one that sported his own curly, brown hair long, finished talking amongst themselves but continued to sip occasionally from their cups of beer. I knew most of them from sitting in on other trials this last year.

Judge North fidgeted with his papers, turned pages, perhaps reminding himself of some detail of what had gone before, while he awaited the silence his gavel demanded. At least four of them were knights: Scroggs, Jones, Levinz and Jeffries, and each was a rough and hardened Protestant. Indeed, it was illegal for a Catholic to be employed by the state, and equally impossible for the Jesuits to be judged by their peers: the jury would be of the Church of England, as was the way of it.

Most of the judges' faces were creased with fifty years or more living, the exception being young Sir Jeffries, who had already made a name for himself in the courts for his scathing attitude towards Catholics and fellow judges alike.

And then there was Sir Scroggs.

Word on the street was that Scroggs had sent the so-called murderers – Berry, Green and Hill – to the gallows without a sincere hearing, and against proof that they were elsewhere at the time of death of the magistrate Sir Edmundbury Godfrey. He had not looked for justice, but revenge. In the words of Tom, the royal blacksmith that I overheard outside the Rainbow Coffee House, 'from what I 'eard, he 'anged 'em to court favour with the King'. Maybe he knew and maybe he did not; there was far too much came from the imagination these days.

Before the interlude, Titus Oates, the main accuser and witness against the Catholics, had spewed his lies all over the courtroom, to stick in the craw of those of us who knew his twisted words were the vilest of stories. He had taken moments of God's own truth and spun them into complicated blasphemy against the very Bible he had kissed upon his oath.

His finger pointed to first one Jesuit then each of the others brought here to be tried today. He brazenly claimed that they had made plans to kill the King and overthrow the country, and then further planned to force the entire three Kingdoms to convert to

Catholicism or die. His accusations reached inside people on the street and in the court, twisting their fears and making them hate. The packed, whispering court seemed willingly to believe him absolutely, occasionally jeering or shouting their assent with what he said.

I was certain, on another day to come, Oates would also enjoy pointing his unctuous, fat finger at James Corker, the sixth Jesuit, for whom the judges had earlier indulged the plea for extra time to prepare a defence and call witnesses.

Less welcome was their indulgence of Oates' inconsistent and imprecise testimony. He could not be sure whether it was this month or that when he had seen such and such person, or whether it was the beginning or middle of the month, vital points for the prisoners to prove their own whereabouts at those times, and yet the judges did not question he could not be precise about any of it!

Not for me to speak out and say they were at fault for this, when no others perceived such, but it seemed to me, each time the prisoners asked for clarification, their queries were swept aside as though the answers could make no difference, despite the importance of those details.

And I was further shocked how the same rules did not count for all. For when the young students from St Omer stood up, and though they were more precise about the time that Oates stayed in their college, and their memories of him being there agreed with each other, even to remembering exactly where he had sat in the dining hall in the college at those times, and stories about him in the garden when he said he was in England, Scroggs had the court laughing at them for not being absolutely certain of some petty detail or another during the cross examination by several judges at once.

As I understood it, Oates' evidence was based on two essential points. The one was about a consult of up to fifty Jesuits in London on the twenty-fourth day of April in the year of 1678 that Oates claimed was got together to plan the murder of the King, and the other was a letter written by one prisoner to another that referred to 'a design', a plan, that was interpreted to be for the killing of the King but, according to the Jesuits, was in fact to organise the aforementioned consult, an annual gathering. Their whole case rested on these two proofs.

And on the testimony of a man that was thrown out of that same Jesuit College for his unseemly and gross behaviour. He had been none too quiet speaking out against Catholics whensoever he had opportunity. His revenge was strong against those that were intolerant to his abhorrences, for which they had thrown this particular viper from their nest. For this, he had snatched so many good innocent people from their homes and condemned them with lies and without fair trial. He could not even keep his lies straight.

Thus far, the answers of the prisoners convinced me of their truth more heartedly than did Oates and the last witness against them, a man called Stephen Dugdale, steward to Lord Aston. It was the latter that had first pointed the finger at, and given evidence against, Lord Powys and the other four lords now in the Tower. Dugdale was so well spoken and had so much wit that he had the manner of one who spoke the truth, yet there were rumours his master had dismissed him for embezzlement…a snake with a silver tongue is still a snake.

The break had been to await the arrival of the next witness after the man Dugdale. I presumed the witness had now arrived. Before he spoke, a voice at my right shoulder said, 'Madam Cellier, I am to fetch some victuals for the young folk of St Omer. Might I also find favour with you and bring something to wet your throat?'

It was Captain Willoughby. Even loving Pierre, I could not prevent the usual flutter behind my ribs at his smooth delivery of words and sincere face.

'If you are in a tavern, a beer would surely wash the dust from my throat, I thank you Sir.' He nodded and smiled at his flirtatious answer.

'For you, madam, I would ride to John O'Groats or Land's End to find such a tavern! Indeed, I would search the world over for one.'

'I do not ask you to travel so far, Captain. Merely fifty paces.'

'I am honoured to do you such service, madam.' With which

he raised his hat from his long false curls and, rather than swirl it in a flourish and bow low as he had when the room was empty, he merely raised it and lowered it once more upon his head. I did not see him for some time after that. I later heard he had stayed longer in the tavern than necessary and had washed his own throat very thoroughly whilst he collected the drinks. This did not surprise me. He was known for frequenting the White Horse Tavern in the Strand for more of the day than he worked. I did not miss him for I had other matters to contemplate.

The judge cleared his throat a couple of times over the constant chatter of the spectators. I returned my attention to the court proceedings. I had many times sat in a courtroom since that time more than a year ago when I was attacked in the street, but that had been in the Sessions. Even then, the nature of the court stirred me. Its dream-like flavour gave me a taste of another world, where every event of the past mattered and shaped the present and future, gave me a yearning to learn more of how the justice process worked.

Any tried for treason would be at the Old Bailey, where serious crimes were dealt with. Something told me I must remember everything, learn how it worked, for that knowledge might, one day, become advantageous. Already, on the first morning, I had learned one could dismiss people assigned to the jury for various reasons. Sir Creswell Levinz had made me burn with rage at his opening speech. He had made clear that this country had 'put up with' the presence of Catholic priests though they be illegal, then he had gone on to proclaim them akin to the bloody murderers that carried out the massacres in Merindol and Paris and Ireland, warning the defendants they would not have the satisfaction of suffering for their religion, that this was not what they were being tried for. It was cleverly done, and turned the court against the prisoners before any testimony was heard, if it were possible to skew opinion more.

And then that pretender, Oates, had told his lies, and called his man, Dugdale, to bear witness to them.

Oates had declared himself part of a design by the Jesuit priests to kill the King, to massacre Protestants and force Catholicism onto the country.

If his story be true, how was it that the Jesuits should be on trial when he was not, though he had apparently partaken of the same crime? He admitted to having converted to Catholicism. Indeed, his crime was far worse, for he had turned against those that had taken him under their wing! How could his word be believed, when the lies of his turncoat witness, Dugdale, were shown in their true colours in court this day. Most unbelievable was when the judges found inconsistencies within his testimony, they corrected for him rather than found it false.

Oates said one thing that could be tested straight away, if they had had a mind to. Dugdale said he recognised the treasonable letters by the hand of Harcourt, yet Harcourt himself stood there and told them the man had not long since been unable to recognise either him nor his hand, when compared to writing by attendant committee members of the House of Commons!

Harcourt revealed that in private, out of Dugdale's sight, some of the gentlemen of the Commons had written Harcourt's name on a piece of paper, and had put them along with that of Harcourt's own hand in front of Dugdale, when he came back into the room. Dugdale could not pick Harcourt's hand out. Yet, when he spoke of this, Harcourt was told his words meant nothing, though their case rested on it.

Why did they not call these gentlemen to test his statement? It was so easily verified, yet they did not do it. In what world this might be considered fair, I could not fathom. Especially, if what he said was the truth. Dugdale had already shown himself a scoundrel and admitted to having given monies towards killing the King and taking over the country.

'I gave them four hundred pounds to pray for my soul, and for the carrying out of this design, and when they told me they doubted they should want for money, I promised them one hundred pounds more for the carrying out of the work,' he told the court, and 'Upon which, Mr Gavan promised me that I should be canonized for a saint,' said Dugdale.

Did they not think this man might not make a good witness?

When Dugdale professed knowledge of the murder of the knight, Sir Edmundbury Godfrey, the noise in court became almost too much to hear him speak. Every Judge vied to question him on that, and seemed to believe all his answers. It was also their wont to ensure the jury particularly heard the parts they wanted them to by repeating certain testimony, and ignoring other.

Even Chetwyn, Dugdale's own witness, spoke against him. He said the testimony where Dugdale said the words, 'This night, Sir Edmundbury Godfrey is dispatched', was not actually in the said letter from Father Harcourt to Father Ewers when it was shown to him, and that he said of the matter, 'it was added later'.

Bedlow also spoke, and knowing how he had admitted in a letter to the man, Stroud, who had confided in Willoughby how he knew none of this before being told it by Oates, his testimony stuck in my craw. I could not help but shout out at one point, 'Lies! 'Tis all lies! He knows nothing about any of it!'

Judge Scroggs looked directly at me, lifted one eyebrow and raised his voice above mine, 'If the lady knows something of this, why does she not take the stand?' before returning to his leading questions, telling Bedlow what to say by how he asked them.

The Judges treated the boys from St Omer disgracefully. When it was their turn to give testimony, they were not let to swear on the Bible, though they wished to, for they were Catholics. One judge had the disrespect to openly tell them that, because of their religion they could not be trusted. His complaint was that a Catholic's first duty was to the Pope before the King, and that would give cause to lie; and that they would not have any compunction about doing so, because they could then be absolved of that sin by confession and a pardon.

Father Harcourt and the others tried to use Dugdale's and Bedlow's criminal past to show they were not trustworthy witnesses, and each time they were told the same thing, that the men were absolved of their previous crimes by having a pardon from the King. I was struck by the irony and hypocrisy of this: they feared the priests and their witnesses had a dispensation to lie and would speak false for only want of a pardon yet they openly allowed and gave credit to the crown's own witnesses standing against them that were criminals just so pardoned by the King in order to give testimony!

Sixteen boys had spoken up that Oates could not have been at the meeting in England when he sat every day at the table by the door in their dining room. And the testimony of each one was denigrated and trodden on as if it had no worth. Why the King saw fit to bring them over for this treatment was a mystery, if they were not to be listened to. And then it took only two lying witnesses from the other side to decide the case against the Jesuits. Their proof might have made a man laugh if it did not have such dire consequences. But instead they laughed loud at those poor boys that had done all they could to defend innocent men the best they could.

When the jury left to decide the Jesuits' fates, there was not a person in the court who had any doubt of the way it would fall. With heavy heart and faint hope justice would be as clear to the jury as it was to me, I took time to look at the eager faces round the room. They came for blood and would not be happy unless they had it. The judges too were talking and laughing as if the priests' lives were not at stake. Did the life of a Catholic mean so little to any of them that they failed to hold a fair trial? They failed to be what they should be – men of the law on the side of right.

But still, some hope in me glimmered. Twelve men sat in judgement of the Jesuits. Surely not all of them were so prejudiced they could not see the truth of the matter!

As it happened, of the twelve men that sat in judgement none of the twelve had sight to see the truth.

When they returned, the judge asked them for their verdict.

'If they are guilty, then you must say so,' he said, 'and their property will be taken for the crown. If they are not guilty, but ran, then their property will be taken for the crown. If they are not guilty and did not run, then say so now. Do you find these men guilty or not guilty?' He then ran through the names of the priests: John Gavan, William Harcourt, Anthony Turner, Thomas Whitbread,

John Fenwick and for each a verdict of 'guilty' was given. None of them would escape the ghastly death of those convicted of treason.

The faces of the priests were neither surprised nor defeated. Neither did they flinch at such unfair judgment. That they had resigned themselves to their fate long before they had reached the court was testament to the kind of trial they had both expected and received. Their calm unnerved me. It made me want to scream out in their defence, but if I did I would not be heard, for the court had gone wild, and the collective joy was at odds to the despair I felt not only for the poor men that were now to be hanged, but for the poor boys, their defenders, who had failed in their task. I searched for them now.

At the back of the court on the other side, the St Omer boys, humiliated and demoralised, stood quietly together. In a room full of movement, their stillness struck me sharply and, if I were not here where seeds of sympathy did not grow, I would have watered them with my tears. I mourned for their own lost innocence, for many of them had truly believed that truth could not fail to reveal itself to all others, and that their testimony to it would be enough to turn the wind of lies from its present course, but the wind merely battered them then blew them away.

The lives of their friends had been entrusted to them, and they had not been able to save them. As one, with heads bent in prayer or dejection, the group turned and left the court, pushed and shoved by the jubilant crowd as they went.

I saw Willoughby some way from them, and wondered at that he had not sat with them; it would have given them moral support to not be so alone. I was glad to be near to the door so that I did not have to push my way through many, but I would have sat with them had I been able.

The last memory I took of the priests was the blessed look of forgiveness they bestowed upon their murderers.

I was sickened for the loss of the reverence of justice and fairness I had once believed to be found in the courtroom, and quickly made my escape.

13

24th day of June, 1679

'I shall not do it, Madam Cellier! You know I would do any thing you ask, but I would rather go one hundred miles than deliver this message to My Lord!'

Like a petulant child, Willoughby thrust the letter back towards me in his tattooed hand, the other hand balled at his side and his face pinched in obstinacy. He did not look so very attractive at that moment, and I more had the notion of placing him over my knee and giving him a spanking than I had of him tilting at windmills in the way of Don Quixote, or as a rakish highwayman the likes of Du Vall that I had once shed a tear for.

If I had tried to save the life of Du Vall, I had tried everything. I had petitioned the King for his mercy, but to no avail. He had stood against too many gentlemen on the road and at the gaming tables, and with their wives in his bed. Tales of his wild escapades filled every coffee shop and, alongside every other lady of the time, I was quite undone by the romantic tale of when he held up a knight and his lady.

She, when she saw they were to be robbed, played heartily on her flageolet. He, the highwayman, Du Vall, was so taken by the music, he drew out his own instrument and played along with her. At the end of their duet, Du Vall asked the knight for his wife's hand in a dance, to which His Lordship could barely refuse, saying, 'I cannot deny a gentleman of such quality and good behaviour anything.' So, they danced a courante with all assuredness, elegance and light-footedness as if the heath were a ballroom.

We ladies had whispered of how, after they finished moving together in a most graceful and dignified fashion, he handed her back up to her husband in the coach, then surprised the knight by saying, 'Have you remembered to pay the musicians?' to which the older man replied, 'I never forget such things'. He then reached under his seat and drew forth a bag holding one hundred pounds. Du Vall took it gracefully and told the knight, for giving the money freely and without force, he would spare him the other three hundred he knew to be hidden whence that hundred came, and that he would be safe from any of his men on the road from that day forth. For that was the sort of decent man he was.

Willoughby had the resemblance of him, though not his character.

'Why do you baulk at such a simple task?' I asked, not taking the letter. 'You have carried notes to him many a time before.' Willoughby's stubbornness on this matter puzzled me.

'He has a temper, Madam. I would rather carry this letter into a lion's den than take this letter to him. He is the Devil, that one!' Willoughby again thrust the letter, but this time into my hand and then took hold of my fingers with both his hands and folded them round it, so I was in no doubt he would not take it.

'What wrong did he do you?'

'My Lord has a temper so vile, I would not trust him to keep it to himself.'

'Surely his temper is not so bad.'

'He swore me to the Devil and said if he saw me again he would have my heart!'

'He did not mean it. Lord Castlemaine is a good man. Did he say more, that you are so discomposed about going to him?'

'I tell you, he was there when I took a message to Powys House for My Lady, and he raged at me. He promised to have me sent to the gallows, or hanged, drawn and quartered. I will not go to him.'

'Why was he so angry?'

'He said I should not have gone to the Tower, so I told him I went on your instruction. I owe you such a great debt; it would have been disloyal to you had I not gone. You know I would do anything for you, Madam.'

There was something ingratiating about Thomas of late.

I would gladly accept a little obligation for our kindness, but he gave his thanks or made some such comment about being in my debt near every conversation, and I owned I was tiring of it. He took it too far. At one time I did begin to think he used the words as a shield to hide insincere thoughts, but his work for Lady Powys and myself and for the cause had been earnest and I was happy to have him on our side.

But there was a distance between us now. I knew not why, only that we were not so cosy as we were before. I could not tell if the change was in him or in me. A memory of how he sat apart from the St Omer boys came into my head, and that air of guilt I caught on his face before he hid it from me. It might have been imagined, though my wits and senses had proved true over and again.

'Then do this for me now,' I said. 'But…I cannot fathom why he was angry with you for taking a message to the Tower. There is no reason in that.'

Willoughby looked as a child caught in mischief, peering up at me through his long lashes with exaggerated down-turned mouth

'I must tell you plain, madam, when I took the message to the Tower, I told them it was from My Lord Castlemaine in order to gain admittance, for they did not believe I came in good spirit.'

'What! Why did you do a thing of such weak judgement? Have you no wits?' It was difficult to believe how a person that knew how dangerous a Roman Catholic's life was in these days might be so completely dull of senses to do a thing so lacking in reason! 'By doing this you implicated him with the lords when their lives are already in peril!'

'It came to me that his nobility would convince them of my innocence. I did not believe any harm would come of it.' 'It was a foolish and dangerous thing to do,' I admonished him. Foolish, foolish man! Why should I hold my tongue and not bawl him out for his thoughtlessness? He put Castlemaine in danger of both his freedom and his life, and mine too. 'Nevertheless, I wish you to take this letter to him.'

124

'I will not do it, Madam,' he said. 'I will not breath the same air as that man. He has said he would have me hanged if he saw me again.'

Nearby, Bennet Dowdal, our tall, thickset coachman, of surprising gentle nature, had come into the yard leading a limping black horse, Thor's Hammer, and became busy clearing packed mud, stones and dung from his shoe. Prance might have had less than all kind thought when he gifted me the young suckling, for we soon discovered him to have a rather tight-sprung hind leg, that might be released on any that happened to walk behind it. We had allowed Dowdal, receiver of the greatest part of the animal's force, to rename him. He had since all but trained the leg to behave, though we were warned never to touch him to be sure of our safety.

'Dowdal, be so kind and come hither.'

Dowdal paused in his task and came over.

"'Tis a stone caught in the frog's cleft,' he said, misunderstanding why I called him.

'I am sure 'tis a simple matter for you, Dowdal,' I dismissed. 'You know Castlemaine, do you not? Tell the Captain he is a good man.'

'Captain, you are a good man,' he said obediently, but frowned as he did so.

'No, no, Dowdal. I mean for you to tell Willoughby that Castlemaine is a good man.'

Obviously still puzzled as to the reason why I tasked him so, Dowdal did as I bid him, 'Yes, yes, he is a fine gentleman. One would search the land and not find better than the likes of him.'

'Well, you deliver this letter to him then!' Willoughby's sulks were an ill-fitting suit on him. Again they made him more a wilful child than a man, a way I now looked at him more often, since the Jesuit trial.

'I thank you kindly, Dowdal. Please return to un-stoning the frog.'

Dowdal moved away slowly, reluctant to relinquish any opportunity to gather information that he might exchange in the stables in return for a shared cup of whatever it was they drunk there of an evening.

125

I waited until he had returned to the horse before saying, 'Captain, let me assure you, I would not send you on an errand to him if I believed he would do you harm. I ask you one time more to take this letter to him.'

'I beg your humble pardon, Madam, but I will not.' Willoughby's persistent refusal to do as I asked irked me, but what was there to do. My only option would be to find another messenger.

'It would make me happier, Captain, if you did not place me in such an awkward position. Is it your intention to hobble me like that poor horse over yonder?' I pointed to Thor's Hammer. 'I have taken you from a cruel fate, and furnished you with clothes, money and a welcoming roof over your head, and found you employment with others too. In return I merely ask you give of your good services for my husband's business and my own, for which I pay you well. This task I give you holds no danger, for I am accountable for it. That you refuse me cuts me to the quick.'

'You have indeed done me more good service than I can repay, Madam Cellier, and I am the first to admit nothing I can ever do will settle the debts of kindnesses shown by you, your husband and Lady Powys. Your rescue of me was the very thing to change my course from rapscallion to honest man. Ask of me anything but that I shall be in sight of Lord Castlemaine again!'

'Fair enough. You make your position clear.' As steadfast as a mule, Willoughby held his ground but, as a man, he must be allowed the final say in his own fate.

'Mean you what you said that, apart from taking a note to Lord Castlemaine, you will do anything to repay me?' At his nod I continued, 'Do you have backbone enough to do another task for our cause?' Again he nodded, more eagerly now he saw I would not force him to Castlemaine. 'You have proved your allegiance and the task I have now cannot be given to any person not honest. Are you with us the whole way? Are you prepared to do what you will to help the cause? I have conceived a deed you might undertake to right the wrongs of those against us.'

'Aye, madam, I have sworn to do anything you ask.'

'Except meet Castlemaine,' I could not resist the jibe, and was pleased the captain looked sheepish but maintained his humour.'

'Except meet Castlemaine,' he agreed, his winsome smile through those dark lashes once again reminiscent of Du Vall, that handsome French highwayman. And his smile cleared the air so that I thought, when he moved his hand to swipe a fly from his face, he would have reached out and touched me, but he did not.

Of late, I had on occasion found myself trying to hide from Pierre how I was snared by this young man's attractions though I feared he might have caught a glimpse of it. With good fortune, Willoughby failed to notice the flush that swept over me now as he looked over to Dowdal, and I fanned my face with my hand. Perhaps he looked away because he did notice.

'I have your word. If you had not given out the pamphlets and broadsides for Father Neville at the coffee houses, that bigot Lord Danby might have secured his release from the Tower and might have won over the Government with his lies. I understand the one titled 'Reflections' with Danby's name on it was very well read. But we cannot take all credit for his downfall. It is all too easy to discredit one that incurs such odium! For your part in this you already have thanks.'

I paused to allow these words to find their target.

'My thoughts are these. Words of a cause are most likely to be read by those that are predisposed towards that cause, or those who wish to overthrow it,' I said, thinking aloud. 'Perhaps we must sow seeds of insight of the Presbyterian treachery in their own garden before they can see the truth of it. But it is not enough to sow the seeds. They must be nurtured until they bear fruit. The belly of our cause is growing, and when it is ripe, justice shall be born unto these three Kingdoms.'

I paused again to see how Captain Willoughby reacted. I did not expect him to answer, but he did.

"'Tis widely spoken now, Madam, by some you would not sup with, that the plot to kill the King was hatched by Shaftsbury to settle King Charles' bastard son, the Duke of Monmouth, to the throne, and those that designed it turned the scheme onto the

Catholics to throw dust in the eyes of any that might see something so plain. They say that Sir Edmundbury Godfrey suspected something of the double plot when Oates swore his affidavit, and that is why he was killed.'

Willoughby went to scratch his scalp, knocking his wig out of place. It was a habit he had not left behind with the lice in Newgate. Unselfconsciously, for we were known to each other around the house, he shifted it around until it sat straight again. Then he looked again to Dowdal now checking the back left hoof, as if what the coachman was doing held great interest, looked down to the ground and back to me again before speaking.

'One servant of Oates, a man named William Osborne, in the employ of a noble man – possibly Danby – plans to speak out about Oates and his sordid affairs, along with two others. I cannot vouch for the truth of it, for I suspect the word of one worm in the stead of another is one you would not wish to believe, but the one to whom I gave my ear also claimed the word is that Oates himself arranged for Sir Godfrey's life to be forfeit under the instruction of Shaftsbury.'

'I suspected this mischief begun with that man! He would have it both ways: his man, Monmouth, on the throne and the Catholics discredited all rolled into one round shot! And Danby is such a hard one against Catholics that he would only speak against Oates to suit himself. If the court had not proclaimed that he had 'dastardly and traitorously concealed the plot', he would likely be enjoying Oates' company!'

'Indeed, people are prone to believe in a Catholic plot against the King, where a Protestant one is questioned,' Willoughby stated what we all oft stated. 'Catholics caused the plague and the Great Fire and every other scourge these three Kingdoms have seen this past century! We – you and I – are an infliction on these three Kingdoms, it would appear.'

The captain again looked to the ground but saw something far from there. I could not deny his words. In this country, our religion would always be blamed for any wrong. All eyes had watched Spain and France and some other countries and seen what happened to any that did not take mass. The persecutions on Protestants in Buckinghamshire when I was a child reflected this same prejudice, when, our family house was ransacked and pillaged by Catholics; and my father and brother paid with their lives for being on the 'wrong' side during the war, as those in the prisons were paying now.

'We must tell the Duke of York! He will know what to do,' I said.

At that moment, there was a small commotion. The horse Dowdal was tending suddenly kicked out and Dowdal sat on the ground with his hand to his chest. Fool man had forgotten the horse did not allow any man, not even the groom, to touch his flank on that side. The man should pay attention to his own business rather than mine! Following my thought, I took my own attention back to where it should be, to Willoughby. He had also seen Dowdal's error, and was smiling, but cleared his face when he realised I was not.

'The Duke would not see me.' Willoughby's words surprised me.

'You have tried?' I said.

'Yes, I tried, but someone recognised me as a witness against that priest, Anderson, six months ago.' Seeing my face he held up his hands as if in defence and added, 'Believe me, I would not have done it if they did not put me on the rack. You must believe me. I swear 'tis true!'

'Father Lionel Anderson? You did not tell me this,' I said.

Though it might be true, I held little respect for those who informed on others, either for their own gain or for weak ethics, at the cost of another's life. I had seen traits of those who had spent time inside The Hole, and Willoughby had none of them. He had no scars from hard irons circling his wrists and ankles, nor did he have the gait of one stretched ruthlessly on the rack… And he had kept knowledge of this betrayal from me. Before I could release my anger, I must know more.

Willoughby spoke first. 'Even with all things I have been condemned for, my behaviour in this was most odious to me and one I did not wish to declare. They forced me to it, else suffer worse.'

'He was hanged on your word? To be hanged, drawn and quartered is a vile death for any man, even for our enemies.' The five priests had suffered that same death only four days since, their last words hanging over the silent crowd, their bodies snuffed out and atrociously desecrated as we watched, all fresh images in my head. And this man had caused another priest to die in the same terrible manner.

'Not only mine, but also of three others.' I shook my head, but it still felt as if I was pulled in all directions at once.

'All as damnable as you?'

'Likely so. Oates was one who spoke and he is an obnoxious man.'

'Seven priests were condemned that day. Did you speak against them all?'

Willoughby's silence told me neither one way nor other. If I were he, nor would I admit to such shame. His big-eyed child face suddenly became sinister and evil to me. This man was responsible for the hanging of at least one good person, and shaming of that person's life where there should have been respect. I could not look upon him any more, my belly churned as though I had eaten poison, and I had to walk away without saying any other thing.

'Do not judge me, Mrs Cellier!' Willoughby's voice chased me to the door. 'You cannot know how it was if you have not had the same done to you as they did to me! You would do the same if they made you!'

I turned then.

'You are wrong, Captain. I would not,' I said, still facing the door, not looking at him. 'What ever did he do to you? Did he give you mass? Did he take your confession?' I turned then and saw by the colour of his face I had hit close to the mark. 'Then you have murdered your own father.'

'My father disowned me when I was a mere boy,' he said, intentionally misunderstanding me, perhaps looking for sympathy.

'Do you also have his death on your conscience?' I advanced

on Willoughby with so much anger in me I believed I could kill him with my bare hands and it would be right that I should do so. My jaw was so hard clamped down I had trouble speaking. 'Or perhaps you have no conscience.'

'He claimed I stole his horses. I did not, but he would not listen.'

'You talk of your birth father who knew you since you were born. He had more reason to believe you than any other, but he did not. Why? Why did he not?'

Again, Willoughby did not answer. I imagined the reason to be simple: his father had not believed him because he knew him too well. How had I been seduced by the same viper as Eve! I could no longer listen to his self pity or his excuses. I turned back to the house, stepped through the door and slammed it shut behind me.

14

27th day of August, 1679

Over the next months, though I could not blame the captain for every wrong done against every Catholic, I most certainly tried. I detested the mere sight of him and chased him from our home with the threat that if I saw him again I would return him to the hole from whence I took him. And I would have done so if I could have found him, but he had gone to earth like the wily fox he was. I could not bear the thought of how I had fallen prey to this cur, believed his pretence of caring for the wrongly accused, when he had stood as the accuser.

Aye, if I could have laid every innocent's death at Willoughby's door I would have, but not even he could extend his reach to Wales whilst still living in London. The dying words of Father Lewis protesting his innocence reached me at the end of August, three days after his hanging.

What had he to protest against? That he was killed for his faith? Or that, as a vessel of the Lord, he had been too generous to the paupers and the destitute of his county of Monmouthshire, and had feloniously relieved them of their suffering?

What sin did that court find, that they would so rejoice in his dying! A man so good, there would surely be more hardship and death now than had they let him live.

But his life was forfeit as soon as they had decided it so. The trial was but a farce, staged to appease weak conscience that justice was done. No man should be so fooled. God would not be.

I stood in the middle of our bed chamber, and read the lengthy paper in my hand, a faithful copy of Father Lewis's final words, written by himself in prison after his trial.

'...in life-moral, I thank God I have suffered lately, and exceedingly, when maliciously, falsely, and most injuriously, I was branded for a public cheat, in pamphlet, in ballad, on stage, and that in the head city of the Kingdom, yes, and over the whole nation, to the huge and great detriment of my good name, which I always was as tender of, as the other I am now quitting...'

I looked up and saw my pale self reflected in the looking glass, hunched shoulders, clasping the pages between my two fisted hands. Though moved by his words, my body was still. I had tasted of the same derision this man suffered, each time I left home, each time I walked the streets to do my business, some drunken beard might threaten me, or some protester against my faith might recognise me and block my way.

In this, it was not hefty men that were most cruel, but my equals, working sisters and other midwives who, like me, were called to duty as often by night as by day. When death whispered in my ear, it was Susanna Atterbury who buried her fist in my belly without warning, not her husband, though when I defended myself against her he needed no further provocation.

I read further.

Lewis declared there was no truth in any of the accusations against him, not in substance nor in circumstance; that it was a story so false, he could have easily defied the face that had attempted to justify it; so sordid a business, a story so ridiculous, that he wondered how any sober Christian, at least who knew him, could as much as incline to believe so open an improbability. In truth, those who knew him and knew that his innocence had satisfied the judge a year and a half before and that the whole was mere fiction of some malicious person or persons against him.

In the next lines he implored God to grant pardon not for himself but for those who had spoken against him, since his own forgiveness for them was 'hearty'. The very words of the executed priest encouraging forgiveness brought up vengeful thoughts in me against the very ones he asked us to forgive. They did not deserve the forgiveness of me nor of any other, so heinous was their crime!

My eyes unfocused from the page. I could not forgive such

maliciousness that would take a good man's life, and that of the many other self-professed innocents. Laurence Hill. Henry Berry. Robert Green. William Ireland. Thomas Pickering. John Grove. John Gavan. Thomas Whitbread. Anthony Turner. William Harcourt. John Fenwick, to name but a few.

Two months had not diminished the horror of the priests' executions. Not even the rabble had been inclined to break the silence before, during and after their several speeches protesting the wrong done them. The crowd knew as well as the false accusers the wickedness of persecuting such fine men. If they had been guilty, saying so would not have hurt them then, for they were to be hanged for the crime already, but, like Father Lewis, they did not ask for forgiveness for themselves, but for those who caused their innocent lives to be lost.

They asked forgiveness for those such as Willoughby, who had spoken against them. I had to ask myself, if they could forgive such people, should I not too? If Willoughby truly had been tortured, then surely I, who never was in that position, should not be the judge of him.

I read on.

Lewis insisted he was innocent of any plot as an infant who had left its mother's womb only yesterday, and that when Oates, Bedlow, Dugdale and Prance had strictly examined him last May in Newgate, London, he had the least knowledge or hint of such plot, and if there had been one, he would have been as zealously nimble in the discovery of it as any of the most loyal subjects His Majesty hath in his three Kingdoms.

He asked that if someone were to speak of him once he was gone, one should do right to his dead ashes and not speak badly of him.

I looked up from the paper once more, and saw how grief stricken was the image of myself looking back at me from the glass. Tears were on my face. I knew the look of that woman, colluded and conspired with her as if she were another. I knew she agreed with me that something must be done to turn the unending tide from the Catholic shore, where black storms whipped up again and again to send waves of anger and persecution and to swallow worthy men and drag them back into the sea to be lost forever. But if Canute, King of Denmark, could not stop the tide, what chance a lesser mortal?

Only a current stronger than the first could turn the tide.

From all accounts of the St Omer boys, those that had been in some coffee houses and in the court, though he was no longer welcome in our house, Captain Willoughby was carrying out my plan and was playing the part of gardener. Perhaps he sought to court favour with me, but his seed planting was growing whispers in the street that the plot against the King was not after all a Catholic plot, but thrown upon our religion as a scapegoat by the Presbyterians.

He carried out our design and filled coffee houses all over town with small pieces of doubt... not so strong he would appear too zealous and on the side of the idea, but sometimes displaying a little hesitation, a small hint or suggestion he might believe it to be the truth. He might have earned a decent wage upon the stage, so convincing was he, and so perfectly did he act the part.

Though I heard he did this, I could not help but think he did it for himself still, that his motives were not pure. But I must also believe the Lord sent me a gift when he guided me to Willoughby in Newgate, a gift it would be foolishness not to accept and use, and use well. The man's charm, handsome looks and breezy wit had beguiled me and all of London's coffee houses, and his attractions were equally effective on both men and women, I observed. So, though I might find his presence an abhorrence, perhaps he was sharp enough and quick enough to influence the crowd and turn the tide.

Were he to reveal details of my plan to any non-Catholic I would be executed for treason for, no matter that I had not myself carried out any act, thoughts were as actions or deeds.

Could I trust him? Regardless of my present feelings toward him, he had not yet failed me in any task I had set him and that he had agreed to. It was not as though he had tried to conceal his warts. I had discovered them almost too easily from tales he told at the dinner table as well as from others in prison.

In Newgate, they told me he had been in a cell for more time than he had been out, and he had frequented more prisons than most anybody anywhere. He freely confessed of his crimes when I asked him, and expressed with the greatest sincerity that he would atone for his sins for the remainder of his life in any way he might. It may be that my trust in him had been persuasive in altering his character so he could now walk out of the gutter, but his past might also once more bring him to do those things he was wont to do. My trust in him could never be absolute.

I read on.

'...*Moreover, know that when last May I was in London under examination concerning the plot, a prime examinant told me, that to save my life and increase my fortunes, I must make some discovery of the plot, or conform; discover a plot, I could not, for I knew of none; conform, I would not, because it was against my conscience; then, by consequence, I must die, and so, now dying, I die for conscience and religion; and dying upon such good scores, as far as human frailty permits, I die with alacrity interior and exterior; from the abundance of the heart, let not only mouths but faces also speak.*'

Oh my lord, I could barely stand!

For all those that had so cruelly died, for all those innocent lives stolen by malicious lies, for all those good men who found the inner truth of their lives revealed to the outside only to be tarnished by the muck of prejudice and fear and anger of our times, a stone stuck in my throat so I could not swallow, and another weighed so heavily on my chest I could not breath. I had an image of him hanging soon after protesting his innocence, as the five priests were hanged only moments after they had protested theirs.

In that moment, I saw them all, every one of them that had died that way, swing before me. I put out my hand to push away the sight, but the sight was not in the room and I could not hide it. My hand touched the looking glass, and the coldness of it on my fingertips made me draw back.

Some of the poor young men who came over from St Omer had gone home to Flanders defeated by how the truth of their many testimonies were made meaningless against the lies of a few servants of the Devil, and devastated by how futile their guileless defence had been to save the lives of their friends. The rest of the boys stayed with us to act as witnesses in other trials, and to discover how these trials fared.

Each day, the prisons filled with more Catholics named by fair-weather friends and neighbours for a few guineas, else a pardon for some past mischief. Too many took absolution to reveal knowledge of the plot against the King, no matter if it was the truth. Such hypocrisy. It was that very reason – that a Catholic could be absolved of the crime of lying for the Catholic cause and so should not be trusted – that they gave for not trusting any who had our faith, and for denying a Catholic man to swear on the Bible!

Almost sightlessly I looked upon the crumpled paper still in my hand and was compelled to finish. These were the man's last words, and deserved to be witnessed and remembered. His words echoed my thoughts about those that had gained from delivering him up and sentencing him, but for each of them he offered forgiveness, which I could not do.

'*Whomever, present or absent, I have ever offended, I humbly desire them to forgive me. As for my enemies, had I as many hearts as I have fingers, with all those hearts would I forgive them. At least, with the single heart I have, I do freely forgive them all: my neighbours that betrayed me; the persons that took me; the justices that committed me; the witnesses that proved against me; the jury that found me; the judge that condemned me; and all others, who out of malice or zeal, covertly or openly, have contributed to my condemnation. But, singularly and especially, I forgive my capital persecutor, who has so long thirsted for my blood. From my soul I forgive him, and wish his soul so well. In the style of our great master, Christ himself, Father forgive them, they know not what they do...*'

But the worst line came at the end of the sheet, written by another: '*His prayers being ended, he was turned off.*'

I openly cried for the man then. There were no more words to read and no more to come. And so came the end of a passionate and caring man, whose only harm was to help those more needy than himself. His life was worth more than any and all of those instruments that took it. This madness had to stop! If no other would attempt to stop it, then I must try mightily to do so myself in whatever way I could.

Aye, I may even ask Willoughby to lend himself further to this task. He had already sworn to repay me, and this would be the payment I ask of him. For his sins against them, he owed recompense to the Catholics still locked behind iron bars, and those yet to be there. If he followed my idea through to fruition, he may yet save other lives, hopefully more than he gave cause to be taken. When he died, he might even find himself closer to God rather than the Devil.

Of course, I would have to speak to him again, but it would be small price to pay if my scheme came off.

15

13th day of October, 1679

'Stand tall, Captain, and desist your incessant prattle! You must act the part when you come before royalty!' I snapped, perhaps a little too harshly, as was evident from his woeful expression.

The moment I spoke, I remembered he was no stranger to royalty; that he had once told me how he had travelled far on the continent as a soldier in his younger days, to Spain, Portugal, Flanders and Holland, and that he had also spent a fair time in the company of William, Prince of Orange. That did not mean I found it any easier to be with him, but it was a necessity I must bear to win this war against us. Willoughby was our only weapon and I must make use of it as best I could.

'It is hardly my fault if I am blessed with a silver tongue and I am of a happy disposition to use it,' he smartly answered only part of my scold and ignored the rest. 'We are all lambs, equal in the eyes of the Lord. I am fine as any man and the King will find no fault in me.' He looked as if he might say more, and I was glad he did not.

Willoughby oft quoted the Bible of late, the insincerity of his hypocrisy catching in my stomach since I had discovered his part in the death of the priest. Seeing my expression he closed his mouth, for which I was entirely grateful. I wished to collect my thoughts before being granted admittance to the Royal Court. He did not allow me the privacy of them for long.

'Madam. Are you aware of the arrests of Mr Pepys and Sir Deane?' It seemed he still wished to converse with me.

'Shhhh!' I hushed him. 'Yes, I have known this awhile.' I took satisfaction he was put out by this and shut his mouth. I returned to thoughts of how we had come to this honour extended to us now.

It had not been such an easy path through the buzzing swarm guarding the King, a more useless collection of drones I had yet to see! But we were in the heart of the hive now, brought into the brood chamber through connections of devotion of one to another, to ultimately be received by a king rather than a queen.

If the Duke and Duchess of York were not abroad, I might have approached Her Ladyship on the matter, for we had an understanding between us, and she considered herself indebted to me for the taking in of the witnesses.

It had been to my benefactor, Lady Powys, to whom I had first presented the dilemma of how to secure an audience with His Majesty. We knew of no straight way to reach our target. If we simply arrived at the gate of St. James's Palace we would fast be cast off. Someone he trusts must introduce us to him. Lady Powys had been perfectly equal to the puzzle, and immediately suggested an exquisite solution.

With great fortune, the King had of late recovered from a dreadful illness, which every loyal subject had concerns over. It happened, while the King was laid to bed, I chanced upon the astrologer, John Gadbury, whom I was impelled to ask how serious was the King's illness, then further asked him if he would discover, from the sign of his birth, whether or not Captain Willoughby might be trusted with the tasks I wished to set him. Pierre had tasked me to do so a long while ago. I know not why I did not do it then, but now it was imperative I should not make a mistake in this.

Whilst Gadbury and I walked through the grounds of Westminster Abbey back toward his rooms, he not only released me from doubt over the employment of Willoughby, but further told me the Duke of York was called home from Brussels to sit by his brother's bed in the event the King might take a turn for the worse. This was good news indeed for our cause, for Lady Powys had connections to the Duke, which she quickly undertook to make good use of.

Lady Powys was undertaking to arrange a marital alliance between her nephew and the daughter of her close acquaintance, Lord Peterborough. She designed to appeal to him to agree a meeting with me that I could introduce him to the Captain, with the further hope that Lord Peterborough would then in turn introduce us to the Duke of York. The beauty of this meeting was that, not only had Lord Peterborough served beneath the Duke in the war with the Netherlands, but he had also set up, and defeated objections to, the marriage between the Duke and his chosen wife, Mary of Modena. The Duke was accordingly indebted to him and was, as hoped, prepared to make allowances for our using him to reach his brother.

The plan came to pass as we imagined, and was declared an outstanding success by all of us.

Lady Powys first introduced me to Lord Peterborough at his leisure. This she did with such aplomb and passion, verily singing my praises so that the upstanding gentleman, a few years our senior, was quite taken by us. Captain Willoughby behaved the eloquent gentleman and won over the lord, so that he told his servants to admit 'his new acquaintance' whenever he came to visit!

It was as well he had not seen him six months earlier with shaved head and prison lethargy. Truly, I had not expected the Captain to shine as he had, and for it to have passed so easily.

Soon afterwards, Lord Peterborough sent us notice that the Duke of York wished for him to present us at his residence, and so we went happily confident of our position. Indeed, we were not disappointed.

'Come forth and show yourself,' said the Duke. His thin face was haggard, as well it might be with the burden of his brother's sickness, yet his clothes were smart and his appearance sharp. The curved lips of his wide mouth curled lopsidedly as he said, 'Lord Peterborough tells me the captain is a young man who appears under a decent figure, a serious behaviour and with common understanding. I trust his judgement faithful in this matter. Madam Cellier,' he turned to me, 'you have denied me the pleasure of your company for many years since last you tended my wife, God rest her soul.'

I had not expected or thought that the King's brother would have noticed my services to the first Duchess of York, Anne, daughter of Earl of Clarendon. She was mother of the princesses of York, Lady Mary and Lady Anne living in Richmond Palace, and the youngest two children, Edgar and Catherine, the poor souls that had joined her in death soon after. She had been a Roman Catholic by conviction even before she took her sacraments and made her communion with Rome at her deathbed, and many believed her the cause of the Duke's own conversion.

'Your kindness in remembering me, Sir, is considerable,' I said curtsying as Willoughby took his hat off, bowed and returned it to his head.

The Duke studied Willoughby's book, wherein he had recorded every meeting he considered of a dubious nature; scribbled lists of whom they concerned and detailed conversations he had recorded those persons as having with each other. I had myself read of the book and was satisfied that the contents were ruinous to the Presbyterians, who plotted against the King with the purpose of blaming the Duke of York.

I observed the King's brother slowly turn each leaf, bent over the sewn pages so that his long brown periwig fell as a curtain to hide his mouth, but I could still see his large protuberant eyes follow his finger over the parchment, marking his progress, and every now and then he exclaimed such as, 'Od's life!' or 'Saints preserve us, it is as I thought!' or 'Fie on it! This will not go unpunished!' as if no ladies were present.

The Duke showed himself keen to ride any road that would alleviate the persecution and suffering of Roman Catholics in London and throughout the three Kingdoms. He asked pertinent questions about Stroud and Bedlow, and of Lord Shaftsbury, Reverend Oates and others of the Green Club, where many of these exchanges occurred, and listened carefully to the answers, asking further questions where he was unclear.

He, being pleasingly perceptive and witty, found Captain Willoughby and myself equally so, and so we left on the best of terms, with his vow he would speak to his brother, the King, on the matter. Though he expressed a doubt whether there was enough to convict any single man of treason, he paid Willoughby the large sum of twenty pounds so that he might continue to discover intrigues and plots in any place where they might be hiding. He then expressed to me the desire to meet again, and proclaimed that, despite circumstance, he had not spent such an enjoyable time in a long while!

When we were almost to the door, he called out to me, 'Madam Cellier!' I turned to him and he added, 'I note the late Duchess of York was indebted to you for the sum of five or six hundred pounds?' I simply nodded, not wanting to impose obligation on him for his previous wife's unpaid debt, the loss of her having brought such sadness to him. 'You did not apply to me for your fee, but you will have it!' Then, with less confidence, 'Perhaps you might... make arrangements to attend... call upon my wife, The Duchess? She has not had great success with child and your reputation for sound advice is famous.' That was common knowledge.

'Gladly will I do so, Sir. I would be most honoured.' He nodded his satisfaction and I curtsied once more before following Captain Willoughby out the door. The Duke of York had been good to his word on both counts. I had received payment for my attendance on his first wife, and he had spoken with King Charles on the subject of Willoughby's discoveries, and we were soon to be admitted to the royal presence.

Though I had seen the King before, I had never spoken with him. He was said to be a discerning and tolerant man if somewhat leaning toward more self-indulgence and extravagance than his brother. It was publicly acknowledged that he openly welcomed the bastards of his many mistresses into the court, including the Duke of Monmouth, though they would never be legitimised as his progeny by the Government. Most considered his rule as nearly frivolous, but preferred the way of that to either the austerity and tyranny of Cromwell or the shambles of anarchy in the years after his death.

I could not help but smooth my dress beneath my cloak, and then straighten my cloak and hat while I waited, noting that I was no better than Willoughby with his prattling. In fact, if anything, Willoughby was more at ease than I. If he had any apprehension about the imminent meeting he appeared calm and self-assured, far distant in poise from the broken man I had found dirty and tearful and curled as an unborn child in Newgate many months ago. If such a one could look calm then so could I! I took some time to work at an appearance of composure and confidence, and raised my head in readiness.

St. James's palace was everything a palace should be. The sumptuous rooms were so enormous, and the ceilings so high I might have been walking outside under some foreign sky, with candelabras as stars and portraits of severe ancestors instead of trees. The corridor to the Throne Room was as long and wide as a metropolis street, yet cleaner and sweeter than the cleanest street on a dry spring day, having been cleansed by the winter rain! If I imagined Heaven, it might be something like this – no mud, no muck and some sort of exotic scent to take away the inevitable smell of dung and smoke that comes with London living. Something about the freshness of the walls and floors made me think of Great Missenden in Buckinghamshire. It was a long while since I had visited the village where I was born.

I considered we had been forgotten when a footman called us to the door and bid us enter.

'Only, be sure to keep your hands out of sight,' I whispered to Willoughby. The sight of the tattoos and scars might prejudice the case against us.

For some unfathomable reason, I imagined King Charles would enter after we had stood for a while. But the moment we entered the great room, which was anything but a throne room, and saw we were even now in the presence of His Majesty, both Willoughby and I fell to one knee and bowed our heads.

'Take down your hood, M'Lady,' I was instructed by the footman before he closed the door behind us. I had been uncertain of the protocol. If I exposed my head might it appear presumptuous? But, if I remained hooded, would it seem as if I hid myself? I quickly uncovered myself as instructed.

'The Duke of York has said you have some information to impart,' said King Charles in a most disinterested voice. 'Come closer so that I may hear you.'

Before we entered, the footman said we should not rise before the King gave permission. Now I did not know if I should shuffle along the floor on my knee into his hearing, or whether I should stand and move with dignity, but perhaps bring the King's ire upon us. Willoughby must have had the same thought, for he had stayed where he was also.

The King laughed. 'Come now. I do not wish to have you shout at me, and I cannot hear you from where you kneel. Have to your feet and come hither!'

Not one in the Kingdom would deny the King's reputation of mischievous humour, and I suspected we had been the source of a secret drollery. To my side, I saw Willoughby gracefully raised his knee, pushed back to his feet and stand tall in one beautiful movement. My eyes still to the floor, I followed suit with less elegance, a more ungainly rise, and scuffled clumsily forward the few steps to stand beside Willoughby.

'Speak now,' commanded the King, seeming to become serious. 'What is this information you have for me? Am I to understand you come to warn me of some plot fouler than all plots before? Then you must tell a good tale for you have great rivalry in this; every other person to enter this chamber comes with the same story!' he said with amusement in his voice. 'And, note this well, I wish to discover plots but not to create them!'

I do not know what I had imagined, but I did not suppose the King to have good humour with so many trying to take his life! He was the King, and being king was a serious duty, one that must demand a solemn demeanour in all those surrounding him, and I had thought we must also be serious in his presence.

'May it please Your Majesty,' I said, 'we are both very relieved you are recovered from your recent sickness, and we are sincerely grateful for your indulgence in granting us audience. I am your humble servant and, as such, my family lives to serve Your Majesty. In the manner my father and brother died in service to your father, the King now deceased, I lay my life before you.'

'Your father and brother were known to me in those troubled times,' the King said, 'and, if for no other reason, for that alone I would see you and offer my thanks to you for their service. And for their lives freely given in defence of my father, I owe you a debt of gratitude I hope it is in my honour and capability to repay.' The King's deep voice was as a cello, reverberating deep in me, drawing on memories of my early life. This was the son of the monarch my father and brother died for. A bond such as theirs should be remembered, and for that I would equally honour both my father and his.

'As the lives of my father and brother were freely given to your service, so is my life,' I reiterated, bowing my head still lower. When the King again spoke, I dared to peek at him through my lashes. 'My brother has told me you tended his wife, Anne, the late Duchess of York. I understand a debt is still due you. We must look to remedy that sad oversight.'

'Thank you, Your Majesty, but the Duke has recently settled it.' I bobbed my knees to a half curtsey; grateful my former attendance was again acknowledged.

'But I am remiss. Who stands this beside you? And what have you to say for yourself?' I imagined the King looked upon Willoughby, so I went to introduce him.

'Your Majesty, this man is the good Captain Thomas Willoughby. The game that once was played against Charles the Great, your father, is now played over with his son. Though you jest about it, he has indeed discovered a plot most foul, and is come to reveal it to you.'

'Begad, a plot!' The King's voice was again underlined with humour and he appeared to be laughing at me. His next words confirmed he was not ready to take us seriously. 'We have plots and plots! Plots in the taverns, plots in the coffee houses, plots on the street corners; and now you are come to tell me of yet another design on my life? I am verily the most murdered King in England!' Other men in the courtroom laughed at the King's jest. I did not know if to laugh or not. The King made light and might expect it of me, but this was no matter for humour. If he did not take it seriously, it might cost him his life. And if I did not take it seriously, it might cost me mine.

'Your Majesty. I humbly beg you take note of this one, for I have heard it with my own ears and know it to be true!'

Willoughby spoke beside me. I sensed he spoke to the floor. 'Your Majesty, I humbly ask your permission to speak?'

'By all means, Willoughby. But first listen to me carefully. If you inform me well, I will reward your service accordingly; but if you steer me along a false path, you will find one of my prisons a familiar home. Be sure to choose your words well, my man. In this room I have listened to many false tales from those who hope to open my purse!'

The laugh had gone from the King's voice, and I sensed he knew too well how readily a man – or woman – would perjure him or her self for the sake of gold in the hand. Then he spoke to me.

'Mrs Cellier, do you vouch for this man?'

Though I knew I must not, I paused momentarily. I freely vouched for him to Lady Powys and Lord Peterborough, and to the Duke of York, but now the King asked me if he could trust him, and I could not be as certain as I had been. He had shown himself sometimes unreliable. Could the King trust his life to this man? If the Captain's tale be false or misled, I would be held accountable for him. But, then, contrary to his original nature, Willoughby had shown himself a good navigator ere now, and had since repented of all his previous sins. He might steer us well, and perhaps save the King's life.

'This man has come in the way of a hard life, Sir…'

'Look me in the eye when you talk, madam. I wish to weigh your sincerity.'

I obeyed the King, and looked into the eyes of a great man. His upturned lips brought up the corner of his moustache in a delightful manner, and his striking smile caused his fine trimmed, three-point beard in the style of 'Van Dyke', made famous by the royal painter, to stand out toward me. And upon my soul, his periwig was a cascade of such immaculate dark brown curls, brushed and oiled to perfection, so it gleamed when he lent his head. Yet, though gaiety marked his face below the nose, his eyes examined me with the seriousness of a man that guards against ever-present danger to his life.

All this I took note of, whilst his regal stance and composure, though I had prepared myself for his company, reminded me to pull my back straight and tall so that I may measure up to even a small part of him. Even more than his presence was the look upon his face. He might jest about the plots, but he was more ready to listen than I had thought.

'The captain has late come from the service of the Prince of Orange and the Duke de Villa Hermosa,' I said to cover that Willoughby had been up to all manner of no good abroad. It was true, the Captain had been in the army in Spain and other places and, though he had been back for some time, that was a piece of the tale that would not lend itself to the King's belief in his story. 'Since his return, he has fallen in with some people of the most obnoxious kind.'

'And this lends him to me?' he asked, echoing my own concern on this matter.

'He has fallen in with them of his own will, Sir, for to discover their deeds and designs, for he was shocked indeed when he heard them speak.'

'What designs and deeds are these?' The King looked directly at Willoughby, who still looked to the ground and so did not see. I elbowed him in the side, and he recoiled as though I poked him with a stick on a sore spot; a noise such as the one he made might be better found in a pig house, though he fast collected himself.

'Designs so dastardly, deeds so dire, Your Majesty, and I heard them spoken with my own ears.'

'Well, man, what are these schemes you speak of?'

For the first time, Willoughby raised his head and looked the King straight in his eyes, a brave and even hardy move, yet a bold one that gave him credence.

'It was not my intention, Your Majesty, to dig myself into the den of the foxes. I put on the crafty fox-coat so that I might run with the cunning creatures and discover their conspiracy, for I had heard them talk of it.'

'Tell me, what did they talk of, and which fox was it that did the talking?'

Willoughby looked carefully and suspiciously at each man surrounding the King. 'Can we speak alone?'

'Speak openly man. I trust each of these men with my life. Anything you have to say to me may be said in front of any of them.'

Willoughby nodded. 'If that is so, I am happy that you are protected so well. This is what I must tell you,' he paused but a moment, I thought, for effect. 'The topic whispered round the coffee table is of how to weigh the appearance of a plot against Your Majesty into the balance of the Catholics, whilst furthering the cause of the Presbyterians. Members of the Green Ribbon Club sit confidently side by side respectable men, spinning their imaginings into plots most wicked.'

The King's eyebrows raised momentarily. 'Get to the point, man.'

'The point is a salient one, Your Majesty, and sharp as a duelling sword that cuts through leather and skin from two steps away. The point is likely to cost Your Majesty's life if it is not heeded well.' Again he paused for effect, and I was both impressed and repulsed by his manipulative nature. 'An army collects in the Netherlands and stands ready for the call to arms! This army awaits but a word from England, an invitation from some that stand beside you and behind you at the throne, so close you might easily think them trusted brethren; so credible that their word, and the word of their stooges, has caused the death of many innocents ere this time.' Now, dramatically, Willoughby looked at each of the men in the room, as if he might identify the traitors merely by their appearance. Wouldst it was so easy!

'Name these vermin, for I will chase them to earth and dig them out with my hounds!'

'Lord Shaftsbury leads the pack, for he has propositioned William of Orange…'

'My brother's son in law?' interrupted Charles.

'Yes Sir. William of the Netherlands, wed to Mary Stuart, daughter of the Duke of York.

'I know my own nephew! Continue!' Even King Charles grew weary of Willoughby's speeches it seemed.

'I fear their plan was to throw the Government of the three Kingdoms into upheaval by the murder of Sir Edmundbury Godfrey, and the casting of blame of that poor man's death onto Catholic hands. I have heard men talk in the taverns and coffee houses and I have listened well.'

'Tell me more of what you have heard,' prompted the King when Willoughby's voice trailed away. I hoped his devotion to the King would not be dissuaded by the fear of retribution amongst those he would speak of.

Fireside talk was that those who spoke up against the Whigs and their plot could easily next day be only a memory in the minds of their family and those once around them. A person could melt away as fast as ice in the springtime, or a shadow brought into sunlight, leaving no trace. Else they could be found beaten in an alley. Willoughby's next words worried me he spoke too much.

'Well, Sir, what you do not know about me is that I was… I was in confinement in one of your finest cells for a spell most recently.' I sensed Willoughby glance quickly at me, most likely to check I was not discomposed at this disclosure. The King only nodded as if he already knew this, giving nothing away. 'While I enjoyed the hospitality of Your Majesty,' he paused again but to smile tentatively, 'I had the dubious pleasure of spending time with a man that knew the Reverend Titus Oates abroad.'

'What has this to do with any new plot?' he said. 'This is one I know of.'

'This is the point I am aiming towards, Sir, and I will reach it shortly, if you will allow me patience. This man I shared bread with, a man named Stroud, he told me how Mr Oates met a friend of his abroad, and employed him to speak out against those that were lately executed for the murder of Sir Godfrey.'

'If this man had information to share of the murder, it was only right he should speak out about it,' said the King in a most strong voice.

'Yes Sir, I would not think to question that. The purpose of my words is not to question what is right, but to inform you of what I know.' Willoughby managed to look uncharacteristically diffident. It was a look that did not sit well on him with my knowledge of him.

'Pray continue,' said the King in a voice that said he was well acquainted with reservations caused by his presence. I willed Willoughby to continue, and he did, with no show of the selfconsciousness of moments before, a sign he should be on the stage, he was so accomplished at changing character at whim.

'The point of all of it is that, in his possession, this man Stroud keeps a letter from his friend, whose name is Bedlow, saying that he did not know of any plot against you, the King, more than he had been told by Reverend Oates. He revealed to me this man had perjured himself for a palm full of gold.'

'Does he say who filled his pockets?'

'This he does, Your Majesty. Pray have patience with my dull story; I am not practiced at telling tales.' Willoughby bowed his head low, but I could see his face and it was not at all submissive.

'Pray continue,' repeated the King, obviously frustrated at not knowing all at once. It occurred to me that there was purpose to Willoughby's pauses. Each time he did so, the King believed the story more. The doubt he showed when Willoughby begun to speak was replaced by impatience for details of the plot. Willoughby held the King's reins and steered him as a skilled coachman, taking him whither he wished to go rather than be instructed on the destination.

'On account of Stroud's story, I have taken it upon myself to discover the truth of the matter. I would not be presumptuous to reveal the story to you before I have acquainted myself with some of those that he talked of to be sure of the truth of it.' Willoughby took all the credit on himself as if I had no involvement. 'What I have discovered will shock Your Majesty.'

'I show great patience, Captain.' The King sighed with exasperation. 'Pray come to the point.'

'Sir, the vilest plotting is discussed openly and most keenly where you think you are safe. More horrid and noxious scheming and designing takes place in the heart of your own government by those you trust most.' Again, Willoughby made a point of looking at each of the men standing in the room as if they might be the ears of the enemy. Again, I imagined he might have acted on the stage at some time, so dramatic was his stance. 'Though abhorrent to me, I have spent time in the company of those who are a danger to you, and written down their speeches so you may judge them your self.'

'What? Is this man not the most loyal and devoted subject!' He spoke to the two men I did not know, who stood behind him, and swept his hand wide towards Willoughby as though he filled the whole room. 'Have you this paper here with you?'

This was the moment we waited for. When he saw proof of the plot, he might be satisfied and take action to protect himself. He would also see what they called the Popish Plot against him was woven to hide other Presbyterian deeds. The table would soon be turned. From beneath his cloak, Willoughby took his bound sheaf of papers, now secured by a length of my red ribbon, and held it in front of him as an offering.

'Bring your papers to me, Captain.'

Head bent, Willoughby approached with suitable humble demeanour, but then took his feathered hat from his periwigged curls and swept it as widely as the King had moments before swept his hand, bowing deeply as he did so, before looked with great daring straight into the King's eyes as he passed him the papers.

'Your Majesty is most kind. I am honoured to share my simple but modest scribblings with hope you might find gratitude for this sincere and heart felt means to serve my King.'

Willoughby understood that sincerity is rarely believed without seeing into a man's soul, and risked himself to prove himself true. It was hard to not admire his practiced audacity and skill, and at that moment I could easily believe how he talked himself in and out of so many escapades as he had described to me in such a short life!

The King untied the ribbon and lay it on his lap. Then he read the pages before him, asking questions to clarify who said what at a particular time when it was not recorded in writing. He also asked questions about the dates when these conversations occurred. Willoughby answered smoothly. It would be hard for the King not to be convinced; all the details were given with confidence. At the end, the King dropped the hand holding the papers into his lap and looked first at Willoughby then at me.

'Will you swear all you say of this before the bench?'

'I will.'

'You have done me the profoundest service bringing me this news. It does indeed deserve gratitude, and gratitude shall you have!' Willoughby again bowed low, widely sweeping the hat in his hand in front of him.

'All I have done in this affair, I have taken upon myself as a humble and devoted subject of your Kingdom. I live only to serve Your Majesty!' In his speech, he again neglected me, and how I had employed him in this business, and took credit for it all upon himself.

'Then you must have payment for your trouble, and for your goodness in bringing this news to me.'

The King called for his purse and, when it arrived, opened it and took out some gold coins. He called Willoughby forward. The captain did as he was bid, and elegantly knelt before His Majesty.

'Take this, and keep your ear to the ground. If you discover any further facts for me, bring them at once.'

With eyes lowered, Willoughby accepted a handful of coins, perhaps as much as the Duke of York had given him, then stood and backed until he reached a few steps away. He then knelt, again for effect, and thanked the King for his graciousness.

'Nay, it is your kindness that I thank you for. You have brought my attention where it was neglected, and for this I am pleased. You may take your leave now.'

Thinking the King had forgotten me, I started backing towards the door, as did Willoughby.

'Mrs Cellier!' As if a whip cracked over me, my head shot up and I looked King Charles in his face, forgetting myself. Should I have curtsied lower? Should I have said something when I did not?

'Your Majesty!' I curtsied to my knee and stayed there.

'Mrs Cellier, I have my purse open and it is incumbent on me to repay some interest on the debt long overdue to you, though my brother has repaid the captial.'

I said nothing. It was not my place to presume to deny the King his generosity, so I waited.

'Will you come forward, Mrs Cellier, and take a small token in lieu of full payment?' I pushed myself to my feet, my legs not as steady as I would have liked them to be, and stepped slowly to the throne. The King held out a bulging fist, and I was obliged to hold my hand beneath it. Without intention, I looked up into our King's face, the second King Charles, and almost jumped when he closed one eye in a saucy wink, the other eye glinting with humour.

The number of years under his hat may be equal to mine, but where the cloak of loose and scandalous life folk would have me wear was imaginary, he wore his so brazenly and boldly none would question it. He audaciously kept his bastards and their mothers in his court, so none would whisper about the issue of his carnal pleasures. I did not know what to do. Likely others in the room too saw his wink so I could not feign blindness. It would be gravely uncivil and ungracious to ignore royalty. But neither could I wink back, complicit in his act. It would not be seemly nor in my heart.

'Why, I am grateful Your Highness remembers my service to the Duchess of York, may her soul rest in peace. I am furthermore happy my service in this present matter might safely deliver the King from such a dreadful plot and that Your Majesty finds himself in such fine spirits once more!'

I accompanied this speech in the manner of Willoughby by fast circling my hands in the fashion of an elaborate flourish and curtsying deep, finishing on my knee with a bow down low to the floor. But I could not resist a quick peep to see how the King would respond, and when I saw he smiled, and those behind him were not looking, I winked so only he could see. At first, he snorted with astonishment as I caught him unaware, and then he released a belly laugh that filled every corner of the chamber that made the men not paying attention behind him jump. Though unaware of the source of amusement, as a flock of sheep, other men in the room baa-ed delicately, for it might be seen as surly not to join in.

'Mrs Cellier! Your actions are most refreshing! Your services are gratefully received!'

With laughter still commanding his face, King Charles clapped his hands at shoulder height. 'Colonel Hallshall,' he addressed the man who came forward. It was His Majesty's cup bearer. 'Be so good as to take Mrs Cellier and Captain Willoughby to the honourable Mr Coventry, and ask him to listen to their tale. He will especially enjoy this one, since it involves his old friend, Lord Shaftsbury!' The King wiped the corner of his eye with the back of his fingers and wiped them on his regal clothes. Then, addressing Willoughby and myself, he dismissed us with the words, 'Mr Secretary Coventry will see to your needs.'

As we backed out of the court, I remembered the words of Lord Powys when supping at the Tower one time, when he laughed at how this Mr Coventry had defended a man of the Government, Mr Samuel Pepys, that was now also falsely accused and in the Tower, by saying, 'There are a great many more Catholics than think themselves so, if having a crucifix will make one'.

He was spoken highly of by all the lords, and if he was so admired by them, then he would have my trust also.

16

17th day of October, 1679

Pierre's fingers teased the curls of his brown horsehair periwig lying on the table between the hide bound ledgers we were working on – previous years balance sheets and Profit and loss books, debtors and creditors – picking at stray hairs and winding them in or pulling them out, tidying them without thinking. On occasion he pulled hard at some hairs until they broke, and other times he gently stroked them in a way that distracted me from my task.

But all the time he recited the things I read out loud until he remembered them. Or thought he remembered them. His memory often failed him these days.

For many long evening hours I guided my husband in what I knew of the business law of our land for, even now, he was familiar with that of France but not of this Kingdom. In the year of 1675, and again in the year of 1677, I had guided him through two business hearings held against him, but now he was come against a tougher case and should know some of the law himself. Together we had studied the fine points yet, whenever I tested him, they skirted his understanding, playfully flirting with him before flitting out of reach.

The candle flickered and spat and threw moving shadows over Pierre's ageing face. I had thought it before, how vulnerable he looked with so little hair on his head, so grey and thin it exposed him for the old man he had become, but it did not compel me to judge him harshly nor did it diminish my esteem for him. He had shot my heart with Cupid's bow so that the arrow had found its mark and stayed true. His good character and fine standing held me forever captive.

Despite my fond feelings for him, I suffered from great fatigue in the effort to impart my knowledge to him. I did not wish to diminish who he was by actions of sinful pride, but I feared his capacity for bookishness was as the stars out of reach. The facts stubbornly refused to settle in his head, more so now than before. The time was come to change the topic under discussion. If I was tired, he was more so.

'Captain Willoughby has done a fine job of collecting, Pierre, but there remains too many outstanding debts. It would be well if you could pay a visit to the more stubborn oysters.'

'If you think I must, *ma chère*, I will take a knife and open them myself.'

Though he could do nothing at this time of evening, Pierre took up his periwig, as if glad to be given some useful action he could follow away from these ledgers, and pulled it close upon his head, hiding the deep worry lines on his forehead behind curls not yet set in place.

I feared concern for his business was the cause of the lines, and prepared to reassure him on this point, but it was upon a different subject he then addressed me.

'Lizzie, my sweet, you and I know the Captain well now we have taken him back into our society. He has lived with us nigh on half a year, and is apt to talk about his past enthusiastically to the extent I fear he takes pride in his roguery...'

'Worry not, my dearest,' I reassured my husband, placing my hand on his. 'It is for this reason he is most right for the collection of debts and for the other tasks we set him.'

'It is not for my business I worry,' he said. 'Though he makes light of his oft-told stories of past villainies and punishments, I sense and fear we must not trust him overly much.'

'Not only has he confessed of his sins, Pierre, he has repented of them. With my own eyes I have seen him stand in the yard and flail himself with Franciscan tails, and he prays fervently for the Lord's forgiveness.'

Before my eyes I saw those silver lines I had spied on Willoughby's bare back whilst he bathed and in the summer sun, so criss-crossed were they that unmarked skin was rare there! I remembered the compassion I had in that moment, and how I would have cared for him tenderly as my own child, had he let me. But he would have none of my attention. He pushed me away, threw his shirt on to cover the welts he had since added to past ones and turned his back on me. 'Save your kindness for one that deserves it,' he had said as he walked away. I did not miss how his voice shook.

'Well, I am not convinced. He still keeps company with those he did mischief with and, as well, a man I did business with said he saw him come from Lord Stafford's home. He is not to be trusted. I wish you to consider this wisdom and avoid his private society when you can.'

'He will do me no harm, dearest one. He is beholden to me, and to you, for his freedom and for paying his debts. I fear you worry needlessly.'

'And I fear not. From what I have heard of him, and what he has told us himself, a worst scoundrel you could not care to find! We are chickens homing a fox under our roof!'

I defended Willoughby, though I knew not why.

'Nature may have made him a fox, but like a tame dog he serves his master. His ways are to our benefit. They are of use to us. If he has sin left in him, I have not seen it since he has stayed in our house. It is not our place to judge him, only to forgive him.'

'If he has sin left in him, like a fox he hides it so we do not see it. One more thing...' Pierre paused as if not knowing how to phrase the next. '...and this is of a nature more delicate. He has earned a...' Still he hesitated. '...name...a reputation with women folk, and that name is Don Juan. I do not question your devotion, but I insist you must not be alone with him any place that could give cause for mischievous tongues. Some have before now whispered in my ear that I would be unwise to leave you and he alone together.'

At the sight of my face he held up his hands in mock defence. 'Of course, I have laughed at them, but it would not do to put yourself in a position where those busy-bodies have substance to talk of…'

Despite his making light of it, Pierre's eyes were serious, and I knew he believed there to be real danger to my reputation.

'I will take care, my dear, but he is too young and I am too old for any ear to believe that wagging tongue!'

'He is a handsome rogue and, from all accounts, does not see wrinkles as a barrier to his amours. Your years have been kind to you, Lizzie, and you are so much younger than me; some believe me already cuckold.'

Before I could catch myself, an image of the captain romancing me, courting me, brought burning to my cheeks. The idea that my many years might not be a barrier to his doing so gave me a moment of stolen satisfaction quite removed from the affection and passion I shared with my husband. I bent my head to hide my guilty blush and turned back the corners of several pages of the nearest ledger, then dropped them back again. I hoped Pierre would think my fluster was from his flattery of me, or perhaps from his revelation that others thought me an adulteress.

'We have spoken of this together many a time, dear one. The only thing meant by your having more years than me is that you were born before me. It is only a matter of time, not of the heart. We were fortunate that we two were born in the same century and close enough in birth for us to find each other! *We are lodged in each other's heart.*' I smiled and kissed his cheek as I quoted our friend and favourite poet, Cowley, that we often read to each other. 'I will guard our reputation as much as I might when my profession prepares fertile ground for seeds of suspicion!'

Pierre grimaced in a way that showed he knew this to be true. My would-be protector had lived long with the good and bad of my trade, but that did not give him acceptance of some parts I was cast, though I was fain to act those parts when I must.

'Now,' I said, wishing to change the subject of our conversation once again, 'if you wish to help your own business, Pierre, you might have Willoughby winkle payments from these, who are not much more than a month overdue with their payments, and not let them become oysters from the first.' At his nod, I continued on the subject we had been so engrossed in before other concerns. 'And when you are in the court, you must carry these books with you,' I said, placing my hand on the pile of finance ledgers. 'You must mind well all I have spoken about this night. In word of the law you have done no wrong to this one you are in court with, but they say they have witnesses to the contrary so we must prove your case.

Pierre placed his hand on mine, in a shared pact with both my hand and the books it rested upon and, with sincere eyes, said, 'I swear I will do justice to your teaching, *ma chèrie.*'

Abruptly, the door burst open with a bang. Pierre withdrew his hand and stood to face the intruder, pushing his chair back with a screech on the polished wood floor. The chair lay tipped over and untouched, our attention turned on our visitors. Masters Townley and Palmer stood a small way inside the chamber, cloaked with cold autumnal air that crept along the floor to our ankles.

Seeing urgency on their faces, my first thought was that a woman needed help birthing, so I also came to my feet and crossed the floor to my midwife's bag next to the comfortable fireside chair, where I had dropped it when I returned earlier.

'Monsieur Cellier! Monsieur Cellier!' Palmer's words halted my hand from taking the handle. It was not me for whom they had come.

'Make haste, Monsieur Cellier! Captain Willoughby…' He looked guiltily at me before continuing. 'Captain Willoughby is… steeped in liquor. You must come now and take him away!'

'It would not be the first time the Captain is in his cups. I am sure his need for a wet-nurse is past.' Pierre's peevishness hinted of more than exasperation for being called to fetch Willoughby home. Perhaps he had after all detected my earlier thought that I now sincerely regretted. Having dismissed any need for his attention, Pierre picked up the chair that had fallen and begun to sit, but halfway to the seat was brought back to his feet by Townley's next words.

'It is not for the Captain I ask you come, but for us. His

intoxication brings danger to us all, with his lack of caution and loose tongue.'

'You say he brings us danger?' I asked. That cursed loosener of tongues!

Townley knew better than to give the answer of my question to Pierre, as some men would have done. He turned to me and said, 'Schemes and designs spill out from him and into many interested ears. His revelations are causing a considerable stir and there are those who stand up and challenge him. We left the coffee house in a most ominous mood. Make haste, before he reveals too much!'

Now I was included in the plea, I came to Pierre's side, took his arm and beseeched him, 'He knows more than he should of our plans, and if he is in his cups and his mouth is so loose we must bring him home before he murders us all!'

'My dear, if he is so intoxicated, his words may be considered those of a drunk fool.'

'I would not be so certain.' I turned back to the Jesuit youths, and asked, 'Where is he?'

'At Farr's, under the sign of the Rainbow.' And, as if my question was an agreement we would come, Townley then turned and left the room, with Palmer following close on his heels. Their urgency suggested it would be prudent not to ignore it. I paused only long enough to see Pierre's nod that he would shadow us, blew out the candle we had been using to read the books, and did likewise.

I could have taken a moment to fetch my cloak against the cold air, and perhaps should have, but did not reflect upon it, when the Rainbow Coffee House was only a short walk from our front door. It was a decision I would regret for every chilly step north along Arundel Street, then East along the Strand past Saint Clement's church on the left; but by the time we reached the Inner Temple Gate in Fleet Street, I was hot and breathless.

Soon after, we turned into Rainbow Court. The entrance to the coffee house lay behind the sign of the Rainbow. I hardly noticed the stray swine that the beadle had missed grubbing in the plants by the door, except to make a point to ensure ours were locked up when we returned home.

My mind raced ahead to the inevitable confrontation with Willoughby: would he be at the rogues' table or the knights'? Captain Willoughby's distinguishing trait was to weave engaging tales to interest and fascinate all, and so he would undoubtedly be welcome at any table at which he chose to sit.

Though wives and mothers proclaimed coffee as a drying liquor, shrivelling their men's seed and enfeebling their men into apes, my own impression on entering divers coffee establishments was of a reverse nature: a man could match any role he might chose in a coffee house, so long as he could read, tell a true tale or debate a point on something of the time. There, where men were equal to each other, it was only women that remained subordinate to men.

Unusually, the pleasant Temple courtyard was not filled with students of the law, so tonight we arrived unseen in the darkness. Even before we reached the door, we heard raised, angry voices. Pierre stepped past our two young visitors that gladly allowed him, and pulled it open. Though womenfolk were not allowed, I followed close behind my husband, for I had been in many places women were banned when that is where some were particularly found.

Plumes of tobacco smoke snaked round the top of the doorjamb and escaped upwards into the star-filled sky, but did nothing to dwindle the thick, choking air inside. My eyes straight away stung with the mingling of wood smoke from the logs burning in the fireplace; spitting pig fat and smoke from the slanted rushlights, hanging glowing on every wall; as well as the copious curls of tobacco smoke from at least one clay pipe at each table.

Through the pane of separating glass at the far side of the room, coffee brewers ground black beans and boiled the huge vats, which we smelt a street away, ready for tomorrow's business, all in sight of the customers who had seen it so regularly they no longer truly saw it. If the lords seated over there beside the bay window looked out into the darkness, I knew they would see Temple Court and, beyond that, the lanthorns of small and large boats glowing east and west upon the Thames, but some talked earnestly and others listened, occasionally looking over to the scene in the middle of the place.

And there he was – scarred but young, handsome, animated and exuding masculine forcefulness – in the midst of a group of gentlemen trying, and failing, to restrain him and suppress his boundless spirit…and his carrying voice!

As usual, he was provoking other regulars with his disposition and the turbulence he exuded wheresoever he went. He could not help it. Though I should disdain it as I would in any other, I could not help but soften at his childishness as he jovially argued with two men that still had sheathed swords, as evidenced by the hilts protruding from their sides. How long would they stay sheathed I did not know, but two things were obvious: if he continued to rile other customers he would soon be at the point of more than one weapon and that he would betray us if he continued to speak out as he was doing.

'The King is in danger, I tell you! There is a plot against him. Do you hear me? They say the plot is by the Catholics, you see, but it is not the Catholics at all, but the Presbyterians, you see… ho! Monsieur Cellier! Tell them about the plot! Oh, and there's the splendid Madam Cellier by his side…come and tell them, Elizabeth. Come and tell them about the Presbyterian plot against the Catholics. A plot the Presbyterians falsely cast upon innocent Catholic shoulders for plotting against the King…a farce as magnificent as any story by Alpha Behn, do you not think?'

'Pierre, make him stop!' I whispered hoarsely, trying not to flinch with each statement the fool threw onto the hotbed of tattle already rife in the coffee houses. 'He throws out indiscretion from his Pandora-box mouth! He can do only harm if his lid is not closed.' That he called me by my given name would add a different injury to Pierre and me.

'No man will listen to such a fool,' said Pierre.

The poetic 'Welcome' displayed inside the door, notified customers of the rules, but did not warn the customer of the remarkable power of transport a few words might take from ears that accidentally overhear to ears that seek out this information. Words insignificant to some might be read as treason by others. When a man might be tried for treason for merely imagining the King's death, what our friend, the good captain, was loudly spouting would surely be pleasing bounty to the wrong ears.

The attention of every lord by the window was entirely on the actions of Willoughby now; as was that of every other man in the room. Even the pot-boys stopped pouring thick black liquor into the dishes on the tables, or paused their task of replacing the spluttering rushlights before they flickered out. He would once more be the talk of the city on the morrow.

Willoughby flailed free from his restrainers and thrust his hands, palms down, upon a nearby table, causing the coffee dishes to jump and one to spill over. One thin man sprung to his feet at the opposite side of the table from Willoughby and drew his rapier sword. His embroidered blue dress coat was not the style of our three Kingdoms, but of a type oft worn by good King Charles on return from his exile in France. An uncommon design, it was trimmed with Flanders lace that Customs House might take notice of, and set off by an undershirt with frilled cuffs over blue silk britches. He wore the feathered hat of a cavalier and a long moustache that turned at the ends over a pointed beard. His voice held the familiarity of being obeyed.

'Do you come prepared for a fight, when here we all are for discussion and debate, a most peaceful pastime? Restrain yourself, man! You carry yourself with the dignity of a baboon and the mouth of a woman!'

Willoughby barely responded to the insults, so intoxicated was he, nor to the sword facing him, nor the raised hand signalling readiness of the cavalier to back up his words. Though he lifted his head to meet the man's slitted eyes, it appeared he had no muscle to lift his hands from the table, but still his bold impudence remained strong.

'And you, sir, are a tailor's dummy! I bring you news of the gravest nature, of import to the King himself, yet your ears are covered in cloth and your actions without sense.'

'To your sword, sir! You tell of this plot and that, and accuse every religion. Look around you, man. This night you have accused every man in this place of conspiracy. Do you see any left to be your knight? We are dignified men here, sir, and your hopbreath does not mingle well. I suggest you leave before you have injury to yourself, else drink a dish or two of Mr Farr's excellent Arabian drink, and quit your ranting!'

Willoughby's expression did not change. He seemed to puzzle over the other's words, but his head was too filled with liquor to be able to do so. Then, without warning, he pushed himself from the table and lurched towards the four of us by the door. He reached the door before he saw us again, then, on seeing us, he stopped suddenly and smiled, and held out his hand.

'Ah, there you are once more, Monsieur et Madame...s'il vous plaît...give me twelve pence in advance of my work. I have erred and offended these gentlemen and must do right by them and pay for a dish each.' He tapped on the pinned up sheet on the wall, displaying the coffee-house rule verse, the like of which is found in so many similar chambers, and read out loud the part that said:

To limit men's expense, we think not fair,
But let him forfeit twelve-pence that shall swear;
He that shall any quarrel here begin,
Shall give each man a dish t'atone the sin

'Non, Monsieur Willoughby. You have had bounty enough,' said my husband. As ever when Willoughby and Pierre stood side by side, I was drawn to compare the two. For once, Pierre's grey age and dignity were so much more preferable to Willoughby's youth and impudent handsome face. 'It seems you have also had ale enough.' Pierre's subtle effort to draw the Captain out without his causing trouble failed.

He was drunkenly rebuffed with a sneer, 'Then I speak to the lady with the purse-strings, Monsieur.' Pierre stopped only for a moment. In that hesitation it was as if he had been run through with the tip of a sharp thrusting-blade, but he fast pushed whatever thought that stilled him aside, and continued towards the bar, ignoring the drunkard. He put a penny on the surface and another on top of that. The man working there had paid attention to the proceeding actions and needed no instruction, but quickly poured a dish of coffee, then another. Pierre picked up the first and advance upon Willoughby with it.

'Drink this,' he said as he held the dish out to the Captain, who looked at the black liquid in horror.

'Give me coins so that I can buy my own poison!'

'Your sort of poison spreads out from the cup to corrupt everything around.' I was uncertain whether Pierre referred to the drink or the man, but at this moment it was a fair point either way.

'How about you give me a pound on account of the work I have done so far?'

'How about you take a sip of this medicine and then we will talk about it.'

'If you Papists are so oyster tight with your money, I will go to Lord Shaftsbury - he will give me plenty!'

'Have you no honour, man? You fly from nest to nest with no loyalty to any but one that holds the golden egg!' Pierre spoke the words quietly, but a rod of iron ran through them. His soft demeanour had fooled many a man to think him a fool for his age, but oftentimes they regretted their hasty judgement.

The thin man with the blade still drawn, again raised his other arm above his head in challenge to fight.

Men at nearby tables had put down their coffee and stilled their pipes to listen with great interest. It was too dark to see who sat in the corners. There might have been some that had a more than natural interest in this event, more than that of an accidental bystander, and this conversation was becoming one that those in other places might pay to hear. I did not wish to frustrate Pierre's efforts, but was impelled to speak to hurry this affair to a conclusion.

As I opened my lips to speak, several things happened at once. The thin man with the sword came round the table towards Willoughby. Willoughby seeing this, attempted, badly, to draw his own sword, but instead struck the dish of coffee from Pierre's hand. The coffee spilt on a poorly dressed man that sat close behind Pierre. Quick on his feet, that man pushed back his chair and shouted at both Pierre and Willoughby, 'Fools! Take your fight into the street where it belongs!' and he too drew his sword.

At that moment, Willoughby unbalanced as he unsheathed his own sword, and rolled back on his heels, falling against the back of a man who had eaten too many meals, and making his chest bang hard into the table with the sound of much expelled air, 'Ooof!'

I was only glad this man did not also have a sword. However, he did have a voice and his angry shout carried to all corners of the room, so that the curiosity of any that had hitherto continued their own conversation stopped to watch the excitement. He also had a strong arm, and thrust Willoughby off him so hard the drunkard flew back towards the poorly dressed man and his sword.

The sniff of a battle, however small, had the effect of waking every man's senses, so that they were all obviously much aroused by the tension. Shouts and cries rose from these sober men as if they had spent the night in a tavern instead of a coffee house, but however different their opinions and debates might be, they happily united against the captain.

I lost sight of Pierre for a moment, but when I next spotted him begging the pardon of the badly dressed man, it was with horror I saw Willoughby bent over and staggering across the floor toward him, sword raised in one hand, and his other outstretched to balance himself. The gentleman that first stood to his feet grabbed the unguarded hand to steady him, so that Willoughby spun fast around, his sharp blade following his body and not caring where it cut. The edge of it struck Pierre's side and he yelled out loud, his hand going to where it hit and coming away with blood on it. He turned on Willoughby, angry now.

'Ungrateful knave! You go too far - you wound me in every way!'

Without further ado, Pierre easily grabbed the sword by the hilt from the shocked and unrepentant fool, that had the empty face of an imbecile, wrenched it from his hand, and threw it to the floor in disgust. With one hand holding his side, he stood tall and grabbed a fist of Willoughby's shirt from his front and pulled the man close to his chest and growled loud enough for every person to hear, 'Get your self together, fool! I am taking you home.'

Then, with the dignity of a man of honour, Pierre, still holding tight on Willoughby's shirt, turned him toward the two men with the sword. 'You have offended these good men and disturbed their night with your prattling nonsense. You must atone for your actions, do right by them.' As he said the last, he let go of Willoughby's shirt and bent to pick up the sword he threw down only moments before. He held it up in front of his face so the silver caught the firelight and, taking a cloth from his pocket, wiped his blood off it. Then, still wiping the cloth up and down as if he were sharpening the blade with it, he looked at the clammed shut captain so hard I swear I saw him flinch.

'If I have offended you, I humbly beg your pardon, sirs.'

Then, as he had in front of the King, he circled his hand two times above his head, swept it wide as the sun's path across the sky and closed the elaborate bow by bending low, where he happened upon his hat that had fallen unnoticed from his head. In a smooth movement he grabbed it, stood up straight and placed the hat back on his head, no matter his periwig lay somewhere beneath some man's feet. He wobbled as he completed this move, and Pierre grabbed him by the arm.

As Pierre left, he threw a shilling to the table closest to him and said to the closest pot-boy, 'Be so good as to fill these gentlemen's dishes, boy.'

With that, he dragged the captain ungallantly behind him and headed for the door. The two boys and myself stood to one side to allow him through, then followed quickly behind, closing the door behind us.

The autumnal night was crisp and cold, especially so after the warmth of the coffee house that had a fire burning night and day to make the drink. I shivered with cold and tension and fervently wished I had remembered my cloak. I almost ran to keep up with Pierre and Willoughby, who Pierre continued to drag behind him with more strength than I would have given him credit for.

Suddenly, Willoughby twisted free from Pierre's grip and stood apart from him.

'You are not my father, monsieur! Do not hold onto me as if you have authority over me!'

Pierre again squared up to the drunk, and I was pleased to see he measured up very well. I had always thought him the smaller of the two, perhaps that his age wilted him, but now he had at least an inch over the small and miserable Willoughby.

'You dare question my right over you, unmuzzled maltworm[13]? I have taken you in and given you employment. I trusted you into my family and home. I have endured endless stories about your deplorable life, borne tales of how you have tricked gallant men of their well-earned savings, abided your arrogance at how you have survived being cast from town to town because no honest men will tolerate you long for your crimes. And all this with the belief that you are a fox changed into the more homely dog. But all the while I have harboured an unrepentant, cheating scoundrel, a thief, a rogue, a villain that does not deserve such kindness!'

'Take it back, Sir. You blacken my name.' The cold air seemed to have sobered Willoughby up somewhat.

'You tarnish your own name, Captain, if that is what you ever were. You behave only as one from the prison not one born of good blood.'

'Kiss my britches! I am of noble blood, I assure you.'

'I have heard it said you stole horses from your own father when you were only a lad, and that your fingers were such limetwigs you could not enter any house that something would not stick to them!'

'You insult me, Monsieur Cellier!'

'I have also heard it said you are a coiner and the marks on your hand are where you were burnt for your deeds.'

'I am outraged…' Willoughby did not seem so sure of himself now. It appeared that some of what Pierre was saying had power over him.

'Furthermore,' continued Pierre relentlessly, 'you told Madame Cellier that the scars on your back were self-inflicted by the claws of a cat to repent your sins, but I have information they are whipping marks from previous convictions. What say you to that!'

'I say you listen to the gossip of women that should not leave a birthing bedside!'

That was the final straw as far as my husband was concerned. He drew back his fist and swung with all his might. The sound that filled the freezing air was satisfying as if I had horse whipped him myself! Willoughby flew back and landed on his buttocks and skidded a short way. His sword belt broke and flew off to the side.

Satisfied he did not stand again, my husband turned on his heel and strode off toward home still holding his side. As I approached Willoughby on my way to catching Pierre he felt his face with his hand and whined pitifully, 'He broke my jaw!'

I reached him and he held out his hand to be pulled to his feet. I ignored it and said, 'I want you out of the house. You must move your things from the garret at once, you ungrateful, ungodly cur! We do not wish our children to be influenced any longer by a man such as you,' and walked on. His present actions having wholly outweighed the benefits of his past that we might have use of. The two priest scholars trailing me also ignored his hand and moved faster to catch up with me.

From the road behind us, I could hear Willoughby still protesting and pleading his cause like a squeaking pig. 'All the world does ride me! I was only following your instructions, yours, and those of Lady Powys and the Duke...'

We left Willoughby's complaining behind and soon found ourselves at home, where I made herbs and bread into a poultice for Pierre's wound and bandaged his side. With good fortune, Willoughby's sword had barely scratched the surface, and although there was blood, it had not cut anything vital.

I worked quietly, not wanting to speak, though I could not help caressing Pierre occasionally and finding a moment to kiss him thoroughly. He had a youthful sparkle and strength about him that I had not seen in him for a long time. He was more attractive to me than he had been since our last child was born and lost.

There was something most becoming, most romantic, about a man who can pick his fights and win.

My thoughts jumped back to Willoughby sitting ungainly in the road.

But what had I become, that I had lost my charity for a fellow man? I should be angry with him for showing his true self. But was it he I was angry with? I was the first to admit it was myself that incurred my ire. Was I so vain I had thought to be the one to change him, to make him an honest man? I had rescued him thinking I was a good woman of charity, taking him from that place, and giving him a home and a job, and changing his course in life. All I had done was move his course through my life, but still it ran where the strength of it would take it.

As I replaced bottles in my bag, Peter stood and came up behind me, put his arms around me and pulled me close. 'He is gone from the house?'

'I have ordered it so,' I said, leaning against him and feeling the warmth of his chest through the open shirt. 'Do I come across as a bawd, Pierre? I am told I am a bawd and a wit.'

'You are a good woman, *ma chère sage-femme*, my sweet flittermouse. Do not think more on coffee house talk nor that of the street. The ones that fill those places have nothing better to do but to comment on the lives of others when they have none of their own.'

'But am I of any use? What if I have done wrong by sending Willoughby from here. We gave him shelter and a job and took him in our home, then cast him out when he was but himself. What kind of charity is that?'

'Your charity has helped more than you remember, *ma chère*. From what I am told, you have made bail for hundreds, maybe a thousand, and you have given relief to more than double with food and blankets and alms. Most of all, you have given many hope they never would otherwise have had. Never doubt it, my dearest, you are a good woman.'

I loved my husband for those words, but he had not reached the end of them.

'And that is only one place in your life…for all the infants and mothers you have saved, you have earned a place beside the angels, and those you have saved will bear witness to that. Think you on all that you have done, and you must see a line of all those lives you have saved or made better in this world!'

I could not help but argue.

'Yet I am spat on in the street, and I have been beaten 'til the last breath of life was only returned to me because your hand held mine, my dear husband, and you were my beacon I used to navigate home through the darkness. As a woman I am given no credence, except what I demand, so long as those that have what I want wish to give it. I am denied an education, only receiving one for that my own mother had an education from her own mother. And as a Catholic, I am unable to work with any but my own kind. And as a midwife, I am considered untrained and uneducated, though I know more than most, and if I am not employed in searching out witch marks, I am marked one myself! I am then ostracised from much of society, my own class, so I cannot practice openly for all that ask me. Nay, I am a monster in the Three Kingdoms.'

Where the outpouring came from, I do not know, but it thankfully fell on my dear husband's ears. If it had fallen on another's, my words might not have received any understanding.

'My dearest Lizzie, come with me to France! I tell you, you would be respected in every house, your rank and circumstance would be a boon, and your fine wit and your good charity would be of the highest grace. Here we are as black sheep in a field of white. In France, we would be black sheep in a flock of black sheep. In a county of non-Catholics, we are considered a hidden cancer that will eventually cause pain and death to all who surround us, yet in France, we would be would be the healthy body. Consider it, *ma chérie*, let us go there where we are not outcasts in the eyes of the law.'

Such temptation was hard to resist, but I was bound by obligation to my craft, to those that needed me.

'One day, Pierre. One day,' I said. 'I cannot leave at this time. I cannot run out on the Catholic mothers who might otherwise be left untended. And who else will look after them! And what of those innocents accused in prison?'

'I knew that would be your answer, my dear Lizzie, but please do not let that day be when I am dead and gone,' he said sadly.

I did not know what to say, for I knew he longed to return to his homeland, but I did not know any other life than this. I could not imagine living in another place. I was needed here, where I could alleviate suffering and make a difference. Though it be safer in France, there would be none that needed me so much.

'We will see your homeland again, Pierre. You have many good years ahead of you yet!'

I could not bring conviction into my voice as I would have liked, but Pierre pulled me close and simply said, 'I know, Lizzie. I know.'

17

23rd day of October, 1679

After Susan closed the door on Henry, the apothecary husband of Rachel my eldest daughter who lived nearby, the same who had once prepared the opium that had failed to loosen Strode's tongue, I returned to the kitchen.

Susan went back to housekeeping since she had to do the work of two now I no longer employed my maid, Margaret. I had dismissed her soon after the Jesuits were hanged, for she slandered me to Rachel saying that Willoughby was 'riding me', and she did not mean he treated me shabbily.

"Tis common truth, Madam Cellier.' With her head raised, Margaret had looked me directly in the eyes when I confronted her.

"Tis the Words that fill every bar and coffee house!'

I might have cut out her wagging tongue had I not encouraged that idea in the jail and fervently wished that was where she had heard it. But, still, hearing tell she told such tales to my own blood, sullying her mind against me, was not to be tolerated.

'You live in this house. Know you this that you told her yourself?' I raised my hand in challenge. 'Have you proof of the tales you tell?' She could not have seen a thing that did not happen.

Margaret blushed, whether from shame of spreading false rumours or from indiscretion, I knew not. She looked to the ground, but did not stay silent. Her voice was still defiant.

'I see how you look at him, Madam. You are not indifferent.'

'He is but a youth, Margaret! What think you, would he look at an old woman as me?' I did not wish to appear that I was fishing for affirmation, so I fast continued, 'Of course he would not, any more than I would want any other than my husband!'

'You spend uncommon time with the man, Madam. He is notorious for being neither fickle of character nor caring of age. I see how he looks at you too.'

Whether I was more angry at Margaret's loose tongue, her insult of me or the truth of her words I could not tell. She had no doubt caught me secretly admiring our young guest now and then – I could not at that time fail to find his stature exceptionally satisfying – and her eye might be equally keen regarding his look to me, though he had done nothing to indicate more than gratitude and respect towards me. However, this did not give her the right to speak up to me as she was doing, nor did it give a maid the right to say as she pleased about one that paid her and to enforce such airy talk from my own home as if it were the truth... My hand of its own volition came up and slapped Margaret's face. The sound of it gave me the tremors for it was not a thing I had ever done to a servant before.

'Margaret,' I said, then stopped. It was wrong of me to smack Margaret, but it had been wrong of her to talk about me around town, worse, to my daughter. I could not have one of so little honour in my service. 'Get out, Margaret. Get out and take your things with you.'

I saw the sudden understanding that she was evicted fill her face from bottom up. First her chin dropped as her mouth fell open, then her cheeks flushed, filling the mark of my hand and last her eyes filled with unshed tears.

'I have served you well for many years, Madam! Have pity on me. Do not throw me on the streets at this hour! My fault is not so harsh I deserve such mean treatment.'

'This is only one lapse I learned of, Margaret, but am I omnipresent that I know of every time you blacken my name? How can I ever know if you besmirch me again? It is bad enough that others talk nonsense of me behind my back, but to have you do so as well is far worse. I should be inclined to trust one that lives in my household, but I cannot trust one that does not stand up for my name, even less one that blows on embers of talk and fires it into full flames! You must go, Margaret, but I will take pity on you this night, and you will leave on the morrow.'

With no word of gratitude for my concession, Margaret bent her head once more, gathered her skirts and left the room. Before she closed the door, she wiped one eye with her hand, and said, 'Dismissing me will not dismiss the talk, Madam. The flame has been burning too long and is as unstoppable as the Great Fire. Your name has long been ashes beneath most decent folk's feet!'

If I had a rejoinder to that, Margaret was no longer there to hear it. She left the next morning and that was all I saw of her since. I had as yet found no replacement and so Susan took over the cooking as much as she was able, and sometimes when my tasks did not fill the day I was able to do some of the household tasks.

This day, after I had gathered the tea cups Henry and I had recently used and taken them to the kitchen, I was pleased I did not have to share the cooking area with Margaret while I worked, since rarely did I have time to make my preparations from the herbs I had dried or steeped in oil months ago. Oh! Could there be a more pleasing way to pass the time? And such an agreeable nosegay of summer scents gone until another year passes.

It was only disagreeable that my son in law had brought news of Willoughby's deeds from the town. Though his ear had merely picked the bones of the matter from gossip rife in the coffee houses, any den where busybodies collect was already replete with the meat of it, and it was enough to know the captain was soon to be returned to the place I had first found him.

Henry was unable to discover all of what had now occurred, but I feared I would not be pleased to know the all of it, particularly as it was only two days since Henry and my husband had once more given bail for Willoughby's release and were forced to give sureties that he would stay free from trouble.

The man was proving a badly chosen nag – more burden than benefit – only discovered after the horse dealer had left town.

On Thursday a week before, which must have been the fifteenth day of October in the thirtieth year of the reign of

King Charles, Willoughby had come to me, his face flushed in excitement, with news he had seen proof of the Presbyterian plot against Catholics and had asked for my guidance on the matter. Forgetting our earlier fight, he had, he told me, held vigil at the Green Ribbon Club, and good fortune had brought him into the acquaintance of one of the most unpopular men of government, Mr Mansell. It transpired that this man had no sense and kept in his rooms damaging papers showing the involvement of himself and others of the plot.

Willoughby informed me that Lady Powys had told him to take rooms near the man and ply him with a drink or two. Then, when Mansell was in his cups, Willoughby should put into the man's pocket some papers revealing his treason.

I was convinced of the dishonesty of putting papers in the man's pocket if they were not there before, but if Willoughby spoke the truth, we could soon see the end to our persecution. I had not forgiven him, but I put aside my own loathing for the sake of the cause to talk to him. So, I told him I was shocked that he should even say such thing about Lady Powys and that I did not believe she was such a woman as to fabricate a plot where there was none, and he must be vigilant to honesty. Furthermore, I told him, I would have no part of any false plot.

'Well, hang me if the plot isn't as real as this table!' he had said, slapping his hand down hard on the surface and making me jump. 'It is only for want of proof he does not hang from the gallows.'

So adamant was he of the man's guilt and that proof of it lay in the man's rooms, I suggested he did as Lady Powys said, and found rooms nearby. 'But,' I told him, 'you must be sure to stay honest, for if you once stray down the path of deceit you will not so easily find the path back to truth. You must find where he keeps these papers you spoke of and then present them to a man of the law.'

On the Saturday two days after that, he returned to me and told me he had taken rooms with Mr Harris in Axe Yard, the very house where Mansell had lodgings. He had, he said, been to the magistrate to obtain a warrant to search Mansell's rooms, but it was refused him. He had then gone to the King, who had shown him to Secretary Coventry, who also refused him.

'Why will they not look?' he shouted, quite agitated. 'The proof is there to be found. I know it is there! If they will not look, he will escape the justice that should be done him. He will be free to plot the King's death and to blame it on such as us, and no one will stop him! What should be done, Mrs Cellier? Tell me what should be done!'

I paused for a moment. I would not play false, but could not bear to think of the King in danger.

'Have you gone to Customs House? I am sure they might be interested to know...'

'Customs House? That is no good to me!' he shouted. 'They are not interested in anything but smuggled goods!'

'And there is your answer, Captain!' I placed my hands on my hips. I could hardly conceal my satisfaction. 'Did you not tell me of your suspicion that Mr Mansell conceals Flanders lace in his rooms?'

'Lace? What would he do with lace! His crime is not to smuggle cloth but to plot and design against the King! He...'

Willoughby was uncommonly slow today, possibly due to another night in the taverns. 'But...are you not of a suspicious nature?' I interrupted, 'and, are you not suspicious of his trips abroad since you have lived in his company?' I was glad to see him at last pause in his ranting. Now I had his attention.

'Madam Cellier,' he had exclaimed suddenly. 'You are brilliant! They would simply have to search Mansell's rooms for contraband and, when the did, they would be sure to find the papers!'

So eager by this idea was he that he forgot our quarrel and came over and hugged me hard. It was quickly over then he was gone without another word. I was left with the smell of day-old ale and sweat, but also of the warmth of a young body against mine, something I had long forgotten. I quickly dispelled that longing with a shake of my head and a reminder to myself of the bounder he was, yet that feeling mixed with the memory of male smell emerged unasked at inconvenient times over the next days, no matter how much I tried to push it away.

That was all I heard of him until after noon on Monday, the twentieth day of October, when he came to our house, with Justice Edmund Warcup and his men following close on his horse's tail. No sooner than Willoughby arrived with news that he had seen to it Mansell's house was searched, and the papers he had seen were found, Warcup and two others came knocking at our door.

'What? You have found your man yet hunt down the one who turns him in?' I said indignantly.

'Nay, Mrs Cellier. That is not why we are here,' said Warcup, the magistrate notorious for his immorality, and for his political leaning toward the Whigs.

The fact he had grown fat on possessions zealously confiscated from those accused of the Roman Catholic faith, heirlooms that never found the way to the King's vaults, also lay heavily against trust in him. Those treasured religious possessions, such as relics, statues and prayer beads, he did not take into his own pocket were burned in street bonfires with so much passion he took the reputation of one of the most hated magistrates of our time.

'We are here to arrest…'

'What!' said Willoughby. 'Has he cried 'whore' first!'

'Who has? Who do you talk about?' I looked at Willoughby through narrowed eyes, resenting his calling me a whore, for there was none other here he could have referred to. 'What say you?'

'Nay, Willoughby. We are here for you,' said Warcup, taking the hilt of his sword, when it looked as if Willoughby might put up a fight. His two men also placed their hands at the ready. 'You are to come before the Privy Council in the morning.'

'What is this? What is your reason?' Now it was Willoughby's turn to be indignant. He let go of his sword hilt now he saw they weren't here to attack him, and stood with his legs apart, backs of fists on waist and his head held proud. 'I have done the King a favour this day! This is how I am to be repaid?'

'The Council wishes to speak with you concerning the papers found at the house of Mr Roderick Mansell,' said Warcup

'Ah, well, that is a grave matter. Tell them I will indeed come in the morning.'

'That is not acceptable,' said Warcup with a sneer. 'The Council are not so certain you will find your way there.'

'I know where it is,' said Willoughby, still haughty.

"Tis not for that reason your presence is doubted. It is believed you have had more than a casual interest in this affair, and might choose to find another place to be on the morrow.'

'Nonsense!' said Willoughby. 'I have only done what any man loyal to the King would do. In fact, I am involved in this business under the instruction of the King himself!'

'That is as may be, but my orders are to bring you to the Council in the morning. That being so, I must keep you in sight until then. It is said you are as a coney, and have the habit of disappearing into a dark hole when your presence is most desired!'

'I will see he comes in front of the Council in the morning,' I said.

'Would that that is enough, Mrs Cellier. What gives you leave to think we might place our trust in one who places a roof over this man's head and food in his mouth?'

'He has not lived under my roof for some past months.' I frowned. These men seemed to know all too much of our business. 'What if I were to offer sureties he will appear at the Privy Council on the morrow?'

Though I did not care overly much if Willoughby spent another night in prison, I would value the chance to further talk with him and discover what this was about.

'We will accept sureties of your husband in this matter, but not from his wife.'

So, this Monday last, Pierre and Henry went with them to give sureties that Willoughby would come to the Council on following morning. When he returned, Pierre could barely conceal his anger at Willoughby. When they found out what he had done, he and Henry spoke severely to the captain at some great length. Of course, he told them about my part in it, and then, when we were in private chambers, Pierre dressed me down for encouraging the captain, and for the danger I placed myself and our family in.

'Lizzie, Lizzie. I understand. You know I do. But do not bring attention to our family in this way! 'Tis not safe at any time, but in these times of trouble we do not wish to be singled out above others. Is it not enough you write to the King and to the parliament about the state of the prisons? And that you visit and feed those accused of treason in the prisons and involve yourself in discovering plots? Each time you do these things, you place us in full view to be judged when we should wish to be invisible. 'Tis not only your own self that you risk here, but our children too. I beg of you, stay away from it.'

I knew he spoke good sense.

Later, Willoughby had little to tell me above what he had already said, but I kept my suspicions he did not tell me everything. He had the look of one that knew which cock would win the fight, perhaps that he had hobbled the other, but would not tell which one. When I asked how they found the papers, he was not shy to admit his part in it.

'What? What did you do there?' I asked, worrying what suspicion that would put upon him.

'Not only was I there, but I found the papers!' he said.

He was brim full of satisfaction, but still I could not help but wonder that he was particularly shifty and it made me ill at ease. I set myself the task to discover what deed he cloaked so imperfectly.

And now my daughter's husband was of the opinion that Willoughby might be in more trouble than we know of. What should I do about this rapscallion? Where once his help had appeared so fortunate to our cause, now at every turn did he undo the work we first had done.

I put my mind to the problem of Willoughby while I worked in the kitchen, bagging raspberry leaves for Mrs Browntree. Her first three babies had come some weeks late causing her considerable discomfort, and raspberry leaf tea might assist the birthing along. I did little more than place the leaves into the sack before the still broken bell over the door jangled discordantly. I resolved to find a person to fix the bell casing when I went out later today

I soon heard Susan's footsteps come past the kitchen towards the door, so I continued to tie the bag of raspberry leaves with some twine. My visitor needed no introduction nor, it seemed did she wish to stand on ceremony. The high voice of Lady Elizabeth Powys found its way to the kitchen the moment the door was opened.

'I wish to speak with Mrs Cellier. Is she at home?'

'Welcome, My Lady.' I heard Susan say in the way I had taught her. 'Please be so kind as to wait while I enquire.'

I wiped my hands on a clean cloth, took off my apron and smoothed my dress down ready move to a more appropriate room to receive my visitor, and was glad I took that moment since I was not given further opportunity to move any place to greet her properly.

'Mrs Cellier, there you are!' Lady Powys stepped so close in Susan's footsteps she almost trod on her heels as they entered the kitchen. She showed every sign of disturbance and did not think it out of order to summarily dismiss my maid with a brusque, 'Susan, please leave us now.'

Susan looked to me and I nodded once.

'Lady Powys,' I bobbed in a curtsy. 'What troubles you?'

'Your man, Captain Willoughby, troubles me.'

He troubles every body, I thought. 'My Lady?'

'I have recently come from Lord Peterborough with disturbing news!'

'What is it, M'Lady? Has something happened upon him?'

'I must warn you, it is not what has been done to him, but what he has done to others.'

A familiar feeling of foreboding came over me. I had seen all manner of faces of the Captain I did not take kindly to, and suspected Lady Powys was about to reveal more of his ungentlemanly nature. He might be the most foolish blunder I had yet made, or would ever make.

'Pray, do not keep it to your self, Elizabeth,' I said with impatience, dropping the formalities, as sometimes we were wont to do. She obliged by speaking frankly.

'After you and he were with the King, you were taken by one Colonel Hallshall to the secretary, Mr Coventry?'

'Aye,' I nodded. 'That we were.'

'It has come to pass that our young man is known to the Colonel as a scoundrel of the very greatest notoriety. The Colonel, you see, is acquainted with Captain Richardson of Newgate, and he has informed him of the rogue's convictions. He is a coiner, a forger, a thief. What think you of that! It is said that any wrong a man can do, this villain has done. He has stood in the pillory for coining, had his hands burned for thieving, his ears nailed for counterfeiting and was whipped out of divers towns for illdoings. Word is out in high circles your young man not only should not be trusted, but should be hanged on the hill.'

I could not tell her I knew some of this news already, for I should have told her before ever I let him near her!

'My suspicions are confirmed. I had not long thrown him from our house for his ungodly conduct before I was forced to give further bail for his conduct,' I said.

'My dear woman, do not mistake my pause for my being at the end of it! I am the bearer of yet worse news. Your husband is Willoughby's master. For this, those who speak harshly of the Captain tar you both with the same brush. Some that know you defend your honour, but I must warn you that your names are joined together with this villain. It does not help that you have written to parliament many times about the maltreating of prisoners, revealing him as a source. This has distinguished you singularly as his voice.'

'What should I have done? Our government would have it we are high above the violence of countries such as Spain and France, claiming we are as angels against their cruelty, yet every day men, and women, are ill-used in prisons in the very streets where we live. If I did not say so, then who would! I will continue to write as long as such abuse goes on.'

'You are a good and charitable woman, Lizzie,' she said, 'but I fear you are the one ill-used. I believe myself maltreated also. We must be careful. It would be wise to avoid any further use of this rogue. Any at all. He will destroy our cause and every thing we have worked for.'

'He came to me two days since for guidance,' I told her.

'Did he indeed.'

I told her about his recent visit. 'He said he had proof of the Presbyterian plot against the Roman Catholics, that he had seen papers in the rooms of a man called Mr Roderick Mansell. He also said that neither the King nor Judge North would give him a search warrant. The reasons for that are clearly those you have told me, that he has been proved untrustworthy by his past deeds.'

'If it is so, that there is proof that will serve to free my husband perhaps, then, I must make use of it.' Despite her so recent assertion that we should no longer use the captain, the wind blew Lady Powys the other way when her husband's life was at stake. She had lived wretchedly in fear for her husband's life for more than a year. Honour comes easy when the life of the man you love is in not in danger. I was in that fortunate position, but not so Lady Powys.

'He came here begging my thoughts on this matter,' I said.

'And pray what did you tell him?'

'I told him, if they would not give him a search warrant to discover the plot, perhaps the customs house might find reason to search the rooms and happen upon the papers. It is only using a different instrument to the same ends. He was delighted with such an idea and declared he would not have thought of that himself.'

'And what has happened since then to put every one of London in such a flutter?'

'I understand Mansell's papers were found as Willoughby said,' I started, but then I stopped. I did not know why, if Willoughby was proved right, the Privy Council and every other person made such quarry of him. 'Willoughby has not told me all of what came to pass at Axe Yard on Monday, but I feel sure he has done some thing he should not have else they would not have such claims on him.'

'We ought not trust him at all. He is a double-edged sword. With one thrust he cuts our enemy, with the next he carves us asunder. He is a dangerous man that does not care which side he harms as long as he has his piece.'

I could hardly deny it. Willoughby had shown he was all for gain. If he had once repented his deeds, he had then repeated them, and that is no repentance at all.

'Well,' I said, 'I shall deny him further entry to this house. He has gone too far!'

As if he had waited in hearing for these very words, the door from the kitchen garden opened, and there he stood, cocky as any rooster in a coup full of hens, strutting in with a tall tail feather in his wide-brimmed cap. He took off his cap and swept it wide as he bowed low.

'My Lady Powys and the good Mrs Cellier! How bountiful to discover you here together!'

'What? Are you here with the magistrate again so soon!' I said haughtily, hardly hiding my anger at his recent conduct.

'Compose your self, madam. My news is practical. I will have myself back in your good favour with the papers I bring.'

'Are they Mansell's?' I asked.

'No madam. I will not reveal to you their exact nature, else the details of it might slip out in an unguarded moment.'

'You cause tongues to waggle all over town yet you think it is I with the loose tongue! You have a wit about you, Captain! In God's name, what have you done the town is in such a bustle about you?'

'I have done nothing to alarm you, madam, but cannot tell you at this time. Only know I have forwarded our cause this day.'

'Do you play games, Captain Willoughby?' Lady Powys seemed to be both angry and curious. 'Lives are close to the gallows. Tell us what you have done!'

'My lady, it is better you do not know. Your innocence might defend you, and your ignorance of the matter will be your best plea.'

Lady Powys took a deep breath. Somehow we now stood side by side facing the rascal, united in extracting his story but, for once, he stood firm and kept his mouth closed.

'Enough, ladies! I must go to my rooms and prepare myself for further examination. I will not tell you what might bring you down.'

'If we are asked, how will we know what we should not speak of if we do not know what it is we should not know of!' I said.

'My humble apology to you ladies. I did not come to have you so disagreeable to me or I to you.' He reached a hand beneath his cloak, unbuttoned the silver buttons on his red tunic, one that he had purchased with the gold from the King and that gave him the false appearance of a lord, or gentleman of means at least, and withdrew a small book of threaded papers tied with red ribbon, similar to that he had shown to the King before. 'Take these and hide them. Hide them well, for they hold proof of the direst treason you did never imagine!'

I took the papers he held out to me. Lady Powys questioned, 'What proof do they hold? Can they help my husband?'

'I can tell you no more, My Lady. Know that what these papers contain is in your favour and can do you no harm, only good.'

'Then why will you not tell us the details inside?'

'My lady, I do not wish you to be part of this. Your purity will bring us through these times.' With that, he bowed deeply once more and left the way he came into the garden.

'Well, upon my soul! What do you make of that!' Lady Powys exclaimed to the closed door.

'I am tempted to open these papers and look. But what if he is right, and knowing their content condemns us.' I went to the bell chord and pulled twice. When the maid appeared, it was not Susan, but Anne Blake, that had been in my service many years, and had proved her loyalty over and over. I instructed her, 'Anne, take this book and hide it where I know not.'

Without question or raised brows, Anne took the bundle, 'Yes Ma'am'.

'And do not read it!' I added as we left the kitchen, though I knew to say so was needless.

I myself saw Lady Powys to the door, where she imparted another piece of news. 'The Captain is being followed at the direction of the King. The King believes he is up to no good. Pray, be vigilant.'

'From whence come you by this snippet?'

'Lord Peterborough has told me it,' she said.

With that, Lady Powys said 'Fare thee well', and I returned to the kitchen to make lotions for my mothers and their infants just as Anne passed me leaving it. Soon the room was filled with scents of simmering herbs and potions.

Things were not going as I had envisaged them going, and I was not at all satisfied about my own part of it. If I had not fallen for Willoughby's charms, we would likely not be in this mess now. I must have no more to do with him, I decided as I bottled my medicines. I would have nothing more to do with him, that is, once he had given me proof of the wicked designs he had told me of.

18

29th day of October, 1679

'Mistress Cellier! Mistress Cellier! Make haste, they come for you!' A large muscular frame filled the doorway.

Little Maggie and Peter abandoned their task of shelling peas opposite me at the table and looked up with open mouths.

'Heavens, Dowdal! What wild beast drives you so hard you forget your manners!' I dropped the chopping knife onto the wooden kitchen table, scored by the making of many family meals and, though scrubbed daily with a brush, stained by many hot pans and cooked meal spills.

'That turncoat, Willoughby, has sent them here. They will lock you up and hang you as soon as walk through that door.'

'What do you mean by this, Dowdal?' I scolded. 'The Captain shared our roof and considered himself a friend to us. He may be indiscreet, he may act the fool and he may even play false, but he would not sell those that saved him to the Devil! Does it not shame you making such accusations?' I did not wish to alarm the children, but they were already shifting from their chairs.

'He is no friend of this house, Mrs Cellier. Just as Oates lay as a snake in the Jesuit nest, Willoughby has turned viper in yours, naming every dwelling and tavern he had dealings in, every Popish man and woman he visited with note or letter or message. I tell you, Madam, the serpent that dwelt amongst us has sent the authorities here and you must go!'

'But, that is impossible, Dowdal.' I looked purposefully at my children that had come round the table to stand behind my skirt. 'Where would I hide with my children? Who would take such fugitives!'

'Forget the children! I will have them. Only go and hide yourself and your husband with haste! Where is Monsieur Cellier?'

'He is gone from here to Manchester on business. He is safe for now, but I cannot leave my children.'

Maggie flung her arm around my skirt and cried, 'Mam!'

Without a thought I rested a hand on her shoulder for a moment. I looked to little Peter, only a year younger than his sister yet so much younger in his mind. He watched without understanding what was occurring, so I turned and crouched low into Maggie's arms and reached out and hugged the two of them together. I could never leave them.

'Get yourself to safety. Go now ere it's too late!' growled Dowdal with such urgency I could not doubt him.

Without further thought, for I trusted Dowdal implicitly, I held my two wide-eyed offspring close one last time, then left both them and the burning stove and fetched my cloak.

Dowdal was dry, and coatless, but my destination was uncertain and, being the last days of October, I might later find myself fugitive in a cold or wet night. Suddenly I stopped and faced my husband's man.

'Why must I run? I have no reason to run.'

'If you have not then that is for you to prove. Willoughby is no Captain, and no gentleman. He is a rogue, with neither the name he gave to you nor even some of the devotion he showed you. Do not try your hand with the courts, they do not care for truth. Go hither, and be safe.'

Willoughby not Willoughby? What nonsense was this! Not content with pitting religion against religion, nor neighbour against neighbour, the Government would as well put the burden of conflict on those within a household. Their spies were in the bosom of every home in London, and perhaps elsewhere too, suckling on the kindness of wet-nurse households, then biting on the nipple that fed them. I never imagined we would embrace such a one in the heart of our own home. I never imagined Willoughby would wilfully harm us.

'Go,' repeated Dowdal. 'I have the children.'

Dowdal stood back and gestured urgently. If fortune should allow me to return to my children I must stay safe for them. I nodded, looked around the kitchen one last time, storing the faces of Maggie and Peter in my mind, then moved quickly towards the door. My foot was no sooner over the threshold than something attached itself to my elbow and halted my escape.

'Whither go you in such haste, Madam Cellier?'

I straightaway recognised the voice beside me as that of the Justice of Middlesex, Sir William Waller, for good reason better known to Catholics as 'The Priest-Catcher'. His zealous Protestant reputation less 'found' its way to me, but more 'fought' its way, cutting left and right along his path of hatred, felling good folk of any other religion with his scythe borrowed from Death.

He was also well known to be tight with Titus Oates at the Green Ribbon Club; some said 'in bed together'. As well, like Justice Warcup, the man was responsible for zealously burning many papal books, vestments, paintings and other documents in large public bonfires. 'I believe I am openly invited to partake of a sip of mulled sac with you?'

It was true that when he came two days before Waller asked me to invite him in for a drink and I told him 'another time', but I never intended that time to come. His visit came shortly before Susan brought news from the gaol of Willoughby's apparent torture, told to her by himself, though I did not then set the two together. Though he searched – I knew not what he expected to find – he proved nothing against me. He took many important and personal financial papers and possessions, and kept them to examine them, but found no evidence I, nor any of my household, had done any wrong. He kept our things still.

That time, he had come with only two men, and had tried to take me from my home to Lord Shaftsbury, again I knew not for what reason. I had told him, 'I have no business with the Earl of Shaftsbury, and if His Lordship has any with me, he might have sent one of his servants to tell me so, and I would have waited on him, as I am still ready to do, without needing a Justice of Peace to take me. But what authority have you to carry me there?'

To his pompous 'His Majesty's Commission of the Peace', I promptly answered, 'Though that empowers you to send me to prison, if I am accused of any crime, it gives you no power to carry me any where else.' He showed surprise at my knowledge of the law, but then went on to accuse me of being a dangerous woman and of keeping correspondence with traitors, and further accused me that I did something wrong by taking in the young Jesuit witnesses come over from France for the Jesuit trials. I was pleased to remind him the King had commanded them to come! I also told him only those convicted of treason can be properly called traitors. 'Do you know of any such I keep correspondence with? I am sure I know none.'

While he talked with me, his men opened cupboard doors, pulling things from inside and letting them drop to the floor. They also turned drawers of papers, cutlery, and any other thing they came across, onto the floor, scaring my little ones by their surly manner, abrupt actions and loud noise, presumably looking for hidden compartments. When they opened my cupboard of medicines, I screamed at them to stop and, surprisingly, they had stopped.

'If you touch my herbs and ointments I'll have the King himself come and find you and whip you! They are my business!'

The men looked from me to Sir Waller, not knowing what to do.

'Look in that cabinet with care, men. We are not here with malicious intent, and would not take this woman's livelihood.' I detected he was not sincere, but the men seemed to think he was, and took the bottles, bags and pots from the shelves and lay them on the table, not as carefully as I would have liked, but careful enough.

In his determination to find me guilty of something, Sir Waller ignored them and returned his steel grey eyes to me.

'Will you take the Oaths of Supremacy and Allegiance?' This challenge was so often made before throwing a good Catholic man or woman in gaol in these days, I was fully expectant of it.

He would have me swear the Oath of Allegiance to test whether I would abide by the four hundred year old law, that every subject of the Kingdom should swear his or her allegiance solely to the King and his heirs. The law stood against all religions but the King's. Since my religion was public knowledge, making me swear the Oath of Supremacy, an allegiance that is a renunciation of the Pope's authority, was an unnecessary ordeal, but one that could become the instrument of my incarceration.

Many feared that if a man's loyalty was to the Pope then he must be set against the King, though this was not the case; most Catholics were loyal to both King and God. That fact did little for the good men that were recently removed, or had resigned, from parliament when they refused to swear these Oaths.

Though the law stood against other beliefs, it was common knowledge a person was never prosecuted unless they had upset a person with power to accuse; for it was not in the King's financial interest to prosecute. Any person not attending weekly church must pay a sum to the King, and if they executed or exiled these people, this income would quickly dry up and leave the King's coffers very much emptier.

It angered me that Sir Waller asked me to speak these Oaths, and so I told him.

'You do not have any authority to ask me this unless another Justice is present. But if there were another here, you should remember, I am a foreign merchant's wife. And my husband, both by the General Law of Nations and those of this Kingdom, should remain unmolested in both his liberty and his property, unless a breach happens between the two Crowns. The King has declared as much in his Royal Proclamation. If you violate the privileges my husband should have as a merchant-stranger, the King of France, whose subject my husband is, has an ambassador here, by whom we will complain to His Majesty, and I hope we should obtain redress!'

He left my upturned house soon after with thin lips and red face. I had hoped he would not return, but perhaps underestimated the desire for vengeance that I gave him. I certainly did not invite the monster back to my home!

But at least he came as a monster, and was not one in disguise as Willoughby had been.

'Come, Madam Cellier, are you not delighted to see me? I warned you I would return.'

Waller was ten years my junior and surprisingly strong for his lesser stature. With very little effort, he dragged me back to the kitchen, where Dowdal leaned against the wall beside the door to the back of the house as yet unseen. Perhaps they did not see him because he held no importance for them. I watched as he slipped away out the door, before the last of Waller's men were even in the room. If only I had left more swiftly, I may have been far away by now.

My children must be somewhere nearby, though they were quiet and did not draw scrutiny to themselves. Perhaps they smelt the wickedness of the Priest-catcher as he approached or sensed the urgency of Dowdal's warning and hid away, else they had preceded Dowdal out of the door. With hope, the last. Either way, not even little Maggie, who rarely stayed quiet, could be heard, for which I could only release my breath in a slow sigh of relief.

'I would gladly supply invited guests with mulled sac or cider, yet must admit to having none to sweeten you with. I fear we midwives drink so much ourselves, we have little left over for entertaining.' My intuition told me I should play the female card, for he saw himself as a man of honour though he was not.

'Do not fret, Madam Cellier, we will make our own entertainment. Perhaps you have superstitious blood we might drink instead?' Waller's men laughed at his supposed wit, casting aspersions on the red wine used in communion. The men all carried swords at their sides, so I swallowed the quip about communion blood running stronger than his own to the King.

'I would be delighted if you would have wine and wafer with me, Sir Waller, but I think you do not have the taste for it.'

'And I would be delighted if you would stand aside while we did the work we came to do but fear you would rather hinder me in the path of justice.'

'I would stand aside if I knew what side to stand on,' I said.

'You stand on the wrong side, Madam Cellier,' he responded. 'You chose the wrong side when you chose to stand on the side of the Devil.' Sir Waller was not amused by my having a voice, and took amusement in degrading me.

'What causes you to think that? I walk with God, and He walks with me.'

The sound of them searching the childrens' bedchamber and ours broke our conversation, and gave me a fervent wish to discover what they were doing. Even in this room where we stood, as before, his men ransacked the same cupboards and drawers they had searched previously, but this time also lifted and moved the cupboards to look behind, and stamped on the wood planks, perhaps hoping to find a secret hole where treasonable things were hidden.

Since I did not know where anything was hidden, I could not react if they came close. In that, the Judas serpent was right. My innocence might save me.

'You are mistaken, madam. He walks with true believers, not with those of superstitious beliefs. You have chosen the Popish ways, and they are against the King's rules and against the King himself. We have testimony that you hide proof of your traitorousness in this house, and we will find them. Your friend, Dangerfield, has told us all we need know of your scheme, and he has revealed that he has seen the proof here. Admit your scheme now, and we will be lighter on you.'

'Who is this Dangerfield? I know him not.'

'You tell me you do not know one who has lived under your very roof with you? This I cannot believe!'

'I know of no Dangerfield,' I insisted.

'Perhaps you know of him by the name of Captain Thomas Willoughby?' he said, then smiled when he saw my understanding grow.

'I know Willoughby, but not Dangerfield,' I reiterated.

'Do not play this game with me, Madam. You must know they are one and the same.' We walked up the stairs whilst we talked. Through the open door to the children's bedchamber, I watched as a man pulled the bed linen off their bed and then lifted the mattress to find nothing beneath. Then he took his knife and slashed the mattresses open and pulled the horse hair out.

'I did not know that,' I said, 'but I have no scheme to tell you.'

'We know the scheme, but if you will save yourself you must admit to it now.'

'Would you have me lie to save myself? '

'No, I would have you tell the truth and admit your plan to kill the King to aid the Duke.'

I followed Waller back down the stairs to the kitchen. I answered to his back. The kitchen was being ransacked.

'I am a loyal subject to both King and Duke and would only protect them with all the honesty and goodness in me.'

As I said this, a man stopped lifting lids off my pewter pans and raised the lid of the butter tub. When he then lifted the larger rice tub lid, I saw he would search the other food tubs too, and called out to him, 'Keep your dirty hands out of my food,' which was a mistake, for immediately he looked at Sir Waller and received a nod of agreement. He plunged his hand deep into the wood barrel right up to his elbow. Rice spilled on the floor as he moved his searching hand inside. I thought he would turn the whole full tub onto the floor.

'Check the other tubs!' said Sir Waller.

They did not take long to find the papers Willoughby or, rather, this man Dangerfield, gave me to hide and that Anne had hidden in the barrel of flour.

'Here is treason!' Triumphantly, the man, his arm surrounded by a cloud of white meal, held the papers high in the air. "Tis hid in the meal tub!'

19

31st day of October, 1679

Back in '44, my father and brother, both, fought side by side with the poet Abraham Cowley at the Battle of Marston Moor in the north, so they wrote us in a letter.

Prince Rupert of the Rhine had led the King's side.

The Duke of Newcastle, both tutor to the King's child, now the second King Charles, and a friend to my father, come to our home after the terrible defeat, bringing sorrow for our loss. My mother lost more than her husband and her eldest son that day; she lost her heart's joy.

But, somehow or other, a connection was made between our lost loved ones and that poet, and through his works she found her consolation.

We would often read Cowley's poems of war together, imagining this connection to my father and brother, knowing that he knew them, and perhaps wrote something poetic whilst he was with them.

It was a sad day when he died at his house in Chertsey little more than two years ago. Having fought so many battles for the King, Fate had her fun when she caused a simple common cold to be the death of him.

Before travelling to Manchester, Pierre read with me 'Friendship in Absence' from my new book of Cowley's Works. It stood strong in my memory and now, in my letter to him, I quoted some remembered lines, and they took more meaning than they did ever before. The first verse I gave him was the last of the poem, but signified my vexatious captivity, and the second I gave told him how much I missed him. With hope, he would as well understand my use of our royalist friend to express myself.

My Dearest Pierre

Should you come home and find I am gone, you will find me at Newgate, where I stay at Captain Richardson's lodgings.

I took myself to The King's Bench Barr yesterday, but they denied me bail, accusing me of treason, and of corresponding with traitors, though I know of none, and they cannot name any.

Today I was there at The King's Bench once more, at the request of counsel and, after they examined me, they informed me I was to go to Newgate. I was so fearful when I was to be sent here, His Majesty took it upon himself to assure me the law would not suffer any torture, which I had told him I feared.

Even so, the dread of being locked up here and attended by felons, or of worse usage, did so oppress my spirits I found myself in convulsions over it which, as you know, is strange for me, so I had to be laid upon a couch to recover. But I need not have worried so; Captain Richardson and his wife are all kindness. I have my own room, and a maid to look out for my needs.

I am reminded of the poem you read to me before you left:

> And, when no art affords me help or ease,
> I seek with verse my griefs t'appease;
> Just as a bird, that flies about
> And beats itself against the cage,
> Finding at last no passage out,
> It sits and sings, and so o'ercomes its rage.

Dowdal and his blessed wife will care for the young ones 'til you can fetch them. It might be a while longer before I can join you by our hearth, which I already miss. I look impatiently for the sight of you when you come!

> I'm there with thee, yet here with me thou art,
> Lodg'd in each other's heart:

Miracles cease not yet in love.
When he his mighty power will try,
Absence itself does bounteous prove,
And strangely ev'n our presence multiply.

With the wind blowing as it does, perhaps some country air might be healthy for you and the children? If you agree I am right, I will join you when I can.

Yours in devotion,
    E.C

I did not tell Pierre everything of the previous days, not only because I knew that any message leaving the prison would be read and copied with hope of discovering proof of some guilty thing, but also Pierre would only worry more.

A thing I certainly did not reveal to him was how, when I told the Privy Council at The King's Bench I had spoken only the truth, the Lord Chancellor told me no person would believe a word I said, and that I would die. Although I bravely sallied, 'I know that My Lord, for I never saw an immortal woman in my life,' I feared they were so set against me, not wishing to hear the truth, and that what he said would surely come true. I would not have Pierre know this.

The men on the counsel had examined me at length before the King, and tried to make me fall over myself. They called forth witnesses, though it was no trial, and judged me though there was no jury.

'When were you in Flanders?' said the Lord Chancellor.

'I never was,' I said.

'You were,' he said.

'I was never out of England,' said I.

Then they made a deal about the story of a man named Adams that Dangerfield and I had drunk too much ale with at the Devil's Tavern, for he had cheated me of five hundred pounds. He would rather I didn't collect it and was bound to speak against me. I denied his insistence I was abroad when I had never been out of the country in my life. Why they were fixed on this, I could not tell, but they came back to it over again. Being neither here nor there whether or not I had crossed the sea, I said, 'If I said so I lied.'

It was a mistake to have said so, for then they did not let that slide.

'If you lied then, how should we know if you tell the truth or not now?' said one skinny fellow with a nose like an axe and a chin with a cleft the nose might have struck.

'My Lord, 'tis one thing to tell a tale in a Tavern, to a man of his understanding, and quite another to tell a lie before a council or court that seeks the truth and where everything said ought to be as an oath. I am not in the habit of lying, nor, like some, do I make a trade of it.'

Then the fellow, Adams, said he would have put more in the deposition, but that I had spoken too bawdy and that it embarrassed him.

This interested the King. He seemed to relish it.

'What? Can she speak bawdy too?' he said.

'She can do anything,' said the Lord Chancellor.

'Well, come now, man. Tell us the story!'

Adams looked to his feet and shuffled them around.

'Come on, man, speak out!'

'She…she…she said she would always have money as long as she had her hands…and as long as…' He blushed to tell the King the rest.

'As long as what?' said the King.

'As long as men kissed their wives,' I went on.

'Well that is no secret.' The King's mouth drooped.

Not to disappoint the King, Adams finished. 'On my oath, she said their mistresses too!'

'Well, what else do they keep their mistresses for if not to kiss!' I said.

'That was very witty,' said the King, 'but only natural to her practice.'

I was happy not to need to explain to him the midwives task of bringing forth a woman's seed when she suffered from melancholy, or when she was wishing to have a child but her seed was not forthcoming. I was also pleased to leave the King on this high note, for I might need to appeal to him for my life.

I had paper, pen and ink enough from the Gate-House, where Sir Waller first sent me, to write some other short notes, and thought to write them to my little Peter and Maggie lest they worry for me, and also one to Lady Powys. In all, I wrote and sent five letters, wrapped with some bottoms of threads I had been using to embroider a cushion for Pierre's chair and still had in my pocket. The last was to Lord Castlemaine, to beg his kindness in providing bail for me. If they had no two witnesses to stand against me, then they could not arraign me and must let me free or release me with bail.

The maid was a woman twenty years my junior, that seemed so happy to share my room I was certain she could have no man to share her bed elsewhere. She was happy to deliver my letters for a small sum, then returned to lie beside me. She was so chummy with me, I was reminded of how Willoughby had pretended cosiness to Stroud to discover information, and was careful to say no more to her than I intended any scheming ear to hear. They tried and tried to catch me out, but I would not wrong-step my foot in their snare.

Four days after I was taken from my house, that rogue Willoughby, or rather Dangerfield, as I now knew him to be, came to my window.

At first I pretended he was not there, and looked away when he called to me, but his persistence was mulish, and he called again and again. When I looked on his face, I saw not the ally I once thought him, but the one who now might take my husband's wife, and my children's mother. The bile rose in my throat, and I swallowed hard and turned away.

'Madam, madam. Pray speak to me, and tell me how you do.'

'I am sick, very sick of you, you bloody barbarous villain.'

'Pray madam, speak low, and do not discompose yourself,' he said, lowering his own voice as if a conspiracy.

'Nothing you do can discompose me. I despise you so much, but I am not angry,' I lied. Of course I was angry. Why would I not be, betrayed as I was.

'I am very glad of it. Then I hope you will have the patience to hear me speak. Pray, how are they treating you?'

I was in no mood for sweet talk, but I did not prevent it. I tried to think why he should be so friendly.

'Much better than I expected,' I said truthfully.

'Have you had any to come and see you?'

'No, nobody.' Who did he expect to come, one of his new cronies?

Dangerfield, it was an unfamiliar name for a familiar face, lifted the material on his arms and showed me where the skin was worn away. If it had been another, I might have had some compassion left for him, but I fast lost any when he began to wail, 'I am sorry you have been confined. I could not help it. Look how I have been tormented. I was unable to bear the misery longer. If I did not accuse you and others, I would have died there!'

'Bloody villain, I am not confined – stone walls and iron bars do not make a prison for innocent conscience. But you are confined. You are one of the Devil's slaves.' I frowned. 'I have been good to you. Which of my good deeds do you seek my life for?'

Dangerfield cried then, 'You shall not die, nor receive any other hurt!'

I stood tall then and faced him. I would not have him think his betrayal hurt me.

'You wicked wretch! I do not fear death, but desire it! Rather that than as you have done. You belie the innocent to save your own infamous life!'

'I tell you I am sorry. I have lived so sinfully, I must not die yet, for if I live longer I may yet repent, and the merciful God may forgive me. The confederates promised me a pardon for joining them. I have unburdened all they wished of me to the King.'

My skin crawled at his self-serving behaviour and I rubbed my arms.

'Do you think you can wipe away your other sins by committing new perjuries and murders?' I asked him.

Then he made me listen to the sorry tale of how he had been deserted by every person in his life, and of how he was so alone that none would have saved him from hanging or, worse, of starving alone in prison. He looked woefully at me then, even though it was me that had arranged for him to be fed every day from my own kitchen.

'Woe is in me that all the world does ride me!' he said, more sorrow for his own situation than I could find in me. Then he complained that if anyone had cared about him enough to even take him before the Bench, he would have been merely pilloried, and would not have been as villainous as he was now. I knew he was so friendly with the stocks he would have been grateful for that small mercy. So, the ungrateful wretch said, since nobody took any care of him, he had good reason to take care of himself.

Then he revealed a new twist to his tale.

'Those I belong to now are very kind to me, and send me great encouragements. I shall have a pardon within two or three days and be set at liberty. Before I go, I should be very glad if you will consider your own condition, and not ruin your family. Your maid Susan will swear against you, and two other persons have been found that will lay worse things to your door than have I.'

I cried out, 'You villain! You know 'tis all lies. I never did a thing wrong.'

'Though you did not,' he said, 'they will swear you did. Come join the most powerful side whilst there is time. I have been told you can make your own conditions.'

It was then I realised that they laid another snare for my life, and had likely set a rogue behind the door to hear what I said. The case for this was made stronger by what Dangerfield did then.

He showed me gold and said, 'See here. This is your reward if you will speak up to the King. 'Tis no use supporting the Duke; he will be destroyed in Scotland. The King himself will soon be gone and there will be a republic, ruled by a government, and the King will be sold out. If you will say the Duke gave you the original papers that were copied and found in your house, and if you say you bid me plant them in Mansell's Chamber and to kill the Earl of Shaftsbury, then we will be well together.'

'How so?' I asked him, not wishing to say anything to darken my case. He gained confidence by my not shooting him down.

'Why, you shall have a pardon like mine, forgiving every thing against you.' He paused, looked to the air for ideas, then added, 'And you will have more money than all the witnesses together have been promised.'

'Oh yes,' I said, leading him. 'And how is that possible?'

'The Earl of Shaftsbury and the rest of the confederate lords will raise ten thousand pounds, and they would make an Act of Parliament to pay you for as long as you live. If you do this, some honourable person will pretend to come and examine you but, instead, they will settle everything to your satisfaction!' Dangerfield showed how well he knew his sponsors, and closed his case as solemn as any man of the law.

I laughed out loud, and said, 'Cowardly wretch, you are worse than your elder brother Judas! At least, having betrayed one innocent, he repented and returned the thirty pieces of silver to those who hired him to seek false witnesses for themselves, and, further, then had courage enough to hang himself. But you have betrayed and belied many innocents, and yet you are such a coward to wait for the hangman. And hanged you will be. He that digs a pit for another shall fall into it himself. Repent now, you rogue, and tell the King who set you on, for you will certainly be damned if you do not.'

Dangerfield lost his composure and howled like a dog with the toothache. Again he showed me his arms, where the skin was worn off with irons or chords.

'Look to my arms, madam! I would never harm you or anyone, but I have been wracked and tortured, and knew not what I said!'

'Cowardly wretch! You shed the blood of so many innocents

to save your worthless life and then are so wicked to try to subvert witnesses to belie the best of men. Look to your elbow and see the Devil stand there. I assure you, he will tear you to pieces alive.'

Dangerfield wrung his hands and continued to howl. 'I am so sorry, so sorry. I shall do as you say. Tomorrow I shall write down the whole intrigue, with the names of the lords and others who have promised to make me comfortable, and I will give it to you, if only you will forgive me the wrong I have done you!'

I assured him, 'I would forgive you, though you are the Devil Incarnate, if you will repent and leave your villainy. But do not pretend piety; for dissembled piety is double wickedness.'

He stopped crying for a moment, and asked, 'Do you think other persons I have accused will forgive me?'

'Yes,' I said, 'if you truly repent, I am in no doubt their charity and prudence will oblige them to forgive you.'

He then blabbed how kind the Earl of Shaftsbury and others were to him, and how they had promised him great things, but he would repent anyway, and tell the truth, so God might have mercy on him. I tired of the scene he was creating with uncertain sincerity, and moved away from the window. I sat on my bed and picked up a book Mrs Richardson had lent me, and pretended to be occupied by it. After a while he went away.

At day break next morning, Dangerfield again stood at his window across the way, and threw little coals at mine to catch my attention. The thought of seeing him tired me, so I ignored him. When he did not go away, I opened the window to tell him to stop. Someone must have visited with him last night; or maybe greed for his life or gratuities had won him over, for he was returned to his usual wickedness.

Straight away, he tried to have me belie the Earl of Peterborough and say he gave me those papers and that I had received a thousand pounds in gold from Sir Allen Apsley to pay Dangerfield to murder the Earl of Shaftsbury, and to raise soldiers against the King.

'How dare you let the Devil speak to me through your mouth, you worst of rogues! '

Again, he told me, 'No harm will come to you,' not understanding anything I said to him yesterday.

I could only reiterate what I said before. 'Innocence fears nothing. If I have done no evil, I cannot fear it.' It was no use speaking to him further; for he was beyond the help I could give him, so I closed the window on him.

All day, I could see him pining outside the window to talk to me, shedding crocodile tears, and begging me with his hands to come and talk with him. The reward he would receive for turning me to the other side would be lost to him if he did not complete his task, but that was for him to mourn, not for me.

About four in the afternoon, I tired of his noise and pathetic expressions, and opened the window.

'Blood-thirsty, ungrateful villain, what have you to say to me?'

He wrung his hands and lamented, 'Madam, please don't be vexed with me. I am fully resolved to tell the truth, and if you would promise I should be pardoned, I will show you how to turn the malicious plans upon their own heads.'

'How can I believe your word when the wind blows it all over the place!'

'Would you believe me if I write it all out for you? I could tie a coal to it and throw it in your window. Here, let me try this apple.'

He flung an apple he had in his hand, but the apple fell short.

'Oh no! I am lost. I hid something in it!'

He suddenly disappeared from view, and I supposed he ran down in great haste to fetch it back, but those who set him up were more fearful I should convert him, than hopes he should pervert me and did not send him to come any more to the window.

Then there was a great clamour in the gaol and the gaoler pretended to discover our interview, though they must have heard it all. Later that evening, Sir John Nicholas came to search and examine me. I told him the truth about everything but that part which related to the Duke, the Earl of Peterborough, and Sir Allen Apsley, for I did not want to implicate them in any way. I also pretended not to understand the reason Dangerfield showed me the gold – though their knowledge before I told them this showed how they had been spying.

Thanks to Dangerfield's act, the gaolers came and nailed the window shutters closed both on that side of the chamber where he was, as well as the other, so I was left with so little air it made me faint. When I tried to take out a pane of glass, which gave little relief, they came and put in another. That gave them another reason to search, with every strictness, my chamber again, even unfolding and searching my linen, and cutting my bread into small pieces, though what they searched for they would not tell. I supposed it might be the blade I took the pane out with, or perhaps they thought Dangerfield had passed me something of importance.

They found nothing, for I was brought there with nothing.

The next day, almost suffocating, I asked the brawny Captain Richardson if I might find some air, and was surprised he let me go into a room on the inner side of the building that looked towards the doctor's garden. I remarked to myself as strange a pair of rough looking men standing in the middle of the room holding hands, but my eyes stayed locked onto the open window, and the clean air. I did not straight away see some others standing at the edge of the room until, suddenly, I was startled by a raucous chorus of two deep voices shouting 'Barley!' followed quickly by a mixed pair of voices from elsewhere shouting 'Break!'

I threw my arms around myself for protection in fright as the room came abruptly alive with many men and women loudly squealing and squeaking like rats and weasels as they tried to run past and dodge the couple in the middle that tried to catch them and make them take their place in 'Hell'. I had not played Barley-Break for many a year. To see prisoners – perhaps guilty, perhaps not, but all that were fortunate in pocket to not be locked with those poor souls in the dank cells of the inner prison – running free as children through the prison seemed incongruent with my present predicament.

There was such a commotion I was sure I did not know how I reached the window, but when I was there, such a noisome smell came from the yard, I gagged and rather chose to be locked up in my own room. My heart raced as I battled my the way back through the ebullient prisoners another time and was shoved and jostled in one direction and another, so I was further certain I would lief die between the walls of my cell than take exercise through there again!

20

25th day of November, 1679

Lady Powys removed the lavender scented hand-kerchief from her nose only long enough to comment, 'Well, if you had seen Mrs Behn's latest play – *The Feign'd Curtizans* – she fair outdid herself last week! I am sure Betty Currer's prologue would have delighted you, Lizzie; how she spouted humour about plots in such delicious manner.'

My Lady might have been reminiscing in the finest drawing room of society if she had not muffled the last of her words as she covered her mouth with the kerchief once more, and if her hand did not betray her discomfort by shaking. I remembered how I was the same when I first came to Newgate a year and more ago, a place so much more vile than here in Richardson's lodgings, so I made an effort to keep my mind on her silly prattle and engage in the pleasantries as if it were mere after dinner conversation.

'What did she say that engaged you so? Can any person truly have an interest in such plays these days?' I asked. 'Surely there are too many real dramas and staged plots acted all around us!'

My own interest in such things had certainly waned. November had followed October, and my many petitions for release had fallen on unfertile ground, yet still I had not been indicted, for they did not have two witnesses against me, and the law says they must have two to arraign me for treason.

Such petty frivolities as the theatre were inconsequential compared to my dire circumstances.

'How extraordinary!' Lady Powys removed her fabric guard once more, so I saw she was smiling, eyes wide. 'That's exactly what Mrs Currer said - she opened the play with just such an observation.

She said that all the plots, suspicions, elections, jealousies,' Lady Powys looked far away as she tried to remember the words, 'and other dramas in this fearful town had made the stage pointless.'

'Well, she was right to say so,' I said. 'Have you heard any more of your own situation?'

'Fortune has not sent me news to alleviate either my situation or my mood since last we met.' Lady Powys replaced the handkerchief over her nose to prevent the stench that seeped over from the main prison from overwhelming her; an odour I was surprised to realise I had now grown used to. Unaccustomed to such tainted air, a tear or two ran from Lady Powys's eyes and soaked into her little piece of lace-edged cloth. "Tis much more than a year now since my husband and the others were accused and committed to the tower.'

'Did you see the Procession last week?' I asked, wishing to take My Lady's thoughts from her woes.

'Oh, but I suppose Pierre has told you all about it! How you were portrayed in that despicable parade was a disgrace so vile it should never have been permitted!'

'Others in here speak freely of my infamy,' I said, 'but Pierre will not talk of it, except to swear those who were part of it are too deep in the Devil's pocket to climb out.'

'Indeed, Mrs Cellier, I am compelled to tell you, their wickedness cannot be measured! Such heinous acts, to have burned an effigy of the Pope,' Lady Powys made a cross with her hand in front of her, 'is not new to London, but what cloven footed creature made them fill it with live cats this time! Yes cats!' She emphasized this last in response to my open-mouth. 'Wriggling and clawing and screeching and screaming – so gruesome, so loathsome, that some of the demons themselves wished they had not done such an ungodly thing and went to slash it open and release the crying creatures; but other more macabre persons stopped them, for there are always those that enjoy the tragedy of death and dying. They said when the cats were squalling it was the Pope talking to the Devil; and also that they signified double-death, both of the Pope and of our religion.'

I had seen some bad sights living in Newgate, and perhaps that should have moderated my sensitive nature, but the combination of people's hate and zealousness still had the power to knock me. The Pope-burning processions started six years ago, when the Duke of York took his Italian bride, Mary of Modena, but I heard the Green Ribbon Club had made this year's parade a much more elaborate affair than those that had gone before, playing to the scared and angry people of London, and to Oates, that wicked man, and his story.

If his finger pointed at the truth, following him would be well, but his condemnation of every Catholic for planning and plotting to kill good King Charles and put his brother on the throne was but fabrication and should not be heard let alone listened to.

And if a person could not have both their own religion as well as the love of their King then justice hid behind the skirt of bad laws.

Lady Powys's husband was one of Oates' accused and remained locked in the Tower with five other lords, now including poor Lord Castlemaine whom, so I heard, Dangerfield had named and condemned as he had me. I had not been struck by Lord Powys as being anything but a good man and a good husband when I met him. There was no indication at all he was the sort of man to plot against his monarch. I suspected the others to be as equally innocent.

'I understand Pierre unwillingness to tell me.'

Now Lady Powys looked in her hand, and unfolded a large piece of paper she had been holding so tight it was as crumpled as tree bark, and passed it to me. As I took it, I saw the smears of dirt on my hand and remembered my revulsion when that same hand had come near Willoughby's, or rather Dangerfield's, last year. How the wind had turned. Now it was me that was untouchable; me, that had always kept myself so meticulously clean, as any good midwife should. Before I read the broadsheet, I wiped my hands on my skirt, being the only suitable cloth I had.

Curious, the things we did miss when they were locked away from us: a bathtub; a table to sit and eat at; sight of the sky overhead; the feel of rain on your cheeks; or even to be needed in your trade… How I longed to see a newborn baby again! Perhaps it was the innocence I longed for – a clean page, with no notions of the world, and with no prejudices, hate or any such thing. This place could make you miss that innocence more even than the trees.

And it had been so long since I had seen my little Pierre and Maggie, and my dearest husband. How I missed them. The older ones that were married had tried to visit, but they had also been denied me. I suspected Lady Powys was only allowed in to catch us out in our 'plotting and planning'. There was, again no doubt, an ear not far from the door or window.

I looked at the picture on the broadside. It took up a full half page and, below it, a half page of writing. Above the picture were the words, *The Solemn Mock Procession of the POPE, Cardinalls, Jesuits, Fryers etc through ye City of London, November ye 17th 1679.* This was dated a week ago, one hundred and twenty one years after the death of Queen Mary, the day that Queen Elizabeth came to the throne, and nineteen days after I was taken here.

In the image, the long, dignified procession snaked from the bottom right corner, up the page in lines right to left, left to right, then right to left again, towards an inset picture in the top left corner, wherein was a contrasting scene of a huge blazing fire surrounded by an angry mob, shaking their raised fists towards the fire in front of the Marble Arch at The Temple. A line of every sort of non-Protestant, religious noteworthies walked in groups before the Pope's pageant towards their death. As the title indicated, there were fryers, priests, cardinals, Jesuits and others. Some were carrying crosses, others were blowing horns, but all appeared blissfully unaware of their destination.

'Look there, there you are at the back of the Procession, at the Pope's feet!' Lady Powys pointed, momentarily forgetting to hold the hand-kerchief over her nose and immediately recovering it. 'They honour you whilst seeking to dishonour.'

She spoke truly. There I was.

None could doubt that it was me wearing the cloak and cap of my trade, sitting to the front of the Pope's wheeled stage and bearing a flag covered in crosses. Beside me sat a man holding another flag the same. Behind the two of us sat the Pope on a throne, proud as any King. My effigy so close to the Pope's marked me as one of the most reviled people in London.

Perhaps it was for this reason Pierre did not talk to me about the Procession. He would not have liked how conspicuous this made our family, making us seen when we should be invisible, and after he had told me I should not bring such attention to us. Though I thought myself strong, a swoon was hard upon me, and I found my voice did not come easy when next I spoke.

'What did I ever do to any of them, that they hate me so…?'

'You need not do a thing to displease them. Our religion is reason enough.' Lady Powys said.

'But they do not target you. I am the only woman whose image was there burned in front of one hundred thousand people of The City and beyond.'

'When they target my husband, they target me. There are broadsheets and whispers enough that portray me with you as a vital conspirator in the plot against the King.'

I could not disagree. She was near as easy a mark as me.

'What news from the courts? How went the trial of our friends John Lane and Thomas Knox, today?' I asked.

Titus Oates had dismissed Lane and another fellow by the name of William Osborne in the spring when he had suspected them of spying for Lord Danby – an accurate insight. Danby had paid the young lawyer, Knox, to persuade the two men to discredit their former master and his false testimony by accusing him of nefarious bed habits with men and boys, including assaults against themselves. The sympathy of the Grand Jury was not with the two workers and the case was thrown out.

Fearing retribution, Lane and Osborne straightaway renounced the accusations against Oates, and later still repented of that renouncement, but it was too late. Knox, Lane and Osborne were indicted for defaming and scandalising Mr Oates and for attempting to hinder justice against all of the lords in the Tower. Lane was to be tried today, as was Knox, but Osborne had moved fast when he saw which way sentiment blew, and had escaped both country and indictment in a timely manner.

Lane had stayed with us a short while in May, when it was feared Oates would use his presence at Powys House as more evidence against Lady Powys and her husband.

'I hear they did not fare so well,' said Lady Powys. They were convicted of misdemeanour and they are each sentenced to a year in prison and a fine; and Lane is to be pilloried also.' Her face was a reflection of the defeat I myself felt at that moment. We had not expected any other verdict, for their testimony had already been rejected, but one could not help but hope for some proof of truth at any time, then be despondent when that time still did not come. 'The court said that they tried to pervert justice, and that what Lane and Osborne told us about Oates' beastliness and how he assaulted them and others was found only as vicious false testimony to sully Oates.'

'So, it was found against them.' All I could do was turn my back for a moment to hide my melancholy, for here every action and feeling was on show, but it occurred to me that Lady Powys must be as miserable as I, perhaps even more so. 'How was the news taken in the Tower?'

Lady Powys placed the back of her free hand to her forehead, a sign she was overwhelmed by either the surroundings or her thoughts.

'They are philosophical about it. No life has been lost, and Knox and Lane will be comfortable in prison, they are visited by your woman Mrs Ayrey, but they are – we all are – of course, disappointed. The Whigs have seemed so invincible that for a time it was a small comfort to think they might have an Achilles Heel.'

'It was well for Osborne that he ran away,' I managed.

'Indeed,' she said, forgetting to cover her mouth. She moved towards the door as if to go, but she had not yet finished talking about the trial. 'The counsel for Knox, my man told me, would have him as a poor duped innocent, taken in by the apparent sincerity of the other two, but it did not wash with the court. He was found equally guilty for his part in managing the whole... and for dropping coins on the table for them to pick up, as payment for their part in it, though he insisted, in truth, he did not hand them any.'

The question of their innocence or guilt was answered by the court, but not by me. Their story had convinced me so I had believed it, but did I do so for reason of wanting to? Had my own desire to disgrace Oates and Bedlow, with their horrid natures, blinded me as to whether or not I should discern the truth? Might my own wish to discredit the man be more a wish for our religion to be redeemed, no matter that truth be lost?

I could not be sure it had not.

I was as much instrumental in encouraging those two as was Lady Powys, her husband and the other lords in the Tower, but perhaps I had done wrong in meddling in this? The flip side of the coin must be, if Lane and Osborne have told the truth about how uncivil Oates had been with them, and their charge of sodomy against him was based on his actions, then a wrong had been done them, as it had been against so many others in prison these days.

Had the court discounted and rejected their testimony as they had for too many innocents, perhaps with a desire for Oates to be pristine and believable. If he was found disgraced they might have to suppose they had killed innocent men on his say so. They would surely not be happy in this.

'All he had done was bring the plight of the young men to light. He should not be punished for that, any more than Lane should be punished for having been assaulted,' I said.

'We are all punished for the actions and words of others. You too will face trial in the stead of another.' The shoulders of Lady Powys hunched as if she tried to make herself small and unseen, but she was as visible as I, and perhaps more so. How she had escaped direct accusation I did not know. She spoke again, but now with less conviction and sound, so I had to listen more carefully to hear. 'Have you thought on how you will defend yourself?'

'I have,' I said. 'Now that Oates is vindicated, 'tis left to me to discredit the one paid to betray us: the serpent that lived amongst us and unwittingly revealed his tender spot. I shall profit from his loose tongue.'

'Dangerfield,' she stated. 'Are you so confident? None have yet escaped the collusion of those venomous witnesses in court! Do you have a weapon none have yet used?'

'I have a weapon some have tried unsharpened,' I said. I could not help look to the closed door and wonder if some ear pressed against it, so I too spoke quietly. 'When they tried to bring his testimony to naught by calling him a criminal, he easily showed the pardon, given to him by the King for his service in speaking against those he formerly ran with…'

'You mean us,' she said.

'Yes. But none have brought true proof of his misdeeds to the jury. I have seen his bit of paper, for he willingly showed it to me and offered me one of my own, and I have seen that his pardon cannot cover every crime he has committed and that he has unwittingly told to me! I will not leave my fate to chance. I am writing to every court house of every place he told me he has passed through. I will find proof of his villainies and convictions. The viper will live only long enough to regret biting his rescuer!'

'Are you so certain they will freely inform you of what you need to know?'

'They must,' I said. "'Tis the law that they must do so.' Her Ladyship looked surprised that I should know this, so I could not keep pride from my voice as I added, 'I have not been idle in my seclusion, My Lady. I would not waste so many weeks and months doing naught to save myself – what other should I do! If I cannot save my life, then any other pastime is worthless. There is a priest here that has found me books and I have read all he could find.'

'Your wit does not limit itself to your tongue, Mrs Cellier. Might I be of assistance to you in this? I am acquainted with some men that might loan you what you need. It is a travesty of law that denies counsel to one accused of treason.'

'It is a travesty of law that denies a person the right to swear oath on the Bible! I am grateful for your kindness and will be further obligated to you if you can find me any book on felonies. It is in this subject I suspect I will find my salvation.'

Lady Powys nodded and, moved closer towards the door,

saying, 'If it will please you, Elizabeth, when I come next, I must as well bring you some little thing to alleviate the gloom and smell of this place. It claws at my nose worse than a pesthouse! Perhaps some scented candles?' She knocked on the door and, when she realised the noise would not be heard, called the guard boldly through the bars and then, as if suddenly remembering her handkerchief, covered her nose and mouth once more as the turnkey undid the lock and the door opened. 'Stay strong, Mrs Cellier,' she said as she left.

The door closed, the key again grated in the lock, and then her footsteps joined the keepers as she walked away along the stone corridor without any further words. I returned my thoughts to the predicament I found myself in. Chief Justice Scroggs had not yet sent me a copy of Dangerfield's pardon as I had requested. I owned little enough paper to this end but I might, perhaps, apply myself to writing once again. My whole defence rested on that other piece of paper.

21

11th day of June, 1680

Neither being fresh to The King's Bench nor any longer holding admiration for the process inside the building, I was not in awe of the ancient law court on the south side of the river at Southwark.

Had it not been a trial for my life I might, however, have delighted in the journey from the prison, sat on the open cart in the hot midsummer sunshine. I might have enjoyed every bump in the road that jolted me and reminded me I was alive after so much stillness. As it was, though the whole time I prayed to the Lord for strength, by the time we arrived outside the courthouse I was stuffed full of panic and dread for what awaited me beyond the crowd.

As wolves drawn by the smell of blood, they awaited my arrival with anticipating of my conviction and death. They would not so happily await my salvation.

Nor, if history were to give an account of now, would the court do any but hang the life from me.

With my hands tied behind my back, the prison guards pulled me in a rough fashion from the back of the cart and ushered me inside through the hostile crowd. Neither encouraging me against their taunts nor protecting me from grabbing hands, they pulled at my clothes as if they would remove them. Indeed, some person took my hat and destroyed it, and they pulled my hair until it hurt. Someone spat in my face, then another did the same. With my hands still tied behind me, I could not wipe the wet away and must endure it sliding down my face.

Once I was past the crowd, still grabbed at and taunted, the ropes around my wrists were removed, and I quickly wiped my wet cheek. It did not wipe away the humiliation and degradation that I would have to carry with me for many years.

I thought on my hands being free now, and looked to see if there were any escape. The crowd had tightened the circle around the edges of the room, removing any chance of making a run for it, even if I were brave enough to try. None would allow me escape and deny them their entertainment! And, where could I go? There was no place I could go they would not find me.

I was pushed behind a rail in the middle of the room, where those being tried are made to stand, with the judges to the front and the jury to my left.

The room was spacious enough that I did not feel bound tight by the walls as I had at the Gate House. Spikes of sunlight shimmered with motes of dust through the window and landed on the faces and periwigs of the judges, and on the crowd of onlookers, both seated and standing, giving a false sense of hope. The sunlight uplifted the spirit in a way that belied the smell of sweat and dung I could only imagine came from the misbegotten worms that accused me that, though I had not yet seen them, must be close by.

As when I stood in that busy court little more than a year ago, for the trial of the Jesuit priests that were condemned that very day, people fanned themselves with any manner of flat thing against the summer heat. I shivered as echoes of the priests' voices passed through me. Such reasoned voices asked only to be heard fairly, but they were not.

I looked over to where Dangerfield had waited on the witnesses from St Omer with such poise and composure, when he had looked so debonair. And then he had attended to me and made me flush with his gallantry. Where he stood then was a different place to where he stood this day. Now he stood falsely and traitorously against me and would be the death of me for none had yet survived the lies of the false witnesses. He may yet consider himself my executioner.

I grabbed hold of the wooden rail supports I stood behind. My fingers poked into sticky cobwebs hanging between the posts, and I imagined the spider hiding somewhere out of sight, just as somewhere nearby a spider watched how I was caught in this courtroom web, waiting for me to tangle myself in its lies until I could not escape. And tangle myself I would, for this spider was an expert at catching flies and not letting them go.

I noticed other breeze-blown, dust-covered, grey threads dangling, unreachable, from the high ceiling and in any corner of the room a broom would not fit. Is it not strange that my thoughts set themselves on a thing so small and insignificant when those very insects that trapped me there would soon suck my life out of me? But everything was both sharp and clear at the same time, as if it were happening not to me but to another. Mine was one more trial, but after I had gone and died, there would be others that I would never know about.

I withdrew my hand from the cobweb, and moved it along the rail, until I found a good support.

The polished woodwork was everywhere smudged by mucky palms, or dirty overcoats, and I quickly withdrew my hands when I touched a place that was rough dried like bark. I did not like to think what filth had left their mark there, though the place I had spent the last months was as bad, if not so much worse. It occurred to me that if I was not so put upon, I might have remarked upon the absurdity of such foolish thoughts.

This was a veritable palace compared to the prison room I had so recently come from. Two hundred and seventy seven days, all counted, I had suffered in that place and I was more than happy to see any other room, even if for so short a time as it would take to convict and hang me. There was no use in holding onto hope, but even if hope had left me I must still do everything to prove my innocence, no matter if I lived or died. Only I stood between life and assured death, for only I was allowed to defend myself.

I clasped in my hand several important pieces of paper, and in my head as many rules of law as it could hold. I must put up a fight for my life with every thing I had, and I was as ready as I could ever be, for I had many months to prepare. A lump in my throat refused to move and let me swallow. Without thinking, I put my hand to my neck and found my crucifix.

I must pray. I imagined my eyes closed, though they stayed open, and I prayed to God for my salvation. Give me strength and wit oh Lord to find a way of proving myself, I prayed. If it was my time to be taken, then I would accept it gladly, for I did not fear death, only leaving life. I did not wish to leave my children and husband to tend themselves, when two were too young and one was too old. I did not remove the cross from its concealed place beneath my dress for fear of drawing attention to it. Instead I rested my hand over where it lay on my chest, fast rising and falling with each agitated breath, and drew strength from it through the fabric.

Many faiths wore the cross, but on this day the very wearing of it might bring prejudice against me. A man might be charged with treason for standing against the King, by following a different faith and, they say, raising the Pope above him. In truth, this was what was meant by treason in this age, and had been so for many years, since the question of the King's successor had arisen. Charles had no true heir but his Catholic brother. The people of the Kingdom rather chose a government of strangers with the right religion than the rightful King of the wrong religion.

Forsooth, I must remain vigilant, I reminded myself. My hazard was a real one. I was to be tried for plotting against the King on the word of perhaps a single man, not for my religion, though that is what it was come to, but for treason. I must keep my eye on the target of acquittal, and shoot arrows at Dangerfield's unworthy testimony.

Hassled witnesses and persons of the law pressed against unknown persons looking for a good show. Catholic-haters shone like lanthorns[14] in the night, hungry anticipation on their faces for a hanging. They had me guilty before any proof was heard. One less foreigner, they would be thinking. I hoped to disappoint them.

As was the custom, every person, whether sinner or sinned against, bowed their heads or stood silent as the judges entered the courtroom. Clothes whispered and feet shuffled as the fortunate few that had seats – the jurors – stood whilst the judges took possession of their own reserved area. Only wooden bars separated the seating areas for the judges and the jury; and the standing areas for the witnesses and spectators.

Once the judges had sat, they either talked quietly amongst themselves or took a good look around the court to see who was in attendance. One peering at the lords and ladies through an eyeglass on a stick, and nodding to one or other of them when his inspection was returned.

Many quenched their thirst with beer or wine, or spilt it as they jostled against each other.

My fear was not allayed by the sight of one judge. Presiding over the court sat the one known to me from earlier interrogations: the judge that condemned many an innocent man based on false evidence of the Oates cohort; the judge that sent men to the gallows on the testimony of rogues; the judge that killed priests with such proof that would have been thrown out of court if it were held against any Protestant.

Lord Chief Justice, Sir William Scroggs.

I would receive neither sympathy nor fairness from him.

I would be disposed of shortly, after all.

'Swear in the jury,' he said with vigour, without more than a brief glance at me. I do not believe he saw me at all.

The twelve men of the jury stood to swear the oath. I recognised two of them from previous juries and, remembering my hours of learning, immediately spoke up, 'I ask for that one be excepted,' I pointed at the man I had seen before, 'and that one too.'

'For what reason, Mrs Cellier?' said the recorder. 'There must be a reason.'

'They were at another trial and that might give them prejudice,' I said. 'I ask for any that have sat on other trials to also be excepted.'

A few minutes later, the two men that were the only ones to admit to sitting on previous trials were replaced by two others.

I did not know any of the other men, and could not see reason why they might not be as good – or bad – as any other, and so the jury was set.

The law was a powerful tool, I surmised, if you knew anything of it. More important, it seemed a person did not have to be a man of the law to use it. But, if I had been pleased that I had used the law to my ends, my triumph was a short-lived minnow.

When the court's clerk read out the indictment against me, buried in his own thorny observations, he was neither an admirer of mine nor was he partial to me in any way. I was disallowed to answer the opening speech. He took advantage of this to convict me before even a single witness was called. His predisposition, to suppose those tried for treason must be guilty, could not be more clearly tangled in his brambled words.

'Here stands Elizabeth Cellier, wife of Peter Cellier, late of the parish of Saint Clement Danes in the county of Middlesex. She stands accused of plotting against our most illustrious and excellent prince, King Charles the Second. False faith prevents her eyes from seeing the almighty God and allows her to be seduced by the Devil and to forget her allegiance to her natural Lord and King. Instead she involves herself in dastardly plans to disturb the peace and tranquillity of this Kingdom.'

And he went on

'On the first day of November 1679, the thirty first year of the good King's reign, at her home in St. Clement Dane, with other, yet unknown, traitors, Elizabeth Cellier devilishly, advisedly, maliciously, cunningly, and traitorously consulted and plotted to depose the King with force and arms and to deprive the said King of his crown, by his death and final destruction. And, furthermore, not satisfied with such terrible imaginings, she has wickedly schemed with all her might to destroy the true religion of this land and to introduce the superstitious worship of the Church of Rome into this Kingdom; to traitorously stir

up a war against the King of this land; and to subversively overturn the ancient government of this realm.'

The man rather revealed his own prejudices than mine, and I was sorely tempted to interrupt and defend myself, but it could hardly have helped my case.

'How say you, Elizabeth Cellier, art thou guilty of the charge of treason whereof thou stand indicted, or not guilty?'

'Not guilty,' I said.

'How wilt thou be tried?' he said.

'By God and my country.' My voice rose to the occasion and reached every person there.

'May God send thee a good deliverance.'

My husband's friend that I had known ten years or more, the astrologer John Gadbury, was sworn in as the first witness. He was brought here to testify against me, and knew enough that he alone might send me to the gallows.

Gadbury was a peculiar man, so often lost in his heavenly world, and rarely anchored entirely in our own. When he did not have his eye to the planets in the heavens he was buried deep in the almanacs he wrote, and was, I believed, as eccentric as he told me the planets were. However, he was a sincere and honest man, and I did hope he would be conscious of the oath he had sworn in the eyes of God, so would be obliged to tell the truth.

Hope, the sweetest of seducers, gave me confidence in the face of doubt.

I had stood comfortably well with Gadbury before I was in Newgate, and before he was also imprisoned. 'It was a recent discovery that Dangerfield had not only turned against me November last, but also Lady Powys, Lord Castlemaine and Gadbury. When I was questioned about him, I was bound to tell the truth and though I did not say a thing but what I knew, they twisted my testimony against him.

The examiners counted only words that came against him, none in his defence.

Scroggs came to his feet and moved to the front of the court. He was coarse and loud mouthed. His prejudice against prisoners tried for any part of the so-called Popish Plot was infamous. But, unexpected diligence in some trials gave me to anticipate he might not be wholly without intelligence or fair spirit, though I might be mistaken in that.

In the last days of April, I wrote to him to clarify whether I would be tried under Common Law, or upon a Statute, and if so, what Statute. I further asked for a copy of Dangerfield's pardon in order to defend myself. The Statute I was to be indicted under, Scroggs wrote back, allowed me as many subpoenas as I wished. He did not know about the said pardon, he continued, but told me to petition the Lord Chancellor for it, which I did, and received it some time afterwards. Given his evident distaste for Catholics, I was surprised he took the time to give me such complete answer.

'Mr Gadbury, what do you know concerning this plot?' asked Scroggs now, coming straight to the point, his mouth twisting contemptuously. If Gadbury did not say something to condemn me, Scroggs would openly belittle him, but if he said any thing my favour, he would be dismissed derisively, as was Scrogg's way.

Gadbury fidgeted guiltily, his eyes darting round the room as if he were hiding something although, to my knowledge, he had no guilty part to play in anything. He straightaway denied any knowledge, as I hoped he would.

'I know nothing of it, neither one way nor another,' he said.

'Do you know of any contrivance of Mrs Cellier's to kill the King and change the Government?'

'No, rather the contrary.' Gadbury was uncommonly quick to talk, not even pausing to think. 'I will tell Your Lordship what I know, if these gentlemen will not be too nimble for me. I have suffered a great deal of prejudice of late in relation to a plot, as if I knew of one but, as God is my witness, I know of none, unless it were a plot to bring Sir Robert Peyton over to the King's interest.'

Oh no, he must not talk about that! How senseless it was

to do so. It had nothing to do with my case and would needlessly bring in a man that need not be there!

'That was the only plot I know about,' Gadbury added, 'but Mrs Cellier was supporting the King, not against him – she could not have acted both for and against the King at the same time!'

Scroggs would not be grateful for Gadbury's championing of me. For that loyalty his testimony would most certainly be discarded.

'Mr Gadbury, you are a man of learning,' Scroggs scolded, 'please say only what you know about Mrs Cellier, not your beliefs.'

Though not a man of wit, Gadbury was a man of intelligence. Dangerfield's betrayal embraced him as tightly as it had me, but it was me his eyes now accused. I had not purposefully said anything to incriminate him, but his next words placed the business firmly on my shoulders. He told Scroggs, 'While I lay in the awful Gatehouse at the prison, believing my life was in danger, Mrs Cellier was a witness against me, so I have no reason to speak for her.'

Silent, his eyes tested the truth of it, if I had betrayed him. Every other person in the court looked to Gadbury so none but he saw me barely shake my head. I was uncertain he saw my denial until he turned back to Scroggs with new boldness in his face. He could have told some false thing but he told fairly.

'If I believed there to be any treasonable plot, I would have discovered something about it.'

I gave him silent thanks. Still he spoke.

'Mr Smith, an old acquaintance of mine, came to me for some important advice in his affairs regarding the lords in the Tower. He told me he knew of something against Mr Oates, and wanted to know if he should use it to make Mr Oates withdraw his evidence. I told him he should not. Then, when I met Mrs Cellier later, she told me Mr Smith and another man named Phillips had some stories about Mr Oates and Mr Bedlow they wanted to tell. I told her how Smith had come to me to ask if he should speak out, and she said she 'did not mind paying ten guineas, if he would be honest and tell the truth.'

Gadbury's story was a true account of events of the day I had asked him if we could trust Willoughby. I was only sorry he offered it so freely.

Scroggs jumped in then. 'So, that was after you did advise Mr Smith not to meddle against Mr Oates?'

Damn his nimbleness. He would twist the astrologer round until the poor man did not know what he was saying. Indeed, Gadbury's face was pure perplexion.

'Yes, My Lord. She said that Mr Dangerfield –we then knew as Captain Willoughby – talked of how the plot against the King they call the Popish Plot, was a deception plotted by Nonconformists to incriminate those of the Romish religion.'

'Did she say that Dangerfield *said* there was a Nonconformists Plot and that he *hoped* the Popish Plot would continue? Or did she say she herself *hoped* the Popish Plot would continue?' As he did in other trials I had seen, Scroggs seemed to refer to something told to him at another time, not in the court, perhaps when they had quizzed Gadbury after indicting him.

'My Lord, I cannot remember particulars,' said Gadbury.

'There's a great deal of difference between Dangerfield saying it and her saying it,' parried Scroggs.

'I have no reason to spare her; she did me the greatest injury in the world,' said Gadbury, looking to me then with reproach in his eyes that I hoped was for the court's sake, 'but I am unwilling to say a thing contrary to the truth.'

Scroggs turned his attention to the plot against the Catholics. 'Why were you talking of a Nonconformists Plot? '

'It was a common talk in the coffee houses.'

Justice Raymond interjected, 'What makes you think it was common talk? Did you hear someone talking about it before she said it?'

'No, not until she spoke of it.'

Then Scroggs took back the questioning. 'So you do not know that Mrs Cellier did not invent the plot. Did she tell you of any Popish priests or Jesuits coming over from beyond the seas?'

'She said she heard there were some coming over.'

'Why were they coming over? '

'God knows. I do not.'

'Did she speak of a plot to kill the King? '

'No,' said Gadbury. 'She reviled plots, otherwise I would not have kept her company.'

Nicely said, my friend!

'Again, I ask you, did she say several priest and Jesuits were coming over, or that she had heard this?'

'My Lord, I think she said she heard it. And several times, when I said to her the Popish plotters would be destroyed, she said she was afraid the nation would be destroyed first.' Again, nicely done, Gadbury, but not quite so honest as I recollected. I had truthfully said the Popish Plot had scared many a good man and woman to leave the country in fear of their lives and it would destroy the nation.

'By the oath you have taken, did she say she was *afraid* the nation would be destroyed first, or that it *would* be? It is important you answer carefully.'

'I clearly remember she said she was afraid the nation would be destroyed for, she said, too many of our nation's best went abroad to live and spend their money, and that weakened and destroyed our own nation.'

'And what did you and Mrs Cellier talk about as you walked through Westminster-Abbey?' The change in tack threw Gadbury for a moment, as it was supposed to do. Since Gadbury had not mentioned our walk in the court, it could only have been talked about ere this day. He frowned in deep thought.

'My Lord, my memory has been exceedingly bruised by time, but I do remember it was a rainy afternoon and, as we admired the architecture, Madam Cellier commented on how the Abbey was formerly filled with Benedictine monks, or some similar thing. She asked, 'What if it should be so again?"

'What is your faith, are you a Protestant or a Papist?' It was a question Scroggs already knew the answer to.

'A Protestant, My Lord,' said Gadbury. He would not have been given grace to swear on the Bible had it not been so.

Scroggs turned to the court, and said, 'He talks like a Papist.' Then, without turning back to Gadbury, asked, 'Was it perhaps, 'what if it should be filled?'' I barely recognised the difference between what Gadbury had said and what Scroggs did. Wouldst that Gadbury could.

Gadbury looked to the roof in thought and repeated, 'She said, 'what if it should be so again?''

'And what did you say to that?'

Gadbury smiled for the first time, as if sharing a joke with his fellow men in the court. 'I only smiled to hear a woman's talk, My Lord.' Many men of the court laughed with him. Surprisingly, Scroggs also smiled. The affect was to put me down as I believe he intended. It might not hurt my case if the Jury saw me as a simple woman, but my pride had me stand taller and glare at them all. Men on different sides of battle would find more in common than with a woman on the same side, so often did they stick together.

Still smiling, Scroggs continued, 'You make all the company laugh, but let us return to serious business. What did she say about the Temple?' Again, the leap in subject to one not mentioned today was further indication Scroggs asked questions from previous knowledge of the matter.

'She said the Temple had also been filled with friars.'

'Did she also talk of filling it again? '

'She said only that the Abbey was once filled with Benedictine monks, and the Temple with friars. That is all.'

'But what else did she say concerning the Temple?' Scroggs chewed on it like a horse on a bit. He would not, or could not, let it go even though it was of no consequence that I could see.

'Nothing My Lord.'

'What else did she say? Remember where you are, and that you are testifying in the presence of God Almighty. Tell it plainly. Make no more of it than it was, nor stifle it.'

'Really,' said Gadbury, 'it was only small talk, nothing more. Only as I've said.'

Another of the King's Bench, a judge that identified himself as Sir Thomas Jones of Shrewsbury, told Gadbury to read what he had written on the paper he held in his hand to remind himself what he had told them before, which Gadbury did. I feared the old Judge's severe interpretation of the law belonged at the turn of this century, from a time of our present King's father's father, King James. And it was common knowledge that Edward Coleman, secretary to the Duchess of York and one of Mr Titus Oates' first victims more than a year ago, was found guilty by this man's strong conviction against him.

'Did she say she hoped to see the Temple filled with Benedictines?' asked Justice Jones, grimacing as he scratched at some crawling creature beneath his extravagant wig.

'My Lord, I do not remember that word 'hope'.'

For one standing on trial for my life and like to lose it, that word 'hope' was the only one the Lord had given me that was of any use to me in these days. What else did I have?

'How long have you known Mrs Cellier?' This was Scroggs again.

Gadbury looked at me as if my face had all our meetings written on it. 'Ten, or perhaps a dozen, years.'

'Did she ever question you about the King?'

Gadbury's eyes shifted to Scroggs and back to me again, perhaps giving him the appearance of guilt. 'My Lord, she questioned me when the King was so ill at Windsor and everyone feared he would die.'

'What did she ask?' said Scroggs, immediately interested.

'Like others, she wanted to know whether I thought His Majesty would live or die. She feared he would die.'

'Did she expect you to know it from your art? Scroggs turned to the common people of the court and raised his eyebrows. They tittered obediently.

'Yes, My Lord. She is one of many that come to me for such answers.'

'And what did you tell her?'

'I never answer questions about my sovereign, My Lord. I told her I would not meddle with this.' How else could Gadbury answer this question, when it was against the law of the land to even imagine the King dying!

'Did she desire you to give a reading after you said you would not meddle with it?'

'No, My Lord, she only asked that question.'

Obviously seeing that this line of questions was leading nowhere, Justice Raymond interrupted, 'What else did she ask?'

What did they desire him to say?

'My Lord, when she realised I would not answer that question, she said to me, 'I see you are afraid of me; I will go to some other astrologer."

'Perhaps she asked if he would live or die for evil intentions. It is your duty to God and your King to declare if she said any more about the King dying than you have told us.'

'She was fearful he would die.'

'Why did she say she would go to another astrologer?'

To his credit, with eyebrows raised, Gadbury's voice held a certain amount of scorn, as if it were a ridiculous question. 'To satisfy her curiosity, as a great many do. And because I refused to meddle with the death of the King.'

'Surely she would have been better to go to one of the clerks than to a conjurer for answers!' I tried not to smile when Gadbury's mouth gaped open. 'Did you answer any other of her curiosities?'

It took Gadbury a little time to recover his composure. He smacked his lips together while he gathered his wits about him.

'She sometimes asked me whether a person would be prosperous in the world, or similar, and I would answer such things, but I am shy of meddling with anything that might be to do with a plot. She did ask how she could get Mr Dangerfield out of prison and, My Lord, she did ask me about some deeds or papers which Dangerfield was to search for, or seize, which concerned Mr Bedlow.'

Did Gadbury know it sounded as if the questions I asked might be to do with the plot?

'You were not shy answering about these things?'

'I did not know for whom I did the reading at the time. It is only since then I discovered it to be for Mr. Dangerfield, then calling himself Willoughby.'

'What? How is it possible to do a reading for a body if you do not know who they are?'

As a teacher talking to a child, Gadbury explained, 'My Lord, Madam Cellier gave me the time of a person's nativity, and I set the figure of the heavens to that sign, to know whether the person could be trusted to collect money for her husband, a French Merchant.'

'So, you mean to say, this might have equally been a reading for a woman! What was the answer?'

'I cannot remember, My Lord.'

'Very convenient that you forget. When did you know the reading was for Dangerfield? '

'I did not know his name until I stood before the court today, My Lord. And as I said, he called himself Willoughby at that time.'

Abruptly, as if he were bored with him, Scroggs finished questioning Gadbury and, turned his back. 'Call another witness.' Whether Gadbury was relieved or affronted by this perfunctory dismissal was hard to see, since he quickly turned away and walked towards the back of the court with his head held as an arrow-head on a back, straight as a shaft.

My curiosity as to whom would be next called was quickly satisfied – my bosom-friend Dangerfield was sworn in.

Immediately, Attorney General Sir Creswell Levinz spoke from beneath his long grey periwig-curls, 'Don't be a mouse now, Dangerfield. Tell us everything you know about this woman.' Levinz's shapely feminine mouth and pink cheeks contradicted his masculine Roman nose and square cleft chin and, unlike the court clerk and Judge Scroggs, revealed little of it, whether he was for or against me.

I returned full attention back to the two-faced scoundrel that bore such a resemblance to the man I knew as Willoughby when he begun to speak. If Dangerfield had no compunction about sullying me with his lies, I had made a weapon to defend myself against them from all he had himself foolishly gifted me while he stayed with us. Then, I had feared his bragging tongue might be our undoing, but now I intended using that very same puffing of feathers to besmirch him and save my neck. I only hoped I had gathered enough skill to use such information he did so freely give of his past to discount him as a witness.

It had not been the easiest task to discover proofs of his every wrong-doing but, in my hand, I clasped papers of all the felonies and misdemeanours he had been charged with in this country alone. I could only hope that not all of these were covered by the pardon so freely given him by His Majesty the King. Some considered that a felon with a pardon was not a felon at all, and that Dangerfield should be considered as innocent as if he had never committed the crime. I did not.

The advice given me by a priest in gaol might not steer me true, and my hand may yet fail, but if I must die, I would not die without casting doubt upon Dangerfield's testimony. If I must die, I would do all I could to take him with me.

Before he could say more than a few words, I spoke with a strong voice.

' My Lord, I have an exception against that witness.'

'Why so? You must show some reason, and then we will do you justice in God's name,' said Scroggs, bored.

'If I can prove he was whipped and transported, pilloried, perjured, etcetera, then he cannot be a witness. When last he stood against me before, he threatened some of my witnesses that, if they would not swear as he would have them, he would kill them,' I said. 'Trust in his word must be based on lies of quicksand.'

Scroggs ignored all but what interested him. He was well known for not listening to, nor remembering, most evidence given against any Catholic that came before him. It was also known he decided a prisoner's guilt and had them executed in his mind even before the trial began, so his next uncharacteristic words gave me reason to pause, to consider what motive might be driving him. 'If you can prove he is convicted of any thing that can by law take away his testimony, then do it.' His eyes did not waiver from mine.

I did take the chance before it could be withdrawn. I straightaway started with the simple crimes. 'He has been convicted for burglary,' I said.

Scroggs turned to Dangerfield and asked him outright, 'Were you convicted for burglary?'

'She will have to prove I was,' said Dangerfield. How silly to ask him - of course he would not admit to it!

I asked for Dangerfield's friend, Ralph Briscoe, who stood nearby, to be sworn in. I did not presume he would be much assistance, but hoped he would at least confirm he knew Dangerfield. Once sworn, Scroggs asked him, 'Do you know this man?'

Though Briscoe knew Dangerfield well, he talked as though this was a long time ago. I noticed he did not meet Dangerfield's eyes.

'I remember one Thomas Dangerfield: I saw him burnt in the hand at the Old Bailey.'

'Is this the same man?'

'I do believe 'tis the same man, but I have not seen him for some years.'

'He lies!' I shouted.

All he had to do was show Dangerfield was convicted of a crime he had not been pardoned for, but Scroggs was not convinced Briscoe knew him well enough and dismissed him. Neither did he hear me.

'So, that is no proof then. Every body has a right to a fair trial. Do you have any more witnesses?'

That he asked showed how he did not know my character. I had done my research.

'My Lord, he was convicted for perjury.'

'Do you have records to prove he was convicted?'

'No.' I had to admit I had failed to find any paper proof of this, though I knew it to be true. Others in earlier trials had tried and failed to discredit Dangerfield in this way.

'Then you cannot prove it,' finished Scroggs, circling his eyes to the roof then round to the crowd. He pursed his lips into a sneer.

'My Lord, I can prove him guilty of forgery.' Dangerfield had bragged over and again that he excelled in his art and, by writing to the many places Dangerfield had been, I had found evidence of this.

'You can only prove it if you have a written record of it.'

The Recorder, whom I recognised as young Judge Jeffries, spoke then to the other judges. 'What she means is counterfeiting guineas, not what the law calls forgery,' he said, showing his knowledge of Dangerfield's reputation was not nothing.

Scroggs nodded at the Judge and continued, 'Can you show he forged any deeds? If you can prove he is a committed forger, but is not convicted, that is no use.'

I nodded at this and handed over a leaf of paper I had held tight to me under my cloak.

Scroggs looked at it briefly, then asked Dangerfield, 'Do you have your pardon? She has proved the conviction of felony, so now prove you have a pardon for it.'

I could not resist adding, 'I have the copies of several records of his convictions here in court, which will be sworn to. He does not have a pardon for all of them!'

'I have my pardon,' he said. I admit to more than a little satisfaction upon seeing him squirm like the worm he was. My papers would prove beyond doubt, even with his pardon, he was still an outlaw.

He was instructed to fetch his pardon so it could be examined and, being yet a free man, he disappeared out the door. I suspected that was the last any of us would see of him. Dangerfield was the only true witness against me but, unfortunately, Judge Jeffries did not want to twiddle his thumbs waiting for his return and ordered other witnesses should be called in the meantime.

They called a man, Thomas Williamson, who aided me in my charitable release of prisoners from Newgate, and who had aided me to free Dangerfield, when I knew him as Willoughby. When he was sworn in, and said who he was, they asked him why I was so kind to Dangerfield. God only knew I regretted my kindness now.

To Williamson's, 'My Lord, I know that not,' Justice asked what I wished to do with him when I had him out of the prison. I knew his aim in this. He, as many others, would rather I was as a loose woman. Indeed, I had played on that when it was necessary to do so, so I hoped that particular snake would not come back and bite me. Williamson had nothing to say, but Judge Jeffries said, 'He is here as a witness that she had a great kindness for Dangerfield.'

That would set him up as an unhelpful witness for them then.

They then swore in my old maid, Margaret, who I fired a year ago for that she had opened her mouth once time too often when she slandered me to my own daughter.

'Margaret Jenkens, what conversations did you hear between Dangerfield and Cellier?' said Scroggs.

Margaret said, 'I only saw them together twice. 'Tis a year since I came from them.'

Scroggs obviously knew the two occasions she talked about, because he forgot to ask her what they were and went straight into asking about them, without giving the court the same benefit.

'When you saw them at dinner or supper together, who else was present?'

'Her husband was with her one time.'

'And what did they talk about? '

'They talked about the condemned prisoners.'

'Was this at her house?'

'No, sir. At my Lady Powys's house.' This was all straight, but I wondered what she would say about the other time, other times, in fact, she saw us together. She had been with us when we did release Dangerfield from prison, and when she brought his suit from the pawn shop. She did as well see him in my room after his bath. She could stir up trouble for me.

'Why were you there?'

'I carried messages for her,' said Margaret.

'And did you ever hear any talk about the Plot?'

'No.' I expected her to add more about Dangerfield and me, but she did not. And that was that. I silently thanked Margaret that she had carried herself with conviction.

Without asking about any other time she had seen Dangerfield and myself together, Scroggs next called on my maid, Susan Edwards. Margaret looked at me as she left the stand, and I had a soft moment for her then. She had been loyal until that day

I dismissed her. She had not done wrong by me this day, when she could have made things worse for me. Perhaps I could forgive her now.

After Susan was sworn, Judge Jeffries leapt in before Scroggs had a chance to. 'What do you know of any intimacy between Dangerfield and Mrs Cellier?'

Scroggs, looked at the Judge, obviously surprised at the interruption, and added, 'Did you ever see them together?'

Susan said, 'Yes, very often, My Lord. She said it outright, that the Popish Plot would turn to a Presbyterian Plot.' And there it was, my betrayer. She may hold no love for me, being a Presbyterian herself, but I had thought she would have some honour and loyalty. My hopes were held too high. Duplicity came from the least expected places.

Scroggs asked if I had said that to Dangerfield, and Susan said no, but that it would not surprise her. She said that Dangerfield had declared to her he had to turn rogue and discover all their Catholic plots.

'What did you say to that?' Scroggs asked curiously.

'I said, he would be no greater rogue than he was before.'

'You were pretty nimble with him,' said the Lord Chief Justice, showing teeth yellowed by ale.

'He thought he should be hanged.' Susan must have been closer to Dangerfield than I had thought.

'What for?'

'He thought he was on the wrong side, and if he did not turn rogue he would be hanged.' Then she turned to me, and, to my chagrin, said in front of the whole court, 'You were very often together in your chamber.' I could have slapped that satisfied smile off her vindictive face.

How good we had been to her. How ungrateful she was, when we had given her every comfort. We had paid her well. She had broken bread with us. I had even given her leave to choose clothes from my wardrobe when I no longer had use for them. 'Who gave you your clothes?' I said.

She ignored my rejoinder and continued to the court, 'One

morning, when her husband was at Church, Dangerfield was with Mrs Cellier in her chamber.'

'What's your purpose in saying this?' Scroggs scrutinised her, as well he should. Even he could see vindictiveness made her say that. But, though it did not look good for me, it was no worse than had been splashed about the coffee houses this last year, according to young Bowden at the prison, who bartered the kindnesses of the bread he oft had from me with snippets from the city.

Young Judge Jeffries again intervened. 'Susan is a civil young woman.'

Meaning, I suppose, her word should be believed?

'I put my life in danger for her, and she said to mind my own business when I told her she should watch what she did!' said Susan.

Ungrateful wretch! How convenient that she forget how much I had done for her.

She was dismissed from the stand, and with certainty from our employ, and my groom, Bennet Dowdal, was sworn in. What would they have him say!

As it happened, he said only he had seen Dangerfield together with me, and that we had tried to make a match between himself and my friend, Mrs Mary Ayrey that I visited Newgate with, but he had never heard us talk about any plot or the King. Scroggs asked Judge Jeffries if there were any more witnesses, and was told we would have to wait until Dangerfield returned with the pardon. He then asked me, 'Do you have any record to show Dangerfield was put in the pillory?'

'Yes, My Lord.' I handed over the record from Salisbury that I had treasured this last month, and he read out how Dangerfield had been pilloried for counterfeiting guineas there. I also handed over a record to show he was an outlaw for a felon he was still wanted for in Salisbury, and Scroggs also read that to the court.

'What say you to this outlawry?' Scroggs asked the Judge.

"Tis not the same person.'

How could the Judge possibly know that! Was he in the pay of the Whigs? Nay, that must not be possible. How could one trust the law that was in the hands of one side and not another! With Scroggs's next words, I relaxed somewhat for, though his reputation was for being partial to the side of the Protestants, his next musings were most surprising.

'We should be very careful we get this right, or it will be a sad day for the country if we stood back and allowed a person who has been immoral and corrupt his whole life before he came to Newgate to be responsible for taking away a woman's life. Persons of his character are employed to discover the way of things, but when they give us the answer we seek, 'tis hard to believe them! He has been gone so long; one might wonder whether he has taken a boat to France.'

Scroggs then said to Captain Richardson, the Gaoler of Newgate, 'Is this Dangerfield the same that broke Chelmsford gaol?'

'Yes, My Lord, I believe it is.'

'He is so convincing, he would have me believe he might fly!' said Scroggs. 'We will not be hoodwinked by such a fellow, guilty of so notorious crimes. Having been in the pillory, if he had been at all modest, he would not look another man in the face. It appears from this record that, not only was he burnt in the hand for theft, but he was then outlawed for felony.'

Scroggs sounded surprised, as if he had no inkling what a scoundrel Dangerfield was, yet I had heard it the subject of many a polite and impolite debate within prison and so it must have been in society.

Still, we waited for Dangerfield's return. I studied the people of the court as they studied me. Some folk talked amongst themselves, and some stood in silence. I found the face of my beloved husband, Pierre, as one such. He stood still and quiet in the middle of the second row, an old man amongst the rowdy rabble.

Around him, men fidgeted and talked either coarsely or quietly with their neighbours but, face tense, his eyes drank me in, like rain after a drought, or a cup of mulled sac[15] after a long day, or as though it was the last he would ever see my face. My case rested upon proving Dangerfield a dishonourable and untrustworthy witness and Pierre had proved himself useful in aiding me, collecting evidence from divers towns fallen down in Dangerfield's trail.

But it was easier for them to punish and convict me than not to do so.

My life was already too long for most every person there.

I could not bear to see Pierre's pained face. He was right. To die for truth was a noble thing, but to leave him and the children was another, one that, in the light of that same truth, I had not truly considered until now. My actions were without heed for my family, when family was all I could trust. What had I done?

We had to wait a further half hour before Dangerfield returned holding his papers high. For him to come back, he must have believed none of it would stick on him. Scroggs took the paper from him, then read the Pardon to the court. It was in Latin, so most would not understand. He emphasize the relevant part, where it said the pardon was for '*Omnia maleficia et utlagaria qualiacunque*', or damage due to outlawry, which Scroggs interpreted as being between two parties, instead of '*utlagaria qualiacunque pro feloniis quibuscunque*,' which would apply to the outlawry of felonies.

Simple as that, they ruled that Dangerfield was still an outlaw for felonies, and that his evidence should be laid aside. For a moment, I touched the fabric of the dress that sat upon the cross around my neck and gave thanks to Almighty God. He had been kind to me this day.

But I must stay vigilant, for all was not over and Scroggs had not yet finished with Dangerfield. He walked right up to the wretch and stood as close as decorum would allow, then took one step more.

'You, sir, must know we are not afraid of such fellows as you. I would like to shake you, and all like you, for your villanies.'

Chastised by the judge, Dangerfield did not wince at this, but took on the double-appearance of a humble man whilst looking

Scroggs straight in the eye as a bold one, in the manner he had with the King. 'My Lord, this is enough to discourage a man from becoming honest!'

That was a mistake on his part. Scrogg's face, so close to Dangerfield's that their noses touched at the tips, became red and his eyes wide. He slammed his hand hard on the bar in front of Dangerfield so the scoundrel jumped backwards and I nearly laughed. 'What! How dare you, who are so notorious a villain and full of the mischief of Hell! How dare you be so impudent!'

Justice Jones also slapped down his hand on the bench where he sat, and his loud growl said it all. 'Indeed, if this is the man so named, he is certainly not fit as a witness!'

'That he is the same man appears to be notorious. Come, Mrs Cellier, have you more to say?'

Scroggs invitation to add to their outrage was welcome, but to be circumspect was prudent in the face of the judge's wrath.

'Enough, My Lord.' I let them decide if my case was proved or not, on what had been spoken, and if we were finished here. Scroggs wiped the spittle from his lips as he returned to his seat, and Dangerfield wiped his face.

'Yes, you have said enough already. You need not prove more. Come, gentlemen of the jury, this is a plain case: here is but one witness in the case of treason, where there should be two, and this one is not believable. Therefore, lay your heads together.'

He did not ask them to leave and make their decision as they should have; he would have them make it there and then.

They found me not guilty, as they should have done.

I silently cheered that it was the task of the horrid Clerk of the Crown, who did open the case with so many barbs, to bid me to get down on my knees, which I did. He could not prevent his mouth pouting as he swallowed his gall and cried, 'God bless the King and the Duke of York!' with which words I was released from captivity and had my freedom.

Though I could now leave, I stopped still as Scroggs raised his voice. 'Where is Dangerfield? Where has the villain gone? Call him back at once!'

Some men at the back shouted he was there, and Dangerfield was compelled forward by hand after hand of the various persons along the aisle. Someone should be punished for today's work, and if it was not to be me, then Dangerfield was a perfect fit for the task.

'Do you have bail for your good behaviour?'

'No, My Lord, but with the leave of the Court I will fetch some.'

'Let a tipstaff go with him, and return before the Court rises.'

Dangerfield, on the point of leaving, said, 'My Lord, that cannot be, for I cannot return so soon.'

With a smug tightening of the lips, as though he suspected, nay desired, this would be the case, Scroggs slapped his hands together and boomed, 'Then let him be committed!' Dangerfield's face as he was led from the court was a picture I happily stored for bringing back time after time whenever it would lift my spirits. I smiled. A more satisfying outcome I could not have imagined.

Before leaving, I was instructed I must give each man a guinea should the jury find me innocent.

I had not come prepared to win and did not have twelve guineas. I knew, from listening to talk in previous trials, these men often came many miles from the city and gave their services for only a single meal as well as whatsoever they were given by an innocent prisoner. My fortune was two-fold for I had also heard that juries for treason trials were given a deal more from the King for finding a prisoner guilty than for finding him innocent. These men had passed over decent payment in order to find me not guilty, and now I had no benefit to offer them.

On impulse, I thanked the spokesman kindly for his wisdom and said, 'Please accept this offer of my most humble service to you and all the worthy gentlemen of your panel. If you please, I will serve your ladies in their deliveries with no less fidelity than you have done me with justice in mine.' This price was worth a good deal to any woman that was with child, but of course, though it was freely and sincerely offered, they could not accept this gift of good value, since they were all of them Protestants and could not be served by a Catholic midwife!

I left a jury, denied fair payment for their good judgement this day, and joined my dear Pierre. He took my hands and led me quickly from the court to murmurs of how I had run rings around the judges and could teach them a thing or two. The moment we reached a place it would be decent to do so, Pierre pulled me close in his arms and kissed me sweetly and at length. After a good while, he stopped and smiled.

'The first you must do, my dearest Lizzie, is to take a bath,' he said, 'for though you are the sweetest treasure God could send, I would prefer it if you smelt a deal sweeter still.'

He had no words back from me. I was done arguing my case for the day.

22

18th day of June, 1680

*M*alice Defeated: Or a Brief Relation of the Accusation and Deliverance of Elizabeth Cellier. A long title, but it read well enough, though I might add some words about the book's content.

'The candles burn low, Lizzie. Come sit awhile with me.'

At the sound of Pierre's voice, the rats, which were come back after the Great Fire, stopped their squealing and clawing behind the cupboards in the sitting room, just as my quill nib ceased scratching across the paper in front of me. I looked at the nib. It was not so good I wanted to write with it, so I took my knife and sliced the end back to an arrow-point, as I liked it.

'I will not keep you long, my turtle. I am checking some details that Edward, my scribe, wrote today in my diary. I wish to be sure everything is as I remember.'

Though one of the longest days of summer had withdrawn most of its yellow light, Pierre had lit the reading lamp and his silhouette against the lamp's warm glow invited me to finish writing and treat with him. He sucked on his pipe and sent tendrils of smoke to the ceiling, then picked up the open book, he had paused in reading, from his knees. The dear man was, as always, patient, but he would soon close his eyes and sleep in his chair. Age demanded it of him. He did not straight away return to his book.

'I grasp the reason you wish for all to know the truth, *ma chérie*, but I must protest! When they see what you have written, I fear your position will have you murdered or executed. Leave this business behind. It cannot do you, nor those you write of, any good.'

'If you were given it, would you forfeit this task, Pierre? Many a time you have said, 'without truth, every lie would become real and would then become the new truth we must live by, and that would not be a world we would wish to live in.'

'Oui, Oui, but 'tis not the same for me. I am a Frenchman; a foreigner is expected to hold foreign beliefs. You are English, and they do not like how it sits on you.'

'It matters not what belief a person lives by – those who wish to find reason to abuse it will do so. I am wiser now, and that wisdom has brought me closer to God. It has likely also brought me closer to the King. How strange that I stood before him a mere fortnight ago! '

'You were in truth a success, my Lizzie. All saw how the King treated you with favour.'

'Pierre, am I wrong to speak out?'

'You will, I know, write whatsoever you chose no matter what I think, will you not?' Without waiting for my nod, he continued, 'So, even if you are taken from me and our children I must support you in writing it.'

He could have sounded bitter uttering those words, but, rather, he sounded defeated. I had no answer for he was right. Drawing long on his pipe then, he looked at the book in his hand as if his next words should appear not to hold importance and started to speak again, quiet but clear enough that I could hear every word.

'I must tell you most strongly, I would prefer that you did not write it. I cannot bear to lose you another time. I was never more lonely in my life than when you were gone before, and when I feared for you each and every day. Good fortune allowed you to escape with your life and come back to me this last time, but you must know, if Dangerfield had not proved such a scoundrel and he had not bragged so loudly of his wrongdoings, you could not have made such a convincing defence. If you publish this book of yours, you will fall into the hands of all those you speak out against, and they will most certainly take you from us. I may yet be made a widow for it.' He paused in deep thought. 'I should forbid you do it.'

I did not remember him making such a speech before.

'Do you regret marrying me?' I asked.

'Never! I will never regret that!' Pierre said this with more passion than ever I expected. 'I love you so my old heart-works might easily stop for drumming so hard whenever you are nearby, and though you are a strong woman, of their own volition, my arms yearn to enfold you and keep you safe from harm. I bathe in your charm and bask in the heat of your wit every day, and each and every time I look upon our children I see you. With sincerest truth you are my life, Lizzie, and if I did not support what you do, I would only be a thorn in your foot.'

'Thank you, Pierre. Merci. Your words mean everything to me! You are so good; your respect fills me to the brim with strength to speak out and say what I must, though the consequence might be dire. You know I have to tell the truth else nothing will change and the torture will continue. What use am I to the Lord then!'

Pierre put his book down and turned old eyes on me, but I swear I never saw a man more determined nor more fearful that I nearly threw down my pen and burned my book right there. I could not stand to see the tears in his eyes as if I had already died.

'You are brave, but dare not think you will dodge the Three Legged Mare at Tyburn only because you are a woman. You have seen with your own eyes how they would hang a woman as a man. 'Tis near a year that the five Jesuits swung high and they did nothing to warrant such an end. You are, in this time, more famous than they were in theirs. You are written about in broadsheets all over London and beyond, and your effigy was burned too gleefully at the Procession. There are many that would take delight in hanging you from the gallows for faith alone, but if that were not all, they would take exception that you are a strong woman with superior wit, and their wives and lovers would have them set your dangling feet dance in time to their music.'

'It will not be so bad as that, my turtle,' I said, trying to untighten the knot inside me. 'I have made myself competent in the law. They would have to prove I wrote the book for them to indict me for it. I will be sure to deny them that proof.'

'But you will have your name on it. Is not that unlawful enough?'

'Yes, love, but do you not see how often are the broadsides in the coffee houses satyrs written by other than it says in the title? No person can be sure who are the authors, but must suppose the names are nonsensical and false.'

'Your name is not nonsensical and false. You are overly known to too many.' Pierre was not often wry, but he was well aware of my reputation around the city. There were those who respected me and those who did not. I gazed down at my words and remembered the Atterbury woman and her husband punching and kicking me.

Pierre's clothes whispered as he stood, put his book on the warmth of his seat and came over from the fireplace to place his shrunken hands on my shoulders. I took my eyes up from the ink I had so recently blotted, barely visible now in the midsummer twilight, and tipped my head over to rest my cheek on his bony fingers. Over my shoulder I caught sight of the greying town outside the window.

Though the day had been hot, the window was closed to the smell of the street that was always there, winter or summer. The stink was worse now in the summer; waste sat on the roads, unwashed by rain. In that waste a rat or two would be racing from gutter to fallen cabbage stalk while, inside, bluebottle flies buzzed ceaselessly against the windows trying to get back to their egg-laying.

Not much else went on in the streets at this late hour. Most horses were stabled and few carts trundled past. Even those persons that had filled public houses until late had finished making drunken noises as they found their way home. Only the occasional footsteps of a man going about some late night business, that maybe he had no business going about, hurried past.

I could barely see the roofs of the buildings opposite, dirty from the soot of fourteen years and a thousand burning winter fires. I did not need to see them to know from the many times I returned home at dusk that the bottom of the walls were painted by the dried on slurry of mud and dung splattered up by carts on many wet London days.

246

My eyes might be on the world outside the window, but my thoughts were on my husband's body touching the back of my head. The memory of him punching Dangerfield onto the ground would forever chase away thoughts of him being old. He was more my hero than any romantic highwayman could ever be. He had saved me as often as every day, and made me a respected woman. His hands pulled me closer still.

'My Lizzie, you have been busy I see.' I knew he referred to the stack of paper on the writing table.

'Would you rather I was busy with you, my turtle? I am finished here for tonight.'

There was a smile in his voice as he said, 'There is nothing I would like better.' His hands left my shoulders and slipped round them until his arms crossed in front of my chest and pulled me close against him.

'Maggie found a beetle this morning,' I said. The conversation came slow and with long pauses as I leaned my head against his belly and we soaked in the moment of warmth and companionship, and his hands caressed my bodice. 'She carried it around with her all day.'

'For what purpose?' That was always a relevant question where little Maggie was concerned. Sometimes her curiosity brought her to simply watch, other times she would physically examine those living things in such a way it was not good for them.

'To race it, I believe. She says it will win against all of the others she has collected. She keeps them in the pearl box wherein she keeps her other special possessions.'

I allowed a smile to wipe the weariness of the day from my face. Our little girl, now five, took her younger brother, Peter, into all sorts of mischief. It pleased me when Pierre told me she took after me.

'It appears she had an interesting day. And what did the day bring you?' Pierre's hands stilled and his arms tightened around me.

'Mrs Bell had her eighth brat without any hardship. I did not take payment; I did so little.'

247

'Did you take time to visit the Palace of Horrors?' That was what Pierre oftentimes called Newgate.

'Yes. They are always glad of some relief from hunger. Mary tells me they are ever in my debt for the air I bring them from outside.'

"Tis the same air, is it not?'

'Not for those inside the cages. I speak not only of the sweet scent of free air. Concealed beneath my cloak I bring wind of the goings on around town, a thing they are agog to hear.' I remembered how, if I placed the desire for news of my family, of the trials and other events, into a balance, they would so often outweigh my physical deterioration and worsening health.

'It would be prudent for you to stay away from there for a while. Your bond with the place is too strong and should be loosened.'

'I grasp the needs of those inside better than most and will not desert them now.'

'You are a good woman, Lizzie. Those who say otherwise cannot know your heart as I do.'

'And you are a good man, Pierre. Without you to stand by me, I would have faltered in my resolve many times.'

'If I was more of a husband, I would not let you be so foolhardy and throw yourself into trouble as you do.'

'That is not so, Pierre. You know what I do is right. You said it yourself. It is only the punishment for it that is wrong.'

"Tis true. Would that a person could speak truth without punishment, then I would not be against doing so at all. But the truth is not wanted here in this city, nor in this Kingdom, this bed of charm. Rather, they would believe lies only keep company in different religions and different countries.'

The unspeakable terror of the screams that came from that poor man, Prance, even now pierced my night dreams and would wake me so that Pierre must hold me until I stopped shaking, proving false the common-held belief that torture was long banished from our shores.

'But, as I have oft said, and you have agreed, if none will tell the truth, the lie will thrive and live in all places from the street to the castle. It may be that no person believes my story, but if I do not tell it, then the truth will hide silent in the darkness. It takes only one to change what passes.'

'I know, I know, but why must that one be you? Will you not leave it to some other that leaves no widower and orphans desolate?'

'Sincerely, my love, I fear that myself, but should I allow fear to sway me from my course? Should I turn my face from those bodily suffering, even as I speak, and every day, for the sakes of my husband and children, who would suffer only in the heart. They will die in gaol of starvation and will never see their loved ones again. And while they die, their bodies are mutilated by the weight of irons that bind their legs and wrists and damage them wholly, completely and without respite. We have every comfort. We want for nothing. Our religion prevents us from doing nothing to help them. We must aid them in every way we can, even if we achieve only our own deaths.'

'I would lief it was another's death. Is there none other that would take up your fight?'

'Knowing how fickle people are, Pierre, you ask this of me? We have been betrayed by too many to trust any other. You know this, yet you can quiz me so?'

I pulled from his close arms and he released me so I could stand and face him. Every time we had this argument, and he did not uphold me fully, it was as if I stood alone.

'Will you stand by me, Pierre?' I said. 'Will you do more than allow me speak out, but also stand proud beside me when I do it? I must know your heart beats together with mine.'

My husband turned from me and I immediately missed him, missed his loving eyes. But it told me what I wished to know: though he would not stop me, he would never approve of what I did.

'You know I am all for speaking the truth, my love, but you place the words on paper, the proof of which will not disappear into the air the moment the words are spoken. This book you write will hold you accountable to any who hold it. Your words hold fast to your name on the cover. They cannot slip away and hide once you have inked them to paper. Your words are outlawed in this land. You know that. The court can, and will, clasp those words in their hands and make you pay for them with your life. Mark well the wisdom of my words, though they not be ink!'

'If the truth is only in the spoken word, it may always hide in the air,' I countered. 'Words may be passed as rumour from one place to the next by those who capture them, but they will never be given substance. Tittle-tattle may be enjoyed and passed on, and may even be believed, but no one will be prepared to act on it, for it disappears the moment it is in another person's ears.'

Pierre, still turned from me, said, 'You have said this to me ere now, and may say so again, but, and again I say, I would lief it was not you that plucked the words from the air and put them on paper.'

'I am not plucking the words from the air,' I said, as the images I wrote of filled my head.

Pierre turned back and grabbed me hard by the shoulders, the old man's hands still strong and his eyes unexpectedly damp. 'I know, Lizzie. I know. But I cannot bear to imagine you back in that dreadful place! If I could only have taken the cell in your stead, I would gladly have done so! 'Tis my fault you had to be in that dreadful place at all, let alone so long, and I cannot stand to let you be taken there again without a fight!'

'Why do you take blame on yourself?' I asked, not pulling from the strong hands that dug into the tops of my arms. 'You played no part in any of it. I placed myself there by my own foolish trust in a man who was not worthy of it, though it was God's will that I did so.' His fingers clenched and bruised me, but I would take so much more than bruises from this man who had nursed me from death.

'We were both taken in by that fox. But I knew you were becoming involved with My Lady Powys and her husband, though I knew them unsafe. Their reputation as meddling Catholics is known by all, but if they want to draw eyes to themselves and die for it, that is their choice. They should play a quieter part as I do. They should never have drawn you into their web. You are a good woman and they played on that. It was my place to stop you.'

'That you did try, Pierre. Do you not remember?' Not for the first time, I was saddened by Pierre's worsening memory. 'You warned me and I heeded your warnings. I am ever careful to hide how close Lord and Lady Powys are to me. You are wrong to think they played me. They are good people and only try to defend their own lives.

I searched Pierre's face for understanding. I would have him laud my efforts rather than condemn them. If I did not have solid foundation to build my confidence at home, then how fast would the walls of my confrontation with the guilty ones crumble! I continued talking, trying to reach him.

'I would never have known the darkness of prison that no one sees or cares about. There are some in there whose only crime is their debt, and yet they are treated as the worst murderers. Someone must speak for them. There are Catholics in there who have done nothing but pray in the wrong fashion. They have not seen their wives or husbands for many months and are then tortured into naming others. Who will speak for them?'

I paused for breath. The tears in Pierre's eyes hung pooled between the lids, but he did not shed them. I did not know if to stay silent, my words being too much, or finish my thoughts. It seemed that, now I had begun, I could not stop myself telling him what I had told him time and again.

'The keepers have no respect for life. Look at poor Mary White. She lost her child at birth after those monsters shackled her ankles and wrists in those wicked bilboes, though she was big with child, and stapled her to the floor without respite. Who will speak out for Mary and her poor lost soul, may he rest in peace? Who? If you had stopped me before, I would not have known so much of this, and I would not be positioned to do something now.'

Pierre knew the truth of this, though he would rather not. He knew that the Almighty God had shown me this path so I might do something for those miserable folk and many others.

He did not speak, but wrapped his arms firmly round me once more and pulled me close to him so that my healed ribs protested. His breathing was deep and ragged, and I knew better than to speak further. Knowing the truth and living with it were two very different things. To do what I had to do, and for him to allow me to, we must draw strength from each other. I held him tight as he held me, imagining my resolve strengthening his backbone, even whilst I took courage from his love.

What fortune to find such a decent man so late in my life. In eleven years of marriage I never doubted him; I trusted him implicitly with every detail of my life. My good husband would stand by me, no matter how much he desired I did not do what I must do.

We did not speak more on my book and the consequences of writing it, but went to our bed and took each other as if the law would take me away that very morning.

23

11th day of September, 1680

Had Pierre's wisdom been written in ink on my heart, he could not have better predicted my fate.

And so it came to pass that I was arrested and imprisoned for the writing of my book, for I was not as quiet about selling my book as I should have been. Now I stood once more before the court. My only hope was that I might rescue myself as before, for this time I had the assistance of counsel, though he pronounced himself wholly against me when first we met at my indictment mere hours before.

The Counsellor for the Crown standing before the court had the arrogant stance of a roost-cock that knew he was King only as long as others gave credence to his crow. 'Mrs Cellier, I warn you to think before you speak. Remember, any Challenges you make will reflect upon you. It is this jury, once sworn in, who will pass their verdict on you.'

'Am I being tried for my life?' I said. If they needed a scapegoat I would not be one, not if I kept my head.

'No,' the court clerk replied, and then, perhaps wary I did not understand the gravity of my case if my life was not forfeit, or perhaps that my reputation preceded me, added, 'but think before you make any Challenges.'

My old friend, the Lord Mayor, dominated the court in his carved wood seat on a dais at the front of the room. In the case that I still misunderstood my position, he raised his leather spectacles and held the round windows to his nose. 'Just watch how you challenge anything, Mrs Cellier.' He dropped his usual familiarity

253

of the bench chambers for the sake of the court. 'If and when you challenge, it must be for a reason.'

He did not fool me with his severity. His eyes were lit with anticipation that I would not only challenge, but challenge often. Why should he wish me to oil proceedings with timidity when every coffee house was full of his commissioned court transcripts, and none wished to read a dull account? Aware the scribes were most ardently scribbling every word, I merely nodded. They would have their story no matter if I did say nothing.

The clerk took the Lord Mayor's words as the sign to swear in the jury.

Each man stood before the clerk was perhaps a tradesman, merchant or labourer and fidgeted with the awkwardness of a person in an unfamiliar role or, perhaps, in a task that did not need him to use his hands as he was used to.

I did not doubt they would sooner pass this time earning a living in their own trade, but they would surely profit today by repeating every word against me to any that would listen. 'I was one bought in to condemn the Papist whore, but she was too quick to catch,' they would say.

Mindful of where I was, I fast hid the smile that crept upon my face from the men that purported to be my peers. In the usual order of things, the jurors were not truly my peers for they were all of them men, and none of them Catholic.

That was not to say the fairer sex, so named with wisdom but more so with wit, would judge me fairer. They might as soon nail me to a cross and place thorns on my crown, for midwives, though essential to childbirth, were often unfairly blamed for the pain of it. As well, some women despised that the midwife was oft used to catch those trying to out-wit the law by pretending to be with child, if that midwife could not be bought.

Nay, I would have no sympathy from one of my own. It was well the judges and jury were men. With little to spur them against me, I might succeed by taking the part of a 'poor hen, pecked into writing my book against my own weak-will'. A more assorted band of men, though, could not be imagined.

The first to be sworn was John Ainger. I could see nothing to either admire or despise. No eye contact. He disregarded me as I would him. The next one was another matter; his eyes stabbed me with hate that curled my insides.

Even as the clerk said his name, 'Swear Richard Boyce,' I raised my arm over the top of the wooden bar and pointed at the man, who had not yet taken his eyes off me. It was there in his eyes, the hate I saw in so many eyes, of both Catholics and Presbyterians, that wariness and distrust of something they not only did not understand, but did not wish nor strive to understand.

'I challenge him!' I said.

The clerk, uncertain what to do, looked not to me, but to the Lord Mayor, who explained, 'Mrs Cellier, as I told you, you must be prepared to explain your challenge.'

As a child I had then been on the wrong side. Then, it was between Protestant Roundheads that wanted an unlawful government and Royalists, the Cavaliers, that wanted the rightful rule of the King. Self-professed 'good' Protestants often pillaged my strong Royalist family home. This same look was in their eyes as they beat my brother and my father, and treated my mother as a whore. As now, the source of hate then was ignorance and fear.

If I only said I did not like the way the man looked at me I would forfeit my right to challenge, but what else could I say?

'I did not know that, My Lord.'

There was little reason to aggravate one I might need later as an ally. The Lord Major asked me to repeat what I said because he could not hear me over the noise of the still rowdy court audience.

Then my counsel, Mr Collins that, when he did visit me before in gaol, told me he did not wish to speak for such an infamous Papist as myself, said, 'You cannot challenge anyone unless you have a cause.'

I bit down some words of reproof that he only advised me of that now and repeated sweetly, 'I did not know that, My Lord. Then I agree he can be sworn.'

Some others sworn to the jury had that same look, as if they were given legitimate opportunity for revenge on all Catholics by

255

judging me. I kept my mouth shut and my face calm. I did not wish them to know they agitated me. One particularly obnoxious man put his hands round his neck, let his tongue hang out the corner of his mouth and rolled his eyes in a gesture symbolising my imminent losing of the case, he hoped. I stuck out my tongue at him. My plan was contrary to his, though every person I spoke with warned me my plan was without hope.

Even my counsel, Mr Collins, warned me ere we came that there were too many witnesses against me. His only instruction was to admit nothing and that was my intention. With difficulty, I roped my mind back to the clerk's speech.

The clerk opened the case against me.

'You Gentleman are now sworn into the Court of Law to try the case of Elizabeth Cellier, who stands indicted, wife of Peter Cellier, of the Parish of St Clement Danes, in the County of Middlesex.'

I looked to the people's area and found Pierre sitting motionless amongst lively men and women of the crowd shouting out or talking between their selves. He had fought my being taken again, but he could not deny what I wrote when proof was held to his face in the shape of my book. But it seemed that, when they took me, they took his spirit too, and that was the hardest to bear. I nodded minutely to him. He barely acknowledged my sign, but I saw it, and it was enough for me.

Meanwhile, the people of the courtroom hushed somewhat in order to hear the clerk proclaim the indictment. He wasted his life in this profession and might have flourished on the stage. As before, he cleverly steered the jury against me with directions to find me guilty.

'This woman of the Popish Religion does not have the fear of God before her eyes, but is moved and seduced by the instigation of the Devil.

'She has falsely and maliciously endeavoured to blacken the name of our Sovereign Lord King Charles the Second, as well as the Government of this Kingdom and, also, the true Protestant Religion of this Kingdom of England. Furthermore, she attempted to bring scandal and infamy upon divers persons produced as witnesses and that gave evidence against her and other persons indicted with high treason on the first day of September in the thirty second year of our sovereign, King Charles the Second.

'Mrs Cellier did, in the Parish of St Clement Danes, in the County of Middlesex, falsely, maliciously and seditiously write and cause to be written, imprinted and published a scandalous libel titled 'Malice Defeated'. Her proceedings, both before and during her confinement, are particularly related, and the mystery of the meal-tub is fully discovered, together with an abstract of her arraignment and trial. She claims it is written by herself for the satisfaction of all lovers of undisguised truth. In this said libellous book are contained these false, feigned, scandalous words following, to wit:

'*I hope it will not seem strange to any honest and loyal person of any religion that I, having been born and bred up under Protestant parents, should now openly profess myself of another church.*' In the case any lacked the wits to understand my words that were clear to any in this court, he looked to the judges and said, 'She means the Church of Rome,' before reading on. '*For my education was in those times when my own parents and relations were persecuted for constant affection to the King, that was himself then murdered, and the loyal party of the Church destroyed, oppressed and ruined.*

'*It was said that the authors of these villainies were Papists to make them odious, yet they assumed the name of Protestants, under which title they pretended to right all things.*

'*An understanding of this produced in me more and more horror of the party that committed them, and made me curious of that religion to which they pretended the greatest antipathy, wherein, I thank God, my innate loyalty not only confirmed, but encouraged me.*

'*These doctrines, agreeing to my public morals, commended charity and devotion to me. So, without scruple, I have hitherto brought myself in communion with both those who were humble instruments of His Majesty's happy preservation from the fatal Battle at Worcester and* to those who, by a pretended Protestant principle, sought his innocent blood.

'And let calumny say what it will, I never heard from any Papists, priest, nor layman anything but that they, and all true Catholics, owe our lives to the defence of our Lawful King, whom I hope that God long and happily preserve as such. I hope these truths may satisfy an indifferent person as to the reason I first changed to the Catholic religion.'

The clerk cleared his throat as the court became noisy, and waited for angry voices to quieten. He read on.

'Nor can anyone wonder at my continuance therein...' She means in the Catholic religion,' he again explained. '...for, notwithstanding that the horrid crimes of treason and murder were laid at the feet of some persons of good quality and fortunes in our party, my religion gives me satisfaction of honesty and honour.

Certainly, when I reflected who were the witnesses and what unlikely things they deposed, and when I observed that many of the main sticklers for the plot were those, or the sons of those, that acted the principal parts in the last tragedy, I was convinced I made the right decision.

I say, these things made me doubtful of the whole circumstance, and the more I searched for truth, the more I stopped doubting that the old enemies of the crown were again at work for its destruction.

I, being fully confirmed in this, thought it my duty, through all sorts of hazards, to relieve the poor imprisoned Catholics that in great numbers were locked up in gaols, starving for want of bread; and this I did some months before I ever saw the Countess of Powys, or any of those honourable persons that were accused, or received one penny of their money directly or indirectly, till about the latter end of January in the year of sixteen hundred and seventy eight.'

Though the clerk delivered the words of my book as energetically as any great orator, when he paused to measure the effect of my supposed libel on the court, it remained unusually soundless and did not give any indication of their understanding of it. Still, he had not finished.

He continued, 'And in another part of the said Libel are contained these false, feigned and scandalous words, to wit:

'About this time, I went daily to the prisons to perform those offices of charity I was obliged to, and on Thursday, the ninth day January of that same year, I dined with the debtors in Newgate in the room called The Castle on the Masters Side. At about four in the afternoon I came down into the Lodge with other women, of which three were Protestants, and we all heard terrible groans and squeaks coming out of the dungeon called the Condemned Hole.

'I asked Harris, the turnkey, what doleful cry it was. He said it was a woman in labour. I bid him put us into the room to her, and we would help her, but he drove us away very rudely, both from the door and out of the lodge. So we went behind the Gate and there listened, and soon found it was the voice of a strong man in torture, and heard between his groans the winding up of some engine.

'When one of the officers of the prison came out in a great haste, seeming to run from the noise, one of us caught hold of him, saying,' Oh! What are they doing in the prison?' He said he dared not tell us. And when I said, "Tis a man upon the rack, I'll lay my life on it!' he said, "Tis something like it.' Then I asked, 'Is it Prance?' he replied, 'Pray, Madam, do not ask me, for I dare not tell you. But it is such that I am not able to hear any longer. Pray let me go.' With that he ran away towards Holborn as fast as he could.

'We heard these groans perfectly to the end of the Old Bailey. They continued till near seven of the clock, and then a person in the habit of a minister, of middle stature, grey-haired, and accompanied by two other men, went into the Lodge.

'The prisoners were locked up, and the outwards door of the Lodge also. I set a person to stand and observe what she could.

'A prisoner loaded with Irons was brought into the Lodge and examined a long time. Some prisoners, that were confined above, crouched down as low as they could to the floor and heard the person examined with great vehemence. They heard him in great agony say over and over, 'I know nothing of it', 'I am innocent' and, 'Will you murder me because I will not belie myself and others?'

'About four of the clock next morning, the prisoners that lay in that place above the Hole heard the same cry again for two hours, and on Saturday morning again. Then, about eight a clock that morning, a person I employed to spy out the truth of the affair did see the Turnkeys carrying a bed into the Hole. They told her it was for Prance, who was gone mad and had torn his bed in pieces. That night the Examiners came again and, after an hour's conference, Prance was led away to the Press-Yard.

'This and many things of the like nature, made me very inquisitive to know what passed in the prison.

'Soon after this, Francis Corral, a coachman that had been put into Newgate upon suspicion of carrying away Sir Godfrey's body, and lay thirteen weeks and three days in great misery, came out. I went to see him, and found him a sad spectacle, having the flesh worn away, and great holes in both his legs by the weight of his Irons and, having been chained so long doubled over that he could not stand upright.

'He told me much of his hard and cruel usage, such as how he had been squeezed and hasped into a thing like a trough, in a dungeon under ground, which put him to inexpressible torment insomuch that he swooned, and that a person in the habit of a minister stood by all the while. He told me that a duke had beaten him, pulled his hair and set his drawn sword to his breast three times, swearing he would run him through.

Another great lord laid down a heap of gold, and told him it was five hundred pounds and that he should have it all, and be taken into the aforesaid Dukes house, if he would confess what they would have him say. One F. A Vintner that lives at the sign of the Half-Moon in Cheape Side, by whose contrivance he was accused, took him aside and bid him name some person that employed him to take up the dead body in Somerset Yard. The lord gave him money for so doing, then told him that if he would do this, both F. and he should have money enough to get by.

Mr Corral also told me that he was kept from Thursday till Sunday without victuals or drink, having his hands every night chained behind him and was, all this time, locked with a chain not above a yard long to a staple driven into the floor. In this great extremity, he was forced to drink his own water for want of any drink given *him. Furthermore, the Gaoler beat Corral's wife, because she brought victuals and prayed that he might have it, then threw the milk she took him onto the ground and bid her begone and not to look at her husband.'*

The clerk raised his sharp little eyes from my book and they leapt from first one to another spectator in the still crowd, and then swept from one judge to another judge. It seemed he did not know where to look, but perhaps he tested his audience if they convicted me, as did he. Of one thing I was certain, his eyes did not seek me, an insignificant actor in this play about me.

I could barely keep from shouting, "Tis not libel if 'tis the truth!' but uncustomary restraint caged my words. I kept my face as an unwritten page. Patience would have my witnesses tell the truth of it all soon enough. I might be made to look foolish, but I was pleased that these things were read out in court; they would become talking points in the coffee houses and ale houses, and that would be no bad thing.

'Another part of the said libel contains, amongst other things,' the clerk turned the leaves of my book and spoke to the court, 'these false, feigned, and scandalous words and figures following, to wit:

In confidence of my own innocence, I continually pressed for my arraignment, so that I could know the charge against me, but I did not then know the danger to my life of encountering the Devil in the worst of his instruments: terrible perjuries encouraged by that profligate wretch, Thomas Dangerfield, that hath since been exposed to the world in his true colours, both at mine, and another's trial thereafter.'

The clerk, still acting his part on the court stage, paused at the derisive jeers that started up then. Into his pause came shouts of, 'Who knows the Devil's instrument better than the Devil's whore!' and 'The cook-pot dares to name the kettle black!' Other shouts hid themselves in the rabble laughs that followed.

When he had given the crowd the stage long enough, the clerk held up his hand towards them to reclaim it, and then continued the indictment in a raised voice. They quietened enough for me to barely hear him speak. The judges leant back in the seats, seemingly indifferent to the happenings that they presided over. Perhaps they also could not hear it. I felt certain they would call for silence, but they did not.

'And in another part of the said libel…' said the clerk. The rest of his words were drowned by another tumultuous swell. He repeated himself louder with a pointed look at the crowd to quiet them, twitching, I thought, because he had dropped the reins of their sentiment he had failed to hold. 'In another part of the said libel are contained these false feigned and scandalous words:

'Nor have I since received anything towards my losses, or the least civility from anyone whilst, as a prisoner for recorded rogueries, Dangerfield was visited by persons of considerable quality with great sums of gold and silver to encourage him to undertake new villainies, not against me alone, but also against good men, both Protestant and Catholic.'

People shouted out again while the clerk turned to the place marked by his forefinger between the pages. He did not look up this time. He knew he had regained the reins enough and could now guide those behind the barrier whichever way he chose. Straight away when he found the place he looked for, he followed his finger with my words.

I listened closely to make sure he did not put in anything I did not write, nor change any word's place so it no longer said what I meant it to. He spoke the words as I wrote them, though he said them in a different way, moulding them into accusation instead of a record of what I discovered.

'And in another part of the said libel, called A Postscript to the Impartial Readers, are contained these false, feigned, and scandalous words following, to wit:

And whensoever His Majesty pleases to make it as safe and honourable to testify the truth as it hath been made gainful and meritorious to do the contrary – creating Hangman's Hounds for weekly pensions or other considerations – we would not want for witnesses to verify far more than I have written.

'This evil and dangerous example of sin offends the peace of our Sovereign Lord the King, his Crown and Dignity', said the clerk. 'Upon this indictment she has been arraigned and has pleaded not guilty unto it and, for her trial, places herself in the hands of the country.

So your issue is to discover whether she is guilty of this offence in the manner and form wherein she stands indicted, or not guilty. If you find her guilty you are to say so, and if you find her not guilty you are to say so and no more. Now hear the evidence.'

I recognised the junior counsel for the crown, the one that opened the indictment, as a young barrister from Buckinghamshire by the name of Robert Dormer Esquire of Lincolns-Inn, near Powys House. From some at the Jesuit trial, I understood he, being not above thirty-one years of age, became a barrister a mere five years since. His family was distantly related to me through my first husband that died at Leghorn when our children were mere infants. I was never formerly introduced to him since his family removed themselves from my circle when I married a second time.

It was common knowledge he had not stood in a court many times before. He had the demeanour of a puppy on his first hunt, not sure of where he should find reassurance: half done gestures, flashes of uncertainty that gave him away. His voice was not unpleasant, if a little staccato.

'May it please Your Lordships and the gentlemen of the jury, Elizabeth Cellier, the gentlewoman at the bar, the wife of Peter Cellier of the parish of St. Clement Danes in the county of Middlesex, stands indicted of being the author and publisher of a libel called Malice Defeated, or a brief Relation of the Accusation and Deliverance of Elizabeth Cellier. You have heard the indictment read. Some clauses of this libel are recited in the words they were written, in Mrs. Cellier's own words. I do not feel necessary to repeat every word to you.

Gentlemen, within this book are contained libels of as many different natures, and against different persons and orders of men, as there are paragraphs. His Majesty, the Protestant religion, our laws, government, magistrates, counsellors of state, courts of judicature, the King's evidence as well as the public justice of this Kingdom are all defamed by the virulence and malice of this woman's pen.'

It was abundantly clear that, whatever tenuous family connection we had, Mr Dormer would allow me no mercy. Indeed, he was set to convict me. If his demeanour did not speak confidence, his words found approval with this audience, and if there were any that supported me here, they would be reluctant to speak for me for fear of retaliation. The noise of the crowd came down for want of hearing what I was charged with. This would be an important part of the tale to be told when they left here today.

'In her book, she casts aspersions on the principles of our religion, the murder of His late Majesty,' said Mr Dormer. 'She accuses those that have done their duty and who are active in discovering The Popish Plot as enemies of the Crown, saying they re-enact the tragedy of our late civil war.

'She further charges our laws with cruelties as inhumane as they are false: in permitting confined prisoners to starve and in admitting the use of racks and tortures to extort perjuries and false evidence against the innocent.

She libels those that give King's evidence, saying they are the Devil's Instruments or the Hangman's Hounds, and defames His Majesty's government, in saying it is not safe to speak truth, but meritorious and gainful to do the contrary.

'You cannot fail to see her as the criminal she is, that has set her name to every page of this scandalous libel and has, since the indictment, owned, published and put value on herself for being the author of so excellent a book.

'To the indictment, she has pleaded not guilty, if the King's evidence prove the charge, you are to find her guilty.'

The prosecution portrayed me a despicable character, a devil's tool worse than any I had discovered in the Popish Plot. I had seen enough of other trials to expect this and had prepared myself for it but, still, I might have convicted myself on Dormer's argument. How easily he twisted unwanted truth into evidence of foul play by the bearer of it.

Mr Weston spoke next. It seemed, twice told, he did not think they fully understood as he wished them as to why I stood before them. Next to my book on the table, he placed down a small stack of papers, very likely details he wrote to remind himself of, then picked up my book.

'Gentlemen, the charge is this. First she is charged with making this book, but there are several clauses in the book she is particularly charged with. The evidence we are about to show will prove, first, the book was owned and published by her, then, that the particulars charged in the indictment were in the book; and finally you will receive the Directions of the Court to sum up the proofs. It is your job to hear the evidence and see the proof.'

Weston returned the book to its place beside the notes.

Mr. Dormer, not the least happy to lose the ears of the court to Mr Weston, roped them back to his side with four words.

'We call our witnesses.'

The first to enter on behalf of the prosecution was the bone-thin William Downing, my publisher. He was ill at ease in the court and, apart from a quick look that acknowledged me standing at the bar, he was apparently disinterested in who was there, as if he had been interrupted in another dozen things and wished to fast return to them.

I fanned my face and tried to not appear out of sorts. This man took my money. We had passed several deep discussions on all manner of details about my book. I was tarnished with the existence of my book with or without his proof. He could not be my downfall, for what could he tell but that I had employed him!

Beside and slightly behind him, hobbled a man with a hooked gait I had seen before, but could not remember in what place. I knew the third person to approach the stand better than I should have liked. If I had doubted him, as I should have doubted any person coming to the door for my book, I would not be fingering cobwebs this day.

This spider cast his web and made sure I stuck on it. As soon as he had my book in his hand, he wrapped me so tight-bound in my own conceit I could do nothing when he arrived with the law and made sure I came to trial. Catching a Catholic in his threads did not give him a robe of respect to the crowd any more than to me. They watched him with as much distrust as did I, for a spider does not change the way he builds a web and catches prey. Even the Lord Mayor looked at him with undisguised distaste.

The three brought to the front of the court were sworn in: William Downing, John Penny and Robert Stevens. John Penny's name did little to enlighten me as to where I knew him. He must have felt my eyes on him, because he looked up and his eyes found mine and stayed on them. It was not maliciousness I saw there, only concern. And apology. He would have to speak against me, I knew, else why would he be here, but he was unhappy to do it. Chance was that he had been threatened into being here and saying what they would have him say against me. I swear he nodded so that only I could see.

Mr Dormer opened the questions by asking William Downing, 'Please tell My Lord, and the jury, what you know of the printing of this libel,' Mr Dormer held up my publication and then continued, 'and who bought these sheets to the press.'

Mr Downing started to answer, 'My Lord, about the 22nd or 23rd of August…' but was interrupted by that impatient fellow Weston.

'Begin with Penny first. Mr Penny, tell us what you have to say about this book.'

So, now this man would be revealed to me. He again looked to me before turning back to Weston and answering, 'My Lord, I was bid to buy a book of that Gentlewoman, and I did so, having asked for her by her name.' Ah, so he was one of the many who did buy a book from me. For what reason this man stood against me, I did not know. Perhaps he needed none.

'By what name?'

'Mrs Cellier.'

Weston pointed towards me. 'Is that the Gentlewoman?'

Neither pause nor thought entered into the man's narrative.

'Yes, that is the Gentlewoman. And she came out of her house and asked what my errand was. I told her it was to have a book. 'That you may have,' she said. I asked her, 'How much is it, Madam?' She said, 'Two shillings.' I asked her if I could not have them any cheaper, and she said, 'No, I have sold them to shopkeepers for 18 shillings a dozen, and I must not sell them under that price to you.' Then she went and fetched me a book, and I gave her the two shillings, and then she gave me another little paper.'

Surprising me, because I thought it was the issue, Weston then said, 'That is not in issue, nor your question now. Did you ask her for the book she published and set out?'

Penny answered, 'Yes, and she acknowledged it was her book.'

'So, she owned the book and told you it was hers?'

Mr. Penny held up my book. 'This is the book I have in my hand, and I read every page of it.' With which he looked at me and did not hide the respect he had for my writing of it. 'And she told me there was another little sheet to be added to it, and if any gentleman wanted it sent to the country, it might be put in a letter and sent by post.'

I remembered that look. It brought to mind when I saw this man before, when he had come to buy my book from our house. It was with respect and goodwill he had looked at me then too, when he had declared himself fortunate to meet the author for, he had said, not many had so little fear for their life that they would lay it down for a book. I had little doubt that spider, Stevens, must have seen him buy it from me and had followed him to make him a witness.

Now I had remembered the meeting, and the words that were spoken, I wondered if I might instil some doubt to my authorship. 'May I ask him a question?'

Weston said, 'Tell me your question, and I will ask it.'

Why I could not ask it when the man stood right before me I did not know, but I did know that courts had strange rules from times long gone by, and I did also know that I did not wish to turn Weston any more against me. So, agreeably, I asked, 'I desire to know if I said any more than you may have a book, or there is a book. And who asked for a book.'

And then, as if I did not longer exist to Weston, he repeated my question to Penny, 'Did she say any more than you may have a book, or this is the book she had published?'

Mr. Penny looked to the rafters and frowned in thought. 'When I got the book, and paid for it, I turned back to her and asked her if it was her own book. She told me it was, and more than that, if she had opportunity, she could have put more in it.'

His answer undid me after all. I had hoped to throw doubt on his words, but they had become all too clear.

Weston suddenly addressed me. 'You did not deny writing this book yesterday, Mrs Cellier. In fact, do you remember when you said, if you could bring in your witnesses, you would prove the truth of it all? Of what you wrote in your book? We told you, the only thing you had to show to prove you were not guilty was that somebody else had published the book, not you. Then you said you had written it yourself, every word with your own hand.'

'Tis with regret I closed my mouth too late. Would that I had sewn my mouth shut before!

'My Lord, if I was a foolish, vain woman and spoke vain words about myself, which I did not understand the consequence of, I hope my vanity shan't be brought against me to convict me of a crime.'

'Mrs Cellier, I scarcely think you would have been so careless to say that of yourself if it were not true.'

He was right, but then I would not have 'carelessly' written any of my book if it had not borne the truth, knowing I would as like find myself in the dungeons as pilloried. My duty was to expose the evil in this city, but I did not want to dwell further in gaol for it. But I would go there, if I must, for the sake of truth and truth alone, though I hoped it would not come to that. My husband, children and customers needed me! I should plead innocence. That was my only chance.

I appealed to them as a woman.

'But I hope you will not take vain words spoken in that foolish way as evidence against me.'

'That will depend on whether the proof shows you guilty.'

He did not try to hide his distaste and he wrinkled his nose. His countenance belied him an objective examiner. He had no sympathy for me, and no subjugation would make it otherwise.

I turned from Mr Weston and again asked Penny to remember my exact words. 'Did I say I wrote it?'

Mr. Penny said, 'You told me it was your book.'

'I told you? Please, My Lord,' I turned back to Weston, 'ask him on the oath he has taken, did I say any more than it was mine and I sold it, not that I wrote it, nor I was the author of it?'

Weston did not, as I hoped, ask the question. Instead, he lectured me in exasperation.

'Mrs Cellier, this book is entitled with your name and sold by your self. Now, in anyone's judgement, this is both an owning of the book, and a publishing of the book. When you sold it, you gave it out as your book, and your name is on the title page as the author of it.'

I could not give up when my fate depended upon it and when I had God and right on my side.

'My Lord,' I said, 'if I could produce my witnesses, I would make my defence, but I am informed that some of them cannot be found. They have looked for them everywhere, all over town, even at Sir Joseph Sheldon's and a great many other places, all to no avail.'

Truth be told, my man, George Grange, that was paid to find the witnesses, told me moments before the trial that many who would speak in favour of me had disappeared. Why this was so was no mystery; it was common enough during a trial. Either they hid because they wanted no attention brought onto themselves for their involvement, or they were taken by those that had an interest to, far from the city so they could not defend me.

Did Weston know of this? I suspected he did not, because he might have pretended to tell me to bring them, knowing they would not come. Instead, he was as a mule, putting me off having them there.

'To what purpose should your witnesses come?'

I held up my chin. 'I should have made my defence with them.'

Again, Weston referred to the previous day. 'If you had said yesterday you had witnesses to prove someone else wrote the book, we would have put off the trial…'

Crafty fox. He referred only to my having written the book and stayed far from the dangerous contents. If I proved the contents true, then it could no longer be called libel, but if he only proved I had written a book that assumed false contents, it would be called so.

He continued, '…but you said you wrote every word of it yourself and so owned the issue. Now you pretend you want witnesses. To what purpose would you have them come?'

His was a bias so clear, it was a wonder he should be allowed to examine me! Surely, he should not be allowed to question a witness when he was so determined to prove them wrong. I barely resisted telling him this.

'My Lord, it is not for the Bench to give evidence, and I hope you will not take advantage of vain words said out of court.'

Weston did not like my citing of the law to him. If he were weary of this whole conversation, even if he were somewhat peeved that I claim the law do right by me, it was my life, my destiny, in question, not his. Mother Destiny did yet await directions where she might take me.

He peevishly asserted, 'It is the honour of the Bench to repeat what you say, when you asked to put off your trial so you can find witnesses, and when the Court asked if you could prove someone else wrote the book you renounced that and admitted to having written it yourself!'

He took himself so serious I could not resist cheeking him. I smiled sweet as honey and said, 'But I hope that is no evidence.' He puffed out his chest like a cock for a fight.

'It was spoken openly in the Court; everybody heard it.'

There was no point continuing in this vein since he was not at all susceptible to a woman's charms, so I only said, 'I am only surprised it is allowed. I have no witnesses.'

Cross, Weston dogged the answer to his question. 'It was easy to pretend you wanted witnesses, but I ask again, for what purpose would you have had them called?'

I did not wish to anger the examiner further, if it may hinder my case, so I turned to Mr Attorney General. 'My Lord, I hope you will please remember, he swore I said only it was mine, not that I was the author.'

Then the Attorney General interrupted, equally exasperated, 'If you sold it, that is a publishing in law and is within the indictment.'

Even then, I did not clam my mouth shut. 'But he did not say I wrote it.'

Weston came to the end of his tether then, and interjected, 'Do not be so sure of that, Mrs Cellier. He said that after he had asked you, 'Is this your book?' you said, 'yes, it is my book and, if I had been aware, I could have put a great deal more in it than I have done.'

'But I did not say I wrote it.'

If I had already lost, it was not for me to admit it. None had told me the very selling of the book was proof of publishing. Too many hours in Newgate I had practiced proving how I had not written the book. My very stubbornness would not have me let it go now, though it might be my downfall. And it surely would be.

Then, Penny spoke, 'You said if it were to be written again, you could put more in it.' He looked at me satisfied as if he had helped me, but I had sooner done without such assistance.

To Weston I repeated, 'I said it was my book, and so it was, because it was my possession, but I did not say I wrote it. This is my fan, but it does not follow I made it.'

If my wit pleased me it counted for nothing to the man before me. Weston frowned that I was not as demure as every woman should be.

'But the question concerned the author of the book,' he

said. He did keep coming back to that. Did he not see that if I had misunderstood the question at the time he could not prove otherwise!

'He asked me no such question.' I said. Then I asked Penny again, 'Did you ask me if I was the author?'

'No, I did not,' he said.

Gratified, I turned raised eyebrows to Weston.

Weston said, 'But what did you ask her? '

'I asked her whether it was her book.'

'And did she own it?'

'Yes, she did,' said Penny.

'So it was mine, in possession,' I stated confidently, as though that was my original meaning.

Still chasing the answer he sought, that dog Weston did not have any of it. 'Did you mean by your question whether that book was hers in property, or that she were the author and publisher of it?'

Penny replied, 'I wanted to know whether it was hers or not.' Frustrated, Weston growled, 'But what was your intention in asking? Was it whether she or any other person had made the book?'

I nearly laughed at Penny's answer, for it only made Weston madder.

'I do not know who made it. She told me it was hers,' he said.

Weston said, 'But what was your meaning in it?'

'My intentions was for fear she should give me another book, to know whether she wrote it or not.'

'My Lord,' I said. 'I am not to be judged by his meaning, but by his question, and my answer, and the time.'

Then Mr. Attorney General intervened with a more specific question. 'Did she tell you she sold more of them?'

Penny said, 'I turned about when I had the book and asked her, if occasion be, could I have any more? She said she had but four or five hundred left, and in a few days she would have more.'

The Attorney General then stated, 'You told us that, she told you how much she sold them for by the dozen.'

'Yes, eighteen shillings the dozen, to the shopkeepers.'

Damned by my own pride; no person would believe I kept more than one or two for my own reading!

Then they swore in Downing, the publisher. Over his skinny bones, he still wore his stained work apron, a sign he was but an unwanted prisoner to the court and would return to his press the moment he was released. I suspected he did not eat not for want of food, but for the want of his body's memory of it. Even as he spoke, his hands shifted and fiddled with the air as if he placed print blocks for each and every spoken word. His eyes did not see the court, but followed his ink-stained fingers, checking for mistakes.

Equally mesmerised by the fidgets of the skinny man, Weston watched them set his next question for some future ghost book.

'Mr Downing,' said Weston, 'pray look upon that book and the title of it.' Downing did so. 'Have you examined that book?'

Mr Downing looked briefly at my book then recorded his answer with his fingers.

'Sir, I printed part of it.'

'But have you examined that very pamphlet?' said Weston.

'Yes, I know it well.'

'Did you Print part of it?'

'Yes, I did,' muttered Downing's fingers.

'Who brought it to you to be printed?'

'Mrs Cellier.'

'She herself?' Weston dragged his eyes from Downing's hands and marked the answer by raising eyebrows to several persons in the jury and the judges. But Downing's talking fingers pulled them back as he went on.

'My Lord, on about the twenty-second day of August, a messenger came and brought me to Mrs Cellier's house in Arundel Buildings and told me she had something to be printed. She told me she had been publicly and wrongfully abused and was resolved to publish her case, and wished to make the world sensible of the wrong she had sustained. When I told her I was a stranger to her concerns, she assured me there was nothing offensive in it, that it was only the truth and I might safely print it. Her discourse was plausible, so I was apt to believe her, and agreed with her to have ten shillings a ream for printing, and I was to print two bundles of every sheet...'

'What is a bundle?' Weston interrupted and Downing's fingers momentarily stopped. With his answer they started up again.

'A bundle is two reams. She wished for four reams of each sheet.'

'She ordered two thousand books? Two thousand for only herself to read!'

Every other person in the room took his laugh as a signal for hilarity, cursing and damning. Many that had opened the day in a local tavern before passing time here shouted and jeered. I did not catch the specifics since they were lost in the confusion of Babylon's tongues. The court became so loud the Councillor for the Crown clapped his hands loudly several times, and called out, 'Silence! Silence! We cannot hear!' By and by, he was heard and the noise diminished.

Downing continued, 'I had printed only half the book when a messenger discovered it printing at my house and carried it before Sir Jenkins, the Secretary. He then granted a warrant to bring us both before him and, having been examined, Mrs Cellier and I were bound to appear the first day of next term in the King's Bench. Since that time, she printed t'other half of her book at another place. And, whereas she promised to indemnify me from all trouble and charge, when I came to pay the fees to the council, she refused to pay them for me. She told me I had betrayed her and so, notwithstanding her promise, I was obliged to pay the fees myself.'

I could not deny that I did renegade that promise, but he had indeed betrayed me. He told them that it was I that had written the book and agreed the publishing of it with him. Though it be the truth, it was not for him to say.

Mr Dormer raised his hand to the still talking crowd and asked, 'Pray Sir, who corrected the sheets?'

Taken by surprise at the changed direction whence came the examination, Downing's fingers again stopped. 'I brought them to her, Sir.' He frowned at Mr Dormer's raised hand, pouting lips and narrowed eyes as if he could not see him. Perhaps he could not. It did seem he saw only as far as his hands from his face, for he had been clumsy with the furniture in my house, and had needed to be shown the door on the way out.

'So she read them and corrected them?' said Dormer.

'Yes, Sir.'

Again, not liking the stage to be taken from him, Weston loudly asked, 'Pray tell me how far it was you printed of the book.'

Quite relieved to see the nearby speaker, Downing said, 'It was to folio twenty two.'

Weston told the court, 'All the clauses in the indictment are contained in those pages.'

Mr Clare, one of the jury, said, 'All but the last in the postscript.'

Weston took no notice of the man and continued, 'Have you read the book since?'

Downing nodded. 'So far, My Lord, as I did print.'

Weston said, 'You take it upon your oath that, to the 22nd folio of that book given in evidence, you printed it by her direction?'

'Aye, I do,' said Downing.

Another nail in my coffin.

'Then set up Stevens,' said Weston.

I could not help but recoil at the look of malice and satisfaction Stevens flaunted at me as he took the Bible in his hand.

'May it please Your Lordship,' said Stevens, 'I saw this book a printing at Mr. Downing's and, reading some passages in it, I asked him, 'Mr Downing, do you know what it is you do?' Barefaced, he told me he printed a truth. Then I asked him for whom he printed it. He said he printed it for Mrs. Cellier...'

I did not know the man but, it seemed, he knew me, and well enough that he wished me harm. Of a certainty, it was my own endeavours that made him busy in my case, for nobody wrote that book but I, but I did not like his enjoyment of my situation. Stevens talked with barely a breath between anything he said, as if he could not wait to reveal everything that would condemn me.

'…I bid him have a care that he did no more than what he could justify. He desired that I would not hurt him, and I was loath to do the poor man wrong, but away I went to the Secretary…'

It was he, then, the messenger for the press responsible for my being in gaol! Without a doubt, it was certain he set me up to catch me out!

'…but before I did I asked him what was become of the sheets, he said he carried them to Mrs Cellier, and, said I, did she bring you the copy? Said he, she sent several, and when I came to her, she did tell me it was her book, and that she kept a man to write it, and she dictated it to another that sat by her, and she often owned it was her book, and she the author of it.'

I did not remember this Secretary's knave coming to the door, nor of telling him about my book. My memory of faces was not so poor I would have forgotten. What travesty of justice allowed – nay demanded – a devil's heinous instrument such as he to swear on the Bible and spit lies! Yet one that does the Lord's work and aids every person in all manner of ways, is denied that solemn right simply for being of the Romish faith!

Was this vengeance for some unknown wrong I did him? For whatever reason he had taken this course, I would not allow him tell lies about me under oath!

'I never said so in my life,' I said. I chomped my teeth together.

Stevens spoke directly to me.

'Mrs Cellier, by the same token as when you sent for bail and you had occasion to write a note, I saw you write it. And I said to you, 'I now find "tis not your hand-writing for there is difference between the note and the pages of the book'.'

Still looking at me, Stevens spoke to others in the court. 'Said she, 'I know that well enough, but I keep a man, by the name of Grange, in the house to write, and I am up very early every morning, preparing and dictating it to him for the press'. One time Grange told me, 'She has put out two sheets since, and this day, at one a clock, she has invited the fleet-footed mercuries[16] and the street hawkers to come and receive a new pamphlet."

Weston said, 'Did she, in front of you, affirm herself to be the author of the book?'

'She did, if it please you, Sir,' said Stevens. 'She claimed to be the author before the Secretary and before the Council. And I myself have seen her sell several of them on separate days.'

Again, that superior look that condemned me as the worst kind of whore mingled with malice that said I was important enough to matter in the wrong way.

Mr Dormer's voice carried up and over the again noisy crowd, 'Swear in Mr Fowler,' and, when that was done, 'Show him the book, if you please.'

Fowler took my book, held out to him, and turned it over. Mr Dormer asked him if he did buy any of my books, to which Fowler said he had bought two for the sum of four shillings. He explained how some of his friends were pleased to joke with him that his name was in it.

Fowler then related how, in particular, a visitor of quality, Mr Henry Killigrew, came one day to his house, and called him into the room and there told him he was notoriously in print and that he was known to be in the company of a great duke and great lords.

So, he had come to me to buy my books and, when I had brought the books to him, he had exclaimed, 'Madam, I believe you have forgotten me!' I had denied having ever seen him in my whole life, and he had become flustered when I further denied his claim that he was the man called 'F' in my book, living at the Half-Moon Tavern in Cheape Side.

Mr Attorney General said, 'You are the man meant by the 'F'? Is there something in this book you are supposed to have done in prison?' Again, the attorney general displayed knowledge outside of the courtroom with which he led the witness.

Fowler said, 'I suppose Corral the coachman laid oath to that, but I also gave my oath for it before the Lord-Mayor himself.'

The crowd, that I was beginning to see as a single angry

beast, growled loudly at the mention of Corral the coachman, and that growling swallowed up the attorney general's voice. I could barely hear him from where I stood closer by. He gestured with his hands to quieten down, cleared his throat and then said over the remaining grumble, 'Pray, for the satisfaction of people here today, tell us what you know of this matter.'

Fowler squinted his eyes and wrinkled his nose. 'The substance of my oath before my Lord Mayor was this: I never did see any of the things that she said in her book, no duke drew his sword, no lord proffered five hundred pounds, nor did I whisper to the coachman that if he should name some great persons then he and I would have money enough! The fact of the matter is that the book is a libel so dire.'

Baron Weston moved closer, perhaps to be better heard, and asked, 'Was Corral the coachman apprehended for carrying away the dead body of Sir Edmundbury Godfrey on your accusation?'

Fowler said, 'As to that, I will tell you the occasion of all our discourse, if it may not be too tedious.' Weston nodded and Fowler went on, 'One day some gentlemen in my Inn called for a coach, but the coachman that came was made to wait too long and so went away again, which the gentlemen were not happy over. There upon another coachman was called, which was the man, Corral, mentioned in this libel. When he went upstairs to fetch the gentlemen, they engaged him to stay and, to make sure he did so, secured his whip.

'While he waited…' He raised his voice for the court to hear him. I doubted they did so even then, for there was such a to-do amongst them. '…he came down to the bar and begged a pipe of tobacco from my wife. 'Aye', said she, 'thou lookest like a good honest fellow, and I believe thou hast no hand in the plot', a common pleasantry at that time. Whereupon the man begins to tell her how he had escaped that danger!

'He swore damn to her that four men had accosted him at St. Clement's Church wall and they would have him do no good and carry Sir Godfrey's body in his coach. He saw the body with his own eyes in a sedan and, loathing to be dragged in, shammed them that he could not carry him for the axletree of his coach was broke.

'Overhearing the fellow talk, I came out from my room and asked him, 'Are you sure of this?' He swore damn the truth of it. Then I asked him if he were master for himself or drove for another. The fellow, being sensible he had been too lavish in his discourse, pretended to light his pipe in haste, and to run out and see if the seats of his coach were not stolen out. I took a candle with me and went after him, but by the time I got to the door, he was already driving away, even though he had left his whip with the gentleman as security for his stay!'

Fowler looked to the court for their blessing he had done right by his questions. It was difficult to tell if they thought it so, for they were to busy talking and jeering amongst themselves.

'The day after, Captain Richardson and the Secondary of the Compter were drinking a glass of wine at my house, so I told them the story, whereupon the captain took the number of his coach that I had set down. They blamed me very much I had not stopped the fellow. Then, the next day, Richardson sent his Janizaries[17] abroad and secured Corral. I believe they kept him in custody for two or three days.'

Baron Weston listened well, then asked, 'When was this?'

Fowler scratched his head. 'Two or three days after the murder was publicly known. To the best of my remembrance, it was Tuesday night that this fellow told me the story, and the next day I told the captain and the secondary.'

Baron Weston said, 'Was that Tuesday after the murder, or the Tuesday seven night after?'

Frowning deeply, Fowler said, 'It was the Tuesday seven-night after. The next day I was ordered to wait upon the lords at Wallingford-house, where the Duke of Buckingham, Lord Shaftsbury, the Marquis of Winchester, two other lords, and Major Wildman, the secretary, examined me upon this thing. And what I have declared to Your Lordships now, I declared to them then. And they brought the fellow in face to face, and there he did confess the whole matter was told to him by two others.'

I wondered at that. If Corral had heard it from two others, surely Fowler this minute inadvertently proved his innocence.

Fowler stopped talking when the crowd became too loud and he was drowned out. Weston turned to the persons making the most noise and waved his hands at them but, again, it took Mr Attorney General as well to hush them. Fowler, impatient for a gap to talk into, begun talking regardless.

'The lords sent for the two persons Corral named and were well satisfied they were both of good reputation, one of them keeping a victualling-house, but they were of the opinion it was mere sham, and that Corral merely named the first persons that came into his mind. Getting nothing out of him, my Lord Duke of Buckingham told him, 'Sir, if you will confess, the King hath promised you shall be protected. My Lord Shaftesbury told him the same, but added that, if he would not confess, and tell them who set him to work, then nothing should be severe enough for him.'

Baron Weston cast the significance of this statement upon the court in a haughty look, his eyebrows raised so high they hid beneath his periwig. 'Upon this accusation was he sent to prison?'

Fowler nodded. 'He was re-ordered to Newgate and there continued for several months.'

Baron Weston asked, 'Were you ever in Newgate, and saw him?'

Fowler, 'Never, not I.'

Baron Weston, 'Did you never see him outwith the chamber with the lords, and at your own tavern?'

Fowler, 'Never.'

Baron Weston, 'Were you ever in Newgate with him, My Lord Duke of Buckingham, or My Lord Shaftesbury, or any other duke, lord or nobleman whatsoever?'

Fowler, 'No.'

Baron Weston, 'Did you see any sword drawn, or money offered or laid down upon a table?'

Fowler, 'There was never a sword drawn, nor any money offered.'

To the judges and then to the jury, Baron Weston summed Fowler's statements. 'He answers very fully to that and denies what

Mrs Cellier writes in her book, that he is accused to be in Newgate in the presence of a Duke and another great Earl, that the Duke drew his sword, and the other nobleman laid down a great deal of gold, amounting to five hundred pounds. This is consequently denial of the whole charge.'

The room was filled with so many shouts and threats, I was enraged by their so despising of me. Though I should not speak, Weston having instructed me so, I could not hold my tongue. 'I did not write that this was true, but I writ that the fellow told me so!'

Baron Weston demanded that the counsellor of the crown should read aloud the passages relating to Fowler's story, and we were made to listen to them for, though it proved nothing, he said, 'Compare it with the record, for she shall have a fair trial, by the grace of Almighty God.'

Baron Weston, 'Now, I must inform you, Mrs Cellier, we have already proved against the clauses in your book that cast great infamy upon our religion and on the whole government.

'Where you say Fowler was barbarously used in prison by nobles, first by drawn sword, next by the temptation of gold, in order to force confession, your words of their bad usage have already been proved false and libellous. Where you allege Prance was tortured in prison to compel him to commit perjury, he will prove against you this day.

'That you accuse the King of making it safer to be a hangman's hound, or to become an accuser for a pension, is a public calumny on the nation, but then to say such things as 'it is not meritorious for a person to speak the truth than to do otherwise' this is a slander that ought earn public rebuke.'

Weston's demeanour became more fervent the longer he stayed on the stage. He played to the audience, but forgot they came not to see him but me.

'Mrs. Cellier has insinuated that the murder of the late King, Charles the First, was sufficient ground to pervert her from Protestantism, when all the world knows that, in that ill period,

281

there were Protestants that were far better subjects, and more loyal, than ever any Papist was in the world. And there were those that suffered as greatly, nay, far more, for their opposition to that dreadful villainy than the Papists can boast of for their loyalty. It is well known there were underhand villains that did encourage all that roguery,' said Weston.

He turned about and addressed me directly.

'You have set a fayre upon the damnable lie that the most arrant rebellious rogues that ever lived are great saints in comparison to Protestants. This, no honest man will believe.'

'I said they call themselves Protestants.' I had to raise my voice to be heard. 'I know the Protestants were great sufferers for the King, and I myself felt it. My family were Protestants, and were several times stripped and plundered for their loyalty. I grant this.'

Weston, his face red and sweating with heat from both without and within, scorned, 'Do you? Then you are an impudent lying woman, or else a villainous lying priest has instructed you to begin your book with such base insinuation against the best of religions! This lie will go upon the public infamy attending your party of notorious liars, among whom falsehood does so much abound. Call Corral and Prance.'

In that way, Weston summarily dismissed me and what I had to say. He took a white lace hand-kerchief from his pocket and wiped the drops of sweat that trickled from beneath his periwig. I clenched my teeth, surprised, once more, he had not pointed to my admittance that I wrote the book. His words had so prodded and riled the mob-Beast, barely held back behind the wooden bar, that it roared and shook and thirsted for my blood. I thanked the Lord that there were soldiers standing by, for it looked as if that bar might not hold, and I would be devoured by the Beast clamouring for my throat.

Swords drawn, the red-coat soldiers positioned themselves before the barrier, their armour easily deflecting stones and small things thrown by an otherwise unarmed audience. Their faces were not so defended, and I saw a woman reach forward and scratch at a soldier's cheek. He hit her hard with the back of his hand so she fell against the men behind her.

I could scarce hear the first part of what Mr Attorney General next said to the jury, but only the last, though I did not think any others heard as much.

'...give ... satisfaction ... jury should know ... does not concern the matter in issue for, in point of law, even if the words of it be true, the publishing of a libel is a crime and deserves punishment.'

It did me no good, then, that I told the truth if the jury had heretofore judged my book a libel and resolved to find me guilty. My only hope was to prove I did not write the book, but the proof weighed heavy in the scales against me and would not tip back lightly.

Weston's shout over the din turned his already red cheeks the colour of good wine. 'But, Mr. Attorney, if we are to set a fine, it will be a satisfaction to the court to disprove the things she alleges. Mayhaps you have witnesses ready?'

If he took offence, Mr Attorney General did not seem so. He leaned sideways in his chair, then slow and off-hand waved some empty pages to cool his face. The scorn in his voice showed a certain ill will that could only have found itself in encounters between them heretofore. 'They are already ordered to be here. Swear Mr. Prance.' His nose could not have risen further in the air without his standing. One judge beside him slept through the din with his mouth open. Prance was sworn in.

Baron Weston was oblivious to the silent-fought battle. 'Mr Prance, pray, were you tortured in prison?'

Mr. Prance, whose haggard look was testament of either ill treatment or ill conscience, had changed his coat so many times he did not know what colour he wore. He changed once more. The puzzle was that he was called back to testify over and over, despite his faulty recollection or barefaced lies.

'No, I never was in my life,' he said.

Weston asked, 'How then were you used?'

Prance said, 'Very well. I had every thing that was fitting. Captain Richardson did take great care of me.'

A triumphant Weston said, 'The truth is, the very book itself implies a contradiction. It says these women heard in prison one strong man roar as a strong man in torture, and yet, presently after that, it says that the prisoner comes up in irons and is examined. Now, any man that knows what the nature of a rack is knows how one so tortured could not even stir or walk let alone heave irons upon his legs. Surely some impudent lying priest dare venture such calumny!

'I did not say it was what happened, but that it was reported,' I said, curious how he should so well know the result of iron when none such were ever allowed. I could not find myself surprised by Prance. I doubted he even knew the truth of any of it any more, he had turned about so many times he must spin.

Mr. Prance slashed my words so they were dropped. 'Dr. Lloyd was together with me many times for half an hour. If there any such thing, it is certain he would have seen it.'

They needed no more 'facts' from Prance, and Francis Corral was called.

I covered my fast beating heart with my hand lest everyone should hear it. Again, my fingers touched the cross beneath the satin on my chest, and I prayed no harm would come to Corral for speaking out for me.

He was called a second time, but still he did not appear. It did not occur to me he would not come.

Captain Richardson slapped some flying thing on his forearm, catching one end of his lace cuff from its fixing so it hung free unnoticed by him, and came into the middle of the room to face the judges.

'Last night I ordered Corral to be here to day, but he is not here. His wife stands in his stead.'

Mrs Corral came to the middle of the room with her eyes to the floor as any good demure woman, or one that daren't do otherwise. When she stopped where she should before the judges, she hung her head so all I could see of her from the side was her white cap and an ear. I did see how tight she held her bent form, a little more weight on her bones than last I saw her, clothed in a plain dress Cromwell would be satisfied with.

Weston spoke with his back to her, facing the jury. 'Good woman, were you ever with your husband in prison?'

Mrs. Corral's head came up and fear lived on her face like a parasite, making it twitch and grimace. She clenched her fist tight into her black puritan skirt and did not look at me.

'I was denied to see him when he was on the Master's-Side.'

Weston turned so abruptly to face Mrs Corral it made her start and look to the floor once more. 'But when he came from prison, how did he tell you he was used? Did he tell you he was compelled to drink his own piss?'

Mrs Corral confirmed what I had said. 'It was Sunday when they called me to bring him victuals so he would not starve. They said he would be dead before I came there if I did not go fast. So, fast as I could, I brought him bread and things, yet I was denied to see him 'til near a fortnight after. Then, I was amazed at the great iron fetters he had on for, if he could barely stand, how could he walk? They told me they had put on those things to keep him warm. I says to my husband, 'Lord, what have you done? You must surely have murdered somebody!''

Impatient for her to tell how they treated her then, I asked, 'Were you ever beaten for bringing your husband victuals?'

Neither by glance nor gesture did she recognise me. 'No indeed, no. I was never beaten. But they would not suffer me to see him while he was on the Master's-Side.'

Did she lie before, when she was comfortable with me, or now when she feared unknown retribution? To be sure, stories abounded of the wife or child of a witness stolen away during a trial that he might be forced do the bidding of a captor. So I did not doubt Mr Corral refused to refute what I said and now suffered for it someplace behind a locked door. Perhaps he owed me his life, but what use was that if it was again forfeit until he was returned home safe! Would I have lied had it been my husband threatened so? Perhaps, but I was not so tested.

It was as if the Lord Mayor had heard my thoughts and taunted me. He said, 'We do not need Mrs Corral. Her husband already denied everything in the book upon oath before me.'

'Mrs Cellier,' Weston ignored the Lord-Mayor, 'You should direct your questions through counsel at the appropriate time.' Then to Mrs Corral, 'Was he ever hurt with screws or any such thing?'

A small shake of her head gave me a clue as to how she would answer. No matter how tight I bound my voice, I could not stop protest and indignation releasing it. 'Had he not holes in his legs?'

Mrs Corral said, 'Yes, he had a great many; I did see holes in his legs.'

Weston was surprised. 'Did you?'

'I did see one,' she said, 'and I can bring the apothecary that brought salve to heal it.'

With false indignation, Captain Richardson stood tall as a mountain, legs parted and with his fists balled on his hips. 'I keep no irons in the house that weighs twelve pound!'

Weston scrutinised Richardson in a manner he refused to accord Mrs Corral. 'They say you have irons called sheers that weigh forty pound.' His eyebrows once more disappeared beneath his periwig. It seemed as if he had already heard this from another place before he heard it from me.

'If there be such a thing I would be hanged for it before I go hence,' said Richardson. If I did not know the untruth of it, I might have been convinced by his conviction. The only way to refute his lies was to have my witnesses testify against him, but would they let me have them now?

'I hope I shall be allowed to make my defence and call my witnesses,' I said.

Weston's eyes narrowed on Richardson as if he still quizzed him, but said, 'Yes, to be sure.'

He did not say more so, shunning Weston's instruction, I used the moment to examine Mrs Corral, before she was dismissed.

'You were present when your husband told me how he was ill-used. Can you state you did not hear him say he was fettered to the floor by a chain not above a yard long, and he was forced to drink his own water?'

'Madam,' she said. 'He was not sensible of what he said.'

Ungrateful wretch! She still did not look me in the eye.

I placed the danger to herself and her husband in one pan of the scales, and my own in the other. They tipped dangerously against me. It was certain I would suffer for the truth, and would suffer more if she did not remember the facts to the court. 'But did not you hear him tell me so?'

'I cannot remember.'

Despite further questioning of her, she cast me an apology with her eyes but did not redeem me.

Weston shrugged the matter from his shoulders. 'We need not hear more of this. For the great matter against you is the death of Sir Godfrey. In that you are tight with Prance's evidence, and turn scrutiny from your own party onto somebody else, though I know not on whom. And so you would be bound to make the World believe that he was tortured into his confession, and that he was mad when he did it.'

'Pray, My Lord,' I said. 'Hear me one word. As to your saying I do it to defend a party, I profess I stand singly and alone. I have been so barbarously used by those you call my own party, and the Protestants have been abundantly more kind to me than they, I would not tell the least lie to do them any good turn.'

I did not expect Weston to believe me but, if he did, it caused him great amusement. 'Then you are a happy woman indeed, that is beloved by both parties. You have not been of good service to both alike, I am sure, but that is no great matter. If the Protestants were so kind as you say, you have requited them ill by such a base libel.'

'I say nothing against them.' I held my head high and looked him in the eye.

'Can you prove you did not write this book?'

'My Lord,' I said, for this was a thing I knew from the Huguenot meetings I attended with my friend Marie Desermeau. The outcast Protestants that escaped France readily accepted and supported some French Catholics, or those related to them, as was I. 'I am not bound to accuse myself. I desire it may be proved.'

Baron Weston's derision was lost in the thunder of outraged

287

talk that came then, but seeing his lips move and seeing his smile of satisfaction I determined his words. 'I think it is fully proved.' If he thought I would cave so easily, and allow him his victory, he was much mistaken. 'I cannot say anything without my witnesses. I desire I may call them,' I said.

Weston folded his arms across his chest, so the loosed lace cuff stood out white against his blue doublet. 'Call whom you will.'

I asked that George Grange should be called.

George Grange was a small man, with a nose suitable for sniffing mischief out of holes wherein it hid or was concealed, that I paid handsomely to find my witnesses. I wouldst that I did not call him, for he harmed me and did me no good. Weston soon had from him that my witnesses had either gone to the country or could not be found. Then he was turned against me.

'Tell me what questions you will ask him,' Weston asked me.

'I desire to know the witnesses he went for? What answers they returned? And where they be?' I said.

Weston did not try to hide his disinterest and impatience. He tapped his still folded elbow with poker fingers and spoke with a thin mouth. 'Well, what witnesses were you sent to look for?'

Grange said, 'I went to look for one Mrs. Sheldon that lives in sir Joseph Sheldon's house, and they told me she was in Essex. Then I went for Mr. Curtis, but his wife did not see him since yesterday before the cock crowed.'

Weston flung his arms wide with exasperation. He asked, 'What were they to have proved?'

Grange said, 'Truly, My Lord, I do not know.'

Then Mr. Dormer asked, 'By the oath you have taken, do you know if Mrs Cellier sold any of these books?'

Grange might be a hound for mischief, but it seemed he was also mischief itself. 'Yes,' he said, 'I know she did sell some of them.'

They needed nothing more of him.

Mr Lord Mayor laughed, 'There, Mrs Cellier. Even your own witness proves against you.' Those of the court that heard him laughed at the irony, but I did not.

Mr Weston befriended me for some small moments then, for he took the court's derision away from me, though not through kindness, I was sure. 'Who else would you have?'

I thought to call my friend, Mary, that came to give alms with me, but she did not appear. When I asked for John Clarke to be fetched from the Gaol, Captain Richardson stepped forward, spilling hops from the cup in his hand onto the dusty floor.

'He is in execution,' he said.

'For what?' asked Weston.

'For debt,' said Capt. Richardson.

'The rules of the prison allow you to bring him hither.'

Capt. Richardson shook his head. Uncertain if they wished it, he looked to Mr Lord Mayor, who waved air at his face with a sheaf of paper. It did not at all diminish the sweat from his hot cheeks. 'If Your Lordship orders it so, I will bring him.'

Lord Mayor was not so gentle on me as Weston. 'She should have brought a Habeas Corpus if she would have had him.'

Mr Attorney General, that moments before had his eyes closed in sleep, as did two elderly judges, sat up sharply in his chair as if a servant had banged a door too loud behind him. 'If he brings him without a Habeas Corpus it will be an escape.'

I rested my hands on the rail and beseeched them, 'I pray a Habeas Corpus to fetch him. I desire to have him come and defend something in my book.'

'What would he prove?' said Weston.

I clasped my hands together before me as if in prayer, imploring them to grant me this wish. 'That I have not belied the Government.'

'In what respect?' said Weston.

'That he was shackled with long sheers and unreasonable irons.' I tried to come over with confidence but, when all I had trusted had already turned against me, I was not so sure that veritable scoundrel, John Clarke, would stand by me either.

Weston said, 'You apply too late. You should have moved the court for one ere now.'

My hope of any witness standing for me waned fast.

'I had no time to prepare for my defence,' I said. 'I did not have sight of the indictment till nine o'clock today, and my counsel had not time to inspect it or speak with me about it.' Mr Lord Mayor lifted his quizzing glasses, making his eyes bigger than should belong to his face, and peered through them at Weston. 'If we dally over this, at what time shall we have done?'

Baron Weston answered question with question. 'Have you a blank Habeas Corpus here?'

The Counsellor of the Peace, I did not know the name of, spoke out. 'They should have to fetch it from the crown-office.'

My counsel, Mr. Collins, came in on the discourse now. He told me, 'You cannot do yourself greater wrong than by such talk as this.' I had no use for his advice, since he had previously informed me, before the trial, that all Papists 'are guilty of everything they are accused of '.

The cryer suddenly shouted above all others, 'Here is Mrs. Smith now.' My friend, Mary Smith, came forward into the room, her eyes down. She nodded at me before taking the oath.

So relieved was I to see a friendly face that again I forgot I should speak only through Weston. I addressed Mary directly. 'What have you heard Corral the coachman say about how he was used in prison?'

''Tis as...' Mary started, but Mr Dormer cut Mary's first words from her gaping mouth and caused her to jump.

'That question is not to be admitted.'

Mary barely spared me a glance before returning her eyes to the floor and saying nothing. I could not judge her, for her husband kept the most vicious head cage, an instrument the like of the one used to bully prisoners in Newgate, though there they called it by another name: discipline. One time, I did see a woman that did not still her tongue and the spikes dug so deep they drew blood only for that she spoke her mind. It was common knowledge when Mary's husband had barbarously illused her with the scold's bridle, for her tongue would be too pained to take victuals or speak.

Weston realised he should have said so himself and frowned. 'What would you have her asked?'

I held my head tall and, in the way he did disrespect me before, I did not look boldly at Weston but at the jury. 'I would have her tell what she heard the coachman say, for I only said he told me so.'

The moment I said it, I rather I had not, though none remarked on the blunder of my owning my book yet again. But then, they need not if they had already weighed against me.

Weston raised his voice high above it all. 'That is no evidence...,' he said. Then louder, 'That is no evidence, I say, for the coachman might have been here, if you had not sent him away.' With that, Mary was dismissed.

Shouts of laughter filled that room so busy with noise that my ears buzzed.

'Nay, I did not. Let his wife testify I did not send him away!' I said.

Captain Richardson again stood as he had stood before, puffed up like a fighting cock. 'They have both sworn before us that she,' he pointed an ironic finger, fattened from his prisoners' pockets at me, 'gave them money and told them she would maintain them.'

He did turn my charitable deed against me, twisting and turning the facts as they had heretofore. But I was not a priest that could rise above such malice. I balled my fists at my side and spoke through clam-teeth to hide my anger.

'You are not an evidence against me, you are not sworn.'

The captain's smug smile did not upturn his moustache in the way a good smile should do. Any dubious kindness he had once shown me was gone. 'But this that I say is already sworn.'

Weston said, 'Go on with your witnesses.'

They did not allow me to call Mary Johnson to prove her fruitless search to find my witnesses, nor would they let me have Mrs Corral answer as to whether or not I had sent her husband away, for they said it did not signify since I could have done it without her knowledge.

If they would not allow me prove my words, I did not know how I might defend myself. I could only cast myself on the mercy of the court now.

'I have done then, My Lord for, not having time to get my witnesses, I cannot make my defence so fully as I would have done.' I raised my chin with my hands once more holding the rail before me. 'I desire you to consider I am a poor ignorant woman. I did not think further than publishing what others had told me. So, if I have erred or offended, I have done so in ignorance.'

For the first time since we were in court together, Weston faced me equally, but his voice held only derision. 'I do verily believe there are more wits than yours concerned in this book, Though you bear the name, I am sure you do not have wit enough that it is yours alone, though you acknowledge your part in it. By doing so, you are against the King, for you must know the King hath set out a proclamation that no books shall be printed without a license.'

I had waited on one to say such thing, though I durst bring it to the trial myself, for I stood on quicksand with it. 'I never heard it. I was under close confinement when the King set it out.'

Weston was triumphant. 'No, I deny that, for you were set free the first day of Trinity-term, and the proclamation came out towards the end of it.' He seemed more knowledgeable of my business than I gave him credit for.

I could not remember all of it, but I was certain he was mistaken in that; Trinity Term ended the day after my release, and I was not out of the company of my husband and children all that day, and that was at home. 'I was not…' I started saying.

'She now does confess she knows of it,' said the triumphant Attorney General over me, 'because she speaks of the time the King made the proclamation, yet that was before her book was written. She wrote her book knowing she did it against the King's will.'

I had verily set myself into a trap, and had been found in it! I looked to Mr Collins, my counsel. I had nothing to lose by roping him in to aid me now. 'I desire my counsel speak for me.'

Mr Collins, that had yet done nothing for me, did nothing more. 'I have nought to say for her,' he said. He turned to me. 'And if you had said less for yourself it would have been better.'

The light shone in Weston's eye. He nimbly summed up

my case. 'He says he hath nothing to say for you. And so there is but one question: guilty or not guilty? The indictment is that you published this libel, and if the matter of it be so proved, as is done, then what can counsel say but that you can disprove the witnesses?'

'Well, My Lord,' I said, 'then I beseech you consider that I am a woman and deal with me in mercy as well as in justice.'

'Mrs. Cellier,' said Weston. 'I have said before, I have reason to suspect that, though you bear the name on this libel, some of your wicked priests are the authors of it. I am not noted to use great severity towards man nor woman, whether or not of your party but, when I see so much malice as is comprised in your book, then I think it not severe that you, who stand at the stake for all, must bear the blame of all. If you will tell us who assisted you in this wicked business, that will be something towards the mitigation of your fine, but if you will take it on yourself, you must suffer the consequence.'

'I beseech you, My Lord,' I said, clasping my hands together, 'have some compassion! His Majesty acknowledged before the council that I had suffered for him. I lost my father and my brother both in a day for him and, if you have no compassion for me, have some commiseration for my loyal parents that lost their estates for him.'

If the judges had any kind of tenderness at all, I prayed my plea would blunt the severity of punishment on me, for now punishment was certain. I had not seen any kindness in any of them, nor did I expect any. Weston's next words proved me right.

'If you have done service for His Majesty and thereby deserved dispensation of him, His Majesty would not fail to recompense you for it, for he is generous of nature, but here we are to proceed according to the rules of law.'

'But pray have some mercy in your justice,' I said one more time, desiring him to change his mind. I wrung my hands in anguish as he dismissed further words from me by facing my supposed twelve peers.

'Gentlemen of the jury,' he said, 'this gentlewoman, the prisoner, stands indicted…'

John Ainger, the indifferent juror, took off his unfashionable brown felt hat and clamped it to his chest in apology. 'Sir, we have not heard one word that hath been said.'

The courtroom thundered and roared with laughter and shouts, as the words of the jury speaker provided them with new fuel.

'Not heard!' Weston wore his horror for all to see. 'That is extraordinary! Why did you not say so! It had been well if you had told us this before.' Weston slipped a finger beneath the front of his periwig and scratched, jiggling it so it did not sit as straight as it should. 'How very strange.'

The Lord Mayor opened and closed his mouth a few times, perhaps not thinking of anything to say, before banging his gavel hard on the wooden block on the table. When that did not immediately quieten the courtroom, he resorted to standing and shouting, 'Silence! Anyone not silent will be removed immediately!'

The Lord Mayor pointed to those that were the noisiest and the men at arms moved to take them out. They struggled and shouted, but the rest of the court became serious. And quiet. Into that hush, Weston spoke again.

'I will acquaint you with as much of the evidence as falls under my information. The business is this, she stands indicted here for writing and publishing of a very scandalous libel. But pray did not you hear Penny prove that she sold it?'

John Ainger said, 'We heard the three first witnesses.'

'That was all that was necessary to hear. Therein was the proof of her libel!'

Nevertheless, Baron Weston took the next ten minutes to explain in full what had gone before. He did not spare me as a villain most terrible in his summation. This time the court was listening. After naming the book as the libel, he placed the evidence into several parts.

The first part, he said, was an insinuation against the Protestant religion, saying how I had turned from Protestants, and accused Protestants of murdering the King, being the first King Charles, and other ungodly deeds. He asked by what right did

I pretend they were called Protestants, and turn Papist, when so many more of that religion adhered to the loyal party of the King?

Then he took the longest part to describe how false was such villainous insinuation; a more rhapsodic speech he could not have made. Rather than nourish and teach seditious principles, he said, there was more fidelity, honesty and generous trust amongst Protestants, than among all the nations of the world.

'For, is it not so, friends in other places will be no better than our enemies here?' he said, raising our countrymen above all others, except the Germans that are famed for their honesty and integrity to one another. He then described the French, the Italian, the Spaniard, or any sort of the Levantine people as living 'like so many wolves, especially in those places where the Popish religion is professed'.

'Pray, My Lord, I say, I only called them Protestants,' I said, for he had missed that part. He took no notice of it now, but clasped the front of his jacket and trod the floor before the jury and went on without a break in his words.

'Now after this insinuation, there is another part of the book recited in the indictment. It is common knowledge that the Popish party labour mightily to cast the horrid barbarous murder of the magistrate, Sir Edmundbury Godfrey, off themselves and onto other persons. For the plot is a thing of so heinous a nature that, if it should stick, it would make their party odious to all mankind.

'Mrs Cellier hath taken upon herself to tell the world that Prance, a principal witness, was tortured, and his evidence against those persons executed for Sir Godfrey's murder was false evidence, extorted from him in gaol by ill and cruel usage.

'As well you know, the laws of the land do not permit torture, the last of that kind being the Jesuit Edmund Campion, stretched upon the rack in the twentieth year of Queen Elizabeth's reign. None other has been racked in any of the reigns since then, not in that of King James nor in that of the first King Charles, and Mighty God in Heaven knows that there hath been none in this King's reign!'

At this, Weston stopped, turned himself to the jury and held his hands wide with the full drama of holding the stage. He paused only briefly, then he rode on:

'Our government is the most lawful and merciful as any nation under Heaven. But, here is Mrs Cellier saying such ways were used against Prance contrary to the law. If this was so, why did she not proceed in a legal way against the persons she supposed made these transgressions of the law? Was it not her duty? If there had been such persons, she ought to have indicted them, for they are highly punishable for such extraordinary ways!'

Then Weston described the events of the day we heard Prance scream; of how Harris, the turnkey, said it was a woman in labour then turned us away when we offered our help; and of how the gaolers dare not tell what was the noise, but that they could not endure it; and how the prisoners heard him cry, 'What would you have me confess? Would you have me belie myself? I know nothing of it', and such other words as these.

'Whereupon, we called Prance,' said Weston.

Weston then described how Prance was today questioned, and upon oath told how he was kindly used in prison, that he was under no compulsion, and that my book was a libel against the Government. Then he recalled how Fowler had turned in Corral the coachman, for his part in the murder of Sir Godfrey. And how, on examination by the Lord Mayor before today, Corral had denied any threat against him in gaol, or attempted corruption of him by the laying down of five hundred pounds, with the offer of more if he should confess.

Weston walked to the middle of the bar, behind which sat the jury, and the spirit that made him passionately pace the floor moved into his hands and face so that he became most animated.

'And Fowler,' said Weston, 'testifies that he was never in gaol with Corral in his life, never with him, nor with any noblemen, and he never saw any such cruel usage as Mrs Cellier wrote. The whole story plays false.'

The last part of it, but the worst, Weston explained, was how I had defamed all persons in my libel, and monstrously defamed and scandalized His Majesty the King and his government.

'She wrote,' he said, reading from his notes, 'Whenever His Majesty shall please to make it as safe and honourable to speak the truth, as it is apparent it hath been gainful and meritorious to do the contrary, their villainy will not want witnesses to testify the truth of more than she had written.

'She supposes, that the King,' he continued, 'by the countenancing of lies, and giving pensions to liars, chokes the truth, and makes it dangerous for those that know the truth to divulge it to the world, which is a very vile scandal upon the King and government.'

With his jaw clamped shut and the muscles in his cheek bulging, Weston grabbed the bar in front of him and, like a man with a fever, came so close he saw himself in each juror's eye. He had not heretofore shown such force of manner.

'And, that still is not the least of it!' he said, 'She said she could have written more!'

The silence that followed this speech was not broken, as it had been throughout the whole trial, by shouts and laughter and persons in all places talking. It went on. In it, all the eyes of the court came and rested on me, until the hatred and anger and desire for my death forced me to look down at my hands, still clasping the bar in front of me. I could not bear to see them so openly exposed, and took them into my cloak. One of the judges put down his fan and, though the clunk of it was not loud, it was heard by all. As I feared was my heart beating in my chest. I had never so dearly desired the return of the noise.

I feared the condemnation of my very soul, by every man and woman there, would be upheld by the Lord as he did all judgements made on Earth, and I near fell to fainting. What had I done but good to deserve such reproach?

It was, perhaps, not so long a time as I thought it, for then Weston continued to talk as if that long silence had not happened at all. I lost hope I could in some way turn it around.

'I must tell you this,' Weston said, 'these are the matters of the libel, in which the clauses are truly set down in the indictment, for I did examine them one by one. The proof of her ownership comes from four sworn witnesses. Downing, the printer, has testified that Mrs Cellier said she wrote the book, and paid for the publishing and correcting of the first twenty two folios. Mr Penny bought her book, and asked her if it was hers, and she told him it was, and that she could have written more. Mr Stevens, the messenger of the press, saw her sell her books on more than one occasion, and was told by the printer that it was her book. And Fowler of the Half-Moon Tavern bought two of the books from her after he was told he was famous in it.

Now, you might doubt she was the author of the book,' he said, 'but the manner she did own it at the publication, by selling it as hers, is to me under the notion of express evidence of the fact. I leave to you as judges of that fact, and expect your verdict in the case'

I looked up to see Weston walk from the jury and return to the table where he had kept my book and his notes.

Mr Attorney General said, 'There are three matters in the indictment. First, that she writ it; second, that she caused it to be printed; and third, that she caused it to be published. Now if you find her guilty of any one of these, though I think you have heard evidence enough for all, you are to find her guilty.'

Then Ainger, the spokesman of the jury, desired they might have the book with them.

Weston said, 'They can have neither the book nor any paper else unless she will consent to it. Mrs. Cellier, will you consent?'

I could see no reason for giving them any thing they wished, if they wished to condemn me with it, so I said, 'No.'

'Then they cannot have it by law,' said Weston.

The jury returned after half an hour, a trifling while to discuss the facts fully. They could not have time to talk about any of it, whether they thought me guilty or not guilty.

The Counsellor of the Crown asked, 'How say you, is Elizabeth Cellier guilty of the writing, printing, and publishing of the libel for which she stands indicted, or not guilty?'

'Guilty,' said Ainger.

There was a great shout of triumph and rejoicing. Did none care that it was not the truth that was tested, but only that I wrote about it? Nay, they would rather silence me.

'She must stand committed to receive the judgement of the court,' said Weston.

'Will you give me leave to speak a word?' I had nothing to lose by asking.

Now Weston had the answer he looked for, he seemed to be less hard. 'I cannot give you any judgement, for by the custom of the city, that is to be done by the recorder or his deputy. So, what you will say to the court, you must say on Monday when the Sessions are done.'

I wished those that condemned me to hear my words, and so I spoke regardless. 'What I would say is only this. I am a woman, and wherein I offended, I offended out of ignorance. And if the offence be mine, let not others suffer for me. Have mercy in judgment, and consider my loyal parents and relations, and the services they did His Majesty. Let this fault be wiped out by that service and duty I and my parents paid him or, at least let the punishment of this offence be mitigated, in consideration that all my life, ever since I had the first use of reason, I have been a loyal subject.

'These things will be considered on Monday, not now,' said Weston haughtily over the jeers and taunts of the courtroom.

24

11th day of September, 1680 (after the trial)

'Hang 'er! 'Hang 'er from the rafters!' shouted one man, with his head gleaming like an egg and not a single hair.

'In the stocks! Let us have her!' called another, better-spoken man, whom I did not see.

'Ay, midwife, here's a stone relic with a cross you can pray to… here, take this!'

This woman's voice was not unlike a frog's. A stone flew toward me across the court, I turned and it hit me on the shoulder. Everyone laughed and the crowd grew rowdy. I looked to see who had thrown the stone but, in so many faces, I saw only the delight that I was to be punished. Any reason was reason enough. I looked down and saw the stone that hit me lying on the floor. Sure enough, there was paint on it that looked like the long body and one arm of a fast drawn cross. The rest of it was hidden on the side of the stone I could not see.

'Oi, Bess, give 'er another 'un!'

None would have stopped the zealous Bess throw another stone. Rather, they would have filled her hands with pebbles from the river shore. The sheriff's men laughed. The judges talked and laughed between themselves, purposefully taking no notice of the goings on before them. Why should they not let the mob have me, and save them the trouble?

Thinking of my speech, if they did not give me leave to speak when it was my trial, they would not give it to me on Monday, when they were already done with me and my fate was decided. I was indebted to the Lord that I was not wholly denied to speak for my cause today. I was unlikely to have any other chance.

Perhaps they would yet treat me with leniency. I was found guilty, and for that I must pay penance, but punishment for libel was not death as it always was for treason. Nay, I should not carry hope, for, if the mood in the court were the basis on which to judge, they would give me the most severe punishment the law would allow. If my fortune followed others that published an unlawful book, I would be stoned to death on the pillory. In the meantime, I was certain to re-acquaint myself with one of Newgate's rooms.

For the first time since I was judged, I dared look for Pierre in the rowdy crowd. When I found him, realisation of what I had done pierced my gut and heart as a hot poker. There he stood, in the midst of a lively group of well-dressed gentlemen that jostled him in their man revelry with no respect for his age. They would have treated him far worse had they known he was my husband. He seemed not to notice or care that he was pitched and tossed like a small boat on a stormy sea between them.

In the stead of the strong husband I had recently remembered respect for, stood a wizened and broken man. His eyes held neither sadness nor anger when they met mine. It was if the last years of his life, his *raison d'être*, were leeched from him. Indeed, no blood stained his face, and his lack of colour gave him the appearance of a laid out corpse. Aching guilt coursed through my belly. I had done this to him. I had taken his life from him. I had flouted his request and written the book against his good judgement.

And… I took myself from him by what I had done. As he had said I would. I did not long enough consider the fairness to him and the children. Perhaps blame could fall on my vanity, for my recent success in court, when I was on trial for treason, had given me false air of competence and invulnerability. I knew the possible consequences of my actions yet my pride had ridden over them.

Looking at the trail of what I had done, I saw with clarity how my fate was pinched with theirs, and my boldness affected them as it did me. Why did I not see it before? I was married to Pierre in more than his bed. I was confidant, business partner and mother to his children. I had wronged him like no other. He depended on my learning of the law in the first years together, and now, when his need was greatest, I was deserting him.

How would he go up against those that tried to trick him in business? Or those that clammed shut their purse when they should pay? My vanity! Oh my vanity! And my sweet, sweet children, what would become of them if Pierre could not care for them, or if he should die when I was gone from them? The burden of what I had done lay heavily upon me.

'I will go home then, and come back Monday,' I said.

Weston was quick to reply, 'No, you do not chose your own requital. You will be committed till then.'

Then came a cry as shrill as an animal of the night that caused my skin to prickle. 'No, no! This cannot be! Do not chain her! Confine her not! She is my life!' He cried then. He cried like I never saw any person cry.

I shivered.

It was Pierre. He knew, as I knew, what would happen to me in prison, guilty of speaking against them. It was as a licence for them to do as they would with me. But the punishment was also his.

'Pierre!' I reached my hands to touch him though he were as if in another country and could do naught to save me now. Richardson grabbed the arm, pinching me, and a man that was the sheriff's assistant at the compter in Cheapside took hold of the other. 'Forgive me, Pierre. The truth was not mine to own!'

The words were all in the world I could say, but were not the ones I would choose. I yearned to tell him I chose to travel a different road but for only a short stretch: our paths would lie side by side until we met again, and that he was right and I should not have meddled. I longed to take every written word back, until, as a fog coming down heavy upon me, surrounding me, memories of the disgusting treatment of prisoners came back. The smell of the holes in Corral's legs filled my nose and I knew I could not have done otherwise.

Pierre did not stop his sobbing. One of Captain Richardson's men shouted, 'Take that squealing pig outside!' They grabbed hold of him and dragged him out of the side door, crying and helpless as a newborn. His whimpers peeled back the veil of my composure so that I was nearly undone. I had done him such wrong.

The more I struggled, the tighter they held me and the more they hurt me. When they had him away out of sight and I could no longer hear him. I was alone in the world. Without Pierre, I was nothing. All fight went from me. I stopped struggling against my captures, lifted my head, and said, 'What gives you pause, my good man? My room for the night awaits me!'

'You cannot talk your way out of this as you did the noose!' The sheriff yanked my arm.

'Neither will you pay your way with coins taken from a book that spoke false against us, Midwife.' Richardson spoke between clamped teeth. 'You know what is to become of you?'

Richardson could not be clearer. For speaking against him and his guards, not only could I expect revengeful treatment in that darksome place, but he would take the greatest of pleasure if it came out worse for me.

Screams of that poor tortured man, Prance – though he lied I knew the truth of it – came to me then and made me cringe back like a dog in his hold. What if they were to place me in his stead? What if they would torture me as they did him? What if they put me on the rack or made me wear a hat of spikes? How would I bear it! They might put me in the Strong Room, with the rats and the putrid stench of rotting bodies! Truly, I could not bear it! I begun to pray as I had never prayed before, but my prayers were interrupted by a brutal tug forward by my guards.

I stumbled. They returned me to my feet.

Then I did the only thing I could do. I walked with my head proud as they allowed me, two tough men with blacksmith's muscles, riding roughshod over a defenceless old woman. I suspected the way they pulled and pushed me between them was so it seemed to the crowd I put up a struggle. I allowed them to play me as a puppet, for I did not, could not, fight them. It would only have added to their pleasure.

Had the judges still been present, I was certain they would turn a blind eye to what next happened, so I did not wish them there.

A women wearing a familiar red cloak spat on me and snarled, 'Popish traitor!'

I had not time to grasp the knife of hate that cut my heart before another person did the same. This time the spittle fell close to my eye. As earlier, I could not wipe it away. Richardson and the other man each held an arm at both the elbow and the wrist. They dragged me toward the door along an aisle between iron barriers, equal in strength against the half-starved drudges from Cheapside as the lords and ladies from the West End.

It transpired, the bar was no more protection for either prisoner or public than a stone on the ground was a barrier to walking a country path. As we passed, a merchant of large stature climbed over it and jumped to the ground in my path. His clothes showed signs of travel: foreign lace, a hat of Dutch style, and breeches more loose than was fashionable.

Richardson grinned, exposing his rare broken and rotten teeth for the first time. Either some prisoner had fought back against his tyranny or he too often found himself in trouble at his local public house.

'What would you do to her?' he asked, not hiding his desire for severity in whatsoever it would be.

'That whore is the Devil's work! Hang her!' He pointed at me, as if any doubted his meaning. 'She sets herself against the King. When she failed to take his life, she besmirched his name and that of our countrymen.'

'Morcock.' Richardson turned to the man on my other arm, "Tis most unfortunate our eyes are only two and we cannot see what hides behind our backs.' He winked at the other man. No other part of his face moved.

Morcock answered with deceptive lightness and so fast, showing that this was not rehearsed as a play.

'Aye, Captain,' he said. "Tis regrettable we are not blessed with the many eyes of that long-legged insect the spider, for then we might see what treachery lies deep in this tangled web in every direction.' The men laughed at their secret, but I understood their code, as well as the merchant. They then both turned their backs on the man, as if discussing something together, whilst leaving me facing him.

Then came the spy-rat Stevens, so I was surrounded by four men, and derided by many more behind them.

Stevens spat the words, 'You weather-beaten lying whore. What gives you cause to blacken my name! How did I wrong you?'

As certain as the cart follows the horse, if I had defended myself and told how he had tried to catch me out and tarnish me with false accusations (for I never did admit to writing my book to him, no matter what he said), my life would be worse than dire. And, no matter what they did to me, there was no thing I could do or say to prevent them from doing what they would to me. I could only worsen my situation by adding to their ire. So, I pursed my lips and refused to be baited.

The spittle fell, a tear of derision, down my cheek.

'Talk, woman! Silence does not befit you! What ails your tongue; can it not move with a fork in it?'

'Make her sing!' shouted my good friend Bess, the croaking creature with a good arm for throwing stones. 'I never heard a snake sing!'

I silently cursed the ungodly toad for wishing me tortured. Such words might give any of these men the confidence to draw the blood she bayed for.

I saw the merchant throw his fist at my chest. I shifted my body so he struck my arm instead.

'Go to Italy where you belong, Popish whore!'

A woman ducked under the bar and came at me. She grabbed the corner of my old cloak and tugged at it. My beloved cloak. I prayed it would not give. With the carrying voice of a boat horn, she said, 'Take off your cloak, whore! 'Tis the scarlet for a midwife, not a loose-lipped strumpet!'

They all laughed. I swallowed down the lump that seemed forever to stick in my craw and stop my breath. They mocked my profession. It would not be the first or last that the two trades were pinched as one.

How dare they mock the profession that was all I had in the

years after losing my first husband at the Battle of Leghorn, then again when my second husband sought the excitement of a foreign land leaving me to fend for the children and myself. The trade Pierre allowed me practice even when I had no further need of it.

Though my notebooks recorded so many losses, my ledgers attested to the wives and babies I had saved over the years. I was married to the art as much as to my husband. I could not delight more in the precious gift the Lord gave with each new life in the world, and for the skill he gave me to save mother and babe when delivery was difficult. That gave me purpose and earned me esteem amongst the Catholics.

It twisted my gut to hear such loose talk of my kind. But this was not a thing I had luxury to dwell on at this time. I should keep my wits on their game. Nay, I would not show them fear. I would not give them satisfaction of that.

Other persons climbed beneath the bar on either side of the aisle and gathered around me. The woman pulled at my cloak harder. Despite every intention otherwise, I could not help but defend myself.

'Unhand me!' I cried. I tried to pull the cloak from her hand by stepping back, but it was curled tight in her fingers and all that my action achieved was to make the Beast of the crowd more rowdy.

Then a hairy arm reached behind my head and grabbed the hood of my cloak, pulling it with such strength the clasp cut sharp into my throat like the back of a sword. Still feigning ignorance, neither Richardson nor Morcock did a thing to prevent it. Whatever the Beast did to me, these two would neither see nor oblige themselves to prevent. They had openly invited the crowd to do as they would with me.

My own cloak strangled me so I thought I would die. I could not draw breath and lights sparkled before my eyes. Darkness filled in from the edges. I could do nothing to help myself except turn my neck and protect my throat but a little; my arms were held still and I could not undo the clasp or pull away. What irony if I should die by the cloak I lived by.

My head turned and turned with the lack of air, and I fell into a whirlpool, the relief of near darkness, a faint. Another person, or perhaps the same, grabbed my cap, pulling the pins from my hair so it fell loose to my shoulders. Hands, all over me, pulled and tugged at my clothes and any thing that hung loose. I no longer cared. Life was distant.

I was back in '78, with the Atterburys beating the very life from me. The blows were theirs as well as of all here. Even from the dark place I hid, I felt the pain, not of being struck, but of being so hated for a truth they could not bear. Still, I was held tight and did not fall. I was a punch bag for all fear and hatred.

'Give her the boot!' A woman far away wished for a piece of me, but could not reach. As if that was their signal, any that once held back were all over me.

I opened my eyes a crack and saw boots and shoes kick at my legs until my skin tore. My legs no longer held me. I stood only by the support of Richardson and Morcock that, rather than moving me from this lynch mob, shoved me amongst them.

Nails scratched at my face, and I closed my eyes to save them. My scalp screamed when some of my hair was pulled from the roots. My weak whisper of, 'Lord save me!' was lost in raucous jeers and taunts and laughter and bared teeth. Then the clasp of my cloak gave way, and coldness surrounded me as the mark of my profession was whipped away, leaving my soul naked and vulnerable.

'My cloak!' I tried to grab it back, but it was too soon gone from my reach. I had only desolation to wrap around me. If once I had fight, it deserted me. Why did the Lord God not take me now, and save me from further pain? I prayed silently for release, but release did not come. If he would not take me, why would he not let me fall into that darkness that surrounded me? If he had forsaken me, why should I care where I fell.

Thank the Lord Pierre was taken away and was spared to see what they did to me! If it did not break his heart, he might have been so angry he would have tried to protect me, and would also have been beaten. His body would not have taken what mine already had.

But I also yearned that he were here to defend me.

That anyone would defend me.

I hung from the arms of the two gaolers that still did not remove me from this unlawful beating. Still the puppets near me did as others bid them:

'Give her one from me!'

'Get me a handful of hair. A fairer relic I will not find!'

'Take that shame from her face!'

Laugh all you like, you will not break me, I thought from a far-away place. One day, people might think for themselves, not think what they are told to think! Not do as they are told to do.

That day was not this day.

Some person, perhaps two, had my hair again, pulling all ways, so I thought I might lose my scalp. The pulling, and kicking, and punching would have unbalanced me had I not been held so tight upright. As if realising that, perhaps on a sign to each other, as one they both let go of me, and I fell face down to the floor and caught a mouthful of so much dry dust, the more I coughed the more I suffocated.

I was straightaway caught in a storm, buffeted and battered in every direction. My legs and arms took hits all over. Why would the Lord not take me from this pain! At the least, blows no longer maimed my front and, if I died here, I would still have enough of my face for them to know who it was they martyred.

Not for the sake of a conscience – a mob had none – my slow murder suddenly ceased. I was suddenly grabbed by my arms and pulled to my feet. I could not stand for my legs were dead to me.

Someone, Perhaps Richardson or Morcock, I dared not open my eyes to see, placed his head through my right armpit, and heaved me up from the ground. There was silence, or seemed to be. For a moment I thought he had stuck a knife in my chest, but soon realised the pain came from within. My ribs, broken once before, were broken twice over.

'C'mon Morcock. Quick, grab t'other arm.'

So it was Richardson that had plucked me from the ground. The other one, his apprentice, followed suit and lifted the other side. My toes caught and bounced on the floorboards as they walked. Through a crack between my lashes, I watched the ground pass beneath me as if I floated face down in a river, the floor a blurred riverbed far below. Perhaps I could die now. Had I not punishment enough?

'You there, what betide this woman?' The well spoken voice might have been familiar, but I could not recall whence it came, nor from whom. The next voice I knew well. It was Richardson's.

'She fainted M'Lord. We're taking her back to Newgate to recover her.'

'Begad! Fainted you say? She appeared to be in fine spirit earlier!'

'It must have been the heat that did it, sir.'

'Really? I thought she fared well in it before.'

'Or maybe it was her husband, Sir. He made such a lot of noise so they had to take him away.'

'Strange. Very strange. I cannot see a strong woman such as this fainting over such a thing. It appears she has been truly raked over. What happened here, man? And where be her red cloak – the mark of her trade she is wont to wear – she recently wore in the stand?'

So, he did know of me. Who was this man?

After a short silence Morcock said, 'A man ran away with it, My Lord. We could not recover it, because we were minding the prisoner.'

'She has a name, use it. But it is a shame about the cloak, I know how fond of it she is. I suppose she will not see it again. Well, be sure to take good care, and I mean very good care, of Mrs Cellier. I am certain she now recognises the madness of writing such a scandalous book, and I am further certain I would not wish any bad thing to happen to her in your care, else it might be misconstrued that her outrageous accusations held truth!'

'She will have good care while she stays with us,' growled Richardson.

'See that she does, good man. I may pay her a visit on the morrow, or perhaps the day following, to see how she recovers from this…' his deliberate pause marked his disbelief, '…faint.'

'Yes M'Lord. You are very welcome.' Richardson moved as if he bowed.

In the dawn and dusk of darkness, I silently thanked the man from the depths of my heart. By saying he might visit he may yet save my life if I did not die of my wounds today. And if he did not visit, it would keep them from doing their worst to me knowing someone kept a watchful eye on them. I again tried to place the voice but, again, failed. Whosoever my guardian Angel was, my debt to him might go forever unpaid.

25

13th day of September, 1680

Two days of lying in Newgate, at the mercy of Captain Richardson and his wife, had done little to improve my body or my spirits. My ribs only missed stabbing my heavy heart for want of trying. Having faced death in court but three months since, I could not find any fear left in me for the sentence this Monday morning. The scheme of my fate was already decided.

And the pain of being bumped in a cart, despite that the surgeon said I was unfit to be moved, was more unbearable than had I walked.

Pain filled me.

My wounds tormented me until not a part of me did not scream with them but, despite my distress, I took satisfaction that the court was not so full this day, it being early and most persons having chores and living to do before the sun grew too hot.

A knight of the realm, that I knew to be Sir George Jeffries, an avid supporter of the King's cause, presided over the courtroom from the dais at the front. I was impressed by the elegance of his figure. He sported a periwig so long it could barely be considered fashionable yet created fashion of its own; long lace collars, I was sure Customs House must have examined closely; fine, yet suitably sombre, black shirt and pantaloons, draped closely with a knee-length velvet brown cloak. In the case any mistook his place as not pinched with the Royal Court, he wore an elaborate gold chain draped over the shoulders of his cloak to lend him to regal society.

The act of speech did not mar this young recorder's countenance, but his Welsh dialect made him mere man, though a formidable one. He was as straight as an arrow to its target, and he faced me most seriously.

'Mrs. Cellier,' he said. 'The court doth think fit, for example sake, that a fine of one thousand pounds be put upon you, and that you be committed in execution till that thousand pounds be paid.'

One thousand pounds? It might as well have been ten thousand, I could neither find it nor pay it!

Jeffries had not finished.

'And because a pecuniary mulct is not a sufficient recompense to the justice you have offended, the court doth likewise pronounce against you that you be put on the pillory three several days, in three different public places.'

The pillory, thrice? Atop of a fine I could never pay? This, the sentence for a few pages of truth, yet, for a lie, great riches and security could be found! I did not have the wherewithal to protest and, even if I had, there would have been no use in it. I looked to a space far away in front of me.

Jeffries swung his arm toward me and fleshed out the details of my sad fortune to the court.

'In the first place, to answer to Mrs Cellier having published and sold this abominable book from her house, it is thought fit that she stand at the May-pole, in the Strand, which is as near her own house as convenient. Let it be for an hour's space between the hours of twelve and one on market day, when there be many witnesses to her shame. The second time, she should stand the like space of time in Convent-Garden on an equally public day. The third time, she should stand an hour at Charing-Cross.'

Cruel! So cruel! I might as well be dead. My character, and my standing in society, was shot! Worse, neither would I have opportunity to redeem myself, for I would be locked away in a dark dungeon, while those I valued would be forced to think me contemptible. But none could make me take back my words. I could not even if I would. Those truths, they had been read by many within and without the court and, though I, the author, might be contained in Newgate for securing them to paper, they were now set free to find fertile fields of thought in which to grow, if that was God's will.

I tried to hold my head high, but such agony as I had rarely felt stabbed me in all places of my chest and heart, so that I had to fold myself over once more to lessen it.

But, what of Pierre? My punishment was his punishment. As my husband and master, his name would be blackened for my deeds. His trade might suffer and our children along with it. For, if he could not trade, he could not feed them. He was not in court to hear my sentence. Had he verily forsaken me?

'And, in the next place,' Jeffries raised his eyebrows at me, 'she must find sureties for good behaviour in her life. This means, Mrs Cellier, someone must come forward and vouch for you.'

Would any speak out for one found guilty of libel against the King? Perhaps none would pledge themselves for my good behaviour and I would be abandoned. But then, since I could not pay the fine and be free, I had little need to concern myself over this.

Jeffries looked down as he turned a leaf of his book. 'And it is ordered that, in every place where she stands on the pillory, some parcels of her books shall be burnt by the hands of the common hangman where she can see them. Last, a notice stating her crime should be placed upon the pillory over her head so that all will know the punishment for dealing with the Devil.'

With no further ado, and with no commotion in the courtroom, I was taken by the arm and led back to the cart with more kindness than I was given to expect. Something of the quiet unsettled me. Perhaps it was that, now they knew how I was to suffer at the hand of the country, they no longer felt the need to punish me further. Or perhaps they had sympathy for for my plight, that I could barely walk let alone sit in a cart.

If I were to be pilloried, perhaps it would kill me and I should have no need to suffer further.

26

18th day of September, 1680

One seven-night ago, with or without his intention, a man had prevented the crowd from finishing me. This day, none could prevent my punishment even if their hearts desired it so. But their hearts would not desire it. It would be their pleasure to set the anger and fear of all that is horrid in this age against me. I had myself seen some so mobbed on the pillory they died before the end of the day. One hour might be enough to end me, but thanks be to the Lord God Almighty it was one hour and no longer!

I held my hand to my stomach, which quietly complained with hunger for the first time in five days. I had eaten but a bare morsel of bread or two since the trial, the agony of my injuries filling my stomach and leaving no corner for appetite. Nor had my gaolers shown me any good will. They gave me water enough I would not keel over if that gentleman, for gentleman he surely was, came to visit me. Enough and no more. The man did not come, but I was thankful he said it *could* be so, for else I might already have been dead.

My mind was sharp, despite my poor condition, on this my day of my punishment. Under my hand, in the stead of my own plump and softening body, I felt the bladder of another, I had procured from Mary at great risk to herself. I pressed and felt the blood inside it move against my palm. My last effort to save myself, when none other had worked. Petitions to the King received no answer. Letters to parliament and influential persons were either without reply or were returned by the messenger unread. I was alone. Not even Pierre had come. Would that he had cut me off for my disobedience, for then he would not be taken down with me.

But, still, he kept my strength from me by his absence.

I shifted from where I had several hours sat in the corner of the dark room fortifying myself for the imminent ordeal. Each day, marking the sun's daily rise and fall, a single blessed beam of light crawled the same path down the wall, over the flea infested bed and across the floor toward the boarded window before disappearing at dusk. For the last two days, when it came near my head on the pillow, I placed my face in the cold light, relishing the link to the outside world. It was as if God had sent this message of hope to take me through the dark days, and what was to come.

Now, I held out my right hand and caught the light in my palm so a spot glowed, then, despite the pain of moving, I raised the hand a few inches towards its source. It was like placing my hand in a falling stream, and catching a piece of the world's soul, a soul so pure it gave me strength to stand up for truth. If I had to die for it, then so be it. That was for God to decide. Only He knew if it was His time to take me. The epiphany filled me with strength, I took the hand from the mound over my belly and found the crucifix around my neck, closed my eyes and prayed for deliverance.

It was not until I sniffed a tear from the tip of my nose did I realise I was crying. With the salty tear, I drew in air thick with the stench of urine and faeces. The marriage of tears and human waste made me gag. Even now, the air clung like a burr to my nostrils, lips and throat worse than any street stink. There was nowhere in this foul place I could avoid it, though the rats did not seem to mind. I was mindful not to break the dried dung crusts and release fresh odour. If only I had some lavender perfume to sprinkle on my hand-kerchief and relieve my sensibilities.

I waited.

Motes of dust hung in the air, not moving, because fresh air had no place here in this hole.

I waited.

The beam of light cut the bed's shadow as a sword slices a man's shirt.

I waited.

Then came the sound of metal on metal as the key to the outer door grated against lock. Then came the creak of metal hinges. And footsteps. They were coming for me. The little ray of light was not enough to show the way, but still I stood and faced the door. I was ready with my scheme.

The footsteps stopped outside, and again I waited with neither breath nor movement.

Keys jangled as the keeper found the right one on the ring. It was only marginally brighter in the corridor outside, barely enough to see the walls, and not enough to see the detail in the keys. He tried several before he found the right one. Then the lock clicked, the door creaked open, and a sun-warmed waft of air wrapped around me and, before I could do any other thing, I breathed it into me and let it fill me with its evocation of freedom.

The air came as a letter with two sides. On the first was thoughts of freedom, but the other side carried the threat of the stocks I would soon face. I breathed in the freedom slow and deep. The breath was so sweet I forgot my design, I had so carefully planned, and took a moment to be thankful God had not yet called me to his side and I was able to take this breath.

Over the last days, between pain and more pain, I dwelled on being imminently locked in the stocks outside my own house for a whole hour. That same mob at the trial would enjoy the spectacle of a pillorying equally as well as any hanging or beheading, and would be sure to be there at the Strand today. Unless he had taken to the countryside, my husband and children would be at home in nearby Arundel Street, a matter of a short walk from there.

The punishment was meant not merely to castigate me and cast disrepute on my character, but, as well, to spur my husband to whip his unbridled wife so that she would keep to the law of the land, no matter that the law be mistaken. My children should not be forced to see me so blackened, for no honest person could find fault in what I had done, and they did not deserve to believe it so. Nor even my Pierre. I prayed he would keep them from this sight and not sully their innocence with my so-called wrongs.

Just as I had witnessed the hangings of good Catholics these last years, so that they be not alone and have a friend amongst all others, good folk would come to witness and report what came to pass today for the sake of adding weight in the scales against false witnesses. These would not wish to see me suffer, but would do so for the sake of truth. I did doubt I would see any of them, for they would not make themselves known to the Beast of the mob. It was enough they be there somewhere.

"ere, Mrs Cellier. 'Tis time.' Young Bowden was one of my guards to the Strand. Bowden. He was very nearly welcome. At the least it was he that came to fetch me, for he had lately shown me some kindness, even while the older ones took pleasure from seeing me cast down. Bowden's look was all doom, and I had no wish to lighten it.

I straightened my dress with grubby hands and thought of my red cloak, a shield against the hard sword of the world, a mark of my status and a symbol of my profession. I was lost without it. Perhaps being pilloried in the cloak would have stained the profession in some eyes but, in mine, it was a symbol of the truth and that would have protected me a little. But, more than this, today it would have cleverly hidden the deception I must undertake to save myself.

Without the cover of a cloak, I may yet be undone.

'Come, Mother Cellier,' said young Bowden in his thick London voice. 'Move y'self along there. They're waitin'.'

After hours praying for strength, I did not feel any more brave. I would lief death came for me now than face the pillory.

'I am ready,' I lied.

A voice came from behind the Bowden boy. 'Don't think any will ease this day for you, that you are a gentlewoman, Cellier. The hounds are baying for your blood, the blood of all Popish Amazons that dare to sully the name of the King and the Government. They will yet see you hanged, Papist whore!'

I squinted at the doorway. The dim light hurt eyes accustomed to no more than a single sunray. Two silhouettes stood with the hilts of their swords sticking out from their sides. The gaoler asked for no answer and I gave him none. I need pay no attention to this rough turnkey, an instrument for Richardson's ghoulish pleasures.

If I was a tool, I was merely an agent for God's work and the honest truth that came from my own realisations, nothing more.

Each man that worked in the prison, or in the Government, was flotsam on the sea of persuasion, particularly the persuasion of hard men, or hard money. They themselves could not turn against the tide for they would soon find they are pushed harder than they could resist. My strength came from standing with my feet planted deep in the sea bed, below the surface of the water and its current, and employing my wits to recognise truth, even when all others would have me say otherwise.

I must act quickly. If not now, I may have no other opportunity.

'Take me to the Strand!' I moved as if to follow the boy out.

After two steps, I clenched my front with both arms and bent over. 'Oh, oh! The pain! The pain!' Then I twisted and pinched the soft pig bladder through the folds of my skirt and felt the loose threads give way. Body-warmed liquid trickled down the insides of my legs toward my ankle. I pressed gently, and the soft skin beneath the fabric emptied. Would it be enough? I lifted the hem of the skirt so that the gaolers could see the colour of blood, and looked to see my stockings were red enough to convince any man, even in the dull light of the cell.

'I am losing it! Oh Oh! I am losing the baby! Help me, help me!' I reached one hand out and grabbed the jacket of young Bowden's arm. He tried to free himself, but I held tight.

'Unhand me, woman! Whence comes that blood?'

'I am losing my baby!' I said. 'Help me to the bed!'

Bowden's dilemma did not prevent him moving a moment longer. He led me to the side of the bed, where I sat heavily, still clutching my gut to be sure the empty bag did not fall and be discovered. Bowden's open jaw in his skeletal face was like week-old death. He cast a helpless look to the men in the doorway. This was a woman's business, not a young man's. His voice cracked as mud in the midday sun.

'Fetch the physician. She carries a child!'

''Tis a trick!' said one at the door.

'Trick or not, a physician will fast discover it,' said the other.

'A midwife should be called to examine her.'

'Nay, a midwife might hide the truth if the reputation of all midwives be in question. We call a physician.'

They argued between themselves as they left the cell and the two shadows became one. Then, without further ado, one gaoler broke free from the joined darkness, his heavy footsteps keeping company with the jangling of his keys as he ran to fetch the physician. Indeed, it struck me he might have gone to fetch Richardson, a thing I did not at all desire, for that man would have me stripped and would quickly discover my invention.

And that would lead to examination of every one of my visitors in order to identify my helper. I had rather place that burden upon myself than those that gave me assistance at risk of their life.

I had to send the other men away so that I might remove the bag.

'Quick. Water. I must have boiled water and a midwife!'

'You have a pillory to go to, woman. You cannot do this now!' This from the man whose face I still could not see. He turned sideways and his round belly blocked the light more fully than his front view. He then spoke to someone coming along the corridor: the turnkey, perhaps, or the physician or even Richardson himself?

'She chooses this day to bleed!' The newcomer's voice was not of a labourer, but perhaps of a merchant or gentleman. 'If she carries a child, why did she not say so?'

Not Richardson, thank the Lord. The voice came louder as the speaker hurried towards my disgraceful quarters.

"'Tis too dark. Bring me light so I might examine her.'

A physician then. Broad and tall as a sapling, himself like a shadow, the man, when he appeared, slipped without effort between the large silhouette and door frame leaving light spare on each side of him. When he came close, the rat-faced man drew out an eye-glass and held it close to inspect me as if I were a gruesome exhibit they displayed in the coffee shops. The overly huge grey eye behind the glass blinked. Without looking at the men behind him, he talked to them.

I had not removed the empty bladder.

'Leave now. I will examine her and, if she is fit for punishment, you may take her.'

They left with no argument.

My heart drummed, but not to a soldier's beat. I held my hands tight over my tummy to prevent the bag slipping. Would he give me away if he found my deception? I swallowed, but there was nothing but pride to swallow. And that I had none of.

'Do you suffer in your belly?' The man went to move my hand. I folded over further so he could not do so. 'Lie back, Mrs Cellier. I must examine you.'

The Bowden lad brought a lit lantern, handed it to the physician and fast retreated.

'I cannot, sir.' I groaned and held myself tight. It had been my misfortune to see too many babies come forth before they were ready, but acting the part of this misfortune might save me if I was able to play the part well.

'Mrs Cellier.' The physician placed his medicine bag beside me on the bed; the floor was too filthy. 'Mrs Cellier, I will be much obliged if you would lie with your head there.'

I did not need to see him gesture to know he meant at the end of the bed, and so was able to employ my whole mind on the subject of how I might escape the plight I had placed myself in. The physician would surely soon discover the pig bladder and I would be undone.

'I will not be examined by a man. Where is the midwife to examine me?'

'I am employed by Captain Richardson to discover any design to escape punishment,' said the bony man, fingering the catch on his bag, but not opening it. 'More men will fake sickness than suffer it, and in this place that is a difficult thing. Being a midwife, you are not to have a midwife examine you. I must tell you, Mrs Cellier, if you are innocent of such lie, you will not see the pillory today. If you have truly lost your baby, I share your sorrow, but you will have to stand. However, if, in this, you scheme against retribution for proven felony, be sure I will reveal it and it will cost you more. Will you save me the examination? It would be better if you lay yourself open now.'

I groaned in the stead of an answer. I had need of more time. A quick glance told me that the turnkeys were nowhere by the door and the physician was busy searching inside his open bag. I might never be given a more fortuitous moment and knew what I must do in that instant. So, I moaned again, and used my elbows to push aside my skirt and reach to the top of my legs to grab the bag before the physician saw how sly I was.

The tips of my fingers touched the neck of the bladder, but they slipped and slid over the bloody, flapping intestines and I could not take hold of it. It took not once, not twice, but thrice to grip the slick skin. At first it would not come free, perhaps caught in the folds of my skirt where I bent over. Frantic, I twisted my finger round and round the neck to better hold it, and pulled sharply. Before I could catch it, the bladder released from whatever grip it was held in and sprung from my fingers. I did not have time to look where it went, for the physician spoke again, his voice louder so I knew he faced me.

'Mrs Cellier,' he said. 'I will not endure this disobedience. I have a task to do, and you will kindly do as I have asked.' I could only pray darkness and the physician's poor eyes would hide the pig bag, wherever it was, until I could dispose of it.

'I do my best, sir! Pain nails me fast to this spot, and I cannot move.' It would not do to provoke him further. 'Aid me, and I will comply,' I said.

Concealing the lie with further moans, I allowed the skinny man to assist me fully onto the bed, ready for examination.

'Your skirt, madam.'

I complied and raised the material of my long skirt to my waist, so he could see the blood on my stocking-clad legs. If I yielded fast, perhaps suspicion would keep from the door. I did not expect that he would see anything amiss by the light of only a lantern. It seemed scrutiny of my more private parts was unnecessary for any opinion on my malaise for, with barely a glance, he spoke in an ill-tempered manner.

'Do you dare use trickery against the crown? What sort of midwife imagines a man of my profession would not recognise a show of menses? It is not that which gives you pain, but the Devil sat in your belly!'

He did not think it a trick, but of a woman's flow. If I could not convince him, he would have me in the pillory within the half hour.

'It cannot be! Do you think a midwife does not know when her body carries an infant, when it has carried so many before? I tell you, I am losing it!'

With that, he took a closer look, and I desired my words unsaid.

"Tis strange, Mrs Cellier. 'Tis a puzzle whence the blood comes, for neither menses nor miscarriage wettens the front of the skirt like this, yet leaves no streak at the tops of the legs…' The man lay my skirt down whilst still looking at my legs, then eyed me with raised eyebrows whilst he awaited a explanation. I could think of none. I had not thought this far of my design.

'That is simple to answer to. My skirt has wiped me clean.'

'That answers to only part of my question, but not the other. Why does blood colour the front of your skirt, and not your back, where it would more likely be?'

I could not think of anything that would suffice, so said the only thing that came to mind.

'I turned my skirt when I found it wet, for it is not a thing that gives a woman comfort!'

'You turned it? You turned your skirt when you were in so much pain? When did you do this? Before or after the turnkeys fetched you? They told me the pain started when they came to take you.'

There was no answer to that. None. But I answered even so.

'I did it when they left to fetch you.'

"Tis a lie!' said a voice out of sight. 'I stayed here and saw her at all times. Hear her not, forsooth it is as you say. She has the Devil in her belly!'

The physician's voice was fuller than his body. 'Come hither, Turnkey! I would speak with you!'

The two fat keepers and young Bowden must have been close by the whole time. They came the moment they were called.

322

'Be she fit for the stretch-neck? Can we have 'er?'

Rather than give me directly to them, the man had a question of his own.

'You say she did not turn her skirt when you were here?'

All three of the gaolers frowned. The biggest of them shrugged and shook his head indicating his 'no'. Seeing this, the other two followed suit.

'I said it as I saw it. She did not,' said the portly one.

'Then you may have her.'

Simple as that, the physician's words marked my fate. They were as a sword in my gut. I had failed. I might never come back to this room, a thing for which I might have been happy a short while since, but now I prayed I would see it again. For, if I did not, I was dead.

'What lies yonder on the floor?'

The eyes of every person in the room followed the fat gaoler's finger to the bloody, mucky skin that lay curled like a scroll against the wall near the bed. The empty bladder. If I had not been undone ere now, this would have unravelled me.

'Fie! We are duped!' The big man stopped pointing at the bladder and turned his finger toward me. "'Tis neither menses nor abortion, but a wicked trick of the darkest devilish kind!'

There was no place for me to hide. The fat gaolers advanced on me, whilst the physician and young Bowden moved to the side and created a path for them to the bed.

'Let the Maypole Nutcrackers have 'er and be damned by the Heavenly Father an' the people of the city of London! We ain't keeping 'em from 'er a moment longer!'

Each rotund gaoler grabbed an arm and hauled me hard from my bed, wrenching the broken bones in my chest and making me howl. With my feet barely touching the ground, they dragged my toes across the floor, my skirt front whipping through the dark, smelly sediment that filled the gaps between the stone pavings, and flowed over to cover the surfaces. They had my arms bent backwards so I was sure they would come free from the shoulders, and my ribs screamed. Or perhaps it was I that screamed.

'Mark me, thou instrument of Rome!' Thou will find me before all others in condemning you.'

I neither answered nor looked at him. The Devil inside me hammered at my ribs. It was all I could do not to faint, though that would have been more tolerable than this torture.

They released my arms the moment we reached the Strand and, with that release, my ribs and my insides again screamed from recent injuries. But no allowance was made either that I was in pain, or that I was a gentlewoman. If I slowed even for a short while to catch breath or wait for the pain to pass, they bid me walk before them and pushed me again.

My failed trick with the bladder had merely delayed my coming to the pillory. I had further delayed coming by making them stop for my dress to be changed. They did not wish to bring me forth covered in blood any more than I wished to look so sullied, for it would only reflect badly upon them.

But the delays had not taken time past the hour that most good folk, and bad, enjoyed castigating criminals on the pillory, for such punishments were always timed to allow this pleasure when most were released from work to eat. It would not be too long before they had to return to work, so I could only hope that I might not endure the whole hour of punishment.

People of all sorts filled the streets, but as yet no crowd surrounded the pillory itself. They would come; slinging stones at criminals in the Neck-Stretcher being a more popular amusement than hangings, for they tended to be nearby and gave every person on the street opportunity to play their part in the discipline. I myself had seen plenty such spectacles in this very spot, being the closest to my house.

As we passed Arundel Street, where I lived, I searched for Pierre amongst the persons milling about the stalls and carrying out their business. I saw no sign of him. Instead, another man I did not know held out his hand to stop me. His plain face did not straight-away bring forth any memory, nor did the long, dark periwig, though such easily removed hair is often changed and cannot be relied upon. I stopped, for how could I not respond to the compassion in his face that gave me to think he meant only kindness.

I noticed he wore a carpenter's tool belt. Something came to mind, only that I knew him, though not from where.

'Wear this; it will offer you some little protection.' His voice was friendly.

In his hand he held toward me a bundle of fabric of familiar red. My spirits rose considerably. It was my midwife cloak, or perhaps one like it. No, it was surely mine, for it was torn from the attack on me outside the courtroom on Saturday. He must have recovered it for me! I begun to thank him for his charity, but my chest again screamed as I was pulled sharply away by the impatient turnkey, and pushed onwards toward the market square.

"Tis meagre repayment for kindness once given,' I heard the man shout after me. I looked back as the men pulled me away, and I swallowed down a familiar lump in my throat. There came to me a memory of a day more than two years past, when this man had stood and thanked me for the life of the baby boy he held in his bandaged hands, though I had been unable to save his wife – Mr Potter, the carpenter.

I soon lost sight of him in the crowd, gathering at the sight of the turnkeys bringing me.

I was not disallowed the cloak so, with difficulty, I swung it onto my shoulders and wrapped it close around me. A certain peace filled me then. If I died in it, I would die whole.

By the time we reached the Maypole itself, the whole square was thick with people awaiting today's sport. I had never seen it so busy, but it seemed that half of the crowd was made of King's soldiers and sheriff's officers, an unusual sight at such an event. I could not think their purpose might be. Did they think one ageing woman so much trouble?

A short way ahead, a group of the sheriff's men stood in file by the wayside then, as we came close, they fell into a tight group around me, still edging me forward. Before they surrounded me, I counted twenty or thirty soldiers round the pillory. What was this?

Protection? Only the city's famous or infamous warranted such guard! If the King granted me these men as a boon for services once given him, it was a strange act, when I was here to be punished for libel against him. Perhaps they were simply employed to keep the peace.

In a weird and unearthly dream, I walked through the throng, with the midday sun on my head, my nose stuffed with stale smells of sweat and ale, knowing I was going toward certain shame and further injury, or even death. Though I could not see them because of the wall of soldiers surrounding me, I could hear the growing roar of The Beast. They cussed me and they threatened me, and bayed for my blood as hounds close to the kill of a wily fox. Despite the pain, I tried to walk tall and not show the fear that grew inside me.

As usual, the pillorying was deliberately chosen to be on the busiest Market day, so many here came to buy animals and wares but would become caught in the excitement of a stoning. My heart hit my ribs trying to get out. I could not draw in enough air, though sweet as any air I ever breathed after the prison, for my lungs would not allow it in.

Every now and then, I caught a glimpse of the wooden beast, the Nutcracker they called it, surrounded by a circle of soldiers. Another row of soldiers now lined each the side of the path I was to follow. I froze. However brave I had felt before, though I could not recall that I did, I never expected so many to turn out, nor did I imagine such fear clawing my belly. I could not take another step forward. When I stopped, so did those behind me, but those in front continued on unaware, leaving empty ground before me.

I was not afraid to die, but I was afraid of suffering as I did so. I told myself the punishment was to be bound to a single hour, shorter than a birthing.

One hour. A short time compared to the labour of a woman. A long time compared to a hanging. Someone pushed me in the small of my back, so I would've tripped had I not caught myself and stepped forward. The pain was enough to give life to my legs again.

And, there he was! There was Pierre at the roadside. The relief of it, of seeing my beloved in that sea of hatred! I must be thankful none of our children stood with him. With an almost imperceptible backward gesture of his head and eyes, he signed for me to go to him. There was nothing more I desired, but feared to bring the crowd against him.

I shook my head and tried to hide from my husband the turmoil that enfeebled me so much it almost stopped me walking. I tried to convey the strength I had always shown him, that I would survive this, one way or other. He beckoned me again, willing me to go thither. I could do nothing other than go to him, and the men round me allowed me this concession. As I came close to Pierre, I was almost hit by some of the shaking fists in the crowd nearby.

I had to pass my poor neighbours, Mr and Mrs Howard, that lived in our building, Arundel-House, and that lost their son two years since. At the trial of the five Jesuits, they had stood as witness against Oates, claiming he was in St Omer at the time of the Jesuit meeting, rather than in London as he claimed. Did these two come for support or for sport? I saw other householders I had visited from time to time.

Perhaps my guards would have stopped me had they seen what I intended, but they were kept busy pushing back some persons that had broken through the hedge of soldiers. I reached out to Pierre, thinking he would embrace me, something I desired as much as I wished this over. Instead, he surprised me by bringing from behind his back a baker's shovel, or perhaps it was a tavoletta, the painted board that a condemned Catholic held before his face on the scaffold until he died. Did he think I was dead to him?

'Take this!' he said. ''Tis all I can do for you now.'

I could not ignore the authority in his voice and so I took it, and straight away stowed it under my cloak, grateful for such kindness from a husband that might have disowned me had he been an unkind man. It was unlikely I could keep the board but, if anyone saw Pierre give it to me, nobody took it from me. I was defenceless against them, should they want it. For now, the rough wood clasped in my hand filled me with hope where my cloak had swathed me in strength; gifts from my husband and a man from the past. I was less naked before those that would strip me of everything.

I looked back, but Pierre was gone from my sight.

When we reached the dais the guards stopped, and so I stopped. A shove from behind told me I was not meant to stop, and a growled, 'Go on, midwife' was the sign I was now utterly alone, and must go forward singly and alone.

I frowned. So I should not hide my shame, my neck and wrists would be locked into the three holes made for them between the two hinged blocks of wood. Who was to do so if only I were to take the steps? I searched the soldier's face, then the sheriff's. Neither contradicted the order, nor made to go with me.

'Go,' confirmed the sheriff.

I breathed the searing, dusty air of the day, pulled my cloak close around me, and slowly took the steps up onto the stage. I had expected to be locked into the contraption of shame, so I did not know what I should do.

Nailed to the pillory, above where my head and hands should have been trapped, was a hastily written paper that said, 'Pilloried one hour for libel against the King'. I took no more notice of it. It was not meant for me as much as for those that came to see me.

The moment I was atop the stand, the soldiers crowded close around it with their faces turned outwards. They were there to guard me! The Lord had answered my prayers for mercy! Perhaps I should not die this day after all.

The Sheriff and the guards that had brought me there, stood to each side of the stage, facing me, to make sure I did not escape. They were not without some wit and had sense enough not to come higher, for they would surely catch some of what was meant for me.

But then, stranger than before, the circle round me widened as the soldiers pushed the crowd several paces further away from me. Although this would not prevent my being hit by more accurate arms, this small belt would save me from those whose aim was less true.

The square filled right back to the church. People surrounded the tall, stone, ribbon-free maypole meant for the spring dance, next to which was a youngster, hoisted up on a dirty man's broad shoulders. I recognised the brat as one I had birthed, and looked to his father, one I knew nearly as well as his wife. Many husbands of the women I had birthed were suspicious of me and resented my role in the bedroom. I had seen the birth of five of this man's brats. Whether he cast a stone I never knew, for I lost sight of him among other people.

At the edge of the crowd, donkeys carried baskets of eggs and rotten vegetables. To the front, some women were let through the wall of soldiers and began to pass out their wares to the nearby crowd.

'Papist whore!'

As if the insult signalled the onset of the assault, it begun.

The stones, and mud, vegetable stalks and oyster shells flew at me, slowly to start with. People had to be strong and accurate to reach me over the heads of the soldiers, but the stronger ones hit hard, mostly on my arms which were the most difficult to protect. All the while, insults flew with more accuracy, more often reaching their aim.

'Home burner!'

'Stinking witch!'

Suddenly, one of the sheriff's men begun shouting and shaking his loaded hands in the air. An oyster shell filled with mud and horse droppings landed nearby, cracking and splattering its contents in my direction. A first miss. They would get better as the hour moved along. This I had seen before. I could only hope they would expend themselves or the missiles ere the hour's end.

Another Oyster shell, and a piece of cauliflower stalk, together hit the leg of the pillory. The shell bounced, the cauliflower burst apart. I thought of the wood paddle beneath my cloak. If I took it out, I could use it to protect myself, but mayhaps it would be taken from me. But, if I did not use it, then what use was it!

Why did the guards neglect to fix me in? That was unusual providence, for it left my hands free to defend myself. Some hard thing flew at me from the other side and caught in my skirt, so it did not hit my leg. I backed into the pillory.

The timber would protect my head from the one side, and my board from the other. I might protect myself quite ably after all. Whether someone had designed this so, I did not know, but for this mercy I was indebted. I took out my paddle and looked out over the scene, filled with fresh courage.

Bitter, dirty faces screamed back at me. Some persons hung out of windows overlooking the street, others used their balcony window seats to cast longer throws, though most of these landed short amongst the people. Sometimes a person would pick up the thing that hit him and throw it back at the window.

The wall of soldiers allowed only over-arm throws, so most weapons rained from above. They hurt, but not nearly so much as a throw straight from the shoulder! Worst were the strong and sure shots from the women within the soldier circle, with close aim at all exposed parts of me, my face most favoured. By and large, I succeeded in batting these away, but those that found me pained me more.

This was a play already written. It would be acted out until its end.

'Papist plotter!'

'Traitor! Traitor!'

'Fire starter! London burner, go back to Italy!'

No matter how great the harm to my body by stones and shells, at this time the anger in the words cut me more, but I could only fend off the tangible. The other hits I must take. The missiles cracked and thudded against the board beside my head with no break. I thanked God and my husband for their protection, and even the sheriff, who did not take the shield from me.

People had collected piles of things to throw at me by their feet, and so they did not run out.

Then I smelt the smoke. It came from behind the people, at the far side of the square. Black plumes rose away from the buildings, for none wished for another city-burning. My books. Any they had found would be in that fire. It may be that none survive to tell my tale. Perhaps every person wishing to read the book had already read it.

If I had hopes my words would make a difference, they were burned in that moment. I could not clearly hear him over the sound of the clattering of stones and shells against my board, but one of the sheriff's men held up each copy and shouted something before he added it to the flames. Persons near him clapped and cheered. A boy grabbed one from the pile and threw it in the flames.

I saw an oyster shell near my foot, filled with manure and mud to give it weight, and stepped my boot down hard on it with a satisfying crunch. A stone hit hard on my paddle and dropped to the ground. I do not know why, but I picked it up and placed it in my pocket. My head became empty of all thoughts.

'Here, she's picking up the stones,' shouted a woman. 'Let's give her more!'

The stones came hard and often; I do not know where they found their fresh supply. I battered as many as I could from my face, but some hit my arms and sides and belly. Each on its own was a sharp punch, the pain short-lived, but the small stones that hit previous bruises hurt worst.

Another pebble landed behind me and rolled towards me feet. Without thinking, I once more picked it up and put it in my pocket to join the first. None would throw it again.

'She thinks she will send them to the Pope, so he can martyr her!' I long since stopped searching for who shouted. Finding one in so many was an impossible task.

My mouth stretched in a straight line, a wry smile, to think of the Pope receiving a bag of stones. I was tempted to do so.

Someone threw a large lump of earth, flattened by a cart's wheel, which fell short on the soldiers below. I had not seen before how many of the missed shots fell on them. They took punishment for something they did not do, but I could not care.

It was the duty of the King's men to defend the monarch. In defending me, they did so. If the words I writ had been untrue, I would have stood against the King and God when I took my oath; yet, though the words were true, they still found me guilty of saying them. I could not be else but guilty. Strange, then, they defended me against the wicked mob!

With defiance I shouted, 'I am innocent! I wrote only the truth!' I did not expect they would hear me, and it merely earned me one of the sheriff's men poking an open sore on the leg with a stick. I kicked it away and spat at him, which only made him laugh when he thought I had missed. I was satisfied to see he did not wipe the white bubbles from his shoulder.

That satisfaction did not live long in me. Amongst rotting and mouldy food, and dry clods of earth, were oyster shells from the river Thames that occasionally caught a glancing blow on the sharp side. Then a large stone hit me solidly above my ear, and a pain shot through the whole of me, shocking my legs so my toes prickled, and my legs buckled. I fell to my knees, throwing my hands forward to catch my fall, and trapped my fingers under the paddle.

Woe betide me should I let go of it.

What was desolation if it was not this!

The handle of the board was just out of reach and, when I went to reach for it, my head spun madly. The missiles stopped, or if they came they did not hit me, for I was below the heads of the soldiers, and they could not see me. I thought to stay there a while, but abrupt hands reached under my armpits and dragged me back to my feet, where I wobbled precariously.

A fresh onslaught came even before the sheriff's men removed themselves from the dais. An egg, the smell of which made me retch, splattered squarely on my brow and dripped down, so my eyes stung. Some touched my lips, and I tasted an age, saved specially for the pillory. I wiped the smelly substance from my eye. Strings of it hung between my face and hand. Bad egg on the face was the like of being spat upon.

When I had regained my balance, I reached down and grabbed the paddle. It would have been so easy for one of the soldiers to grab it, or for one of the sheriff's men to kick it off the dais, but they had not. Nor had they taken it from me. Odds teeth, a strange mercy!

Did they not see? Any one of those that stood before me might one day thank me, when they were cast in the debtors' prison, or wrongly accused and left without victuals to die, that I spoke up for them. My pride did not prevent fresh pummelling. I dared them to throw something, and they did. Another stone rattled to the boards and I bent to retrieve and pocket it. I had a few now, maybe eight or ten. The weight of them banged against my leg as I batted away another.

How much time had passed, fifty minutes, an hour? The church clock had not yet struck. Surely I had done my penance. If each minute tarried more, I believe the clock would stop altogether and run backwards!

There was Mrs Chenery, a neighbour, come to see the spectacle. Her sole interest would be to gather tasty tidbits to share. My story would be told as far and wide as Oxford tonight, and in Gretna Green, no doubt, by the morning. Watching another's torment was a miserable bedfellow to such curiosity, but such a one as she did the work of the law, spreading news of what should happen if a person dared speak against Government or King.

In my naïve days, I knew, with conviction, any found guilty in the court of law must be so, but now I knew, with equal conviction, innocence or guilt of any wrong-doing was uncertain. Again, I tilted back my chin and looked in the face of the mob. Stones, shells and rotting things were small reparation for speaking the truth. My conscience must speak out. If need be, I must stand alone until others stood beside me for, if I would stand down, there would be none with whom others could stand with.

I waited for the church bell to strike one, but still it did not. If I did not know the mechanical precision of it, I might have thought they had stopped the clock to make me suffer further.

A tiny hurled pebble clattered against the paddle and I batted it away. Again, I tottered and lost balance, and again the sheriff and his men were quick to pull me back to my feet. Would they allow me no respite?

The soldiers around me took nearly as much flak as I. Apart from missiles slung from the crowd, an occasional stone I batted away would land hard on one of my protectors. I did not care enough about it to alter my aim.

Though somewhat guarded by the soldiers, my arms ached from batting stones, my head hurt from the strain, and my eyes wished to flow, not merely from the wrong done to me, but from pieces of dirt and shell that shattered off the paddle. I refused to wipe the grit away lest the crowd thought I cried. But I could not prevent my eyes blinking.

The name-calling did not abate. If what they said was true, I was the cause of all that ailed London.

I have done you no wrong! It was not I! I clammed my mouth. Denial would give reason for more anger.

At length, the clock struck one. At last, I was done.

The sheriff and his men did not move. Nor did the crowd beast go back to work and leave me be.

'My time is up.' I shouted. I shook my fist. If the sheriff heard, he did not show it. 'Sheriff! I have done my time!' Again I shouted. This time he turned and in his eyes and the set of his mouth was determination. He would not yet finish this. If he did not enjoy the occasional stone or root hitting him, he enjoyed that I was the target.

Suddenly, without seeing any end, what was unbearable became torture. Perhaps he wished for some hard thing to hit my eye, as it had done a man a few years ago, then he could give my husband leave to take my broken remains back to our house and he would have none more of me.

If I pleaded, if I begged, there was no use in it. Somewhere amongst the other voices, drowned in the opposing clamouring sea, one shout for my release.

The sheriff shouted back, 'We did not start at twelve; we will not end at one!'

There was no point to returning the argument. It was true that I had started after I was supposed to start, so I conceded they should finish after I was supposed to finish. Unless higher authority spoke against this, his was the voice the soldiers would obey.

But it was not mere minutes I stood there longer. Another hour passed ere the sheriff ended the mob's rule, and only then because the crowd that should have returned to work became unruly.

Perhaps some of them protested how the rules had been broken, and once a single rule is broken, who can tell what rules might be kept and what others might not? Skirmishes broke out, and a few tried to break the wall of soldiers. All told, there must have been four hundred soldiers in the square. I thanked the Lord for that, for otherwise the Beast would surely have torn me to pieces.

When the men lost control, the sheriff gave the command, 'Bring her down!' Two soldiers, that had likely taken some battering themselves, climbed on the dais and took an arm each. They pulled me down, and now, at ground level, I was out of sight of most of the crowd. I was dragged roughly, and without consideration, through the alleyway the soldiers formed to hold back the throng, back towards Newgate.

I had been pilloried one time out of three and had two more times ahead, yet, in one day I had done the time of two. I vowed the King would hear of this!

I was thrown into another cell, different from before, and thanked our Father for the mercy, for I could lie on the mangy, flea-filled bedding and nurse the considerable bruises I did not even like to look at.

In pain I slept until the cock crowed the following day.

Revealing the truth hurt, but my life was yet spared.

27

18th day of November, 1683

'Hold tight to life, most beloved flittermouse. Do not let go now, I beg of you. It be not your fate to leave me, but mine to leave you.'

'Let me go, Pierre. I cannot bear more. If only I might walk beneath the sky once more or...or...' My voice broke. 'Or...if I might see my children one last time, I could die. Even one sniff of that vile Arabian coffee house brew might prevent Death from entering this door.'

A stay of three years and more at the King's pleasure, with but two months' freedom between the two times in court, had pinched flesh from my bones and fortitude from my heart. I would rather lie down in the grave next to truth that had long since died than stay another day in that place.

'It does not please me to hear you discouraged, Lizzie. You will be revived, I am certain.' For days, the rowdy prison noises surrounded our silence, closing us in together. Pierre never left my side. I laboured to slide my arm over the thin blanket and find his hand, desiring the warmth of his old, warm skin on mine. I could find no strength to take it further than the edge of the bed.

'Pierre.' I said his name and it was enough for him take my hand and raise it to his lips. His cheeks were damp. He would likely follow me from this world sooner than live without me. I thought of the children as orphans. 'You must find someone to care for our children, Pierre, a mother for them.'

'They need no other mother than you, Lizzie. They yearn for your return home, as do I. You cannot die. I am old and I refuse you to die before me. If ever you obey me, you must obey me in this. Do you recall that time when life was near beaten from you?'

I did. I recalled pain so grim that I prayed for God to relieve me. This malady that ailed me now had crept upon me in a manner most insidious, rather than that infliction of violence.

That they took light and freedom from me, could not alone bring me to languish in this way. There was no place in this world where God could not be with me, and so long as this was so, my spirit was free and I had no reason to die that I might find him. But, if this prison was my sole world, then I no longer had reason to live. In this place, I could not be a mother, nor a wife, nor a midwife. I could ask for charity, but not give it. And, in taking, I was no longer the woman I knew myself to be.

I likely slept awhile, for then Pierre was talking.

'...the incompetence of the hangman. I tell thee, Lizzie, 'tis a noise I cannot forget, ever...in the same way you could never forget the screams from the gaol that night. Remember you that? The people did scream, not for the entertainment of the execution, but for the axe to be taken from him before he struck again. They dare not see him miss his mark one more time. It was a sight most gruesome, most grisly. Not even the distance of three score paces to Powys House, could prevent Lady Powys faint at the sight of blood spraying from his gaping neck onto the spectators! I never liked the dreadful man, a greater traitor there never was, but I could not wish such a death on the Devil.

'And if you had heard his screams as I did,' said Pierre, 'you might have mistaken him for the Devil, for I assure you, it was all too grim! A man close to the beheading told me that, even in death he had berated that hangman, Ketch, for such shoddy work, for he had paid well for a quick strike. Though his head hung half on and half off, he called the man a dog for treating him so barbarically.'

Pierre's voice faded. In the dimming light, I saw he was shaking his head, perhaps to cast out the ghastly image.

'Was it...was it someone we know, Pierre?' It seemed there would be no end to such undeserved Catholic deaths.

'Lord Russell, my dear. May his soul rest in peace. Have you forgot? You asked me about his death but a short while ago.'

'Lord William Russell? But does he not stand against the Duke of York becoming King for his faith?'

''Tis your fever that makes you forget. It was four months since he died, and I have told you of it time and again, but I cannot rid myself of such horrid sight. Remember? He was condemned for his fiendish part in the Rye House Plot.'

'As I was condemned for the Meal-Tub Plot,' I murmured.

'No, *ma chérie*. You were never proved guilty of that. You were found guilty of another deed. You exposed the Government and King's prison in a way they could not like. That is not treason.'

The fog would not go, no matter that I tried to push it away. It closed around me so I was comforted. I slept some more. When I next awoke, Pierre's forehead rested on our joined hands on the rough blanket. I ached. My arms ached and my back ached. My legs ached. All my old wounds from the beating and the pillory pained me. Every part of me had seen enough of this place. Most of all, my heart ached, and I hungered for a taste of home.

Though my body was sore, I stayed still. I did not wish to disturb my poor husband, who had kept vigil so long and now rested. How much must he have given the gaolers to allow him to stay, that I did not know, but I was glad for his companionship in my last days. His periwig had come loose and slipped over one ear, leaving the other exposed. I stroked the length of his cheek along the edge, and then gently straightened it. He stirred, but did not wake. We had found each other when we both had the greatest need for a companion, after my husband was gone and after his wife, Margaret, was dead. His love was the staff I leaned on through the years, and even now he propped me up, though he was frail and old.

Ten months ago I had dictated a petition to the King to release me. I told him how I was thrice near stoned to death, and how I now lay weak and sick. Pierre had added the part about how I prayed for remission of the fine and should be put into the next Old Bailey Pardon, if it pleased His Majesty. A heartier plea could not have written and sent, yet all I had received in reply was neglect and silence. If ever I lost faith at that time, Pierre's belief in me spilled over and filled the both of us.

But his faith had yet to set me free.

I would be loyal to the King until the last time I closed my eyes to sleep, yet he forgot so easily all that I had done for him, and for his family. It seemed I was to die in this filth and my children would be full-grown without a mother to guide them. Perhaps without a father too. Without me, Pierre's business had quickly failed, for he was a merchant but no businessman, so he had little enough to pay the daily squeeze let alone the thousand pounds to free me from that ungodly place.

Pierre stirred. I used his movement to slip my hand from beneath his, and turn on my side for comfort, then I laid my hand back on his.

'Pierre? Do you sleep?' He did not answer. No sooner than I closed my eyes, the ugly prison cell was replaced by darkness, worse than darkness.

Memories that hurt me in earlier years came back to hurt me twice over: a man dragging us into the rain whilst others pillaged my childhood home; waking and finding my first husband unmoving and cold next to me; plague wretches followed by people running frightened through the streets from the Great Fire; the snarling madness of that Atterbury woman as she beat me again and again; judges laughing at me in court…laughing, laughing…with such exultation as they pelted me with vilest dung and vegetables mixed with rosary beads and crucifixes.

Somehow I knew memories had turned to dream, but it may as well have been real as they stomped on statues of the Virgin Mary, then filed into a procession with Jesuits and monks and priests, and forced me to follow with them behind a burning effigy of the Pope, stuffed with screaming, writhing cats.

When we reached the home of the Green Ribbon Club, they grabbed my arms, and forced me towards a huge bonfire of a burning church. It seemed no person but me saw flames and sparks from the church spire fly across the square behind us and catch hold on the roofs there. We were surrounded by fire, but they continued to force me behind the Pope towards the burning church. People screamed for our death and the crackling heat became unbearable.

The judges threw the plague dead into the church and then, one by one, those in front of me, uncaring of their religion, and then the accusers as well as accused. Judges followed each other into the fire. Then it was my turn.

I knew I dreamed the horrors, but still the heat of the flames burned my skin and cooked me even as I fought to escape.

I opened my eyes with a start. There *was* no escape. I was haunted awake as surely I was haunted in sleep. The scene played over as I stared at the cold grey stone, hung with spider webs and wet dust. Tiny streaks of dirty water trickled from cracks by the window and followed a slow course inwards, along crevices in the stone, and culminated in dirty drops that occasionally fell to the floor. The rain on the city rained through the prison, but did little to cleanse this palace.

'They hate us because they fear, though we have the same appearance,' I drew a breath and heard it rasp in my throat, 'we hide an unfathomable religion on the inside, and they cannot see the proof of it. They cannot see the target, so they blindly shoot arrows in every direction with the hope one of them might strike the bull's-eye! But I am weary of the barbs piercing me, Pierre. My wounds are too many. What manner of test of my faith will I have next? I am weary to my very bones.'

'You must not say such things, Lizzie.' Pierre spoke into my dress, not raising his head. 'The Lord challenges us with trials to let us chose the right path. You are tested more than most, for he asks you to walk your path with more certainty, even when everyone around you shouts disbelief. You have more strength than any, the hope of so many. In this place,' he raised his head, let go of my hand and gestured to my lavish chamber, 'I have heard men and women tell how you have helped them. You have given them food and warmth when they had none. You have given them rosaries and bibles when they had no hope. You have given freedom though it was taken from you. For that, your name is spoken of most highly.'

Pierre further straightened his periwig with nary a pause in his words. His eyes were old; his mouth drooped as if it had long forgotten how to smile.

'Without your goodness and your charity, many in here would be dead long since. Even now, your good work continues and the helpers you taught continue to relieve the suffering of so many. It is your light that has guided them. So do not speak ill of your trials, *ma chérie*. They are the road that has led you to do these good deeds.'

I squeezed his hand and felt the thin parchment skin move easily over his bones, but warmth came from it and it was a comfort to me.

'Yet my strength comes from you, Pierre, so all those deeds are yours rather than mine.'

'You are too kind, *ma chérie*.'

The usual grinding of iron on iron, groans, shouts, and occasional laughter – for a man's spirit is indomitable – were muffled by wood and stone yet for a moment seemed in the room with us. With time came the clanging of keys and clanking of leg chains, and the moans of a neighbouring prisoner. When I did not loathe that hard oak door for that it did hold me in, it pleased me, for it also kept the prison from me.

In the dark of the night, with but a single candle to keep Satan's scuttling vermin away, it also kept eyes from me when I cried for home, or for the life I missed, or when I knelt down to pray. Every man and woman must need some time in their own company for necessary things, such as washing or sitting in the corner. Not every room had a solid door. In that I was fortunate. Those locked behind iron bars were scrutinized by every other prisoner and turnkey, enduring exposure that no decent person should endure.

'Your kind words are a salve on the festering wound that is Richard Whittington's Newgate. I give you sincere gratitude, Pierre, for I find I am unable to aid myself now, let alone any other. I despair for my life and my freedom. I do not think I will last many more moons.'

As if I'd stuck him with a hot poker, Pierre sat up suddenly then took to his feet. 'You do not deserve such treatment, Lizzie, and he must know this. I will demand to see the King myself. I will remind him what you did for him and ask that he show you mercy. Begad! He must give you a pardon!'

'A pardon should not so easily be given to a person that has done wrong, but a person should not have need of a pardon when they have done no wrong.' I could not see his face and tried to pull myself off the scratchy blanket to see him clearer, but let my head fall back when I found I could not hold it up.

'No Lizzie, they should not. But the law of the land oft finds a man, or woman, guilty, so then they must be punished, no matter that the law would better be altered.'

'The law that shut me here should be changed, for truth should not be punished.' Each breath, each word, wore another layer of life from me. I closed my eyes and felt water wet my lashes and run on my skin and into my hair. 'They did not want to know if the words in my book were true, only if I wrote them. They did not go to the prisons and question those who could tell them the truth, but brought to them those who would tell anything they wished to hear for a handful of coins.'

'We must pray that some day the veil of lies will be lifted to reveal the truth, and when they are, you shall have handsome reward for all you have done.'

'I will be rewarded by God, for I will no longer need mortal things.'

'Do not say so, Lizzie. You are a heroine already to all those whose lives you have aided…'

'…and a villain to all others.'

'But those that know the truth of it are fortified by your deeds, and that is as a chain that others can hold onto as an anchor in these dark days.'

'I have had much time to think, Pierre,' I turned to a subject I wished to talk of. 'I have had thoughts of things I have talked of before…'

'No, Lizzie. 'Tis best you do not concern yourself further with such schemes. Any more interference in the way of things will have you hanged at Tyburn.'

"Tis not plotting and treason I concern myself with on this instant. More often than I care for, I lay here with mere thoughts for company, and they have told me, should I survive this dire time, which I have told them I will not, I must do all I can to change the way of the midwife, to protect mothers and their newborn infants.'

I saw by my husband's surprise and confusion that I must elaborate.

'My thoughts are haunted by so many wicked deeds done by false midwives. I have oft told you how they murder infants with their ignorance and butchering ways. The infants and their mothers die for lack of proper care.'

'Aye, we have talked of this. And I see this cause kindles you, even when your embers lie smothered in ashes. It would be well for you to think more of this after all.

'Twas as if he saw me drowning in the river and threw me a rope. I grasped that twine so tight it hurt me, and with each word I uttered hereafter, I pulled closer back to him.

'Husband, have I not oft spoken of the true lore of the midwife? How it is secure in but a few women? They cannot teach this to any but their own daughters. Only a few surgeons hold intimate knowledge of the lore, and their knowledge is not about delivery but about the physical, the body, so they have too little to teach.'

Pierre was slow of body, but still had his wits about him, and saw what I tried to say.

'But what if a midwife might teach those who wish to practice?'

'Then they could not. The law says that no woman can learn anything but what she can learn in her own home. She cannot join men in a place of learning to do so.'

I dropped my head on the side so I could see Pierre as he reclaimed my hand. It was too much to do more. I blinked tears from my eyes, for it seemed he kept me talking for fear if I would stop. "Tis the subject of my thoughts, Pierre, that it must be wrong when a man can learn skill in a college, but a woman cannot learn

343

more than her parents or husband are willing to teach her at home. Are a woman's needs unequal to that of a man?'

'As with treason and plots, we return to the law of the land. It matters not if it is right or wrong, the law is as it is and must be followed. A woman cannot go to college, for there is no place for her there.'

'Not even a college run by women, meant for women?'

'Such a preposterous thought would not be given credence.' If I did not know hope in Pierre's voice, I might have been indignant for being so summarily dismissed, but as he breathed life into me, I breathed life into him.

'By whom?' I asked. 'Would these very men conceive that 'tis their own infants and wives that are at risk from ignorant and unskilled services of false midwives? 'Tis they who should be most eager to change this law!'

'Forsooth, you are right, Lizzie! 'Tis every man that should look to the midwife for the well-being of his wife and for the safe delivery of his sons and daughters.'

'And how can he be sure of this if he does not know where she has learned her trade.'

'He does as we are all wont to do, he goes by the word of another.'

'Would it not be a fairer thing if a man could trust every midwife?' Pierre's face lightened as he begun to see where my thoughts took him.

'Indeed, my love.' A crafty expression came upon him then. 'And what better judge of character than a midwife to the ladies of court…Lizzie, you are matchless for the task of teacher. It must be you!'

'I fear 'tis not my fate to do more than set out the plan, Pierre, but you must see to it that my ideas are explained to the King that he might change the law.'

He frowned, 'You must not talk that way. I cannot do your work for you. I have not your skill with words and I fear to fail where you would succeed. You must recover yourself and I will plead with the King for your release, that you may stand before him in this matter.'

Despair blew through me as an early winter wind. I was weak and worsening, and would not again see the sky. In the silence Pierre turned away. He sniffed. I need not see his face to know he cried for me and I had no will to tell him not to. I closed my eyes and rested. When I awoke, Pierre was gone, leaving behind only his tears. They welled up in me. I could not remember such a time when I could not see any light to guide me. Even the light Pierre often lent me did not guide me this night. Darkness filled the cell as it filled my heart.

'Mrs Cellier! Mrs Cellier! Hear this!' The rough voice of the turnkey came to me through layers of sleep. I did not feel disposed to answer. I could hardly move my lids but, working at them, gained a crack and saw the sun must be above the rooftops. It came to me I had heard the cocks crow for some while.

'Mother Cellier!' Metal ground against metal as the key turned and unbolted the lock. A man that once was obedient to my command not to enter without my by your leave came to the bedside. The skinny Bowden boy was a strapping man now. I was only grateful he had continued to treat me with reasonable dignity and consideration. 'Mrs Cellier, the sun shines on you today. Put your your feet in your boots and your boots to the floor – you are to go from here!'

'Come you to gloat over my lost cause? Go away, man.'

'Forsooth, Madam Cellier, prithee hear my words. You are free!'

'Tis a cruel game you play with me.' I said. For a piece of time, the sun shone on me, lighting an ember of warmth in my cold guts. I doused it for fear of it being falsely lit.

'I play no game, Madam. You are released by command of the King. You are to return home.' Young Bowden's hands clasped my shoulders and pulled me to sitting. 'Do you not hear me? You are free!'

Then he cast off the blanket from my legs and with strong fingers, as though I were but a puppet, pulled my legs round to hang loose from the bedside. Though I loathed his hands on me, for a touch anywhere caused me pain, there was an aspect of his sincerity that reached through the heavy gloom filling me.

'Do you speak truly?' I asked. He said he had no reason to tell me so if it was not so.

'A messenger even now fetches Mister Cellier, your husband. He is to bring you home. Your freedom has been spoken for.'

If he be laying a trap for me, perhaps tricking me to saying something on my release I might not otherwise say, I would say nothing on it. But it might be that Lady Powys or Lord Peterborough, or even my Pierre, had secured an audience with the King and pleaded for my freedom. I suppose I should know what means my freedom came by, if it were so.

'Am I free with a pardon? Or am I free because I am wronged?' I asked.

'I heard nothing of a pardon, nor of bail.'

If he told me I had a pardon, though I should have refused freedom by rights of not needing one, I would surely have left that place by any means offered to me. The taste of fresh air was distant and I craved it.

As Bowden, the turnkey, instructed, I pulled on my boots and placed my feet to the ground and he assisted by tying the laces. Finally, though I was weak and barely able to move, he helped me stand. I weighed as little as my bones and no more, so he easily braced my shaking body against him and, together, we walked along the cold, dank corridor toward the gate.

I had walked this way so often ere I had a place there that every shadow in the wall was familiar to me. Knowing the place held no comfort for me. It was as cold a place as ever it was, tasting of my soul even as I left it. Bowden took me to the outer gate and left me there.

'Wait here, Mrs Cellier. Your husband will fetch you.' The man's heavy footsteps marked two steps away, then two steps back again. 'Here is bounty given with the good grace of the King.' At which he pulled a bag full of coins from his belt and handed it to

346

me. 'There be ninety pounds and no less, Madam. Of that, you can be certain, for I have guarded it myself.'

With that, I was completely alone, leaning against the wall with no strength to stop my legs buckling beneath me. The weight of the bag so heavy, I slid down the wall until I sat in the wet mud.

But the sweet air I breathed worked some kind of magic on me. And when I held out my hand it became wet. It was raining.

Icy water ran down my arm and drenched my sleeve. As I watched, I saw the dirt and shame wash out of it. Somehow, climbing the wall with my hands, I pulled the rest of me back to standing. The water trickled over my face and hair, through my filthy cloak and dress and over my disgusting dung covered boots. At that moment, I swear nothing could have made me happier. Dame Nature bathed and cleansed me in a way no lavender bath ever could, so I held my face skyward and allowed her full reign.

While the water drops purged three years of prison from me, the sight of sky restored some semblance of hope. Still with my face upturned, I laughed. It was not a genteel laugh, but a loud uncontrollable laugh. And once begun could not be stopped. A hand took my arm, and with my free hand I wiped the rain from my eyes so I could see. Pierre. Within an instant, his arms were around me, and I was crying. And laughing. As was he.

'Lizzie, my dearest flittermouse, are you able to walk?' he asked.

'Aye. I will walk,' I said.

"'Tis not far. Monsieur Hobry's cart lies yonder.' I must have shown my puzzlement, for he added, 'Our coach was too long to make ready, so widow Desermeau has loaned us her new husband's cart.'

'Marie? My friend Marie?'

'Aye. I will tell you the news of it on the way home. Come, Lizzie, the children await you.'

These were the dearest words I ever did hear.

Pierre helped me up onto the cart, lifting me easily, and we took the short road home, my head resting on Pierre's shoulder. Home. Side by side with my husband, cool rain trickling over my cheeks and hands, home meant all sorts of things.

Home had stayed inside me the whole time I was locked away, but I no longer knew what it was to me. It had changed from the place I had once daily returned to, the family home that bustled around me whensoever I was not practicing midwifery, into that other place, the distant place filled by my children and husband, that I was a part of only by inclination but not by presence.

Soon I would pinch the two together again, make my home where I both wished to be and where I be, but, for now, I wished only to hold Pierre's hand and rest my head on him and enjoy how even the shine of the lanterns on the street mud was as beautiful as a meadow of flowers. Street lanterns. Strange how many hung outside buildings along the wayside where there were so few before.

Even the pain the stones in the road gave me as we went over them did not stop strength seeping gently between us from him to me and from me to him. I closed my eyes and I smiled.

28

22nd day of June, 1685 (first year of the reign of King James II)

From aloft, Lady Powys looked down at me from her elegant four-horse Berlin coach. The sun came from behind a cloud and she shielded her blue eyes with a Spanish lace fan. She could not hide her stirring fever for the forthcoming castigation.

'Do you not yearn to see that spawn of Hell wriggle and writhe upon the pillory? Thou art more harmed by his venomous devilry than any other, and I should have thought…not that I suggest you be not forgiving…but I imagined you might have relished fortune's fair play?'

'Nay,' I said. 'I do not wish to set eyes upon that legless creature again at any other time in my whole life!' That was a thing of which I could not have been more certain. I desired to live free from his vicious poison. Any punishment Dangerfield took that day would not change that. 'And fortune cannot be credited for the judgement against him, when we have worked so hard to put him there!'

The truth of the matter was that we had stood for hours in court, examined and examined twice over, but the tide had changed in our favour whilst I was in Newgate and, this time, the court was with us and turned against him. Oates and all his cabal were shown to have lied and perjured and falsified their testimony, so none was left to support them.

Dangerfield's lot was more particular, and he was despised upon his own merits of being a scoundrel, thief, coiner and criminal as well as letting that lying Devil speak from his belly.

Retribution would never be enough. His crime was far worse than to write a book – I could never forgive him his testimony against poor Father Lewis that died– yet he would merely stand on the pillory for libel just as I did. The whipping he would have today brought me little satisfaction; it did not balance years locked in a small, loathsome cell away from my children and husband. Besides, he had so oft whipped himself it would be no special hardship for him at all.

'But, Madam Cellier…Elizabeth…it is right justice is done in our name and all others he has falsely condemned. That worm has out-hissed every other viper in that nest of snakes, biting even his own kind. It is thus fitting that we watch this sentence carried out against him.'

'Your Ladyship.' I bobbed my respect. In my mind's eye I remembered blood and skin fly from the whip Ketch so recent drew back to strike Oates again and again. 'I am in a quandary. I am convinced the Lord wishes I should forgive, as those that died on the gallows forgave the ones that condemned them but, though I have searched for it, I have found neither the mercy nor the generosity to do so. I anticipated that seeing the flesh publicly whipped from the back of Oates would alleviate my desire for retribution. Seeing it did none of that. I fear to so indulge myself by enjoying Dangerfield's whipping will only fuel burning vengeance rather than damp it down.'

Forebodingly, the sun moved behind a dark cloud and I shivered. Lady Powys, seeing me stand in darkness, closed her fan and pointed it at me.

'If Oates had died as he should have died, as those innocent men he condemned did die, it would be some compensation, though the fate he deserves is far worse than that of those innocent men.' Aloud, but to herself, she added, 'If a worse death can be had than theirs.' Then she looked right through me. 'The Lord knows, his life should be forfeit for what he has done. Our good friend, Lord Stafford, that was in the Tower with my Lord Powys for more than a year, died at his hand. For though he did not himself cleave the man's neck with the axe, he did put him on Tower Hill as every person knows. Their deception is now discovered and they are to be punished for it. Will you not stand with me next to Lord Powys and have a little satisfaction?'

I looked to the ground and my dust-covered boots. When I spoke, I did not say any new thing, but the words that came were those that had to be said.

'It was no punishment when Oates stood in shame on the pillory after he took the lives of the best of men, nor did a whipping balance even one life, let alone that of so many. Indeed, his own life should be forfeit for such treachery. As should Dangerfield, his nest-fellow. They should rather be punished for murder than perjury. Is it so wrong to wish death upon him?'

'Forsooth, Madam, 'tis as you say. Oates has alas recovered and come back from the dead after his thrashing. But surely 'tis better that he be held to task at all for what he has done than exalted as he was ere now. Nay, the punishment is no fit for his crime, but at the very least it is punishment. In balance, it is better that Dangerfield, too, is whipped, though it be not enough.'

I shuffled my feet and then looked directly up into the confident eyes of Lady Powys. With her husband back at her side, she was once more strong where, before and without him, she was undone. Together they made formidable opponents, as they had at the King's Bench in the last days of May when we stood as witnesses together with Lord Peterborough against Thomas Dangerfield. I drew my own boldness from knowing that God had stayed by me these last years when he need not have done. I feared no retribution.

'Go then and see him whipped. He cares not for such small penance. He oft took a flail to his own skin and is hardened to it. If your destination today was the three-leg tree at Tyburn to see him hang for the lives he took, I would gladly take a place beside you, but at the end of this day he will still live to slither deviously and sneakily amongst better folk. He will still live as others have not.' I spat on the ground to show my distaste.

Lady Powys withdrew her head and spoke some words to another occupant of the coach, her husband William, Earl of

Powys. Though I oft visited with the lords in the Tower when they were there, and though they were released a year ago, I rarely saw him since that time. He barely showed his face in public. I could well imagine the hardship in recovering life with his wife, son and five daughters, for I had some little experience of that myself, but that of society was a different and more difficult matter. Society was not as forgiving, nor did it so easily forget.

After some deliberation, Lady Powys poked her head through the window once more.

'I cannot fault your reflections on this matter, and can only respect your decision. Lord Powys and myself will see Dangerfield punished today on your behalf, and I will, if you would be so good as to allow it, relay news of it back to you.'

'You are too kind, My Lady. You have a stronger stomach than I, for I would be sick that he does not suffer more.'

I stepped back from the coach and bowed my head, dismissing any further conversation.

"Tis fair reason, Madam Cellier. I will come by and see you after noon. Coachman, drive on!'

With that, the horses broke into a trot, and the leather sprung coach rumbled smoothly over the cobbles toward Ald-Gate, just as another carriage passed in the same direction. Was I the only one not on my way to the whipping? Perhaps I would walk to Newgate, where Dangerfield's whipping was to end, to see his suffering at its greatest, even if that were little enough, but the very desiring of it defiled my better feelings of charity. It would never return the lost years to those that had died.

Besides, I was not dressed for such a spectacle, but for better things. One should not tarry when summoned to the Palace. It would not do to keep the King waiting.

I did not take our coach, but walked, as I was wont to do, though it sometimes took more courage to do so. Danger did not keep to the shadows, but walked the streets in the form of every other person. And I avoided the river path in order not to be late. The Strand, Pall Mall and Saint James's Street were considerably emptier than

I was used to at noon. A woman with a basket of vegetables bade me good day. A chandler, with candles hanging between gritted teeth while trying to hang others from his shop sign, nodded his greeting. Some folk that knew me bade me walk on by, if they saw me at all.

The day was a pleasant enough. I swiped an occasional fly from my face but, otherwise, the only noteworthy observation to make was that the direction I took was the opposite to that of most others. Any that were free to, headed somewhere between Ald-Gate and Newgate to see the infamous Dangerfield whipped.

It was a short brisk walk to St James's Street, and took me less than half an hour to get there. One of the two guards that stood before the twin doors on either side of the tall oak palace tower gates pulled the large iron bell chain, the other shouted through a pipe to the side.

'Mrs Cellier to see His Majesty!'

I did not need to study the immense, rust coloured brick building, for I had done so before. The towers reached six floors above the ground, each door and window framed by that lighter stone oft used in some churches and regal buildings, sculpted to give a more splendid appearance.

I was accompanied from the magnificent main entrance to the throne room that the eighth King Henry had built one hundred and fifty years before. The King, when he was Duke of York, once said how the palace had been built on a leper hospital and that ghosts walked the corridors at night. The only ghosts this day were those of His Majesty's brother and father, two Kings that would live on in the hearts of many.

The corridor was as I remembered it, with ceilings so high and so ornate that reflections of gold and sparkles of chandeliers were as of stars twinkling at twilight, except that it was day. I could nearly see my own reflection in the gold-shine.

'Mrs Cellier.' A guard at the door greeted me, for I was expected. 'Unhood yourself and open your cloak.' Warm day as it was, as ever, I had worn my cloak so all might know my trade. I held it open, and the guard made sure I carried no weapon to kill the King. I had none, so he bid me leave my midwife bag at the door, a thing I was reluctant to do, for I knew how light-fingered some could be, but I did as I was instructed and found myself instantly naked without the tools of my trade. While I waited to be hailed, I straightened my skirt and my hood. I saw that the guard's shoes were clean and wax-polished, and withdrew my dusty boots beneath my skirt. They sullied the royal chambers, the shining tiled floor, so that I was in no doubt I did not belong in there but in the streets.

'His Majesty bids you enter, Mrs Cellier.'

I drew courage from the air and stepped inside the room, a great hall in any other house. King James sat where his brother had sat some six years since. He did not look as if taking his place on the throne this last winter were any discomfort to him. Rather, he sat as he might have sat every day since he were a child, managing the state of the country, on the edge of the ornate seat. I almost thought he would get up and greet me personally, as he had when I had met him as a Duke. He did not yet smile a greeting and I remembered myself to courtesy to the floor.

'Madam Cellier. Pray, come hither into the chamber so that I might see your countenance. Some time has passed, has it not? I hope you are recovered in wit and are of rude health after your ordeal in Newgate?'

I took myself closer to the throne and curtsied once more, but this time a short bob.

'Indeed, Your Majesty. You are uncommonly kind to think of me. Permit me, I beg of you, to present you with my most humble gratitude.'

'Nay, Madam Cellier. It is you that should allow me to extend every manner of sincere remorse, for I am beholden to you for a superior service in exposing those loathsome and despicable betrayers, whose fork-tongues did bring foul play against you and others, for which I cannot atone for. And the King's justice did hold and inconvenience you overly long when you awaited trial for treason against my brother. For this I must sincerely beg your pardon.'

With that pretty speech, the King did seem quite impressed with himself. He peered at me through slitted eyes and his satisfied smile seemed to await my refusal to accept his obligation in this matter, which I wasted no time in doing.

'You do me great disservice in thinking I would allow your desire for pardon when yours was neither the villainous lies that sent me there nor did your hand turn the key in the lock. I do not consider fault for any of it to be on your head, Your Majesty.'

'You are kindness itself, Madam.'

The King bowed his head to acknowledge his acquittal of any debt he had considered himself to owe me. His heavy-oiled, long, brown periwig caught the sunlight and shone as bright as any gold furnishings surrounding him. He looked at the ceiling as if to remember a further matter he wished to address to me. Once remembered, he returned his attention to me.

'Mrs Cellier.' He stopped in that unsuitable place and took up a silver tankard of ale from a nearby table. After wiping the froth from his beard, he came to the end of his thoughts slowly, so I must be impatient for them.

'Mrs Cellier, at the time of your first trial, you may have felt it incumbent upon yourself to battle alone against every lie aimed to bring you down. In this belief you are in part correct, for you were, as any person tried for treason, obliged to defend yourself. But I must press upon you that my brother spoke strongly in your favour, for he did not believe a wit of the testimony against you, though it was not for him to prove one way or another. I must congratulate you in your defence, for...' Again my patience for the last of his thought was tested as he took another swig of ale. And again he wiped the ale from his mouth. It seemed he might have been drinking a little fast and a little early and that perhaps he was in his cups. 'Now where was I? Oh yes. It is reported that your defence of yourself in court was of a superior nature and could not be bested! Jolly well done, I say!'

'"Tis most generous...' I cut my thanks short, for he continued talking, and to speak over the King was an offence most grave.

'Another matter I take it upon myself to address, is that of your second stay in prison. I believe you, along with your husband and other genteel persons, wrote to King Charles, God rest his soul, to plead Mercy, and for him to commute your sentence. In this he was generous, and you were freed on his word near two years ago. But you were not freed from the sentence itself, and it is this I first wish to address.' His eyes searched me so thoroughly, I was careful to hide my thoughts in case he should find them wanting. I did not try to speak into the silence, as was my wont and character, for he had not yet ended. 'I have heard you are against a pardon for your crime of writing your book, but I wonder if one would not be the worst thing you could have. Will you change your mind?'

In my answer I was certain, and hoped I spoke with as much conviction as I always held on this matter. 'I would neither presume to ask it, nor…and I beg your indulgence in my plain speaking… would I wish it a thing to be offered. I could never accept a pardon for a wrong I do not think I did.' I paused, then realised my words might be seen as ingratitude, and I did not wish to seem insensible to his kindness, nor bring down his ire for speaking against his judgement. 'I do hope that I do not offend Your Majesty in my boldness or my words.' I bowed my head and bobbed a curtsey.

The King shouted out at that. His sudden outburst caused me to bring my head up sharply, for I thought he was angry, but his face was alight and his guffaw turned into a laugh. 'Oh you are as quick as ever, Madam Cellier. I thought you might have become dull after your stay in Newgate, but I am delighted you still think on your toes!'

Just then, the guard opened the door from outside and announced a messenger.

'What? Cannot you see I am in audience here?' he said, his laughter drying in his throat. I could not help but be gratified that he wished to give me his undivided attention.

"Tis something of importance Your Majesty may wish to hear,' said the guard.

'Well, make haste and come forth then,' said King James. 'What is of such import I should be interrupted?' His elaborate gestures reminded me of Dangerfield at his most charming.

The messenger, a well-fed man of diminutive stature, beautifully coiffured hair that appeared to be his own and a nose that appeared not to be, for it was too big and too dark, spoke surprisingly well.

'Your Highness, I am come from the city with news of the convict, Mr Dangerfield, that was to have a whipping this day,' he said.

I wrinkled my nose. I could not escape the man even here in the palace.

'Well, what news do you bring me?' said the King.

'He is dead, Your Highness.'

'Dead? Dead, you say.' The King's face scrunched up, his mind likely imagining the dead Dangerfield. I do not know if my face was equally ridiculous, but the King's next remarks indicated that might have been the case. He raised himself almost to standing, wobbled, and then sat down once more. 'Begad! Am I not verily the most bad-mannered of hosts!'

My eyes and mouth were wide, and I did not know if I could close them. I could not answer the King, though he did not seem to await anything from me.

He went on, 'For now I have thrice wronged you. The first was as we spoke of a while ago, for your extended time in gaol. The second was to forget the punishment of that dastardly Dangerfield was today and you would wish to witness it. It was remiss of me to have done so.' He paused and practiced a look of astonishment. 'Why ever did you not say so?' Then he ended with a flourish, 'And the last was preventing your seeing the last breath taken from him. In that, I am equally destitute, for he offended against me when he accused me of plotting the killing of my brother just as he did you!' As an afterthought, he turned back to the messenger.

'Was he whipped to death?'

'No Your Majesty. He was stabbed.' The messenger appeared to enjoy the telling of this.

'He was, you say! Was it murder?'

'They say it was so, Your Highness. Some say he did not mean to do it.'

The King asked the question I wished to know. 'Who was the man that did all life this favour?'

My imagination awoke from its confusion. Unbidden came to mind Dangerfield in many guises: in Newgate, begging for my help; a broken man in a lonely cell; the silver lines shining on his tanned naked back in the courtyard; himself cutting a dash in the trial of the Jesuits with his pearl earring; his laughing and telling thrilling, bawdy or stirring tales around the dining table at home. Then, last, came an image of him standing against me in court.

Dead.

He was dead to me long ago, yet these visions invited sorrow to make a home in my belly. I had to know the facts of the matter.

'What was the manner of his death? Did he die outright?' I said.

'Aye,' said the King. 'Tell us all you know.'

The messenger answered first the King, and then me, relating his tale with the passion of one relating many.

"Twas a gentleman of the law, Your Majesty. A barrister of Gray's Inn by the name of Robert Frances. 'Twas his fortune, whether ill or good, that the coach taking Mr Dangerfield back to prison happened to pass him along the way at Hatton-Garden in Holborn. Mr Frances, curious, rapped on the side of the coach and asked Mr Dangerfield, 'How now, friend. Have you had your heat this morning?' meaning his whipping,' explained the messenger, 'and Mr Dangerfield, not knowing him, was uncivil and asked him 'What have you to do with me?' and spat on him. They tell me Mr Frances then spoke some words of derision to Mr Dangerfield and called him 'so much scum upon the dregs of life in the street' and said he 'should die by a thousand cuts'!'

Then, still facing the King, but his eyes at me, the messenger carried on in his best story-telling voice. 'Mr Dangerfield spoke such scurrilous words, after which curses he called Mr Frances 'the son of a whore'. That enraged the barrister so that he shook his bamboo cane at the man, and when Mr Dangerfield went to grab it, Mr Frances shook the stick harder still and ran it right through Mr Dangerfield's left eye and into his brain!'

Yes, I wished him dead, at times with all my heart, but this was not as I had imagined it.

'Did his death come fast?' I asked. That he did not suffer was unkind to any that had suffered by his false accusations. He had turned on me when I had saved him, and now I was deprived of this last sight of him! And, yet, he was still a man.

'Nay, Madam. He is dying still.

'Alas,' said the King. 'If they try the barrister in court, I must allow sentence, for he has murdered a man, but, truly, I would rather shake his hand. He has done us all a great service! Have they taken him in?'

'Aye, Your Highness, they have. He was seized as he ran into Saint Thavie's Inn in Holborn and is yet held in Newgate.'

'And where is Dangerfield now?' I asked. I had thoughts of seeing his last breath.

'He is returned to gaol and laid to bed.'

'Thank you, good man. You may go.'

The messenger was thus dismissed. The King was thoughtful. He took up his ale and looked within it for awhile without drinking. Then he spoke most cheerfully.

'Gads! This is verily too much ado and did only arrest for a short while what I wish to say to you. If you did wonder at my summoning you to the palace, I will allay any fear it was for bad and assure you it was only for good. I have now thrice wronged you. Is it not fortunate I am come prepared to offer reparation?' The King opened his arms in grand gesture. 'You are, as is every person, aware no male heir of mine has survived birth nor infancy. I have heard it from the most virtuous and reliable sources, one being Catherine, the Queen Dowager and another is my first wife, Anne, God rest her soul, that you are the midwife that brings forth healthy babies when none are forthcoming. The Queen invites you do so for her. I am requested to task you with this but, in the stead of a task, I wish to bestow this as a gift upon you, for it can only better your position in society.'

'Naturally, Your Majesty, it is a gift of the most generous kind!' Could my heart be more tumultuous? Both news of Dangerfield and an invitation to attend the Queen all mixed in one bag! 'Please convey to Her Majesty I am honoured and will attend her at her convenience.'

I left the palace soon after, with a purse of gold in my pocket and a heart of gilded lead beating in my breast.

29

3rd day of June, 1687

'Mon Dieu! Can this be so, Lizzie?' asked Pierre 'A more terrible loss I cannot imagine!'

Most times, Pierre showed little interest in the findings of my searches and asked few questions, for he was taken up with his own business, but when I recounted how many infants and mothers I had found died at birth, or soon after, as recorded by each and every church in the city, that was his remark. I wrote the sad figures in my journal.

'That is the whole of my design, dear heart, if more be trained in the old ways, more lives might be saved...' I said. "Tis not enough we preserve life in childbirth. That Devil's left hand man, Poverty, takes a particularly terrible toll. I have found that in such a place as Cheapside every new mouth is a burden ill afforded, and many babies are abandoned to charity or death.'

'If mothers deny the infants, who would take them?'

'A midwife college. I make my plan for a college that will take such infants.'

'What use to take such infants of the nature of the very fathers and mothers that abandoned them? What use to save them only to return them later to the poverty whence they came!'

'Nay, Pierre. Remember how our own children were once helpless babes? And now they are grown into strong character. See how they laugh and cry and converse on the worldly nature of things. Each of these abandoned infants, unwanted only for lack of food and shelter, would grow as our children grew, to be Godloving, and educated in the ways of the world, and they would be useful in our society. 'Tis only for the lack of this attention they turn out to be villains and rogues. With good care, they might be as worthy as any child born in good society'

'And who will pay for this, my dear? I think the King will not care to dig too deep into his pockets for these brats!' Pierre came and stood behind me and read my figures. Soon the warmth of his gentle fingers caressing my shoulder ran like a river through me. It was the touch of affection rather than invitation to bed, for we were wrapped up together in the discussing of my work.

'Now here is my coup, *mon chéri*!' I showed Pierre the papers I had written and re-written until I was satisfied with them. 'I have made a design so clever it will floor you,' I smiled. "Tis the midwives themselves that will pay for everything: the building of the college and the training of them, as well as the rescue and care of foundling babies. And if more money is needed, alms boxes might be placed in churches and public places for people to give charity if they so choose. But though this can be done, the most of what is necessary will come from annual membership fees, paid by the midwives from their richer coffers, for a well trained midwife will earn more than an ignorant one.'

'Will it be enough?'

'It will,' I said. 'I have worked out a sum that should cover it.'

'I will raise my hat to you if the King will allow womenfolk this freedom, but if anyone can make pretty speeches and persuade His Majesty of the benefits of this scheme, 'tis you.'

'Bless you for you sincere kindness, my dear. I have near finished the plan. I hope 'tis as complete as any could be. And if those buzzing around the King cannot find fault in it,' I said, 'then it might please the King, for he can give it his royal name, and it can be a monument to his goodness.'

Pierre returned to the fireplace and smiled indulgently. 'That is a pretty touch indeed. I am sure that might persuade His Majesty if he is undecided. It cannot harm his reputation to be seen as a benefactor for his people.' Something in the way he stood reminded me of the man he once was. In particular, a vision of him punching Dangerfield made me smile back.

Then, unbidden, for he was never welcome there, the memory spun about and I was looking at Dangerfield, or Captain Willoughby, as we knew him then. He was sat on the frozen ground rubbing his jaw after Pierre hit it, and looked a poor example of a man, the poorer still for having been easily floored by an ageing one.

It was not only he that fell that day, but my estimation of him, if I had any left. Before I could think on it, the image was fast replaced by another gruesome and grisly one: Dangerfield lying on a bed of blood with a ragged black hole where his beautiful long-lashed eye once was, and dried blood on his cheek. I remember it was the day I came from the palace, after hearing of his injury, and on the spur of the moment changed direction toward the gaol.

'Are you come to save me or to see me die?' he had said.

'I saved you once and you repaid me with betrayal. The value of your life, once lost, was never recovered. I do not want it.'

I could not take my eyes from the mangled wretch. If he tried to move, the wounds from the whipping made him cringe and curl, though he could not escape the affliction. Lady Powys later told me his skin was torn from his back so there was more blood than skin left. The straw he lay on was testimony to this, for blood spilled from beneath him in a soggy puddle and, even in the dark, shone wet.

'Though you are come to see me die, you are the only one that has come. For that I give you thanks.' He spat out the words between long moments of agony and retching. Red dribbled from the corners of his mouth.

'I do not want your thanks, you ungrateful cur,' I said. 'I am here to see if the Devil sits in the room with you for, if he is not yet here, he will come to keep you company soon.'

Dangerfield wailed. Coldly, I watched him writhe, surprised I did not have even so much sympathy I had for the cats burned at The Processions.

'Do not say so! Pray for me, Madam, I beg of you. Pray for

my soul.' Every word cost him dear.

'Do you repent? Have you confessed?' It was of little interest to me if he did or did not.

'I do!' Then he screamed, 'My eye! My eye!' Then he became still and said nothing for some time. I turned to go when I had seen enough. 'Fetch the priest.'

I turned back to him. His lids were closed now.

'You do not believe in our religion. Why would you have a priest come?'

Without his disquieting single eye watching me, I took the opportunity to look at him. Now his contortions were ended, and he was nearly a corpse, the anger went out of me. He begun to rattle. Was that it? Was he finished? Through some extraordinary draw on reserves, when he should be dead, he came back to life again.

'I will…confess…before I die.' His words barely reached my ears, still the rattle between them, but I knew what they were.

I was divided. My faith would have me fetch a priest; it was the right, the charitable, thing to do. I did not want to be charitable to that man. I did not want to aid him to Heaven. If it were the will of the Almighty God to bring me there, I would not wish to meet him, for then it would not be Heaven for me. The rattle came loudly then and filled the room, and I could bear it no longer.

'Gaoler! Gaoler! This man wishes for a priest!' The gaoler, I knew, was nearby, waiting to let me out. He answered.

'Thee be in the wrong place for a priest, Madam. Ain't none 'ere!'

Death made so much noise coming now, I feared he came for me too.

'Find a priest. He needs one now!' I tried for authority.

He laughed. I heard him shout to someone further away, 'She be seeking a priest.' He went on laughing, joined by that other person. 'Weren't that one swinging from the gallows?'

It was no use. The rattle was slower now. Irregular. Against every inclination, I returned to Dangerfield's side. I could not help myself; I took his hand and knelt beside him and prayed for his soul. And then he was gone.

I shook my head and dipped my pen nib into the ink. Would that inconsiderate man never leave me be!

'I have found that a woman who wishes a man to hear what she says can best do so by first telling him his feathers are as fine as a peacock's, his craftiness could outwit a fox, and his wisdom surpasses that of an owl. He is then so caught up by preening, his mind stays in the most receptive frame! I then hold myself up as a looking glass that he might better preen his feathers and not be distracted from his receptive mind-set.'

'Yes, my dear. You have thus used me effectively many a time.' Pierre laughed. I smiled as we shared this moment together, and then I begun my evening's writing. My presentation must claim perfection if it was to hold up against scrutiny, and it would be examined many times before even the King would be allowed the slightest sight of it.

30

8th day of October, 1687

Five months. Five months since the King bestowed his mercy upon me. Pierre warned me that I must not cleave to the anger, which was my constant companion for the seven horrid years since I was first sentenced and imprisoned. He told me I must act grateful for such kindness, that it had not been necessary to give it, since I did, as a matter of inescapable fact, act against the law of the Three Kingdoms. I must obey the law as did every person and, if I did not, I should be punished as was every other that did not.

But I could not have faith in a law that said writing a book such as Malice Defeated was worthy of so high punishment as I had borne, no matter the boldness of it. The King's mercy could not bring the full redemption it should. I would forever carry the mark of a criminal, though I was guilty of no other thing than compassion.

If they thought truth could so easily be shut away, they were wrong. It could never be. There would always be some that talked and kept it alive. And, if they thought we should not care about truth, that we should not see it, nor do a thing about it, then they deceived themselves. No law could close every person's eyes and cover every person's ears, no matter the degree of coercion.

Old man Cellier rubbed his hands as he doddered toward the fireplace. His clothes were awry. He scratched his bare head as he sat, no longer caring for a periwig about the home, and took his pipe from the table. I smiled and returned to my writing.

After a few lines I was disturbed again when Pierre pushed to his feet and patted his jacket pockets, looking for tobacco.

"Tis where you left it, on the sideboard,' I said.

I gathered folios of paper together in a neat heap on the desk as Pierre walked to the sideboard and found his pouch of dried leaves tucked into a fine china cup, displayed there as part of our best table service. I did not much like the smoke of many pipes together, but a single one I found I could endure most comfortably, and certainly it was a better habit than the snuff taking that some gentlemen took to. Did we not see enough of that sneezing over persons during the Black Death of '65?

Pierre moved slowly, his bones not so ready to do his bidding as he would like them to. He took up the small pipe tongs from beside the fireplace and picked a glowing wood ember to light his pipe. Once he had sunk back into his chair, I returned to rereading my proposal. I was inordinately pleased with it. It was entitled:

A Scheme for the Foundation of a Royal Hospital, and Raising a Revenue of Five Or Six-thousand Pounds a Year by, and for, the Maintenance of a Corporation of Skilful Midwives, and Such Foundlings Or Exposed Children as Shall be Admitted Therein, Etc.

My wordy title did not bore the King and I was satisfied that he showed himself more receptive to my ideas than his brother, may The Lord protect his soul. His fast approval was especially satisfying, since it was given before the Queen had found she was with child.

It pleased me that the copious records I had set down in this account of horrid treatment and deaths of infant-bearing women and their babies, through the bad training of midwives, had served their high purpose. But I did not wrap it up so tight. Since I had spun my web of ideas of how the midwife college might take under its wing all the abandoned babies and infants of the city I had added further details to the scheme. The King was impressed that the wherewithal for it all would be raised from the training fees of the midwives themselves. The sum of five or six thousand pounds a year would cover not only the building of the hospital, and the maintaining of it, but also the training of a corporation of skilful midwives with not a penny coming from his own vault.

I took my quill and adjusted the nib to write another piece. Some person, a physician with little or no sense of our craft, had misused my idea for a hospital to attack women as midwives. That was a thing I would not allow! Indeed, I would hone my answer as an arrow and shoot it straight to the arrogant heart of him. I would not let him dissemble an honour that was centuries in the making. Nor would I allow him his barbed pokes at me! I would publish an open answer to him as he had done to me.

With my pen poised over the inkpot, I thought of the years since I had come from prison. I had been as a toad crawling from pond scum that none would look upon without smelling the prison, long after I had washed the last muck off me. Aversion was naked in the eyes of every person I knew, no matter how they tried to dress it. Furthermore, they were wont to choose any but me to do a midwife's work until I lost the spirit to wear my cloak with pride when it was so plain unwanted.

How different it was then and now.

'Lizzie, did'st thou find the Queen in good spirits and robust health?' Pierre smacked his lips about his pipe.

'I am pleased with her thus far. I am hopeful she will stay with child if she stays faithful to every instruction I have given.'

'When will it come?'

'In the summer, after fledglings have left their nests and before the corn is fat in the fields. She must practice patience for many months ere her son comes forth.'

'Begad! A son, you say! Can you be so sure of it? I pray you have not talked wide of this.'

'I have told any that ask.'

'Show caution, dear flittermouse. Not all will greet this news with joy. Many are satisfied the King's line will pass to Mary, his daughter, on his death, for her reign would remove any alliance with the Catholic religion from the throne. If it is truly a son, then many will defend the crown from him!'

'I have done tests, and I am confident the Queen carries a boy-child in her belly.'

'Then you must not declare it. You may endanger the Queen's life by saying so. You may also endanger your new position.'

I smiled. Though I argued for it handsomely, and held high hopes the King had wits enough to see how suitable I was as Secretary to the Company of Midwives, my proposed midwife college, I was unready for him to so readily agree. He did straight away declare how perfect I was for the commission and said he would make it official in due course. I held hope my forthcoming exalted status in St. James' Palace would wash the last of the prison from me and I would be once more acceptable in society.

31

9th day of December, 1688

Mermaid Inn, Rye
ere the cock crows
Stay clear of London Road
Faith guide the blind

The ruddy-cheeked messenger that delivered this short missive limped away, still huffing and puffing as a horse from unnatural exertions. He asked for no answer by return, nor awaited one. His task here was done, though his whole task was not. He held a fistful of warning notes for all those he was instructed to call upon.

The use of the words 'Faith guide the blind' was the signal they had told us to expect at the last Huguenot meeting. 'If the words come to you in any form, then you must run, and run fast. Take nothing with you.'

'Faith guide the blind.'

Our vain hopes that we would not ever hear these words in our lives were dashed, for they signalled, truly, that our faith must now be tested by strangers in whom we had never learned trust. The words signalled that King James had either fled or died. Either way, the King had lost the battle for the throne and we must flee ere the sun heralded a new day. If we stayed, we risked everything. We risked our lives.

Pierre collected a single trunk hid in the cupboard. We had packed the trunk with personal items months earlier, back when news of the young prince caused mutterings of unrest, in readiness of this day.

I woke Isabelle, and she helped with the younger children. Maggie, ever wiser and quicker witted than her thirteen years could account for, awoke on the instant, grabbed her small, carved pearl box of cherished trinkets, where once she kept beetles, butterflies and pressed flowers, and made for the door. It took more to wake young Peter from his slumber, and longer still for our urgency to convey itself to him, for his head was full of things children should dream of: brave knights and the defending of our land from invading Dutchmen. There was no time to call the maid to dress him, so I helped him don his coat over his long-johns.

'Ready yourself by the door. We should leave soon.'

Pierre left us with that instruction and called upon the servant quarters to warn them it was time for us to make good our escape. Those that were to come with us fast readied themselves, but those that chose to stay must also leave. They should not be found in our home for they were tainted by us and would suffer a fate no different than our own.

'Have you fetched all that you ought?' Pierre asked. We had oft planned this instant, when staying would be more dangerous than leaving. Before now, the right time did not present itself. Another infant would need my help to be born, another lucrative deal would call Pierre to seal it, but tidings of the King's fall cut short our dawdling for it marked the time to flee for France.

As Catholics famous in our position, the risk to our lives was intolerable.

'Aye.' My nod was sharp. 'Think you our Lord and Lady Powys have already learned what has come to pass?'

It was a mere stone throw into the past, some few months since, that Powys House was odiously attacked and ransacked; the second time such abominable events had occurred since Lord Powys was released from the Tower. In the first instance, they lost most every one of their possessions and barely escaped with their lives. With good fortune, this last time, His Lordship and Her Ladyship were partaking of country air when the mob stormed their house. Their home was lost, but they were not.

371

Though the new knick-knacks with which Lord and Lady Powys had since filled the house did not raise any needless sentimentality, this barely diminished how distraught they were on their return to find, once more, their house was barren and destroyed, and razed from proud stately home to burnt ruin, as after the Great Fire. Such act of malice, reminiscent of those done against my own childhood family, near finished Lady Powys, and would indeed have done so had her husband not been once more at her side.

It was then in that horrid time we made a pact that, if such a time came that staying here in this country was no longer tenable, we would together travel to the coast and purchase passage to France. There, good King Louis would protect us, for he had told King James his Royal Court would be welcomed. We were of that court: Lady Powys as Principal Lady of the Bedchamber and I, as principal advisor to the Queen's midwife, Mrs Wilkes. My success in bringing the Queen to full term had hoisted me high in the King's estimation and secured my place in the court.

'I was in the city today. Lord Powys did stop his coach by me.' Pierre bobbed his head toward the other side of the trunk as he spoke, indicating I should take the other strap. Together we carried the trunk to the door, where our three children still at home awaited us. What of our other children? I could not think of them. I could only hope they were making their own way to the port or had fled to the countryside. 'He told me, if the worst acts were played out, and the Dutch came close, he would accompany the King and follow the Queen and Lady Powys to Paris and safety.'

So rumours were true, Queen Mary had already left the country, taking Lady Powys with her.

'Did it seem as if he knew today would bring such sore news? He might have obliged us and given us fairer warning!'

I could not prevent a moment's derision, though this warning was not unexpected. We had hung on tenters since news reached us a day or so ago, that the King's married nephew, William of Orange, and first-born daughter, Mary, had landed with an army at the coast and were making their way to London. Successive messengers came with news the Dutch were closer and then closer still, but it was not dread we saw in the eyes and faces of the people of London. It was hope. No invasion this. It was by invitation. All for fear the infant boy-child would step into his father's Papist shoes.

I had no thought there would be so much turmoil with the birth of James Francis Edward Stuart, the new Prince of Wales and healthy heir to the throne. It seems a Catholic King that has shown his colours might be forborne as long as the line ends with him, but a Catholic King that was a mere swaddling babe and might live longer than many of his subjects was more than could be endured. Religious tolerance shown by the father was not a prediction of his son's actions. For who could read the character of one so far from manhood (unless you are the astrologer, Gadbury, I suppose)?

Furthermore, there were accusations that the Queen's own female child had died at birth and was swapped for a changeling, a healthy boy, using a warming pan. Those who made this claim cannot have seen the size of her warming pan, if they thought a baby could fit into one. But this ludicrous claim was given credence by any who wished to believe it, rather than by those that sought the truth.

There never was any use talking to such persons. I had tried and failed. But, as well, I had tried to show them how their own religion and beliefs were as little tolerant of other beliefs as they accused of the Roman Church. Perhaps it was so, that every country destroyed all that did not comply with its majority.

We five of us stood on the threshold of the living room and looked this house once more in the eye that everyone knew was the hearth, or heart, of the place. It was as it had always looked, but it already missed us around the flame. I had called this home for eighteen years, notwithstanding my times in prison. I remembered my first children and my husband's children playing around that hearth. They were ghosts that sang songs, read books and talked by candlelight long after sundown. I could see them – us – happy spirits, sad spirits that were ourselves. The only home these youngest three children had ever known, begged of me stay. So many memories clamoured for me to say goodbye, but I did not have time for them all.

This house had seen its fill of staying guests over the years – some pleasing and some that seemed honest until they removed their topcoat and revealed a Devil's tail – all the spirits of them now came to life before my eyes, as if they had so much life in them still.

The boys from St Omer were some of those ghosts that now haunted the room. There they were sitting around the fireplace after a pleasing meal. Despite the danger of this dark night, one side of my mouth turned up, remembering lively debates and heated conversations that had brought us together and made all else about that terrible time bearable.

Unstoppable, Captain Willoughby, as we then knew him, came unbidden to my mind just as he came unbidden to our home, and joined our society of spirits. Despite that he later changed his name to Judas, at that time he was the biggest wit amongst us. Oftentimes, that jolly fellow, when he was one, had us laughing through the darkness of the night with his flowery language, ornate gestures and mimicking of persons of notoriety.

Toe to heel behind such congenial thoughts came the reminder of how, after many months breaking bread with him as one of the family, Willoughby had from that trusted place stuck the dagger deep into the vulnerable heart of us.

And if he was not of the name Captain Willoughby, nor of Judas, he was Thomas Dangerfield, villain and fiend who, in the likeness of the snake in Eden, came sliding into our warm nest, curled around us and leeched the warmth of life from us.

We thought we had released a harmless cage bird that sung his pretty song and preened his fancy feathers for the reason of his merely knowing he was a pretty bird, but, all the while, he was not a bird at all. He was a wily fox that bit the hand that freed him. I shook deceptive memories from my head.

'Come Lizzie,' said Pierre. Not waiting to see if I did as he bid me, he went to pick up one side of the trunk. He might be frail, but he was ever determined to prove he could do as well as any young man.

'One moment more, Pierre. 'Tis too quick and I would take a moment longer.'

'This occasion is not blessed with endlessness. We must leave now. They might already be coming for us!'

Nevertheless, I could not move until the apparitions were gone from that place. The phantom of Dangerfield raised his face to the roof and laughed that infectious laugh that had all persons around him find amusement where none would otherwise be. Facing that one was another spectre, the one that pleaded with me for his freedom from the odiousness of gaol. A more sorry sight one could not see, unless it was that of him as he was whipped through the city, the like of which I did not see.

Did Dangerfield deserve the nature of his death? I could not bear thinking of the man who had shared our meals and done such good service for us, our fine and quick-witted companion.

But for the thief in him, the coiner and turncoat, his death was seemly and fitted him as a glove. I would never forgive him his sins, may the Lord have mercy on me. To my continuing shame, I could not acquit him with whole heart as did the poor Fathers that died on the gallows their false condemners.

Fast after Dangerfield disappeared from my sight came a vision of Titus Oates being whipped 'til the skin came from his back. His life was spared though he cost good men their lives.

'Mama! Mama!' Isabelle took my arm and pulled. Her sob swept my family, the boys, Dangerfield and Oates from my inner sight. 'We cannot tarry longer, Mama! They come for us!'

I frowned and shook my head. With difficulty, I banished the ghosts and in the instant saw Pierre and the children waiting for me, concern or, perhaps, urgency, holding them remarkably still, watching me. When I looked at Pierre, I saw not Pierre as he was now, but as he was when we took to being together in this house, and also the solace of seeing him standing at the edge of the crowd as I walked to the pillory when he gave me the baton. The strength he did give me then, and through all other times, did the same for me now, and I straightened my back.

'Forgive me, I dwell too long in the past. Let us go.' My voice trembled more than I liked. I firmly tied the ribbons of my black bonnet under my chin and pulled the black cloak tight around me. My red midwife cloak and bonnet were packed in my case along with other of my midwife things, things I hoped to use again in France once we were settled.

'Come, Lizzie. Come children. Make haste. Our boat will not await us!' said Pierre.

We followed him to the door where our coach now stood. Dowdal wrapped the reins around the holding strap, jumped down without using the step, and helped Pierre load our trunk and the children's' meagre baggage on the back in silence. Icy fog formed from their lips as they did so. There was room enough for only our family in this coach, two facing where we would go, two facing from whence we came. Maggie and little Peter squashed together as one. Any servants wishing to stay in our employ would close up the house and meet us at the boat to join the King in St Germaine-en-Laye.

In readiness, the groom held down the horses, fresh and braying, rightly surprised by their night time journey. The midwinter nights were long, and the ends of many trips came in the dark, but not so many beginnings. None of us spoke as we took our places inside, but soon the creaks of the springs and rattle of the harnesses covered our silence.

No sooner did we turn the corner than the reason for our leaving stopped our coach. A mob of bawling men and some women stood in the middle of the street blocking our way. A person grabbed the bridle with such speed that the nearest horse to him jumped and bucked so I thought the coach would tip over. Through the blinds, I saw a rough man with a long beard and crushed hat coming towards the door and braced myself for confrontation.

'Where do you run to with your packed cases in the night? Surely, you do not mean to leave the city and deny the new King! Oh? Did you not hear, we have a new King. Long live King William!'

'Long live King William! Long live Queen Mary!' The crowd took their cue from the ringleader and chanted loud and together.

'Let us through!' said Dowdal with, I was pleased to note, more authority than request.

'Running like rats from a fire! Stay and meet the new King! He itches to meet you!' said a man different than the one that spoke before. The blinds hid most of the beast-crowd. I could barely see any man or woman, only an arm here or the back of one there now they were gathered close in front of the horses. Where was the man that had been coming to the coach door?

'Shall we see what these rats look like ere their tails are all left behind!' A woman, loud and close by. Raucous laughter. The handle moved and the door opened a crack. I grabbed the inside handle and pulled it back with a bang. It was straight away pulled harder, jarring my arms, and the woman shouted to the others, 'Look! The rat hides in his hole! Come on out, Mister Rat, there are no mousers here!' This time the door opened with such strength I could barely hold it. Pierre held his own side shut and could do nothing for me. The coach rocked violently from side to side as we tried and failed to hold the doors closed. Isabelle's hands closed over mine, and Pierre's, 'Maggie, Peter, hold tight!' told me they were helping him. The doors were little more protection than a cloak against a sword.

They rocked the coach harder and harder, so hard I feared it would tip over.

'I cannot hold much longer! They are too many,' I shouted.

Rough voices encouraged those pulling at the doors outside, and the blinds were torn away. Arms reached in to grab us. I saw Dowdal pulled from the coach to the ground, where he struggled against punches thrown at him by a puny and dirty yellow haired boy hardly out of britches, one that would hardly have made a mark on a milk jelly had our man not been held down by two monstrous fat oafs and a woman with yellow hair. The last was likely the boy's mother. She screeched, 'Go on lad, harder!'

'Pierre, they have Dowdal!'

'Pierre? Gads! We got ourselves a French rat in here!' crowed the woman by my window whose talons bit into my flesh. I could not but dislike this woman with the greatest of intensity befitting the Devil himself. I braced my feet braced against the coach wall and, for a moment, the wavering door shut once more.

Pierre shouted through the window, 'Leave the man be! He did nothing to you!'

'Nought but carry Popish rats around the country!' shouted one on Pierre's side that I could not see. The man growled as if he had swallowed a dog and it spoke through him.

'Shove over, Mrs Round. Let me 'ave 'er.'

Suddenly, the face of the biggest man I ever saw, a giant in this world of men, more hairy than a standing bear, appeared behind the woman. For a moment none pulled the other side of the door and it slammed shut, but it was merely the still before a terrible storm. Even with my feet strong on the wall, and both hands braced against the handle with Isabelle's on mine, we did not give the man the slightest trouble turning it. Single-handed, he pulled it down as if it were a gale against a mere feather.

The sharpness of the pull caught me off my guard, and the door flew open taking us flying into the heart of the mob.

I hit my head on the step as I fell.

'Leave my children!' I moaned. 'They are innocent!'

The giant grabbed my arm tight so it hurt and dragged me to where Dowdal still struggled against the grip of three. He was making hard work for them, and the lad's punches were as of a mosquito, barely touching him. The giant discarded me beside him like a corn husk, and then returned to the coach. Too many surrounded me to see what happened with Pierre and the children, but soon Isabelle was flung down next to me.

'See here, more rats!'

'Leave them alone! Pierre, help them!' Pierre was no doubt doing all he could, but he was, alas, an old man that could do no more than a child.

A raggedy woman with slitted eyes came from the far side of the coach and eyed me up and down. 'Look 'ere! It's the infamous Popish Midwife!'

'The Popish Midwife?' said the dirty, yellow-haired woman.

'Aye, with her brats and foreign husband!'

'That's the one that tricked 'em out of 'anging 'er,' shouted the yellow-haired woman to the crowd. 'String her up, I say! String them all up!'

My children. My husband. This was no court and I could do nothing. I tried to stand, but felt something rock-hard hit the back of my head, and spun to the ground. I shouted, 'Pierre!' as I fell, but I could not move, and I could not keep my eyes from closing.

When I came to, my hands were bound together and my arms were pulling from my shoulders as I was dragged and bumped face up over rough road. I heard a slopping noise. The next moment I passed through something hot and wet. It seeped through my skirt. Horse dung. I was being dragged through the street by a horse. I tried to raise my head to find my children, but could not.

For a moment, a heavy boot stepped on my cloak and it tightened round my throat leaving me gasping. 'She's choking!' cried a voice close by. Isabelle. I could not see her, but her voice wobbled as if she too was bumped as was I.

'She aint yet started choking!' came a laugh. 'Sir Death is coming for her.'

I struggled to pull my hands free, but could neither see the children nor Pierre. His voice was not of those I could hear.

'Leave my children be!' I sounded weak even to me. 'They have done nought to anyone.'

'Quiet woman. If they behave, we will let them watch you swing as you should 'ave swung eight years ago.'

'Let us burn her as she burnt at the processions!' said another. It was not their laughs I wished to hear, but word from Pierre. A stab of fear pierced me. Did they kill my husband, or did they show him mercy? What of the children?

My back and legs and sides were so bruised as my poor broken body was tossed over mud and stones that I would cry had I the strength. If it was summer I would have been damaged worse.

I saw familiar rooftops and black sky. It was a route I had so oft taken towards Lincoln Fields Inn and Powys House. My arms burned and would surely pull free of my shoulders if they dragged me much further. Where was Dowdal? Did they kill him? Why did they not finish me and have it over with! I did not wish to live without my family.

Isabelle. She at least lived. I must find a way free to help her escape. This was a reason to hold on.

'Where do you take me?' I asked, not expecting an answer. 'To Tyburn. You are to dance the jig you should have danced long since!'

Tyburn. To hang. If that was so, the Lord had merely lent me eight years, delayed but not changed the sentence I once thought to have escaped. They took me to the Three-Legged Mare, where too many good men and women died alongside murderers.

In some strange form of escape, my mind lingered on that charming French highway thief, Du Vall, I saw hang not long before I married Pierre. Some words of the poem I wrote for him came to me now:

And Love (though know it) disdains so small a Prize,
Which makes thee bold, and glad to venture where
Thou think'st there is not the least room for fear.
This shows thy Narrow Soul, thy Little Merit,
This shows thou art all Gall, and hast no Spirit.

There was not the least room for fear.

The road was harder here and I talked no more. Every stone in the road found a mark in my back, buttocks or legs.

I tried to stand to my feet, but straight away my foot caught on the fabric of my dress and I twisted round so now I faced the ground and my knees and boots caught the bumps. My shoulders suffered more and my back near broke. Nor could I now see the rooftops or sky, only the horse's hooves and the mud. Only my closeness to the animal prevented my face from dragging in the mud where I would have been smothered by it. I was not well pleased at my bungled handiwork.

Each time I tried to turn my face back up, I came close to claiming a foothold beneath me, but then the horse jerked forward and I lost it. After a while of trying, I turned my feet to the side to stop them catching, but the thought of my making it easy for them had me digging them back in, even if it pained me. And it did pain me.

Over the sounds of the rowdy mob, that no doubt shared a good deal of blood between them, came a thunder of horses' hooves, not a single horse but many.

'Ho! What passes here!' The horse pulling me stopped and I dropped my knees in the thick mud. Though weary, and the mud slippery, and though it pained me beyond measure, I used the moment to walk my knees towards my hands then struggled to standing and looked about me.

A group of masked horsemen had stopped in the path of the mob. I now saw, by the dark mark on the back leg, I was dragged by my own horse, Thor's Hammer, they took from the coach. They used my own animal to drag me to my death! Isabelle, with her hands tied behind her, was held at the elbow by the yellow haired youth. I could not see Peter or Maggie.

'Out o' our way. This is nought to do with you!' The man's voice was that of the hairy ringleader that attacked our coach.

I stretched my beaten legs and pulled my back straight then, carefully, shifted round the horse's flank to better see the horsemen.

'The judge does his own work,' he said. His deep welsh voice sounded familiar. Lord Powys? Had he not left for the coast? He sat tall in his seat as a country gentleman, but wore no periwig. His right hand crossed his saddle and rested on the hilt of his sword, though he did not make a move to withdraw it. 'What wrong has this woman done you that you punish her so?'

'If it be something, it aint nowt to you, Sir. This 'ere is a matter intimate to ourselves and 'er.' One of the twin fat men pointed as he spoke trying, and failing, to sound rich and gentlemanly. I tiptoed to better see if he or the other still held Dowdal. No sign of him.

'A judgement is a public matter, man, and a matter only for the courts. Release the woman.' His voice held neither violence nor tyranny only calm authority. It was a voice that expected, rather than asked, to be obeyed.

'Nay, we will not! Fortune has brought The Popish Midwife

into our company this night that we might deliver her to the gallows she cheated Destiny of before. Go about your business, Sir, and let us go about ours.'

The fat man waved his under-sized rapier high in the air in a show of defiance. The horseman stayed still, and when his men came forward behind him, he held up his free hand and they stopped. His right hand did not move from his own sword. He spoke with the same commanding voice, but I sensed, rather than saw, a change in his mood.

'The King wishes an audience with this woman at the palace.'

'The King must not be sullied by this contagious whore's presence. We take her to Tyburn.' The man seemed to think the exact same threat he made to me but a short time ago was now a rescue of the King's well-being.

'You disobey His Majesty's direct order?'

'Why should the King wish an audience with this traitor?' jeered the fat brother of the first speaker.

'Is it for you to question His Majesty?' With this, the masked horseman, still calm, drew his broad sword and lay it across the horse's mane.

The act was warning enough to any person with sense, but there is rarely sense to a mob's words or actions, nor do they closely observe the words or actions of others.

Even unbalanced that I was after my ordeal, the glint of the sword behind the horse's ears was clear, but the fat twin did not even think to flinch as the horse galloped towards him. Steel on steel, the horseman's blade slid along the length of the fat man's skinny blade and twisted it neatly and skilfully from his fat hand in a masterful gambit. As stars fallen from the sky, sparks lit the dark street and the thin sword flew high over the crowd and clattered, metal against stone wall of a potter's shop. The horseman ended the dashing move with his sword at the fat man's throat.

His fool twin raised his sword in his defence, but another of the riders intervened and easily knocked it from his hand.

The mob acted as one, first hesitant while assessing that the men on the ground outnumbered the horsemen two to one and then confident as they rushed the riders at once. So taken up was I by the events that unravelled before me, I was not prepared for the hands that grabbed me from behind and pulled me backwards. As a midwife, I had walk the roads at night for more than thirty years, but never before had any taken a knife to my throat. The cold metal surprised me and stung my skin.

I could not turn with my hands still tied to the horse and I could not pull free for fear of having my throat cut.

I had but one advantage, and that was knowledge. Slow – slower than the receding ice of winter – so that my attacker did not squeeze that knife across my neck, I inched to the side of Thor's Hammer. Once there, I leaned sideways, still slow, so slow I might have been mistaken in my movement and reached out my hand and touched the horse's left flank. I could not fault the horse's reaction. Already unsettled by the crowd, he kicked back hard as ever he did into the person that held me and, in that moment, I felt myself released and twisted out of his grip.

But it was not a man that had held me. Once again my assailant was a woman, the yellow-haired woman. Bent double on her knees, she held one hand close to her chest and the other hand with the knife far away to avoid stabbing herself. Wouldst that the knife was closer; I would cut myself free. I could do nothing. Then she tried to find her feet and, as she staggered, I did a thing I had not done since I was on my father's knee. I stuck my leg before her and tipped her balance in my favour. She landed with a satisfying splash in the mud. I dropped beside her, placed the knife handle between my knees and ran the rope binding me to the horse back and forth along the blade until it first frayed then tore apart. I was free.

But I remained trapped in the midst of those who wished me to meet that reaper, Death, before Death was ready to greet me, and my hands were still tight bound. I could only be grateful for the chaos around me. While I tried to loose the knots around my wrists, I saw horsemen chase some of the mob down the street, but one turned back and galloped fast toward me.

'Watch to your back, Madam!' he cried.

I turned just as the yellow-haired woman, knife reclaimed, bore down on me. I had nothing with which to defend myself but fast action that brought me more pain. I dodged to the side. It was enough. It gave the rider time to reach me. He hung low from the side of his horse, reached out and grabbed me onto the horse in front of him as he rode away.

'Isabelle! We must find Isabelle. She is back there somewhere.' He seemed not to hear my shout.

We rode a street or two from that place before he slowed to a canter.

'Isabelle is safe. She awaits you with your family at home, but your husband is in pieces over you!'

'You know my husband?' I asked, my earlier suspicion of his identity renewed.

'But of course, Madam Cellier. Know you not who I am?' Now that I was close and might study his face beneath the mask, I turned to do so.

'Lord Powys. It is you!'

'At your service, Madam Cellier.'

'I believed you to have left for the coast with the Queen,' I said, confused despite that I had suspected as such.

'Indeed, my coach left two hours ago, when we sent word to you, but I was not in it. Lady Powys took our youngest two and rides to the port to meet with the Queen. You must go with all speed to join them. She will hold the boat for you if she can. I have unfinished work here.'

'That is too kind of my Lady.'

'She holds you in great affection, my dear lady, as do I,' said Lord Powys. 'Although I have little affection for your smell at this time,' he said less gallantly, turning his nose away.

I remembered the horse dung and wrinkled my nose. His saddle would hold that smell after I had dismounted.

'Many apologies, My Lord. I did not have the luxury of a bath since my recent horse ride.'

Lord Powys laughed the deep, vibrant laugh I had known since my first visit to the Tower many years ago.

'Why did you not escape with your coach, Lord Powys?'

'For this reason,' he said, gesturing whence we came. 'Since the King's nephew and daughter have come to usurp him, mobs in every street wait as foxes for any chicken that tries to fly, and then they beat them or hang them. I fear your life was as close to the gallows as any person's!'

'I am forever beholden to you, My Lord,' I said.

'As I am to you, madam. Your service to Lady Powys, myself and my friends in the Tower will never be forgotten. Aye and your acts of kind charity in the prisons and in our homes are renown to every Roman Catholic in this city, and I will see to it they are known in France too.'

'You have my further gratitude, Sir.'

Four other horsemen joined us then, one following behind holding the reins of Thor's Hammer. Wouldst that I could take him with us. I would at least be sure he was well stabled before I left the country.

'I believe you will be safe now,' said Lord Powys as he reached our coach. There stood Dowdal, no less shifting and spooked than our other horse, Troy, he stood beside. The coach door opened and my husband climbed out and hurried towards us no sooner than Lord Powys set me down. Behind him came Isabelle, Maggie and little Peter, each with a bloody and bruised face.

'Hold out thy hands, madam,' said my rescuer, 'that I might set you free.' With trust, I held my hands out before me, and with the competence of a skilled swordsman he used the tip of the sword to slice between my wrists. My hands swung apart as if they repulsed each other. At last, I was free. I rubbed where the ropes had cut the skin and thanked Lord Powys once more for his kindness.

'Lord Powys,' said my husband. 'I have heard your home was taken by William, and has been given to Lord Delaware to use?'

'That is so, Monsieur Cellier.'

'I beg you, sir, make free with our house as your home until you are ready to leave!' continued Pierre.

'Accept my gratitude, monsieur.' Then, before he might answer more, the other riders shouted, 'Long live King James!' and rode away in the direction of his house. Lord Powys bowed his head. 'Carry my regards to Lady Powys. Please inform her I will join her at Saint Germaine!' And, with that, he was gone.

Immediately I turned to my husband to embrace him, but Isabelle and Margaret came and held me hard. Young Peter grabbed Pierre's middle, then, tears in his eyes, Pierre put his arm around all of us and drew us together.

'Come, Lizzie, children. We have not long to get to the boat. The wind is rising, and Powys tells me the boat must leave as the tide turns. We leave late already. You must reveal all that has happened, and about the part our gallant protector played as we ride.'

Whilst Pierre talked, Dowdal re-harnessed Thor's Hammer. When he finished, I went to him and said, 'I thank the Lord you are unharmed Dowdal. I feared for your life.'

'I am grateful for your kindness, madam,' he said. 'We thought you were dead when they knocked you out. We could not prevent them taking you. 'Twas the best of good fortune that we happened upon those gentlemen aiding another family.'

'We must go, Lizzie. We will talk as we ride.' He sniffed, reminding me of my dreadful condition.

'Have I time to change?' I asked.

'Nay, we must bear the smell of you until the coast,' he added.

We alighted the coach for the second time that evening. The door on my side, where it had been forced open, did not properly close, but I was only glad to be in it and on the way from there. Who knew when – if – it might be safe to return, but in this moment, my attachment to London and England was a frayed tether and I wished to cut it loose. I closed the drape over the window and allowed my youngest two into my arms once we started to move. Soon, my greatest wish was to have Pierre hold me. Now I was safe, I could not stop shaking.

'Come hither, Lizzie,' Pierre read me as a book. I did as he said. I slid out from behind the children and moved into his arms. He held me tight as we rattled and bounced over rough road and, as a family, we prayed to safely reach the rendezvous.

32

10th day of December, 1689 (dawn)

Seawater intermittently and gently lapped against the side of the rowing boat between the steady clunk... clunk... clunk of oars in the wishbone oarlocks. The right hand man of Mr Cadman, landlord of the Mermaid Inn, rowed us to our rendezvous. The blades sliced the water in near silence, but the thick fog embraced us together with the oarsman's grunts and groans as he heaved mightily against the sea. His back to me, his face hidden from me, I imagined that huge age-whipped grey beard of his to be blown from his cavernous, large-lipped mouth with each slow growl.

Each time the man drew back the oars, a rain of cold salt water splashed over me and young Peter. I pressed my lips together and half-closed my eyes against it, but I was happy to smell it. The fresh wide ocean was the smell of freedom and safety, the largest moat a country might have to protect it, a barrier both ways. The more water between us and the land of England, the better I would like it.

Twisting behind me to look in front of the boat, I could see no more than a few feet from the boat into the darkness, for we used no lantern, and I puzzled by what uncommon gift the oarsman knew our whereabouts and in which direction we moved, if we moved at all, for it seemed we did not. I turned back to face the flat trail of bubbles we left behind us, the only sign to show from whence we came and the progress we were making.

Isabelle and Margaret, tears long spent, leaned into Pierre's arms at the back of the boat and faced the oarsman. He held them close; relief and satisfaction leaving no place on his face for fear. He had travelled back to France many times on his travels as a merchant, but this was perhaps the last time; this time Lady Fortune had invited him home to die.

Young Peter sat still and quiet beside me, made a man this night by his bravery in the face of the danger we had endured. He stared past his father and sisters toward the land we were leaving behind. He may never see it again, but then he had seen enough this night that he may never wish to.

None of us would ever again in our lives wish to witness the scenes we saw as we left London: men and women that did not fare so well as us were left strung up from signs, others hanging from windows, cut open by their very neighbours; torch-carrying mobs searching the streets for more to torture; children crying in those torch lit streets, newly orphaned, that we could not aid for fear of our being caught further in the terrible events. We must be grateful we did escape such horrid demise, yet we would never forget to mourn those that did not have our fortune.

I wriggled my toes in ice-cold water that had filled through the fresh-made holes in my boots when we waded out to the waiting boat and I shivered. Digging in my feet as I was dragged through the street was perhaps not the cleverest thing I had done. My wet dress clung as a limpet to my boots and legs and I plucked at it, fidgeting with my so recently torn lace cuffs. I would not sigh my relief until we had left these shores far behind. Boats might yet lie in wait for us just beyond our sight, and we would never know it until they were upon us. 'Twas certain they would search for us. Our only hope was this God-given fog sent to hide us.

The oarsman stopped rowing and stowed the oars under the boat's seat. Suddenly, we were jolted backward then forward as the bow crunched hard against something solid. First I feared we had hit rock, but the oarsman, obviously expecting the collision, stood and took a coil of sopping rope from the puddle at our feet. Once we had righted ourselves, I turned to see what we crashed into and was surprised to find ourselves bumping against the side of a massive ship, silently moored beside us.

The oarsman yelled something, I did not know in what tongue, then used both arms to swing the rope upwards, to whom

I knew not, while his yell still echoed in the small fogless cavern surrounding us. An answering, equally unintelligible shout from above must have told our man the rope had been caught. At least, that's what I guessed, for it did not fall back down beside us, and the oarsman secured our tiny open boat next to the giant. Then a second rope fell loosely alongside the first.

'Step your feet down firmly, M'Lady,' said the oarsman, who I was no more familiar with than when we had climbed over the side of his boat on the beach. I expected him to say more, but that was all he said. He gestured towards the slats of wood nailed one above the other onto the side of the boat as a ladder, then reached his hand toward me that I might take it.

I'm sure I could not be faulted for my obedience, so eager was I to be away from this bobbing twig and onto the sturdy trunk. I dithered not an instant, but came so fast to my feet, my legs being aquiver from the ride, I fell before even I could take his offered hand. The boat rocked precariously.

'Lizzie!'

'Mama!'

I would not have them think the less of me. I could do this. I slapped my hands on the seat our oarsman had so recently quit until I stilled first myself and then the boat. Some warmth lingered where the oarsman had sat and somehow that gave me strength where his hand had not. When I was certain I had the boat stilled once more, I raised myself straight and tall, with my head upraised. I could do this.

The oarsman struggled to hold the boat still against the ship as it was pulled hither and thither by the swells and my actions.

Pierre's expensive shoes were made for solid land and did not grip the slippery wood well. He wobbled perilously close to the edge as he stood yet, ever the gentleman, he stepped to the middle of the boat with more grace than I credit him and, as well, offered his hand to me. I accepted his over the oarsman's, for though my husband was old and frail, and the oarsman steady, I rather trusted Pierre with my life. Though circumstance dictate I must, I had rather not trust a stranger.

I stepped over the middle seat to where the boat was pinched with the ship and looked up. Without the ladder, the ship's side was a smooth, shiny cliff. With the ladder, I still did not know how I could climb it in my long dress, for the fabric would surely catch on my feet. The oarsman grunted with impatience and, modesty to the wind, I hitched up the skirt and apron and tucked the hems beneath the string around my waist holding up the undergarments I was happy now to have had the foresight to wear when it was my wont not to do so.

With my free hand, I grabbed the rope and tugged it hard to make sure it was firm. It seemed to be.

'I will stand beneath you should you should fall, Lizzie.' Pierre kissed my hand then released it. 'Be brave.'

I took a shoulder high slat, pulled myself onto the side of the ship and climbed. The rungs were wet and slippery, and sometimes there were slimy things I did not want to grasp, but grasp them I did. I ignored the pains spearing every limb, the trophies of our recent dangerous encounter in the city. I had never climbed a ladder in my life, let alone one so high. So I stepped upward with the greatest care and made sure of each hand and foothold before taking the next. My heart ran faster than a deer, and beat louder than its hooves. At one point my foot slipped and I was forced to hold tight whilst I steadied myself. Dimmed by fog, far below, my husband's upturned face still conveyed his concern. I could barely see those of my still seated children, not much further, but on the edge of the fog.

'Keep going, dear flittermouse. We follow you.'

I could do this. I must. I must do this.

What if I fell? I saw myself falling. My whole body stiffened and I could not bring myself to reach for the next rung. I was like ice clinging to the ladder.

'Reach out and grab the next slat, Lizzie.' Pierre so well knew me, he knew I had lost the courage I had held onto for so long.

'I only rest, my dear,' I lied. 'I ask only for one or two breaths.'

Easy to say. Not as simple to do. I concentrated on releasing my left hand and raising it to the next piece of wood. My slow and inflexible fingers clasped the cold, slippery surface, soft rotting wood filling my nails, and I looked up rather than down, searching for the top. The fog thinned for a moment and I now saw the rail was closer than I thought. From the bottom I had only seen as far as I was now, but here I was in a position to see both up and down equally well, and judged myself half way. I could either go up or down. If I returned to the bottom, I would still have the ship to climb, and that made no sense. I must go up.

I cannot recall how I managed to reach the top, but I must have done so, for a waiting hand took my arm and pulled me the last of the way. I stood on solid wood. The relief of that had me bend over, nearly sick, with my hands rested on my knees for support, and I breathed deeply. I wished never to do that again!

Mortified, I saw my skirt remained tucked into my under clothes. I should be ashamed if royalty should observe such vulgar display and fast loosened it so it fell to the floor before bringing myself upright to peer through the damp air at my rescuer.

He already busied himself at the rail to secure first the children, then Pierre as they reached the top, aiding them as he had aided me. The boatman did not follow. He was to return to shore and fetch any others that came after us.

From a thick metal post, the man unwound a rope, presumably the rope the oarsman cast up, and dropped it over the edge, shouting words as unfathomable as his last. Strange that we could hear the rope smack the water when the fog smothered so many other sounds, but then came the noise of water slurping and sucking between the two vessels, the clunking of oars into the oarlocks, then silence.

I pulled my cloak close around me. We strained to hear the boat move away. There. It was somehow eerie to hear the oars hit the water, receding yet still so close. That was the sound of our path changing, of leaving one life behind and starting another anew.

If I was sad to leave the old life, it was sorrow for so much good and bad.

I had won prestige in the highest royal palace, yet been reviled in the lowest inn. I had been a bringer of life, yet also a plotter of death. I had lived with different religions, yet my faith in truth had been constant and I always had God at my side. The years in prison were worse than anything I could have imagined, yet from this place I had received my redemption – a royal pardon for my loyalty to the King, a place on this ship to France and a future in the Royal Court of Saint-Germaine-en-Laye.

To go with King James in his exile, at his request and with his blessing, was honour and reward enough for a lifetime of loyalty to the kings of this land. Yea, the fate of such terrible betrayal by his own faithless daughter and her coughing, orange husband was a mystery perhaps only God knew the reason of, yet surely he had seen how I had done his work for him, and gifted me and my dear Pierre a chance of happiness to end our days.

If fortune should decide it so, I would still practice as a midwife. Most women in France were Catholic and would gladly receive my services. 'Twas ever my calling and what I wished to do until I died. I could but regret my College for Midwives would never be built in England in my life, unless the King would return there.

As we stood there at the dripping iron rail of that ship with others of the Royal Court and watched more persons brought on board in the manner Pierre and I had been, my remembered life wended a path from my ransacked comfortable beginnings in Buckinghamshire; to near destitution after my husband left me with five children to feed; to meeting and loving Pierre, and his support throughout every year I lived in and out of prison; and to my final release and esteem given to me by His Royal Highness and his beautiful wife.

Perhaps sensing the trail of my thoughts, Pierre wrapped his arms around my waist from behind and stood with me in silence, looking out to sea.

'What of my children?' I had no way of knowing my older children's fate, and prayed our warnings of late had sent them out of the city and to the safety from persecution ere now. I clasped Pierre's arms to me as a cloak to ward off pain that I may never meet with them again.

'As with mine, we will find them, or they will find us.' Pierre leaned over my shoulder to place his cheek next to mine. It was cold, soft, old, but it reassured me.

We stood a while more. It was near dawn, and thin light turned the fog grey.

Hairy men were all places on deck, doing things sailors knew to do. Then, finally, a line of strong seamen turned the large cogged wheel that hauled the heavy chain and rusting barnacle covered anchor on board. With that, they pulled ropes and released ropes and raised large flapping sails as tight-woven as my memories. The gentlest breeze touched my face as we begun to move. I shivered, and Pierre held me tighter.

'I own, my hospital was a fanciful dream, Pierre. I suppose such places can never be.'

'You do your dream injustice, my Lizzie. Be assured, such fine ideas merely foreshadow another time, a time that has not yet come, when one great King or another will follow your plan, and he will build it and honour you for it.'

I smiled at Pierre's faith in me. His faith in the woman I was held me fast to truth and goodness when I might have failed in courage, rivalling only the backbone given to me by my calling as a midwife, which, though it had always sustained me before, would not on its own have been enough in these last years.

Still, I was The Popish Midwife, and honoured to be so entitled.

Not for the first time, I thought of my family's motto: *Semper Eadem* – Ever the Same. Being true to myself, and to truth itself, might have changed our destiny and won us the prize of a better and safer life in the Royal Court, but it had done nothing for those we left behind. We left everything the same.

I could do nothing now for those poor souls in England, but I would always remember their tragedies and tell any that would listen of them.

THE END

Endnotes

1 Catholic. Often used in a derogatory way.

2 Archaic term for eighth day of April.

3 Catholic. Like Popish, often used in a derogatory way.

4 bright red resin

5 17th Century form of *ambergris*, waxy substance from intestines of a sperm whale

6 stony mass from a ruminant's stomach

7 resin of Mastic tree

8 archaic for bat, the mammal, used as term of endearment.

9 A burning torch made from rushes.

10 scandalmonger

11 someone who chatters/talks a lot

12 bottled/preserved juice made from unripe (green), still sour, fruit and used to flavour sauces and dishes.

13 drunkard

14 A candle lantern, where thin, opaque horn is used instead of glass.

15 (or mulled sack): a type of Spanish white wine, warmed with spices.

16 Messengers, particularly carrying news.

17 Policemen

With Thanks

Despite being written in solitude, a book is never written entirely in isolation.

The worst of crimes are enacted by the writer against his or her family, so I now take this belated opportunity to apologise to my children's skeletal remains, poised by their empty plates at the table, still waiting for dinner to be served. Kids, yes, it was me that caused you all to get your asses kicked on 'games night', when my thirty open windows of research crashed the internet. Oh, and thanks for doing all the housework for weeks at the time while I chatted on Twit…I mean, immersed myself in the seventeenth century. Joe, Carmen, Connor and Rhianna – you rock!

My sisters and their families deserve thanks for their unswerving support. To Helen Cleary, for her belief in me as well as years of pushing me to do something with my writing, and to Karen Gray, for her encouraging feedback - *it wasn't as hard to read as I expected it to be!*

Special thanks to my beta readers for such detailed and helpful thoughts: Tim Savage, for being my writing rock and friend across the Atlantic for many years. I am also eternally grateful to Tim for formatting this edition of *The Popish Midwife* and helping me through the self-publishing process. And to Paul Scales, who persisted in reading a genre so alien to him, I thought he'd side-stepped into another universe to escape! Hands together, also, for Will Kent, for his invaluable advice on some details about Catholicism.

Another special thanks goes to Carmen Christensen for her awesome cover design – it's exactly as I imagined it! Thanks, also, to Charlotte Mouncey for formatting the first editions of my debut novel.

Thanks to James Essinger for the encouragement to write and independently publish this book.

And, last, I crossed time to meet The Popish Midwife, a remarkable and inspirational woman, who upheld the truth regardless of the risk to her life. Thank you, Elizabeth Cellier, for allowing me to tell your story.

About the Author

Annelisa Christensen was born in Sussex, took a psychology degree at the University of Stirling in Scotland, then returned to the south to partner in a fashion design company with her childhood friend, Julia. They had fun selling to shops and in street markets all over London, but dissolved the business when children came along, both believing in putting their families first. Delighted to be offered the job of laboratory technician in the local secondary school, in which she had herself been Head Girl twenty years earlier, she simultaneously wrote a magical realism series (as yet unpublished). She wrote *The Popish Midwife* after falling in love with Elizabeth Cellier in some 300-year-old disbound pages of a trial she bought off the internet. The more she discovered about this woman, the more she wanted to share this amazing woman's story. *The Popish Midwife* is the result of years of research and writing

Please support the Author

Annelisa would be delighted to hear what you thought of *The Popish Midwife*. Please, also, tell others about it and leave a review on Amazon, Goodreads and any other place you hang out. Annelisa can be found online:

- Daily on Twitter: @Alpha_Annelisa
  twitter.com/Alpha_Annelisa

- At her website, *Script Alchemy*
  www.scriptalchemy.com

- And at her *Script Alchemy* Facebook page
  www.facebook.com/ScriptAlchemy

While you're there, sign up to her newsletter (bit.ly/2iYS3Kl) and get the latest news and offers. (No spam!)

A preview from
𝕿𝖍𝖊 𝕸𝖎𝖉𝖓𝖎𝖌𝖍𝖙 𝕸𝖎𝖉𝖜𝖎𝖋𝖊
Third in the *Seventeenth Century Midwives* series

A cold wind rushed past me as I pulled open the door and pushed myself into the shadow of morning light. Even before the wind caught the door and slammed it shut, the welcome smell of new-baked bread from Mr Brown's bakery enticed me forward. Sometimes it seemed Mr Brown never did sleep, for he had already lit the lanthorn outside his shop ready for early customers. Even if I came betimes, before any other man or woman opened their eyes, he and I would pass that early morning time exchanging observations about life, only ending when Gabriel rang to call the town to Angelus and the apprentices to a new day.

This morning, as usual, Mr Brown let me in so we could share the morning news as we were wont to do. As it happened, there was no news of any great note to discuss, so we talked of the farrier newly arrived at the blacksmith's and how he seemed of decent character.

'I have heard he is come from London with a son but without a wife.'

'And what is that to do with me?' I asked, understanding Mr Brown full well.

Mr Brown, a man a mere five years my senior, had in my opinion but two faults.

His greatest fault was Mrs Mabel Brown, his wife. He adored her with all his heart though he could have had his pickings from any number of suitable women. Blinded by marital affection, he believed the happiness he had with Mrs Brown to be something extraordinary, she apparently being a 'charmingly congenial woman' of 'inestimable delightful wit and intelligence'. If I had equally often thought otherwise, I did not say so. In my experience, the nature of his wife was entirely opposite to everything he believed it to be.

Apart from this serious blindness with regard to his wife, his own disposition was not without integrity and honesty, and his reputation for fair weighing of the loaves beyond dispute. He was in ruddy health and his almost plain face was very nearly always friendly after six o'clock in the morning. Almost plain, I say, for his insistence on keeping his crow's nest of an unruly red beard upon his chin gave him the appearance of a scoundrel pirate which, being in the middle of Hertfordshire, stood absurdly out of place.

Of more curiosity than fault was that his wearing it long seemed to defy intelligent nature, its presence quite contradicting the twofold reason he gave for never wearing a periwig whilst baking. Often did I argue with him against the foolishness of keeping it so long. If he had apologised once, he had apologised a hundred times for not wearing his periwig, but nerry once did he admit fault in his unfathomable beard.

In the case of the periwig, he was more conscientious. Oftentimes did he beg pardon that the heat of the oven made it too unbearable to wear one and at other times claimed that it could not be at all clever to risk long hair by an open fire. To prove him right in this, much of his beard was singed into tight fragile curls at the ends or scorched right off. As for his head, it was only unfortunate that he had lost so much hair at such a young age and had been quite bald for nigh on the thirty years I knew him.

His second fault, and fault it most certainly was, made him insensible to my discomfort when he told me I was in need of a good husband.

'Is it not time you found yourself a man to marry and help you with your girls?'

'I do not need assistance, Mr Brown. If ever I had need of any, it was twenty-one years ago when I took on young Mary. Finding a nursemaid to care for her when I was so green a midwife and had little enough work was a testing time. But I am done with rearing the girls now and, if I must take on any more, for it seems it is in my nature to do so, the girls will help me with it as Mary has done with the younger ones. I make no complaint now, for they each pay for their living and I am content with the way of things.'

'No need to chop off my head for only noticing what's what, Abigale. It seemed to me that the farrier is in need of a wife and you are in need of a husband.'

'Indeed, no, Mr Brown. You are very much mistaken. And I will have you keep such things you notice to yourself and not say them to other persons. Talk is rife enough without your adding to it!'

'I beg your pardon, I am sure. My opinion is for you, Abigale, and no other, of that you can be certain. And though you are not of the mind, perhaps it would not be too unwelcome for you to think on it awhile and see if I am not right.'

His sadness in offending me was sincere and I could not but feel regret for my sharp tongue.

'Accept my apology, Mr Brown. I am out of sorts this morning, for I have had little sleep. The girls chitter-chattered all night, or so it did seem!'

Mr Brown put down the batch of bread he had just withdrawn from the oven and scratched the remaining tuft of hair above his left ear as if it bothered him it was alone. Then he returned his attention to taking the buns and placing them on the cooling tray.

'Talking of your girls, Abigale - Mrs Harris - I must bring to your attention another thing you will have great interest in,' he said, using my last name so that I should place myself in a more formal manner of thinking

'Oh?' I said. 'And what might that be?'

'Before I tell you, I must remind you I am partial to my head and do not wish to be parted from it.' I nodded to encourage him continue. 'I see Mary and Elin being close as sisters should be, but I should warn you there is some talk of them being in the way of more than sisterly, if you understand my meaning.'

I gingerly took a hot bun from his cooling tray, as much

to give myself time to compose myself before next I spoke than because I was hungry. Deep in my pocket I found a penny and placed it on the side. It was enough for this bun and three more for the girls to fetch later. Then I pinched off a small piece of the crust and enjoyed watching the steam rise from the middle, breathing deeply of the hot sweet cinnamon. I blew on it.

'I do not, Mr Brown. What do you imply? They are sisters in every way but blood. How else should they be with one another?' I placed the bread in my mouth and chewed. It was not a small pleasure to break fresh bread so early in the morning. Many a time the warm comfort of it carried me through a hard day.

Mr Brown again scratched his head, bringing blood to the skin's surface.

'I am not so bold I know how to go on, Abigale. You and I are known to each other since we came of age and we have been friends for many of those years. That is so, is it not?' I nodded. 'And you know that I am not shy of giving you a piece of my mind if it seems right to do so. Is that not also so?'

I nodded again and placed another piece of bread in my mouth. I chewed slowly, keeping my mind on it so I did not act on whatever Mr Brown seemed to take so long to lead me to.

'Well, then,' he said, 'you must understand I am a tolerant sort of fellow and not one to lean toward making a quick judgement on the lives of persons I have no right to judge. That being said, I hear what others less tolerant than myself say as they stand and talk in the shop, and am of the belief that some things that are talked of should go no further.'

Again, he looked for my understanding of what he was trying to say. I nodded that he should go on with his point to reach the target.

'Our town is not so large, Abigale,' he said, using my first name once again. 'I have said nothing of this before now, you understand, for I am, as I say, of a tolerant nature and it is not my place to be a busy-body and poke my nose where it is not wanted, but I must speak now on this matter, before it becomes a larger issue.'

I was still thinking of what he had said some moments ago. Yesterday, I had bristled when his wife had said almost precisely the same words. Perhaps they had talked to each other on it. But where her intentions were unclear, Mr Brown's held truth that blew on the embers of growing disquiet. I found I was not so tolerant as Mr Brown in hearing the opinions of others. Nor was I so patient.

'Go on, Mr Brown. I am listening.'

'You are well liked, Abigale,' he said, 'and have earned the respect of most persons of this town, but I have heard some call you by the name of Mother Midnight.'

My smile stretched thin and did not gather enough strength to raise the edges of my mouth. It was not uncommon to give a midwife that dark name when she took in unwanted girls of the parish and, though the parish might have given payment for their upkeep, many assumed the midwife used those girls to make her home a bawdy-house and that she sold the girls' flesh to lusty men by night. But if others did such, I did not. I was no Mother Midnight. My girls were as my own daughters.

'You tell me nothing I do not already know, my friend. That is oftentimes a name erroneously paired with my trade. I am listening, but I do not have all day. I have a client to attend. Do you have more to say to me than this?' It seemed I must be direct if he should no longer dodge what he wished to say, for he would skirt it all day if he was not brought to it. Wariness made my words sharper than I meant them to be.

'I do. I will reveal to you my suspicions of the secret you have kept for all these years. I am not blind, Abigale. I have watched Mary next door as a child and then when she passed through the turbulent years to become full-grown. In my privileged position I have seen things that others will not have seen, heard thing others will not have heard.'

As he spoke, he took a bowl from the side and removed the cloth that covered it. Then he started with the next batch of buns: taking chunks of dough, placing them on the scales and rolling them between his hands into balls, and finally arranging each on the greased pan ready for the oven.

I was all ears. No matter how careful I had been over the years, I did wonder a time or two if anyone had seen anything when we were less discreet than we should have been. Never hearing a murmur about it, I had hoped good fortune was on our side and we had escaped notice completely. It seemed that perhaps we were not as clever as I had thought us. How much did he know?

'Well?' I said. 'Bring your point to the target, Mr Brown. I see you are reluctant to spill what you know, but if none of it is new to me, you may be certain you will not surprise me.'

'I am sure you must speak true,' he said. 'The rights and wrongs of it are not for me to judge, nor for me to be secret about. If you know what it is I talk about without me saying it, I need not then tell you. But if you ask it of me I will freely do so.' He stopped rolling the piece of dough he was holding and leaned toward me over the table. Even though there was no other person in the shop, nor yet would there be for some time, his voice was low and confiding. 'I *know*, Abigale...'

Get *The Midnight Midwife* here:
books2read.com/themidnightmidwife

RECEIVED AUG – – 2019

Made in the USA
Middletown, DE
25 July 2019